for
CHRISTMAS

A *Daddy* for CHRISTMAS

CATHERINE
MANN

ALISON
ROBERTS

TERESA
CARPENTER

MILLS & BOON

First Published in Great Britain 2016
By Mills & Boon, an imprint of HarperCollins*Publishers*
1 London Bridge Street, London, SE1 9GF

A DADDY FOR CHRISTMAS © 2016 Harlequin Books S.A.

Yuletide Baby Surprise © 2013 Catherine Mann
Maybe This Christmas…? © 2012 Alison Roberts
The Sheriff's Doorstep Baby © 2012 Teresa Carpenter

ISBN: 978-0-263-92738-2

9-1216

Our policy is to use papers that are natural, renewable and recyclable products and made from wood grown in sustainable forests. The logging and manufacturing processes conform to the legal environmental regulations of the country of origin.

Printed and bound in Spain
by CPI, Barcelona

YULETIDE BABY SURPRISE

CATHERINE MANN

To Savannah

USA TODAY bestseller and RITA® Award winner **Catherine Mann** has penned over fifty novels, released in more than twenty countries. After years as a military spouse bringing up four children, Catherine is now a snowbird – sorta – splitting time between the Florida beach and somewhat chillier beach in her home state of South Carolina. The nest didn't stay empty long, though, as Catherine is an active board member for the Sunshine State Animal Rescue. www.CatherineMann.com

One

Dr. Mariama Mandara had always been the last picked for a team in gym class. With good reason. Athletics? Not her thing. But when it came to spelling bees, debate squads and math competitions, she'd racked up requests by the dozens.

Too bad her academic skills couldn't help her sprint faster down the posh hotel corridor.

More than ever, she needed speed to escape the royal watchers tracking her at the Cape Verde beachside resort off the coast of West Africa, which was like a North Atlantic Hawaii, a horseshoe grouping of ten islands. They were staying on the largest island, Santiago.

No matter where she hid, determined legions were all too eager for a photo with a princess. Why couldn't they accept she was here for a business conference, not socializing?

Panting, Mari braced a hand against the wall as she

stumbled past a potted areca silk palm strung with twinkling Christmas lights. Evading relentless pursuers wasn't as easy as it appeared in the movies, especially if you weren't inclined to blow things up or leap from windows. The nearest stairwell door was blocked by two tourists poring over some sightseeing pamphlet. A cleaning cart blocked another escape route. She could only keep moving forward.

Regaining her balance, she power-walked, since running would draw even more attention or send her tripping over her own feet. Her low-heeled pumps thud-thud-thudded along the plush carpet in time with a polyrhythmic version of "Hark! The Herald Angels Sing" wafting from the sound system. She just wanted to finish this medical conference and return to her research lab, where she could ride out the holiday madness in peace, crunching data rather than candy canes.

For most people, Christmas meant love, joy and family. But for her, the "season to be jolly" brought epic family battles even twenty years after her parents' divorce. If her mom and dad had lived next door to each other—or even on the same continent—the holidays would not have been so painful. But they'd played transcontinental tug-of-war over their only child for decades. Growing up, she'd spent more time in the Atlanta airport and on planes with her nanny than actually celebrating by a fireside with cocoa. She'd even spent one Christmas in a hotel, her connecting flight canceled for snow.

The occasional cart in the hall now reminded her of that year's room-service Christmas meal. Call her crazy, but once she had gained more control over her world, she preferred a simpler Christmas.

Although simple wasn't always possible for someone

born into royalty. Her mother had crumbled under the pressure of the constant spotlight, divorced her Prince Charming in Western Africa and returned to her Atlanta, Georgia, home. Mari, however, couldn't divorce herself from her heritage.

If only her father and his subjects understood she could best serve their small region through her research at the university lab using her clinical brain, rather than smiling endlessly through the status quo of ribbon-cutting ceremonies. She craved her comfy, shapeless clothes, instead of worrying about keeping herself neat as a pin for photo ops.

Finally, she spotted an unguarded stairwell. Peering inside, she found it empty but for the echo of "Hark! The Herald Angels Sing" segueing into "Away in a Manger." She just needed to make it from the ground level to her fifth-floor room, where she could hole up for the night before facing the rest of the week's symposiums. Exhausted from a fourteen-hour day of presentations about her research on antiviral medications, she was a rumpled mess and just didn't have it in her to smile pretty for the camera or field questions that would be captured on video phone. Especially since anything she said could gain a life of its own on the internet in seconds these days.

She grasped the rail and all but hauled herself up step after step. Urgency pumped her pulse in her ears. Gasping, she paused for a second at the third floor to catch her breath before trudging up the last flights. Shoving through the fifth-floor door, she almost slammed into a mother and teenage daughter leaving their room. The teen did a double take and Mari turned away quickly, adrenaline surging through her exhaustion and powering her down the hall. Except now she was going in the opposite direction, damn it.

Simply strolling back into the hall wasn't an option until she could be sure the path was clear. But she couldn't simply stand here indefinitely, either. If only she had a disguise, something to throw people off the scent. Head tucked down, she searched the hall through her eyelashes, taking in a brass luggage rack and monstrously big pots of African feather grass.

Her gaze landed on the perfect answer—a room-service cart. Apparently abandoned. She scanned for anyone in a hotel uniform, but saw only the retreating back of a woman walking away quickly, a cell phone pressed to her ear. Mari chewed her lip for half a second then sprinted forward and stopped just short of the cloth-draped trolley.

She peeked under the silver tray. The mouth-watering scent of saffron-braised karoo lamb made her stomach rumble. And the tiramisu particularly tempted her to find the nearest closet and feast after a long day of talking without a break for more than coffee and water. She shook off indulgent thoughts. The sooner she worked her way back to her room, the sooner she could end this crazy day with a hot shower, her own tray of food and a soft bed.

Delivering the room-service cart now offered her best means of disguise. A hotel jacket was even draped over the handle and a slip of paper clearly listed Suite 5A as the recipient.

The sound of the elevator doors opening spurred her into action.

Mari shrugged the voluminous forest-green jacket over her rumpled black suit. A red Father Christmas hat slipped from underneath the hotel uniform. All the better for extra camouflaging. She yanked on the hat over her upswept hair and started pushing the heavily laden cart toward the suite at the end of the hall, just as voices swelled behind her.

"Do you see her?" a female teen asked in Portuguese, her squeaky tones drifting down the corridor. "I thought you said she ran up the stairs to the fifth floor."

"Are you sure it wasn't the fourth?" another high-pitched girl answered.

"I'm certain," a third voice snapped. "Get your phone ready. We can sell these for a fortune."

Not a chance.

Mari shoved the cart. China rattled and the wheels creaked. Damn, this thing was heavier than it looked. She dug her heels in deeper and pushed harder. Step by step, past carved masks and a pottery elephant planter, she walked closer to suite 5A.

The conspiring trio drew closer. "Maybe we can ask that lady with the cart if she's seen her...."

Apprehension lifted the hair on the back of Mari's neck. The photos would be all the more mortifying if they caught her in this disguise. She needed to get inside suite 5A. Now. The numbered brass plaque told her she was at the right place.

Mari jabbed the buzzer, twice, fast.

"Room service," she called, keeping her head low.

Seconds ticked by. The risk of stepping inside and hiding her identity from one person seemed far less daunting than hanging out here with the determined group and heaven only knew who else.

Just when she started to panic that time would run out, the door opened, thank God. She rushed past, her arms straining at the weight of the cart and her nose catching a whiff of manly soap. Her favorite scent—

clean and crisp rather than cloying and obvious. Her feet tangled for a second.

Tripping over her own feet as she shoved the cart was far from dignified. But she'd always been too gangly to be a glamour girl. She was more of a cerebral type, a proud nerd, much to the frustration of her family's press secretary, who expected her to present herself in a more dignified manner.

Still, even in her rush to get inside, curiosity nipped at her. What type of man would choose such a simple smell while staying in such opulence? But she didn't dare risk a peek at him.

She eyed the suite for other occupants, even though the room-service cart only held one meal. One very weighty meal. She shoved the rattling cart past a teak lion. The room appeared empty, the lighting low. Fat leather sofas and a thick wooden table filled the main space. Floor-to-ceiling shutters had been slid aside to reveal the moonlit beach outside a panoramic window. Lights from stars and yachts dotted the horizon. Palms and fruit trees with lanterns illuminated the shore. On a distant islet, a stone church perched on a hill.

She cleared her throat and started toward the table by the window. "I'll set everything up on the table for you."

"Thanks," rumbled a hauntingly familiar voice that froze her in her tracks. "But you can just leave it there by the fireplace."

Her brain needed less than a second to identify those deep bass tones. Ice trickled down her spine as if snow had hit her African Christmas after all.

She didn't have to turn around to confirm that fate was having a big laugh at her expense. She'd run from an irritation straight into a major frustration. Out of all the hotel suites she could have entered, somehow she'd landed in the room of Dr. Rowan Boothe.

Her professional nemesis.

A physician whose inventions she'd all but ridiculed in public.

What the hell was he doing here? She'd reviewed the entire program of speakers and she could have sworn he wasn't listed on the docket until the end of the week.

The door clicked shut behind her. The tread of his footsteps closed in, steady, deliberate, bringing the scent of him drifting her way. She kept her face down, studying his loafers and the well-washed hem of his faded jeans.

She held on to the hope that he wouldn't recognize her. "I'll leave your meal right here then," she said softly. "Have a nice evening."

His tall, solid body blocked her path. God, she was caught between a rock and a hard place. Her eyes skated to his chest.

A very hard, muscle-bound place encased in a white button-down with the sleeves rolled up and the tail untucked. She remembered well every muscular—annoying—inch of him.

She just prayed he wouldn't recognize her from their last encounter five months ago at a conference in London. Already the heat of embarrassment flamed over her.

Even with her face averted, she didn't need to look further to refresh her memory of that too handsome face of his. Weathered by the sun, his Brad Pitt–level good looks only increased. His sandy blond hair would have been too shaggy for any other medical professional to carry off. But somehow he simply appeared too immersed in philanthropic deeds to be bothered with anything as mundane as a trip to the barber.

The world thought he was Dr. Hot Perfection but she simply couldn't condone the way he circumvented rules.

"Ma'am," he said, ducking his head as if to catch her attention, "is there a problem?"

Just keep calm. There was no way for him to identify her from the back. She would rather brave a few pictures in the press than face this man while she wore a flipping Santa Claus hat.

A broad hand slid into view with cash folded over into a tip. "Merry Christmas."

If she didn't take the money, that would appear suspicious. She pinched the edge of the folded bills, doing her best to avoid touching him. She plucked the cash free and made a mental note to donate the tip to charity. "Thank you for your generosity."

"You're very welcome." His smooth bass was too appealing coming from such an obnoxiously perfect man.

Exhaling hard, she angled past him. Almost home free. Her hand closed around the cool brass door handle.

"Dr. Mandara, are you really going so soon?" he asked with unmistakable sarcasm. He'd recognized her. Damn. He was probably smirking, too, the bastard.

He took a step closer, the heat of his breath caressing her cheek. "And here I thought you'd gone to all this trouble to sneak into my room so you could seduce me."

Dr. Rowan Boothe waited for his words to sink in, the possibility of sparring with the sexy princess/research scientist already pumping excitement through his veins. He didn't know what it was about Mariama Mandara that turned him inside out, but he'd given up analyzing the why of it long ago. His attraction to Mari was simply a fact of life now.

Her disdain for him was an equally undeniable fact, and to be honest, it was quite possibly part of her allure.

He grew weary with the whole notion of the world painting him as some kind of saint just because he'd rejected the offer of a lucrative practice in North Carolina and opened a clinic in Africa. These days, he had money to burn after his invention of a computerized medical diagnostics program—a program Mari missed no opportunity to dismiss as faux, shortcut medicine. Funding the clinic hadn't even put a dent in his portfolio so he didn't see it as worthy of hoopla. Real philanthropy involved sacrifice. And he wasn't particularly adept at denying himself things he wanted.

Right now, he wanted Mari.

Although from the look of horror on her face, his half-joking come-on line hadn't struck gold.

She opened and closed her mouth twice, for once at a loss for words. Fine by him. He was cool with just soaking up the sight of her. He leaned back against the wet bar, taking in her long, elegant lines. Others might miss the fine-boned grace beneath the bulky clothes she wore, but he'd studied her often enough to catch the brush of every subtle curve. He could almost feel her, ached to peel her clothes away and taste every inch of her café-au-lait skin.

Some of the heat must have shown on his face because she snapped out of her shock. "You have got to be joking. You can't honestly believe I would ever make a move on you, much less one so incredibly blatant."

Damn, but her indignation was so sexy and yeah, even cute with the incongruity of that Santa hat perched on her head. He couldn't stop himself from grinning.

She stomped her foot. "Don't you dare laugh at me."

He tapped his head lightly. "Nice hat."

Growling, she flung aside the hat and shrugged out of the hotel jacket. "Believe me, if I'd known you were in here, I wouldn't have chosen this room to hide out."

"Hide out?" he said absently, half following her words.

As she pulled her arms free of the jacket to review a rumpled black suit, the tug of her white business shirt against her breasts sent an unwelcome surge of arousal through him. He'd been fighting a damned inconvenient arousal around this woman for more than two years, ever since she'd stepped behind a podium in front of an auditorium full of people and proceeded to shoot holes in his work. She thought his computerized diagnostics tool was too simplistic. She'd accused him of taking the human element out of medicine. His jaw flexed, any urge to smile fading.

If anyone was too impersonal, it was her. And, God, how he ached to rattle her composure, to see her tawny eyes go sleepy with all-consuming passion.

Crap.

He was five seconds away from an obvious erection. He reined himself in and faced the problem at hand— the woman—as a more likely reason for her arrival smoked through his brain. "Is this some sort of professional espionage?"

"What in the hell are you talking about?" She fidgeted with the loose waistband on her tweedy skirt.

Who would have thought tweed would turn him inside out? Yet he found himself fantasizing about pulling those practical clunky shoes off her feet. He would kiss his way up under her skirt, discover the silken inside of her calf...

He cleared his throat and brought his focus up to her heart-shaped face. "Playing dumb does not suit you." He knew full well she had a genius IQ. "But if that's the way you want this to roll, then okay. Were you hoping to obtain insider information on the latest upgrade to my computerized diagnostics tool?"

"Not likely." She smoothed a hand over her swept-back hair. "I never would have pegged you as the conspiracy theorist sort since you're a man of science. Sort of."

He cocked an eyebrow. "So you're not here for information, Mari." If he'd wanted distance he should have called her Dr. Mandara, but too late to go back. "Then why are you sneaking into my suite?"

Sighing, she crossed her arms over her chest. "Fine. I'll tell you, but you have to promise not to laugh."

"Scout's honor." He crossed his heart.

"You were a Boy Scout? Figures."

Before he'd been sent to a military reform school, but he didn't like to talk about those days and the things he'd done. Things he could never atone for even if he opened free clinics on every continent, every year for the rest of his life. But he kept trying, by saving one life at a time, to make up for the past.

"You were going to tell me how you ended up in my suite."

She glanced at the door, then sat gingerly on the arm of the leather sofa. "Royal watchers have been trailing me with their phones to take photos and videos for their five seconds of fame. A group of them followed me out the back exit after my last seminar."

Protective instincts flamed to life inside him. "Doesn't your father provide you with bodyguards?"

"I choose not to use them," she said without explanation, her chin tipping regally in a way that shouted the subject wasn't open for discussion. "My attempt to slip away wasn't going well. The lady pushing this room-service cart was distracted by a phone call. I saw my chance to go incognito and I took it."

The thought of her alone out there had him biting back the urge to chew out someone—namely her father. So what if she rejected guards? Her dad should have insisted.

Mari continued, "I know I should probably just grin for the camera and move on, but the images they capture aren't…professional. I have serious work to do, a reputation to maintain." She tipped her head back, her mouth pursed tight in frustration for a telling moment before she rambled on with a weary shake of her head. "I didn't sign on for this."

Her exhaustion pulled at him, made him want to rest his hands on her drooping shoulders and ease those tense muscles. Except she would likely clobber him with the silver chafing dish on the serving cart. He opted for the surefire way to take her mind off the stress.

Shoving away from the bar, he strode past the cart toward her again. "Poor little rich princess."

Mari's cat eyes narrowed. "You're not very nice."

"You're the only one who seems to think so." He stopped twelve inches shy of touching her.

Slowly, she stood, facing him. "Well, pardon me for not being a member of *your* fan club."

"You genuinely didn't know this was my room?" he asked again, even though he could see the truth in her eyes.

"No. I didn't." She shook her head, the heartbeat throbbing faster in her elegant neck. "The cart only had your room number. Not your name."

"If you'd realized ahead of time that this was my room, my meal—" he scooped up the hotel jacket and Santa hat "—would you have surrendered yourself to the camera-toting brigade out there rather than ask me for help?"

Her lips quivered with the first hint of a smile. "I guess we'll never know the answer to that, will we?" She tugged at the jacket. "Enjoy your supper."

He didn't let go. "There's plenty of food here. You could join me, hide out for a while longer."

"Did you just invite me to dinner?" The light of humor in her eyes animated her face until the air damn near crackled between them. "Or are you secretly trying to poison me?"

She nibbled her bottom lip and he could have sworn she swayed toward him. If he hooked a finger in the vee of her shirt and pulled, she would be in his arms.

Instead, he simply reached out and skimmed back the stray lock of sleek black hair curving just under her chin. "Mari, there are a lot of things I would like to do to you, but I can assure you that poisoning you is nowhere on that list."

Confusion chased across her face, but she wasn't running from the room or laughing. In fact, he could swear he saw reluctant interest. Enough to make him wonder what might happen if…

A whimper snapped him out of his passion fog.

The sound wasn't coming from Mari. She looked over his shoulder and he turned toward the sound. The cry swelled louder, into a full-out wail, swelling from across the room.

From under the room-service cart?

He glanced at Mari. "What the hell?"

She shook her head, her hands up. "Don't look at me."

He charged across the room, sweeping aside the linen cloth covering the service cart to reveal a squalling infant.

Two

The infant's wail echoed in the hotel suite. Shock resounded just as loudly inside of Mari as she stared at the screaming baby in a plastic carrier wedged inside the room-service trolley. No wonder the cart had felt heavier than normal. If only she'd investigated she might have found the baby right away. Her brain had been tapping her with the logic that something was off, and she'd been too caught up in her own selfish fears about a few photos to notice.

To think that poor little one had been under there all this time. So tiny. So defenseless. The child, maybe two or three months old, wore a diaper and a plain white T-shirt, a green blanket tangled around its tiny, kicking feet.

Mari swallowed hard, her brain not making connections as she was too dumbstruck to think. "Oh, my God, is that a baby?"

"It's not a puppy." Rowan washed his hands at the wet-bar sink then knelt beside the lower rack holding the infant seat. He visibly went into doctor mode as he checked the squalling tyke over, sliding his hands under and scooping the child up in his large, confident hands. Chubby little mocha-brown arms and legs flailed before the baby settled against Rowan's chest with a hiccupping sigh.

"What in the world is it doing under there?" She stepped away, clearing a path for him to walk over to the sofa.

"I'm not the one who brought the room service in," he countered offhandedly, sliding a finger into the baby's tiny bow mouth. Checking for a cleft palate perhaps?

"Well, I didn't put the baby there."

A boy or girl? She couldn't tell. The wriggling bundle wore no distinguishing pink or blue. There wasn't even a hair bow in the cap of black curls.

Rowan elbowed aside an animal-print throw pillow and sat on the leather couch, resting the baby on his knees while he continued assessing.

She tucked her hands behind her back. "Is it okay? He or she?"

"Her," he said, closing the cloth diaper. "She's a girl, approximately three months old, but that's just a guess."

"We should call the authorities. What if whoever abandoned her is still in the building?" Unlikely given how long she'd hung out in here flirting with Rowan. "There was a woman walking away from the cart earlier. I assumed she was just taking a cell phone call, but maybe that was the baby's mother?"

"Definitely something to investigate. Hopefully there will be security footage of her. You need to think through what you're going to tell the authorities, review every detail in your mind while it's fresh." He sounded more like a detective than a doctor. "Did you see anyone else around the cart before you took it?"

"Are you blaming this on me?"

"Of course not."

Still, she couldn't help but feel guilty. "What if this is my fault for taking that cart? Maybe the baby wasn't abandoned at all. What if some mother was just trying to bring her child to work? She must be frantic looking for her daughter."

"Or frantic she's going to be in trouble," he replied dryly.

"Or he. The parent could be a father." She reached for the phone on the marble bar. "I really need to ring the front desk now."

"Before you call, could you pass over her seat? It may hold some clues to her family. Or at least some supplies to take care of her while we settle this."

"Sure, hold on."

She eased the battered plastic seat from under the cart, winging a quick prayer of thankfulness that the child hadn't come to some harm out there alone in the hall. The thought that someone would so recklessly care for a precious life made her grind her teeth in frustration. She set the gray carrier beside Rowan on the sofa, the green blanket trailing off the side.

Finally, she could call for help. Without taking her eyes off Rowan and the baby, she dialed the front desk.

The phone rang four times before someone picked up. "Could you hold, please? Thank you," a harried-sounding hotel operator said without giving Mari a chance to shout "No!" The line went straight to Christmas carols, "O Holy Night" lulling in her ear.

Sighing, she sagged a hip against the garland-draped wet bar. "They put me on hold."

Rowan glanced up, his pure blue eyes darkened with an answering frustration. "Whoever decided to schedule a conference at this time of year needs to have his head examined. The hotel was already jam-packed with holiday tourists, now conventioneers, too. Insane."

"For once, you and I agree on something one hundred percent." The music on the phone transitioned to "The Little Drummer Boy" as she watched Rowan cradle the infant in a way that made him even more handsome. Unwilling to get distracted by traveling down that mental path again, she shifted to look out the window at the scenic view. Multicolored lights blinked from the sailboats and ferries.

The Christmas spirit was definitely in full swing on the resort island. Back on the mainland, her father's country included more of a blend of religions than many realized. Christmas wasn't as elaborate as in the States, but still celebrated. Cape Verde had an especially deep-rooted Christmas tradition, having been originally settled by the Portuguese.

Since moving out on her own, she'd been more than happy to downplay the holiday mayhem personally, but she couldn't ignore the importance, the message of hope that should come this time of year. That a parent could abandon a child at the holidays seemed somehow especially tragic.

Her arms suddenly ached to scoop up the baby, but she had no experience and heaven forbid she did something wrong. The little girl was clearly in better hands with Rowan.

He cursed softly and she turned back to face him. He

held the baby in the crook of his arm while he searched the infant seat with the other.

"What?" she asked, covering the phone's mouthpiece. "Is something the matter with the baby?"

"No, something's the matter with the parents. You can stop worrying that some mom or dad brought their baby to work." He held up a slip of paper, baby cradled in the other arm. "I found this note tucked under the liner in the carrier."

He held up a piece of hotel stationary.

Mari rushed to sit beside him on the sofa, phone still in hand. "What does it say?"

"The baby's mother intended for her to be in this cart, in *my* room." He passed the note. "Read this."

Dr. Boothe, you are known for your charity and generosity. Please look over my baby girl, Issa. My husband died in a border battle and I cannot give Issa what she needs. Tell her I love her and will think of her always.

Mari reread the note in disbelief, barely able to process that someone could give away their child so easily, with no guarantees that she would be safe. "Do people dump babies on your doorstep on a regular basis?"

"It's happened a couple of times at my clinic, but never anything remotely like this." He held out the baby toward her. "Take Issa. I have some contacts I can reach out to with extra resources. They can look into this while we're waiting for the damn hotel operator to take you off hold."

Mari stepped back sharply. "I don't have much experience with babies. No experience actually, other than kissing them on the forehead in crowds during photo ops."

"Didn't you ever babysit in high school?" He cradled the infant in one arm while fishing out his cell phone with his other hand. "Or do princesses not babysit?"

"I skipped secondary education and went straight to college." As a result, her social skills sucked as much as her fashion sense, but that had never mattered much. Until now. Mari smoothed a hand down her wrinkled, baggy skirt. "Looks to me like you have Issa and your phone well in hand."

Competently—enticingly so. No wonder he'd been featured in magazines around the globe as one of the world's most eligible bachelors. Intellectually, she'd understood he was an attractive—albeit irritating—man. But until this moment, she hadn't comprehended the full impact of his appeal.

Her body flamed to life, her senses homing in on this moment, on *him*. Rowan. The last man on the planet she should be swept away by or attracted to.

This must be some sort of primal, hormonal thing. Her ticking biological clock was playing tricks on her mind because he held a baby. She could have felt this way about any man.

Right?

God, she hoped so. Because she couldn't wrap her brain around the notion that she could be this drawn to a man so totally wrong for her.

The music ended on the phone a second before the operator returned. "May I help you?"

Heaven yes, she wanted to shout. She needed Issa safe and settled. She also needed to put space between herself and the increasingly intriguing man in front of her.

She couldn't get out of this suite soon enough.

"Yes, you can help. There's been a baby abandoned just outside Suite 5A, the room of Dr. Rowan Boothe."

Rowan didn't foresee a speedy conclusion to the baby mystery. Not tonight, anyway. The kind of person who threw away their child and trusted her to a man based solely on his professional reputation was probably long gone by now.

Walking the floor with the infant, he patted her back for a burp after the bottle she'd downed. Mari was reading a formula can, her forehead furrowed, her shirt half-untucked. Fresh baby supplies had been sent up by the hotel's concierge since Rowan didn't trust anything in the diaper bag.

There were no reports from hotel security or authorities of a missing child that matched this baby's description. So far security hadn't found any helpful footage, just images of a woman's back as she walked away from the cart as Mari stepped up to take it. Mari had called the police next, but they hadn't seemed to be in any hurry since no one's life was in danger and even the fact that a princess was involved didn't have them moving faster. Delays like this only made it more probable the press would grab hold of information about the situation. He needed to keep this under control. His connections could help him with that, but they couldn't fix the entire system here.

Eventually, the police would make their way over with someone from child services. Thoughts of this baby getting lost in an overburdened, underfunded network tore at him. On a realistic level, he understood he couldn't save everyone who crossed his path, but something about this vulnerable child abandoned at Christmas tore at his heart all the more.

Had to be because the kid was a baby, his weak spot.

He shrugged off distracting thoughts of how badly he'd screwed up as a teenager and focused on the present. Issa burped, then cooed. But Rowan wasn't fooled into thinking she was full. As fast as the kid had downed that first small bottle, he suspected she still needed more. "Issa's ready for the extra couple of ounces if you're ready."

Mari shook the measured powder and distilled water together, her pretty face still stressed. "I think I have it right. But maybe you should double-check."

"Seriously, I'm certain you can handle a two-to-one mixture." He grinned at seeing her flustered for the first time ever. Did she have any idea how cute she looked? Not that she would be happy with the "cute" label. "Just think of it as a lab experiment."

She swiped a wrist over the beads of sweat on her forehead, a simple watch sliding down her slim arm. "If I got the proportions wrong—"

"You didn't." He held out a hand for the fresh bottle. "Trust me."

Reluctantly, she passed it over. "She just looks so fragile."

"Actually, she appears healthy, well fed and clean." Her mother may have dumped her off, but someone had taken good care of the baby before that. Was the woman already regretting her decision? God, he hoped so. There were already far too few homes for orphans here. "There are no signs she's been mistreated."

"She seems cuddly," Mari said with a wistful smile.

"Are you sure you wouldn't like to hold her while I make a call?"

She shook her head quickly, tucking a stray strand of hair back into the loose knot at her neck. "Your special contacts?"

He almost smiled at her weak attempt to distract him from passing over the baby. And he definitely wasn't in a position to share much of anything about his unorthodox contacts with her. "It would be easier if I didn't have to juggle the kid and the bottle while I talk."

"Okay, if you're sure I won't break her." She chewed her bottom lip. "But let me sit down first."

Seeing Mari unsure of herself was strange, to say the least. She always commanded the room with her confidence and knowledge, even when he didn't agree with her conclusions. There was something vulnerable, approachable even, about her now.

He set the baby into her arms, catching a whiff of Mari's perfume, something flowery and surprisingly whimsical for such a practical woman. "Just be careful to support her head and hold the bottle up enough that she isn't drinking air."

Mari eyed the bottle skeptically before popping it into Issa's mouth. "Someone really should invent a more precise way to do this. There's too much room for human error."

"But babies like the human touch. Notice how she's pressing her ear against your heart?" Still leaning in, he could see Mari's pulse throbbing in her neck. The steady throb made him burn to kiss her right there, to taste her, inhale her scent. "That heartbeat is a constant in a baby's life in utero. They find comfort in it after birth, as well."

Her deep golden gaze held his and he could swear something, an awareness, flashed in her eyes as they played out this little family tableau.

"Um, Rowan—" her voice came out a hint breathier than normal "—make your call, please."

Yeah, probably a good idea to retreat and regroup while he figured out what to do about the baby—and about having Mari show up unexpectedly in his suite.

He stepped into his bedroom and opened the French door onto the balcony. The night air was that perfect temperature—not too hot or cold. Decembers in Cape Verde usually maxed out at between seventy-five and eighty degrees Fahrenheit. A hint of salt clung to the air and on a normal night he would find sitting out here with a drink the closest thing to a vacation he'd had in... He'd lost count of the years.

But tonight he had other things on his mind.

Fishing out his phone, he leaned on the balcony rail so he could still see Mari through the picture window in the sitting area. His gaze roved over her lithe body, which was almost completely hidden under her ill-fitting suit. At least she wouldn't be able to hear him. His contacts were out of the normal scale and the fewer people who knew about them, the better. Those ties traced back far, all the way to high school.

After he'd derailed his life in a drunk-driving accident as a teen, he'd landed in a military reform school with a bunch of screwups like himself. He'd formed lifetime friendships there with the group that had dubbed themselves the Alpha Brotherhood. Years later after college graduation, they'd all been stunned to learn their headmaster had connections with Interpol. He'd recruited a handful of them as freelance agents. Their troubled pasts—and large bank accounts—gave them a cover story to move freely in powerful and sometimes seedy circles.

Rowan was only tapped for missions maybe once

a year, but it felt damn good to help clean up underworld crime. He saw the fallout too often in the battles between warlords that erupted in regions neighboring his clinic.

The phone stopped ringing and a familiar voice said, "Speak to me, Boothe."

"Colonel, I need your help."

The Colonel laughed softly. "Tell me something new. Which one of your patients is in trouble? Or is it another cause you've taken on? Or—"

"Sir, it's a baby."

The sound of a chair squeaking echoed over the phone lines and Rowan could envision his old headmaster sitting up straighter, his full attention on the moment. "You have a baby?"

"Not *my* baby. *A* baby." He didn't expect to ever have children. His life was too consumed with his work, his mission. It wouldn't be fair to a child to have to compete with third-world problems for his father's attention. Still, Rowan's eyes locked in on Mari holding Issa so fiercely, as if still afraid she might drop her. "Someone abandoned an infant in my suite along with a note asking me to care for her."

"A little girl. I always wanted a little girl." The nostalgia in the Colonel's voice was at odds with the stern exterior he presented to the world. Even his clothes said stark long after he'd stopped wearing a uniform. These days, in his Interpol life, Salvatore wore nothing but gray suits with a red tie. "But back to your problem at hand. What do the authorities say?"

"No one has reported a child missing to the hotel security or to local authorities. Surveillance footage hasn't shown anything, but there are reports of a woman walking away from the cart where the baby was abandoned. The police are dragging their feet on showing up here to investigate further. So I need to get ahead of the curve here."

"In what way?"

"You and I both know the child welfare system here is overburdened to the crumbling point." Rowan found a plan forming in his mind, a crazy plan, but one that felt somehow right. Hell, there wasn't any option that sat completely right with his conscience. "I want to have temporary custody of the child while the authorities look into finding the mother or placing her in a home."

He might not be the best parental candidate for the baby, but he was a helluva lot better than an overflowing orphanage. If he had help…

His gaze zeroed in on the endearing tableau in his hotel sitting room. The plan came into sharper focus as he thought of spending more time with Mari.

Yet as soon as he considered the idea, obstacles piled in his path. How would he sell her on such an unconventional solution? She freaked out over feeding the kid a bottle.

"Excuse me for asking the obvious, Boothe, but how in the hell do you intend to play papa and save the world at the same time?"

"It's only temporary." He definitely couldn't see himself doing the family gig long-term. Even thinking of growing up with his own family sent his stomach roiling. Mari made it clear her work consumed her, as well. So a temporary arrangement could suit them both well. "And I'll have help…from someone."

"Ah, now I understand."

"How do you understand from a continent away?" Rowan hated to think he was that transparent.

"After my wife wised up and left me, when I had our

son for the weekend, I always had trouble matching up outfits for him to wear. So she would send everything paired up for me." He paused, the sound of clinking ice carrying over the phone line.

Where was Salvatore going with this story? Rowan wasn't sure, but he'd learned long ago that the man had more wisdom in one thumb that most people had in their entire brain. God knows, he'd saved and redirected dozens of misfit teenagers at the military high school.

Salvatore continued, "This one time, my son flipped his suitcase and mixed his clothes up. I did the best I could, but apparently, green plaid shorts, an orange striped shirt and cowboy boots don't match."

"You don't say." The image of Salvatore in his uniform or one of those generic suits of his, walking beside a mismatched kid, made Rowan grin. Salvatore didn't offer personal insights often. This was a golden moment and Rowan just let him keep talking.

"Sure, I knew the outfit didn't match, although I didn't know how to fix it. In the end, I learned a valuable lesson. When you're in the grocery store with the kid, that outfit shouts 'single dad' to a bevy of interested women."

"You used your son to pick up women?"

"Not intentionally. But that's what happened. Sounds to me like you may be partaking of the same strategy with this 'someone' who's helping you."

Busted. Although he felt compelled to defend himself. "I would be asking for help with the kid even if Mari wasn't here."

"Mariama Mandara?" Salvatore's stunned voice reverberated. "You have a thing for a local princess?"

Funny how Rowan sometimes forgot about the princess part. He thought of her as a research scientist. A professional colleague—and sometimes adversary. But most of all, he thought of her as a desirable woman, someone he suddenly didn't feel comfortable discussing with Salvatore. "Could we get back on topic here? Can you help me investigate the baby's parents or not?"

"Of course I can handle that." The Colonel's tone returned to all business, story time over.

"Thank you, sir. I can't tell you how much I appreciate this." Regardless of his attraction to Mari, Rowan couldn't lose sight of the fact that a defenseless child's future hung in the balance here.

"Just send me photos, fingerprints, footprints and any other data you've picked up."

"Roger. I know the drill."

"And good luck with the princess," Salvatore said, chuckling softly before he hung up.

Rowan drew in a deep breath of salty sea air before returning to the suite. He hated being confined. He missed his clinic, the wide-open spaces around it and the people he helped in a tangible way rather than by giving speeches.

Except once he returned home in a week to prepare for Christmas, his window of time with Mari would be done. Back to business.

He walked across the balcony and entered the door by the picture window, stepping into the sitting room. Mari didn't look up, her focus totally on the baby.

Seeing Mari in an unguarded moment was rare. The woman kept major walls up, giving off a prickly air. Right now, she sat on the sofa with her arms cradling the baby—even her body seemed to wrap inward protectively around this child. Mari might think she knew nothing about children, but her instincts were good. He'd watched enough new moms in his career to identify the ones who would have trouble versus the ones who sensed the kid's needs.

The tableau had a Madonna-and-child air. Maybe it was just the holidays messing with his head. If he wanted his half-baked plan to work, he needed to keep his head on straight and figure out how to get her on board with helping him.

"How's Issa doing?"

Mari looked up quickly, as if startled. She held up the empty bottle. "All done with her feeding."

"I'm surprised you're still sticking around. Your fans must have given up by now. The coast will be clear back to your room."

Saying that, he realized he should have mentioned those overzealous royal watchers to Salvatore. Perhaps some private security might be in order. There was a time he didn't have the funds for things like that, back in the days when he was buried in the debt of school loans, before he'd gone into partnership with a computer-whiz classmate of his.

"Mari? Are you going back to your room?" he repeated.

"I still feel responsible for her." Mari smoothed a finger along the baby's chubby cheek. "And the police will want to speak to me. If I'm here, it will move things along faster."

"You do realize the odds are low that her parents will be found tonight," he said, laying the groundwork for getting her to stick around.

"Of course, I understand." She thumbed aside a hint of milk in the corner of the infant's mouth. "That doesn't stop me from hoping she'll have good news soon."

"You sure seem like a natural with her. Earlier, you said you never babysat."

She shrugged self-consciously. "I was always busy studying."

"There were no children in your world at all?" He sat beside her, drawing in the scent of her flowery perfume. Curiosity consumed him, a desperate need to know exactly what flower she smelled like, what she preferred.

"My mother and father don't have siblings. I'm the only child of only children."

This was the closest to a real conversation they'd ever exchanged, talk that didn't involve work or bickering. He couldn't make a move on her, not with the baby right here in the room. But he could feel her relaxing around him. He wanted more of that, more of her, this exciting woman who kept him on his toes.

What would she do if he casually stretched his arm along the back of the sofa? Her eyes held his and instead of moving, he stayed stock-still, looking back at her, unwilling to risk breaking the connection—

The phone jangled harshly across the room.

Mari jolted. The baby squawked.

And Rowan smiled. This particular moment to get closer to Mari may have ended. But make no mistake, he wasn't giving up. He finally had a chance to explore the tenacious desire that had been dogging him since he'd first seen her.

Anticipation ramped through him at the thought of persuading her to see this connection through to its natural—and satisfying—conclusion.

Three

Pacing in front of the sitting room window, Mari cradled the baby against her shoulder as Rowan talked with the local police. Sure, the infant had seemed three months old when she'd looked at her, but holding her? Little Issa felt younger, more fragile.

Helpless.

So much about this evening didn't add up. The child had been abandoned yet she seemed well cared for. Beyond her chubby arms and legs, she had neatly trimmed fingernails and toenails. Her clothes were simple, but clean. She smelled freshly bathed. Could she have been kidnapped as revenge on someone? Growing up, Mari had been constantly warned of the dangers of people who would try to hurt her to get back at her father, as well as people would use her to get *close* to her father. Trusting anyone had been all but impossible.

She shook off the paranoid thoughts and focused on

the little life in her arms. Mari stroked the baby's impossibly soft cheeks, tapped the dimple in her chin. Did she look like her mother or father? Was she missed? Round chocolate-brown eyes blinked up at her trustingly.

Her heart squeezed tight in her chest in a totally illogical way. She'd only just met the child, for heaven's sake, and she ached to press a kiss to her forehead.

Mari glanced to the side to see if Rowan had observed her weak moment, but he was in the middle of finishing up his phone conversation with the police.

Did he practice looking so hot? Even in jeans, he owned the room. Her eyes were drawn to the breadth of his shoulders, the flex of muscles in his legs as he shuffled from foot to foot, his loafers expensive but well worn. He exuded power and wealth without waste or conspicuous consumption. How could he be such a good man and so annoying at the same time?

Rowan hung up the phone and turned, catching her studying him. He cocked an eyebrow. She forced herself to stare back innocently, her chin tipping even as her body tingled with awareness.

"What did the police say?" she asked casually, swaying from side to side in a way she'd found the baby liked.

"They're just arriving outside the hotel." He closed the three feet between them. "They're on their way up to take her."

"That's it?" Her arms tightened around Issa. "She'll be gone minutes from now? Did they say where they will be sending her? I have connections of my own. Maybe I can help."

His blue eyes were compassionate, weary. "You and I both already know what will happen to her. She will be sent to a local orphanage while the police use their limited resources to look into her past, along with all the other cases and other abandoned kids they have in their stacks of files to investigate. Tough to hear, I realize. But that's how it is. We do what we can, when we can."

"I understand." That didn't stop the frustration or the need to change things for this innocent child in her arms and all the children living in poverty in her country.

He scooped the baby from her before she could protest. "But that's not how it has to be today. We *can* do something this time."

"What do you mean?" She crossed her empty arms over her chest, hope niggling at her that Rowan had a reasonable solution.

"We only have a few more minutes before they arrive so I need to make this quick." He hefted the baby onto his shoulder and rubbed her back in small, hypnotic circles. "I think we should offer to watch Issa."

Thank heaven he was holding the child because he'd stunned Mari numb. She watched his hand smoothing along the baby's back and tried to gather her thoughts. "Um, what did you say?"

"We're both clearly qualified and capable adults." His voice reverberated in soothing waves. "It would be in the best interest of the child, a great Christmas message of goodwill, for us to keep her."

Keep her?

Mari's legs folded out from under her and she sank to the edge of the leather sofa. She couldn't have heard him right. She'd let her attraction to him distract her. "What did you say?"

He sat beside her, his thigh pressing warm and solid against hers. "We can have temporary custody of her, just for a couple of weeks to give the police a chance to find out if she has biological relatives able to care for her."

"Have you lost your mind?" Or maybe she had lost hers because she was actually tempted by his crazy plan.

"Not that I know of."

She pressed the back of her wrist to her forehead, stunned that he was serious. Concerns cycled through her head about work and the hoopla of a media circus. "This is a big decision for both of us, something that should be thought over carefully."

"In medicine I have to think fast. I don't always have the luxury of a slow and steady scientific exam," he said, with a wry twist to his lips. "Years of going with my gut have honed my instincts, and my instincts say this is the right thing to do."

Her mind settled on his words and while she never would have gotten to that point on her own, the thought of this baby staying with him rather than in some institution was appealing. "So you'll be her temporary guardian?"

"Our case is more powerful if we offer to do this as a partnership. Both of us." His deep bass and logic drew her in. "Think of the positive PR you'll receive. Your father's press corps will be all over this philanthropic act of yours, which should take some pressure off you at the holidays," he offered, so logically she could almost believe him.

"It isn't as simple as that. The press can twist things, rumors will start about both of us." What if they thought it was *her* baby? She squeezed her eyes closed and bolted off the sofa. "I need more time."

The buzzer rang at the door. Her heart went into her throat.

She heard Rowan follow her. Felt the heat of him at her back. Felt the urgency.

"Issa doesn't have time, Mari. You need to decide if you'll do this. Decide to commit now."

She turned sharply to find him standing so close the three of them made a little family circle. "But you could take her on your own—"

"Maybe the authorities would accept that. But maybe not. We should lead with our strongest case. For her." He cradled the baby's head. "We didn't ask for this, but we're here." Fine lines fanned from the corners of his eyes, attesting to years of worry and long hours in the sun. "We may disagree on a lot of things, but we're people who help."

"You're guilt-tripping me," she accused in the small space between them, her words crackling like small snaps of electricity. And the guilt was working. Her concerns about gossip felt absolutely pathetic in light of the plight of this baby.

As much as she gave Rowan hell about his computer inventions, she knew all about his humanitarian work at the charity clinic. He devoted his life to helping others. He had good qualities underneath that arrogant charm.

"Well, people like us who help in high-stakes situations learn to use whatever means are at our disposal." He half smiled, creasing the lines deeper. "Is it working?"

Those lines from worry and work were real. She might disapprove of his methods, but she couldn't question his motivations, his altruistic spirit. Seeing him deftly rock the baby to sleep ended any argument. For this one time at least, she was on his team.

For Issa.

"Open the door and you'll find out."

* * *

Three hours later, Mari watched Rowan close the hotel door after the police. Stacks of paperwork rested on the table, making it official. She and Rowan had temporary custody of the baby while the police investigated further and tried to track down the employee who'd walked away from the cart.

Issa slept in her infant seat, secure for now.

Mari sighed in relief, slumping in exhaustion back onto the sofa. She'd done it. She'd played the princess card and all but demanded the police obey her "request" to care for the baby until Christmas—less than two weeks away—or until more information could be found about Issa's parents. She'd agreed to care for the child with Rowan Boothe, a doctor who'd saved countless young lives. The police had seemed relieved to have the problem resolved so easily. They'd taken photos of the baby and prints. They would look into the matter, but their faces said they didn't hold out much hope of finding answers.

Maybe she should hire a private detective to look deeper than the police. Except it was almost midnight now. Any other plans would have to wait until morning.

Rowan rested a hand on Mari's shoulder. "Would you get my medical bag so I can do a more thorough checkup? It's in the bedroom by my shaving kit. I'd like to listen to her heart."

He squeezed her shoulder once, deliciously so, until her mouth dried right up from that simple touch.

"Medical bag." She shot to her feet. "Right, of course."

She was too tired and too unsettled to fight off the sensual allure of him right now. She stepped into Rowan's bedroom, her eyes drawn to the hints of him everywhere. A suit was draped over the back of a rattan rocker by sliding doors that led out to a balcony. She didn't consider herself a romantic by any stretch but the thought of sitting out there under the stars with someone...

God, what was the matter with her? This man had driven her bat crazy for years. Now she was daydreaming about an under-the-stars make-out session that would lead back into the bedroom. His bedroom.

Her eyes skated to the sprawling four-poster draped with gauzy netting, a dangerous place to look with his provocative glances still steaming up her memories. An e-reader rested on the bedside table, his computer laptop tucked underneath. Her mind filled with images of him sprawled in that massive bed—working, reading—details about a man she'd done her best to avoid. She pulled her eyes away.

The bathroom was only a few feet away. She charged across the plush carpet, pushing the door wide. The scent of him was stronger in here, and she couldn't resist breathing in the soapy aroma clinging to the air—patchouli, perhaps. She swallowed hard as goose bumps of awareness rose on her skin, her senses on overload.

A whimpering baby cry from the main room reminded her of her mission here. She shook off frivolous thoughts and snagged the medical bag from the marble vanity. She wrapped her hands around the well-worn leather with his name on a scratched brass plate. The dichotomy of a man this wealthy carrying such a battered bag added layers to her previously clear-cut image of him.

Clutching the bag to her stomach, she returned to the sitting room. Rowan set aside a bottle and settled the baby girl against his shoulder, his broad palm patting her back.

How exactly were they going to work this baby bargain? She had absolutely no idea.

For the first time in her life, she'd done something completely irrational. The notion that Rowan Boothe had that much power over her behavior rattled her to her toes.

She really was losing it. She needed to finish this day, get some sleep and find some clarity.

From this point forward, she would keep a firmer grip on herself. And that meant no more drooling over the sexy doc, and definitely no more sniffing his tempting aftershave.

Rowan tapped through the images on his laptop, reviewing the file on the baby, including the note he'd scanned in before passing it over to the police. He'd sent a copy of everything to Colonel Salvatore. Even though it was too early to expect results, he still hoped for some news, for the child's sake.

Meanwhile, though, he'd accomplished a freaking miracle in buying himself time with Mari. A week or so at the most, likely more, but possibly less since her staying rested solely on the child. If relatives were found quickly, she'd be headed home. He didn't doubt his decision, even if part of his motivation was selfish. This baby provided the perfect opportunity to spend more time with Mari, to learn more about her and figure out what made her tick. Then, hopefully, she would no longer be a thorn in his side—or a pain in his libido.

He tapped the screen back to the scanned image of the note that had been left with the baby.

Dr. Boothe, you are known for your charity and generosity. Please look over my baby girl, Issa.

My husband died in a border battle and I cannot give Issa what she needs. Tell her I love her and will think of her always.

His ears tuned in to the sound of Mari walking toward him, then the floral scent of her wrapped around him. She stood behind him without speaking and he realized she was reading over his shoulder, taking in the note.

"Loves her?" Mari sighed heavily. "The woman abandoned her to a stranger based on that person's reputation in the press."

"I take it your heart isn't tugged." He closed the laptop and turned to face her.

"My heart is broken for this child—" she waved toward the sleeping infant in the baby seat "—and what's in store for her if we don't find answers, along with a truly loving and responsible family."

"I'm hopeful that my contacts will have some information sooner than the police." A reminder that he needed to make the most of his time with Mari. What if Salvatore called with concrete news tomorrow? He looked over at Mari, imagining being with her, drawing her into his bedroom, so close to where they were now. "Let's talk about how we'll look after the baby here during the conference."

"Now?" She jolted in surprise. "It's past midnight."

"There are things to take care of, like ordering more baby gear, meeting with the hotel's babysitting service." He ticked off each point on his fingers. "Just trying to fill in the details on our plan."

"You actually want to plan?" Her kissable lips twitched with a smile.

"No need to be insulting," he bantered right back, enjoying the way she never treated him like some freaking saint just because of where he chose to work. He wasn't the good guy the press painted him to be just because he'd reformed. The past didn't simply go away. He still had debts that could never be made right.

"I'm being careful—finally. Like I should have been earlier." Mari fidgeted with the hem of her untucked shirt, weariness straining her face, dark circles under her eyes. "She's a child. A human being. We can't just fly by the seat of our pants."

He wanted to haul Mari into his arms and let her sleep against his chest, tell her she didn't have to be so serious, she didn't have to take the weight of the world on her shoulders. She could share the load with him.

Instead, he dragged a chair from the tiny teak table by the window and gestured for her to sit, to rest. "I'm not exactly without the means or ability to care for a child. It's only for a short time until we figure out more about her past so we don't have to fly by the seat of our pants." He dragged over a chair for himself as well and sat across from her.

"How is it so easy for you to disregard the rules?" She slumped back.

"You're free to go if you wish."

She shook her head. "I brought her in here. She's my responsibility."

Ah, so she wasn't in a rush to run out the door. "Do you intend to personally watch over her while details are sorted out?"

"I can hire someone."

"Ah, that's right. You're a princess with endless re-sources," he teased, taking her hands in his.

She pulled back. "Are you calling me spoiled?"

He squeezed her fingers, holding on, liking the feel

of her hands in his. "I would never dare insult you, Princess. You should know that well enough from the provocative things I said to you five minutes ago."

"Oh. Okay." She nibbled on her bottom lip, surprise flickering through her eyes.

"First things first." He thumbed the inside of her wrists.

"Your plan?" Her breathing seemed to hitch.

"We pretend to be dating and since we're dating, and we'd be spending this holiday time together anyway, we decided to help with the child. How does that work for a plan?"

"What?" She gasped in surprise. "Do you really think people are going to believe we went from professional adversaries to lovers in a heartbeat?"

He saw her pulse throb faster, ramping up his in response.

"Lovers, huh? I like the sound of that."

"You said—"

"I said dating." He squeezed her hands again. "But I like your plan better."

"This isn't a plan." She pulled free, inching her chair back. "It's insanity."

"A plan that will work. People will believe it. More than that, they will eat it up. Everyone will want to hear more about the aloof princess finding romance and playing Good Samaritan at Christmastime. If they have an actual human interest piece to write about you it will distract them from digging around to create a story."

Her eyes went wide with panic, but she stayed in her seat. She wasn't running. Yet. He'd pushed as far as he could for tonight. Tomorrow would offer up a whole new day for making his case.

He shoved to his feet. "Time for bed."

"Oh, um," she squeaked, standing, as well. "Bed?"

He could see in her eyes that she'd envisioned them sharing a bed before this moment. He didn't doubt for a second what he saw and it gave him a surge of victory. Definitely best to bide his time and wait for a moment when she wasn't skittish. A time when she would be all in, as fully committed as he was to exploring this crazy attraction.

"Yes, Mari, bed. I'll watch the baby tonight and if you're comfortable, we can alternate the night shift."

She blinked in surprise. "Right. The night schedule. Are you sure you can handle a baby at night and still participate in the conference?"

"I'm a doctor. I've pulled far longer shifts with no sleep in the hospital. I'll be fine."

"Of course. Then I'll call the front desk to move me to a larger suite so I'll have enough space for the baby and the daytime sitter."

"No need to do that. This suite is plenty large enough for all of us."

Her jaw dropped. "Excuse me?"

"All of us," he said calmly, holding her with his eyes as fully as he'd held her hand, gauging her every blink. Needing to win her over. "It makes sense if we're going to watch the baby, we should do it together for efficiency. The concierge already sent someone to pack your things."

Her chest rose faster and faster, the gentle curves of her breasts pressing against the wrinkled silk of her blouse. "You've actually made quite a few plans."

"Sometimes flying by the seat of your pants works quite well." Otherwise he never would have had this chance to win her over. "A bellhop will be delivering your luggage shortly along with more baby gear that I ordered."

"Here? The two—three—of us? In one suite?" she asked, although he noticed she didn't say no.

Victory was so close.

"There's plenty of space for the baby. You can have your own room. Unless you want to sleep in mine." He grinned. "You have to know I wouldn't object."

Four

Buttoning up her navy blue power suit the next morning, Mari couldn't believe she'd actually spent the night in Rowan Boothe's hotel suite. Not his room, but a mere wall away. He'd cared for the baby until morning as he'd promised. A good thing, since she needed to learn a lot more before she trusted herself to care for Issa.

She tucked pins into her swept-back hair, but the mirror showed her to be the same slightly rumpled academic she'd always been. While she wasn't a total innocent when it came to men, she wasn't the wild and reckless type who agreed to spend the night in the same suite as a guy she'd never actually dated. She'd expected to toss and turn all night after the confusing turn of events. She couldn't believe she'd agreed.

Yet in spite of all her doubts, she'd slept better than anytime she could remember. Perhaps because the odds of anyone finding her here were next to nil. Her longtime professional feud with him was well-known, and they hadn't yet gone public with this strange idea of joint custody of an abandoned baby. The hotel staff or someone on the police force would likely leak juicy tidbits about the royal family to the press, but it would all be gossip and conjecture until she and Rowan made their official statement verifying the situation.

Soon enough the world would know. Eventually the cameras would start snapping. Her gut clenched at the thought of all those stalkers and the press feeding on the tiniest of details, the least scrap of her life. What if they fed on the innocence of the baby?

Or what if they picked up on the attraction between her and Rowan?

There was still time to back out, write it all off as simple gossip. The urge was strong to put back on that Christmas hat and slip away, to hide in her lab, far, far from the stress of being on show and always falling short. She craved the peace of her laboratory and cubby-hole office, where she truly reigned supreme. Here, in Rowan's suite, she felt so off-kilter, so out of control.

A coo from the other room reminded her she needed to hurry. She stepped away from the mirror and slid her feet into her low, blue pumps. She pulled open her bed-room door, then sagged to rest against the doorjamb. The sight of the little one in a ruffled pink sleeper, rest-ing against Rowan's shoulder, looked like something straight off a greeting card. So perfect.

Except that perfection was an illusion.

Even though Rowan had the baby well in hand, the child was helpless outside their protection. Issa had no one to fight for her, not really, not if Mari and Rowan gave up on her. Even if Mari left and Rowan stayed, he couldn't offer the baby everything Mari could. Her fame—that fame she so resented—could be Issa's salvation.

The baby would get an exposure the police never could have provided. In these days of DNA testing, it wasn't as if fake relatives could step forward to claim a precious infant. So Mari wasn't going anywhere, except to give her presentation at the medical conference, then she'd take the baby for a walk with Rowan.

Looking around the suite strewn with baby paraphernalia, anyone would believe they were truly guardians of the child. Rowan had ordered a veritable nursery set up with top-of-the-line gear. A portable bassinet rested in the corner of the main room, a monitor perched beside it. He'd ordered a swing, a car seat, plus enough clothes, food and diapers for three babies for a month.

He knew what an infant needed, or at least he knew who to call.

Hopefully that call had included a sitter since he was dressed for work as well, in a black Savile Row suit with a Christmas-red tie. God, he was handsome, with his blond hair damp and combed back, his broad hand patting the baby's back. His face wore a perpetual five-o'clock shadow, just enough to be nighttime sexy without sliding over into scruffy.

He filled out the expensive suit with ease. Was there any realm that made this man uncomfortable? He'd taken care of the baby through the night and still looked totally put together.

His eyes searched hers and she shivered, wondering what he saw as he stood there holding Issa so easily. The man was a multitasker. He was also someone with an uncanny knack for getting into a person's mind. He'd found her vulnerable spot in one evening. After all of her tense and bicontinental Christmases, she simply

couldn't bear for this child to spend the holidays confused and scared while the system figured out what to
do with her—and the other thousands of orphans in
their care.

She couldn't replace the child's mother, but she could
make sure the child was held, cared for, secure. To do
that, she needed to keep her mind off the charismatic
man a few feet away.

He looked over at her as if he'd known she was there
the whole time. "Good morning. Coffee's ready along
with a tray of pastries."

And some sweet, sticky *bouili* dipping sauce.

Her mouth watered for the food almost as much as
for the man. She walked to the granite countertop and
poured herself a mug of coffee from the silver carafe.
She inhaled the rich java fragrance steaming up from
the dark roast with hints of fruity overtones. "Did she
sleep well?"

"Well enough, just as I would expect from a baby
who's experienced so much change," he said, tucking
the baby into a swing with expert hands. "The hotel's
sending up a sitter for the day. I verified her references
and qualifications. They seem solid, so we should be
covered through our lecture presentations. Tonight we
can take Issa out for dinner and a stroll incognito, kill
time while we let the cops finish their initial investiga-
tion. If they haven't found out anything by tomorrow,
we can go public."

Dinner out? Revealing their plan to the world? Her
heart pounded with nerves, but it was too late to go back
now. The world would already be buzzing with leaked
news. Best to make things official on their own terms.

If Issa's family wasn't found by tomorrow, she would
have to call her parents and let them know about her

strange partnership with Rowan. First, she had to decide how she wanted to spin it so her parents didn't jump to the wrong conclusions—or try to interfere. This needed to be a good thing for the baby, not just about positive press. She would play it by ear today and call them tonight once she had a firmer idea of what she'd gotten herself into.

Maybe Issa would be back with relatives before supper. A good thing, right?

Rowan started the baby swing in motion. The click-click-click mingled with a low nursery tune.

Mari cleared her throat. "I'll check on Issa during lunch and make sure all's going well with the sitter."

"That's a good idea. Thank you." He cradled a cup in strong hands that could so easily crush the fine china.

She shrugged dismissively. It was no hardship to skip the luncheon. She disliked the idle table chitchat at these sorts of functions anyway. "No big sacrifice. Nobody likes conference lunch food."

Laughing softly, he eyed her over his cup of coffee. "I appreciate your working with me on this."

"You didn't leave me much choice, Dr. Guilt Trip."

His smile creased dimples into his face. "Who'd have thought you'd have a sense of humor?"

"That's not nice." She traced the rim of her cup.

"Neither is saying I coerced you." He tapped the tip of her scrunched nose. "People always have a choice."

Of course he was right. She could always walk, but thinking overlong about her compulsion to stay made her edgy. She sat at the table, the morning sun glistening off the ocean waters outside. "Of course I'm doing this of my own free will, for Issa's sake. It has absolutely nothing to do with you."

"Hello? I thought we weren't going to play games."

She avoided his eyes and sipped her steaming java. "What do you mean, games?"

"Fine. I'll spell it out." He set down his cup on the table and sat beside her, their knees almost touching. "You have made it your life's mission to tear down my research and to keep me at arm's length. Yet you chose to stay here, for the baby, but you and I both know there's more to it than that. There's a chemistry between us, sparks."

"Those sparks—" she proceeded warily "—are just a part of our disagreements."

"Disagreements? You've publically denounced my work. That's a little more than a disagreement."

Of course he wouldn't forget that. "See, sparks. Just like I said."

His eyes narrowed. If only he could understand her point. She only wanted to get past his impulsive, pigheaded mindset and improve his programs.

"Mari, you're damn good at diverting from the topic."

"I'm right on point," she said primly. "This is about our work and you refused to consider that I see things from another angle. You've made it your life's mission to ignore any pertinent input I might have for your technological inventions. I am a scientist."

He scraped a hand over his drying hair. "Then why are you so against my computer program?"

"I thought we were talking about what's best for Issa." She glanced at the baby girl still snoozing in the swing with the lullaby playing.

"Princess, you are making my head spin." He sagged back. "We're here for Issa, but that doesn't mean we can't talk about other things, so quit changing the subject every three seconds. In the interest of getting along better during these next couple of weeks, let's discuss your public disdain for my life's work."

Was he serious? Did he really want to hash that out now? He certainly looked serious, drinking his coffee and downing bites of breakfast. Maybe he was one of those people who wanted to make peace at the holidays in spite of bickering all year round. She knew plenty about that. Which should have taught her well. Problems couldn't be avoided or the resolutions delayed. Best to confront them when given the opening.

"Your program is just too much of a snapshot of a diagnosis, too much of a quick fix. It's like fast-food medicine. It doesn't take into account enough variables." Now she waited for the explosion.

He inhaled a deep breath and tipped back in his chair before answering. "I can see your point. To a degree, I agree. I would welcome the chance to give every patient the hands-on medical treatment of the best clinic in the world. But I'm treating the masses with a skeleton team of medical professionals. That computer program helps us triage in half the time."

"What about people who use your program to cut corners?"

Rowan frowned. "What do you mean?"

"You can't truly believe the world is as altruistic as you? What about the clinics using that program to funnel more patients through just to make more money?"

His chair legs hit the floor, his jaw tightening. "I can't be the conscience for the world," he said in an even tone although a tic had started in the corner of his azure-blue eye. "I can only deal with the problems in front of me. I'm working my tail off to come up with help. Would I prefer more doctors and nurses, PAs and midwives, human hands? Hell, yes. But I make do with what I have and I do what I can so those of us who are here can be as efficient as possible under conditions they didn't come close to teaching us about during my residency."

"So you admit the program isn't optimal?" She couldn't believe he'd admitted to the program's short-comings.

"Really?" He threw up his hands. "That's your take-away from my whole rambling speech? I'm being prac-tical, and you're being idealistic in your ivory tower of research. I'm sorry if that makes you angry to hear."

"I'm not the volatile sort." She pursed her lips tightly to resist the temptation to snap at him for devaluing her work.

Slowly, he grinned, leaning closer. "That's too bad."

"Pardon me?" she asked, not following his logic at all.

"Because when you get all flustered, you're really hot."

Her eyes shot open wide, surprise skittering through her, followed by skepticism. "Does that line really work for you?"

"I've never tried it before." He angled closer until his mouth almost brushed hers. "You'll have to let me know."

Before she could gasp in half a breath of air, he brushed his mouth over hers. Shock quickly turned to something else entirely as delicious tingles shimmered through her. Her body warmed to the feel of him, the newness of his kiss, their first kiss, a moment already burning itself into her memory, searing through her with liquid heat.

Her hand fluttered to his chest, flattening, feeling the steady, strong beat of his heart under her palm matching the thrumming heartbeat in her ears. His kiss was nothing like she would have imagined. She'd expected him to be out of control, wild. Instead, he held her like spun glass. He touched her with deft, sensitive hands, surgeon's hands that knew just the right places to graze, stroke, tease for maximum payoff. Her body thrilled at the caress down her spine that cupped her bottom, bringing her closer.

Already she could feel herself sinking into a spiral of lush sensation. Her limbs went languid with desire. She wanted more of this, more of him, but they were a heartbeat away from tossing away their clothes and inhibitions. Too risky for a multitude of reasons, not the least of which was the possibility of someone discovering them.

Those sorts of exposé photos she absolutely did not want circulating on the internet or anywhere else.

Then, too soon he pulled away. How embarrassing that he was the one to stop since she already knew the kiss had to end. Never had she lost control this quickly.

Cool air and embarrassment washed over her as she sat stunned in her chair. He'd completely knocked the world out from under her with one simple kiss. Had he even been half as affected as she was by the moment? She looked quickly at him, but his back was to her already and she realized he was walking toward the door.

"Rowan?"

He glanced over his shoulder. "The buzzer—" Was that a hint of hoarseness in his voice? "The baby sitter has arrived."

Mari pressed her fingers to her still tingling lips, wondering if a day apart would be enough time to shore up her defenses again before their evening out.

* * *

That evening, Rowan pushed the baby stroller along the marketplace road. Vendors lined the street, and he eyed the place for potential trouble spots. Even with bodyguards trailing them, he kept watch. The baby in the stroller depended on him.

And so did the woman beside him. Mari wore her business suit, without the jacket, just the skirt and blouse, a scarf wrapped over her head and large sunglasses on for disguise, looking like a leggy 1940s movie star.

She strolled beside him, her hand trailing along stalls that overflowed with handwoven cloths and colorful beads. Bins of fresh fruits and vegetables sat out, the scent of roasting turkey and goat carrying on the salty beach breeze. Waves crashed in the distance, adding to the rhythmic percussion of a local band playing Christmas tunes while children danced. Locals and tourists angled past in a crush, multiple languages coming at him in stereo—Cape Verdean Creole, Portuguese, French, English…and heaven knew how many others.

Tonight, he finally had Mari out of the work world and alone with him. Okay, alone with him, a baby, bodyguards and a crush of shoppers.

The last rays of the day bathed Mari in a crimson glow. She hadn't referenced their kiss earlier, so he'd followed her lead on that, counting it a victory that she wasn't running. Clearly, she'd been as turned on as he was. But still, she hadn't run.

With the taste of her etched in his memory, there was not a chance in hell he was going anywhere. More than ever, he was determined to get closer to her, to sample a hell of a lot more than her lips.

But he was smart enough to take his time. This

woman was smart—and skittish. He made his living off reading subtle signs, deciphering puzzles, but this woman? She was the most complex individual he'd ever met.

Could that be a part of her appeal? The mysterious element? The puzzle?

The "why" of it didn't matter so much to him right now. He just wanted to make the most of this evening out and hopefully gain some traction in identifying Issa's family. While they'd gotten a few curious looks from people and a few surreptitiously snapped photos, so far, no one had openly approached them.

He checked left and right again, reconfirming their unobtrusive security detail, ensuring the men were close enough to intervene if needed. Colonel Salvatore had been very accommodating about rounding up the best in the business ASAP, although he still had no answers on the baby's identity. Issa's footprints hadn't come up in any databases, but then the child could have been a home birth, unregistered. Salvatore had insisted he hadn't come close to exhausting all their investigative options yet.

For now, their best lead would come from controlled press exposure, getting the child seen and praying some legit relative stepped up to claim her.

Meanwhile, Rowan finally had his chance to be with Mari, to romance her, and what better place than in this country he loved, with holiday festivities lightening the air. He would have cared for the baby even if Mari had opted out, so he didn't feel guilty about using the child to persuade Mari to stay. He was just surprised she'd agreed so easily.

That gave him pause—and encouragement.

She hesitated at a stall of clay bowls painted with

scenes of everyday life. She trailed her fingers along a piece before moving on to the jewelry, where she stopped for the longest time yet. He'd found her weakness. He wouldn't have pegged her as the type to enjoy those sorts of baubles, but her face lit up as she sifted through beads, necklaces. She seemed to lean more toward practical clothes and loose-fitting suits or dresses. Tonight she wore a long jean jumper and thick leather sandals.

Her hand lingered on the bracelets before she stepped back, the wistfulness disappearing from her golden eyes. "We should find somewhere to eat dinner. The conference food has left me starving for something substantial."

"Point the way. Ladies choice tonight," he said, curious to know what she would choose, what she liked, the way he'd just learned her preferences on the bracelets. Shoppers bustled past, cloth sacks bulging with purchases, everything from souvenirs to groceries.

Instinctively, she moved between the baby stroller and the hurrying masses. "How about we eat at a streetside café while we watch the performances?"

"Sounds good to me." He could keep watch better that way, but then he always kept his guard up. His work with Interpol showed him too well that crime didn't always lurk in the expected places.

He glanced down the street, taking in the carolers playing drums and pipes. Farther down, a group of children acted out the nativity in simple costumes. The sun hadn't gone down yet, so there was less worry about crime.

Rowan pointed to the nearby café with blue tables and fresh fish. "What about there?"

"Perfect, I'll be able to see royal watchers coming."

"Although your fan club seems to have taken a break." He wheeled the stroller toward the restaurant where the waitress instructed them to seat themselves. Issa still slept hard, sucking on a fist and looking too cute for words in a red Christmas sleeper.

Mari laughed, the scarf sliding down off her head, hanging loosely around her neck. "Funny how I couldn't escape photo-happy sorts at the hotel—" she tugged at either end of the silky scarf "—and yet now no one seems to notice me when some notoriety could serve some good."

"Issa's photo has already been released to law enforcement. If nothing comes of it by tomorrow morning, the story will break about our involvement and add an extra push. For now, anyway, the baby and I make good camouflage for you to savor your dinner."

"Mama-flage," she said as he held out her chair for her.

"Nice! I'm enjoying your sense of humor more and more." And he was enjoying a lot more about her as well this evening. He caught the sweet floral scent on her neck as he eased her chair into place.

His mind filled with images of her wearing only perfume and an assortment of the colorful beads from the marketplace. Damn, and now he would be awake all night thinking about the lithe figure she hid under her shapeless suits.

Mari glanced back at him, peering over her sunglasses, her amber eyes reflecting the setting sun. "Is something the matter?"

"Of course not." He took his seat across from her, his foot firmly on the stroller even knowing there were a half-dozen highly trained bodyguards stationed anonymously around them. She might not use them, but he'd made sure to hire a crew for the safety of both Mari and Issa.

The waitress brought glasses and a pitcher of fruit juice—guava and mango—not showing the least sign of recognizing the royal customer she served. This was a good dry run for when they would announce their joint custody publicly.

"What a cute baby," the waitress cooed without even looking at them. "I just love her little red Christmas outfit. She looks like an adorable elf." She toyed with toes in tiny green booties.

"Thank you," Mari said, then mouthed at Rowan, "Mama-flage."

After they'd placed their order for swordfish with *cachupa*—a mixture of corn and beans—Mari leaned back in her chair, appearing far more relaxed than the woman who'd taken refuge in his suite the night before. She eased the sunglasses up to rest on top of her head.

"You look like you've had a couple of servings of grogue." Grogue was a sugar cane liquor drunk with honey that flowed freely here.

"No alcohol for me tonight, thank you." She lifted a hand. "My turn to watch the baby."

"I don't mind taking the night shift if you're not comfortable."

She raised a delicately arched dark eyebrow. "Somewhere in the world, a couple dozen new moms just swooned and they don't know why."

"I'm just trying to be helpful. You have the heavier presentation load."

She stirred sugar into her coffee. "Are you trying to coerce me into kissing you again?"

"As I recall, I kissed you and you didn't object."

She set her spoon down with a decisive clink. "Well, you shouldn't count on doing it again."

"Request duly noted," he replied, not daunted in the least. He saw the speeding of her pulse, the flush of awareness along her dusky skin.

He started to reach for her, just to brush his knuckles along that pulse under the pretense of brushing something aside—except a movement just out of the corner of his eye snagged his attention. Alert, he turned to see an older touristy-looking couple moving toward them.

Mari sat back abruptly, her hand fluttering to her throat. Rowan assessed the pair. Trouble could come in any form, at any age. The bodyguards' attention ramped up as they stalked along the perimeter, closing the circle of protection. Mari reached for her sunglasses. Rowan didn't see any signs of concealed weapons, but he slid his hand inside his jacket, resting his palm on his 9 mm, just in case.

The elderly husband, wearing a camera and a man-purse over his shoulder, stopped beside Mari.

"Excuse us, but would you mind answering a question?" he asked with a thick New Jersey accent.

Was their cover busted? If so, did it really matter that they went public a few hours early? Not for him or the baby, but because he didn't want Mari upset, bolting away from the press, terrified, like the night before.

She tipped her head regally, her shoulders braced as she placed the sunglasses on the table. "Go ahead."

The wife angled in eagerly. "Are the two of you from around here?"

Rowan's mouth twitched. Not busted at all. "Not from the island, ma'am. We both live on the mainland."

"Oh, all right, I see." She furrowed her brow. "Maybe

you can still help me. Where's the Kwanzaa celebration?"

Mari's eyes went wide with surprise, then a hint of humor glinted before her face went politely neutral. "Ma'am, that's an American tradition."

"Oh, I didn't realize." Her forehead furrowed as she adjusted her fanny pack. "I just didn't expect so much Christmas celebration."

Mari glanced at the children finishing up their nativity play and accepting donations for their church. "Africa has a varied cultural and religious heritage. How much of each you find depends on which portion of the continent you're visiting. This area was settled by the Portuguese," she explained patiently, "which accounts for the larger influence of Christian traditions than you might find in other regions."

"Thank you for being so patient in explaining." The wife pulled out a travel guide and passed it to her husband, her eyes staying on Mari. "You look very familiar, dear. Have I seen you somewhere before?"

Pausing for a second, Mari eyed them, then said, "People say I look like the Princess Mariama Mandara. Sometimes I even let folks believe that."

She winked, grinning mischievously.

The older woman laughed. "What a wicked thing to do, young lady. But then I imagine people deserve what they get if they like to sneak photos for the internet."

"Would you like a photo of me with the baby on your phone?" Mari leaned closer to the stroller, sweeping back the cover so baby Issa's face was in clear view. "I'll put on my best princess smile."

"Oh, I wouldn't even know how to work the camera on that new phone our kids gave us for our fiftieth anniversary." She elbowed her husband. "We just use our old Polaroid, isn't that right, Nils?"

"I'm getting it out, Meg, hold on a minute." He fished around inside his man-purse.

Mari extended her arm. "Meg, why don't you get in the photo, too?"

"Oh, yes, thank you. The grandkids will love it." She fluffed her bobbed gray hair with her fingers then leaned in to smile while her husband's old Polaroid spit out picture after picture. "Now you and your husband lean in to pose for one with your daughter."

Daughter? Rowan jolted, the fun of the moment suddenly taking on a different spin. He liked kids and he sure as hell wanted Mari, but the notion of a pretend marriage? That threatened to give him hives. He swallowed down the bite of bile over the family he'd wrecked so many years ago and pretended for the moment life could be normal for him. He kneeled beside Mari and the baby, forcing his face into the requisite smile. He was a good actor.

He'd had lots of practice.

The couple finished their photo shoot, doling out thanks and leaving an extra Polaroid shot behind for them. The image developed in front of him, blurry shapes coming into focus, much like his thoughts, his need to have Mari.

Rowan sank back into his chair as the waitress brought their food. Once she left, he asked Mari, "Why didn't you tell that couple the truth about us, about yourself? It was the perfect opening."

"There were so many people around. If I had, they would have been mobbed out of the photo. When the official story about us fostering the baby hits the news in the morning, they'll realize their photo of a princess is real and they'll have a great story to tell their grand-children. We still get what we want and they get their cool story."

"That was nice of you to do for them." He draped a napkin over his knee. "I know how much you hate the notoriety of being royalty."

She twisted her napkin between her fingers before dropping it on her lap. "I'm not an awful person."

Had he hurt her feelings? He'd never imagined this boldly confident woman might be insecure. "I never said you were. I think your research is admirable."

"Really? I seem to recall a particular magazine in-terview where you accused me of trying to sabotage your work. In fact, when I came into your suite with the room-service cart, you accused me of espionage."

"My word choices may have been a bit harsh. The stakes were high." And yeah, he liked seeing her riled up with fire in her eyes. "My work world just doesn't give me the luxury of the time you have in yours."

"I simply prefer life to be on my terms when possi-ble. So much in this world is beyond anyone's control."

Her eyes took on a faraway look that made him burn to reel her back into the moment, to finish the thought out loud so he could keep learning more about what made this woman tick. But she'd already distanced her-self from him, deep in thought, looking off down the road at the musicians.

He needed those insights if he expected to get a sec-ond kiss—and more from her. But he was beginning to realize that if he wanted more, he was going to have to pony up some confidences of his own. An uncom-fortable prospect.

As he looked at Mari swaying absently in time with the music, her lithe body at ease and graceful, he knew having her would be well worth any cost.

Five

Mari soaked in the sound of street music mellowing the warm evening air. The steady beat of the *bougarabou* drum with the players' jangling bracelets enriching the percussion reminded her of childhood days. Back when her parents were still together and she lived in Africa full-time, other than visits to the States to see her maternal grandparents.

Those first seven years of her life had been idyllic—or so she'd thought. She hadn't known anything about the painful undercurrents already rippling through her parents' marriage. She hadn't sensed the tension in their voices over royal pressures and her mother's homesickness.

For a genius, she'd missed all the obvious signs. But then, she'd never had the same skill reading people that she had for reading data. She'd barely registered that her mother was traveling to Atlanta more and more frequently. Her first clue had come near the end when she'd overheard her mom talking about buying a home in the States during their Christmas vacation. They wouldn't be staying with her grandparents any longer during U.S. visits. They would have their own place, not a room with family. Her parents had officially split up and filed for divorce over the holidays.

Christmas music never sounded quite the same to her again, on either continent.

The sway melted away from her shoulders and Mari stilled in her wrought-iron seat. The wind still wound around her as they sat at the patio dining area, but her senses moved on from the music to the air of roasting meat from the kitchen and the sound of laughing children. All of it was almost strong enough to distract her from the weight of Rowan's gaze.

Almost.

She glanced over at him self-consciously. "Why are you staring at me? I must be a mess." She touched her hair, tucking a stray strand back into the twist, then smoothed her rumpled suit shirt and adjusted the silver scarf draped around her neck. "It's been a long day and the breeze is strong tonight."

Since when had she cared about her appearance for more than the sake of photos? She forced her hands back to her lap.

Rowan's tanned face creased with his confident grin. "Your smile is radiant." He waved a broad hand to encompass the festivities playing out around them. "The way you're taking in everything, appreciating the joy of the smallest details, your pleasure in it all is... mesmerizing."

His blue eyes downright twinkled like the stars in the night sky.

Was he flirting with her? She studied him suspiciously. The restaurant window behind him filled with the movement of diners and waiters, the edges blurred by the spray of fake snow. She'd always been entranced by those pretend snowy displays in the middle of a warm island Christmas.

"Joy? It's December, Rowan. The Christmas season of *joy*. Of course I'm happy." She thought fast, desperate to defer conversation about her. Talking about Rowan's past felt a lot more comfortable than worrying about tucking in her shirt, for God's sake. "What kind of traditions did you enjoy with your family growing up?"

He leaned back in his chair, his gaze still homed in solely on Mari in spite of the festivities going on around them. "We did the regular holiday stuff like a tree, carols, lots of food."

"What kind of food?" she asked just as Issa squirmed in the stroller.

He shrugged, adjusting the baby's pacifier until the infant settled back to sleep. "Regular Christmas stuff."

His ease with the baby was admirable—and heart-tugging. "Come on," Mari persisted, "fill in the blanks for me. There are lots of ways to celebrate Christmas and regular food here isn't the same as regular food somewhere else. Besides, I grew up with chefs. Cooking is still a fascinating mystery to me."

He forked up a bite of swordfish. "It's just like following the steps in a chemistry experiment."

"Maybe in theory." She sipped her fruit juice, the blend bursting along her taste buds with a hint of coconut, her senses hyperaware since Rowan kissed her. "Suffice it to say I'm a better scientist than a cook. But back to you. What was your favorite Christmas treat?"

He set his fork aside, his foot gently tapping the

stroller back and forth. "My mom liked to decorate sugar cookies, but my brother, Dylan, and I weren't all that into it. We ate more of the frosting than went on the cookies."

The image wrapped around her like a comfortable blanket. "That sounds perfect. I always wanted a sibling to share moments like that with. Tell me more. Details... Trains or dump trucks? Bikes or ugly sweaters?"

"We didn't have a lot of money, so my folks saved and tucked away gifts all year long. They always seemed a bit embarrassed that they couldn't give us more, but we were happy. And God knows, it's more than most of the kids I work with will ever have."

"You sound like you had a close family. That's a priceless gift."

Something flickered through his eyes that she couldn't quite identify, like gray clouds over a blue sky, but then they cleared so fast she figured she must have been mistaken. She focused on his words, more curious about this man than any she'd ever known.

"At around three-thirty on Christmas morning, Dylan and I would slip out of our bunk beds and sneak downstairs to see what Santa brought." He shared the memory, but the gray had slipped into his tone of voice now, darkening the lightness of his story. "We would play with everything for about an hour, then put it back like we found it, even if the toy was in a box. We would tiptoe back into our room and wait for our parents to wake us up. We always pretended like we were completely surprised by the gifts."

What was she missing here? Setting aside her napkin, she leaned closer. "Sounds like you and your brother share a special bond."

"Shared," he said flatly. "Dylan's dead."

She couldn't hold back the gasp of shock or the empathetic stab of pain for his loss. For an awkward moment, the chorus of "Silver Bells" seemed to blare louder, the happy music at odds with this sudden revelation. "I'm so sorry, Rowan. I didn't know that."

"You had no reason to know. He died in a car accident when he was twenty."

She searched for something appropriate to say. Her lack of social skills had never bothered her before now. "How old were you when he died?"

"Eighteen." He fidgeted with her sunglasses on the table.

"That had to be so horrible for you and for your parents."

"It was," he said simply, still toying with her wide-rimmed shades.

An awkward silence fell, the echoes of Christmas ringing hollow now. She chewed her lip and pulled the first question from her brain that she could scavenge. "Were you still at the military reform school?"

"It was graduation week."

Her heart squeezed tightly at the thought of him losing so much, especially at a time when he should have been celebrating completing his sentence in that school.

Without thinking or hesitating, she pushed aside her sunglasses and covered Rowan's hand. "Rowan, I don't even know what to say."

"There's nothing to say." He flipped his hand, skimming his thumb along the inside of her wrist. "I just wanted you to know I'm trusting you with a part of my past here."

Heat seeped through her veins at each stroke of his thumb across her pulse. "You're telling me about yourself to…?"

His eyes were completely readable now, sensual and steaming over her. "To get closer to you. To let you know that kiss wasn't just an accident. I'm nowhere near the saint the press likes to paint me."

Heat warmed to full-out sparks of electricity arcing along her every nerve ending. She wasn't imagining or exaggerating anything. Rowan Boothe *wanted* her.

And she wanted to sleep with him.

The inescapable truth of that rocked the ground underneath her.

The noise of a backfiring truck snapped Rowan back into the moment. Mari jolted, blinking quickly before making a huge deal out of attacking her plate of swordfish and *cachupa,* gulping coffee between bites.

The sputtering engine still ringing in his ears, Rowan scanned the marketplace, checking the position of their bodyguards. He took in the honeymooners settling in at the next table. The elderly couple that had photographed them earlier was paying their bill. A family of vacationers filled a long stretch of table.

The place was as safe as anywhere out in public.

He knew he couldn't keep Mari and the baby under lock and key. He had the security detail and he hoped Mari would find peace in being out in public with the proper protection. The thought of her being chased down hallways for the rest of her life made him grind his teeth in frustration. She deserved better than to live in the shadows.

He owed little Issa a lot for how she'd brought them together. He was moved by the sensitive side of Mari he'd never known she had, the sweetly awkward humanity beneath the brilliant scientific brain and regal royal heritage.

Leaning toward the stroller, Rowan adjusted the baby's bib, reassured by the steady beat of her little heart. He'd given her a thorough physical and thank God she was healthy, but she was still a helpless, fragile infant. He needed to take care of her future. And he would. He felt confident he could, with the help of Salvatore either finding the baby's family or lining up a solid adoption.

The outcome of his situation with Mari, however, was less certain. There was no mistaking the desire in her golden eyes. Desire mixed with wariness.

A tactical retreat was in order while he waited for the appropriate moment to resume his advances. He hadn't meant to reveal Dylan's death to her, but their talk about the past had lulled him into old memories. He wouldn't let that happen again.

He poured coffee from the earthen pot into his mug and hers. "You must have seen some lavish Christmas celebrations with your father."

Her eyes were shielded, but her hand trembled slightly as she reached for her mug. "My father keeps things fairly scaled back. The country's economy is stabilizing thanks to an increase in cocoa export, but the national treasury isn't flush with cash, by any means. I was brought up to appreciate my responsibilities to my people."

"You don't have a sibling to share the responsibility."

The words fell out of his mouth before he thought them through, probably because of all those memories of his brother knocking around in his gut. All the ways he'd failed to save Dylan's life. If only he'd made different decisions... He forced his attention back into the present, on Mari.

"Both of my parents remarried other people, divorced again, no more kids, though." She spread her hands, sunglasses dangling from her fingers. "So I'm it. The future of my country."

"You don't sound enthusiastic."

"I just think there has to be someone better equipped." She tossed aside the glasses again and picked up her coffee. "What? Why the surprised look? You can't think I'm the best bet for my people. I would rather lock myself in a research lab with the coffeemaker maxed out than deal with the day-to-day events of leading people."

"I think you will succeed at anything life puts in your path." Who had torn down this woman's confidence? If only she saw—believed in—her magnificence. "When you walk in a room, you damn near light up the place. You own the space with your presence, lady."

She blew into her mug of coffee, eyeing him. "Thanks for the vote of confidence. But people and all their intangibles like 'magnificence' are beyond me. I like concrete facts."

"I would say some people would appreciate logic in a leader."

She looked away quickly, busying herself with adjusting the netting around the baby's stroller. "I wasn't always this way."

"What do you mean?"

"So precise." She darted a quick glance at him out of the corner of her eye. "I was actually a very scatterbrained child. I lost my hair ribbons in hotels, left my doll or book on the airplane. I was always oversleeping or sluggish in the morning, running late for important events. The staff was given instructions to wake me up a half hour ahead of time."

His mom had woken him and Dylan up through elementary school, then bought them an alarm clock—a really obnoxious clock that clanged like a cowbell. No one overslept. "Did this happen in your mother's or your father's home?"

"Both places. My internal clock just wasn't impressed by alarms or schedules."

She was a kid juggling a bicontinental lifestyle, the pressures of royal scrutiny along with the social awkwardness of being at least five grades ahead of her peers.

When did she ever get to relax? "Sounds to me like you traveled quite a bit in your life. I'm sure you know that losing things during travel is as common as jet lag, even for adults."

"You're kind to make excuses." She brushed aside his explanation. "I just learned to make lists and structure my world more carefully."

"Such as?" he asked, suddenly finding the need to learn more about what shaped her life every bit as important as tasting her lips again.

"Always sitting in the same seat on an airplane. Creating a routine for the transatlantic trips, traveling at the same time." She shrugged her elegant shoulders. "The world seemed less confusing that way."

"Confusing?" he repeated.

She chewed her bottom lip, which was still glistening from a sip of coffee. "Forget I said anything."

"Too late. I remember everything you say." And what a time to realize how true that was.

"Ah, you're one of those photographic-memory sorts. I imagine that helps with your work."

"Hmm…" Not a photographic memory, except when it came to her. But she didn't need to know that.

"I'm sure my routines sound a bit overboard to you. But my life feels crazy most of the time. I'm a princess.

There's no escaping that fact." She set her mug down carefully. "I have to accept that no matter how many lists I make, my world will never be predictable."

"Sometimes unpredictable has its advantages, as well." He ached to trace the lines of her heart-shaped face and finish with a tap to her chin.

Her throat moved in a long swallow. "Is this where you surprise me with another kiss?"

He leaned in, a breath away, and said, "I was thinking this time you could surprise me."

She stared back at him so long he was sure she would laugh at him for suggesting such a thing, especially out in public. Not that the public problem bothered the honeymooners at the next table. Just when Rowan was certain she would tell him to go to hell—

Mari kissed him. She closed those last two inches between them and pressed her lips to his. Closemouthed but steady. He felt drunk even though he hadn't had anything but coffee and fruit juice all evening. The same drinks he tasted on Mari's lips. Her hands, soft and smooth, covered his on the table. Need, hard and insistent, coursed through his body over an essentially simple kiss with a table between them.

And just that fast, she let go, pushing on his chest and dropping back into her chair.

A flush spread from her face down the vee of her blouse. "That was not... I didn't mean..."

"Shhh." He pressed a finger to her lips, confidence singing through him along with the hammering pulse of desire. "Some things don't need to be analyzed. Some things simply are. Let's finish supper so we can turn in early."

"Are you propositioning me?" Her lips moved under his finger.

Deliberately seductive? Either way, an extra jolt of want shot through him, a want he saw echoed in her eyes.

He spread his arms wide. "Why would you think that?" he asked with a hint of the devil in his voice. "I want to turn in early. It's your night with the baby."

The tension eased from her shoulders and she smiled back, an ease settling between them as they bantered. God, she was incredible, smart and lithe, earnest and exotic all at once. He covered her hand with his—

A squeal from the next table split the air. "Oh, my God, it's her." The honeymooner at the next table tapped her husband's arm insistently. "That princess... Mariama! I want a picture with her. Get me a photo, pretty please, pookie."

Apparently the mama-flage had stopped working. They didn't have until the morning for Mari to become comfortable with the renewed public attention. The story about them taking care of a baby—*together*—was about to leak.

Big-time.

Two hours later, Mari patted Issa's back in the bassinet to be sure she was deeply asleep then flopped onto the bed in the hotel suite she shared with Rowan.

Alone in her bedroom.

Once that woman shouted to the whole restaurant that a princess sat at the next table, the camera phones started snapping before her head could stop reeling from that impulsive kiss. A kiss that still tingled all the way to the roots of her hair.

Rowan had handled the curious masses with a simple explanation that they were watching a baby in foster care. More information would be forthcoming at a morning press conference. Easy as pie.

Although she was still curious as to where all the bodyguards had come from. She intended to confront her father about that later and find out why he'd decided to disregard her wishes now of all times.

Granted, she could see the wisdom in a bit more protection for Issa's sake and she liked to think she would have arranged for something tomorrow...on a smaller scale. The guards had discreetly escorted her from the restaurant, along with Rowan and the baby, and all the way back to the hotel. No ducking into bathrooms or racing down hallways. Just a wall of protection around her as Rowan continued to repeat with a smile and a firm tone, "No further comment tonight."

Without question, the papers would be buzzing by morning. That press conference would be packed. Her father's promo guru couldn't have planned it better.... Had Rowan known that when they kissed? Did he have an agenda? She couldn't help but wonder since most people in her life had their own agendas—with extras to spare.

This was not the first time the thought had come to her. By the time she'd exited the elevator, she was already second-guessing the kiss, the flirting, the whole crazy plan. She knew that Rowan wanted her. She just couldn't figure out why.

Until she had more answers, she couldn't even consider taking things further.

She sat up again, swinging her legs off the side of the bed. Besides, she had a baby to take care of and a phone call to make. Since Issa still slept blissfully in the lacy bassinet after her bottle, Mari could get to that other pressing concern.

Her father.

She swiped her cell phone off the teak end table and thumbed auto-dial…two rings later, a familiar voice answered and Mari blurted out, "Papa, we need to talk…."

Her father's booming laugh filled the earpiece. "About the boyfriend and the baby you've been hiding from me?"

Mari squeezed her eyes shut, envisioning her lanky father sprawled in his favorite leather chair on the lanai, where he preferred to work. He vowed he felt closer to nature out there, closer to his country, even though three barriers of walls and guards protected him.

Sighing, she pressed two fingers to her head and massaged her temples. "How did you hear about Rowan and Issa? Have you had spies watching me? And why did you assign bodyguards without consulting me?"

"One question at a time, daughter dear. First, I heard about your affiliation with Dr. Boothe and the baby on the internet. Second, I do not spy on my family—not often, anyway. And third, whatever bodyguards you're referring to, they're not mine. I assume they're on your boyfriend's payroll."

Her head throbbed over Rowan hiring bodyguards without consulting her. Her life was snowballing out of control.

"He's not my boyfriend—" even though they'd kissed and she'd enjoyed the hell out of it "—and Issa is not our baby. She's a foster child, just like Rowan said at the restaurant."

Even though her heart was already moved beyond measure by the chubby bundle sleeping in the frilly bassinet next to her bed.

"I know the baby's not yours, Mariama."

"The internet strikes again?" She flopped back, rolling to her side and holding a pillow to her stomach as she monitored the steady rise and fall of Issa's chest as she slept.

"I keep tabs on you, daughter dear. You haven't been pregnant and you've never been a fan of Rowan Boothe."

An image flashed in her mind of Rowan pacing the sitting room with Issa in his arms. "The baby was abandoned in Dr. Boothe's hotel room and we are both watching over her while the authorities try to find her relatives. You know how overburdened Africa is with orphans. We just couldn't let her go into the system when we had the power to help her."

"Hmm..." The sound of him clicking computer keys filtered through the phone line—her father never rested, always worked. He took his position as leader seriously, no puppet leadership role for him. "And why are you working with a man you can't stand to help a child you've never met? He could have taken care of this on his own."

"I'm a philanthropist?"

"True," her dad conceded. "But you're also a poor liar. How did the child become your responsibility?"

She'd never been able to get anything past her wily father. "I was trying to get away from a group of tourists trying to steal a photo of me at the end of a very long day. I grabbed a room-service tray and delivered it." The whole crazy night rolled through her mind again and she wondered what had possessed her to act so rashly. Never, though, could she have foreseen how it would end. "Turns out it was for Rowan Boothe and there was an abandoned baby inside. There's nothing going on between us."

A squawk from Issa sent her jolting upright again to

pat the baby's back. An instant later, a tap sounded on the door from the suite beyond. She covered the mouthpiece on the phone. "We're okay."

Still, the bedroom door opened, a quizzical look on Rowan's face. "Everything all right?"

"I've got it." She uncovered the phone. "Dad, I need to go."

Rowan lounged against the doorjamb, his eyes questioning. Pressing the phone against her shoulder to hold it to her ear, she tugged her skirt over her knees, curling her bare toes.

"Mari, dear," her father said, "I do believe you have gotten better at lying after all. Seems like there's a lot going on in your life I don't know about."

Her pulse sped up, affirming her father was indeed right. This wasn't just about Issa. She was lying to herself in thinking there was nothing more going on with Rowan. His eyes enticed her from across the room, like a blue-hot flame drawing a moth.

But her father waited on the other end of the line. Best to deflect the conversation, especially while the object of her current hormonal turmoil stood a few feet away. "You should be thrilled about this whole setup. It will make for great publicity, a wonderful story for your press people to spin over the holidays. Papa, for once I'm not a disappointment."

Rowan scowled and Mari wished she could call back the words that had somehow slipped free. But she felt the weight of the knowledge all the same. The frustration of never measuring up to her parents' expectations.

"Mari, dear," her father said, his voice hoarse, "you have never been a disappointment."

A bittersweet smile welled from the inside out.

"You're worse at lying than I am. But I love you anyway. Good night, Papa."

She thumped the off button and swung her bare feet to the floor. Her nerves were a jangled mess from the emotions stirred up by talking to her dad...not to mention the smoldering embers from kissing Rowan. The stroke of his eyes over her told her they were a simple step, a simple word away from far more than a kiss.

But those tangled nerves and mixed-up feelings also told her this was not the time to make such a momentous decision. Too much was at stake, the well-being of the infant in their care...

And Mari's peace of mind. Because it would be far too easy to lose complete control when it came to this man.

Six

Refusing to back down from Rowan's heated gaze, Mari stiffened her spine and her resolve, closing the last three feet between them. "Why did you order bodyguards without consulting me?"

He frowned. "Where did you think they'd come from?"

"My father."

"I just did what he should have. I made sure to look after your safety," he said smoothly, arrogantly.

Her chin tipped defiantly. He might have been right about them needing bodyguards—for Issa's sake—but she wasn't backing down on everything. "Just because I kissed you at the restaurant does *not* mean I intend to invite you into my bed."

Grinning wickedly, he clamped a hand over his heart. "Damn. My spirit is crushed."

"You're joking, of course." She stopped just shy of

touching him, the banter sparkling through her like champagne bubbles.

"Possibly. But make no mistake, I do want to sleep with you and every day I wait is…torture." The barely restrained passion in his voice sent those intoxicating bubbles straight to her head. "I'm just reasonable enough to accept it isn't going to happen tonight."

"And if it never happens?" she asked, unwilling to let him know how deeply he affected her.

"Ah, you said 'if.'" He flicked a loose strand of hair over her shoulder, just barely skimming his knuckles across her skin. "Princess, that means we're already halfway to naked."

Before she could find air to breathe, he backed away, slowly, deliberately closing the door after him.

And she'd thought her nerves were a tangled, jangled mess before. Her legs folded under her as she dropped to sit on the edge of the bed.

A suddenly very cold and empty bed.

Rowan walked through the hotel sliding doors that led out to the sprawling shoreline. The cool night breeze did little to ease the heat pumping through his body. Leaving Mari alone in her hotel room had been one of the toughest things he'd ever done, but he'd had no choice for two reasons.

First, it was too soon to make his move. He didn't want to risk Mari changing her mind about staying with him. She had to be sure—very sure—when they made love.

Second reason he'd needed to put some distance between himself and her right now? He had an important meeting scheduled with an Interpol contact outside the hotel. An old school friend of his and the person responsible for their security detail tonight.

Rowan jogged down the long steps from the pool area to the beach. Late-night vacationers splashed under the fake waterfall, others floated, some sprawled in deck loungers with drinks, the party running deep into the night.

His appointment would take place in cabana number two, away from prying eyes and with the sound of the roaring surf to cover conversation. His loafers sank into the gritty sand, the teak shelter a dozen yards away, with a grassy roof and canvas walls flapping lightly in the wind. Ships bobbed on the horizon, lights echoing the stars overhead.

Rowan swept aside the fabric and stepped inside. "Sorry I'm late, my friend."

His old school pal Elliot Starc lounged in a recliner under the cabana in their designated meeting spot as planned, both loungers overlooking the endless stretch of ocean. "Nothing better to do."

Strictly speaking that couldn't be true. The freelance Interpol agent used his job as a world-renowned Formula One race-car driver to slip in and out of countries without question. He ran in high-powered circles. But then that very lifestyle was the sort their handler, Colonel Salvatore, capitalized on—using the tarnished reputations of his old students to gain access to underworld types.

Of course, Salvatore gave Rowan hell periodically for being a do-gooder. Rowan winced. The label pinched, a poor fit at best. "Well, thanks all the same for dropping everything to come to Cape Verde."

Elliot scratched his hand over his buzzed short hair. "I'm made of time since my fiancée dumped me."

"Sorry about that." Talk about headline news. Elliot's past—his vast past—with women, filled headlines across multiple continents. The world thought that's what had broken up the engagement, but Rowan suspected the truth. Elliot's fiancée had been freaked out by the Interpol work. The job had risked more than one relationship for the Brotherhood.

What would Mari think if she knew?

"Crap happens." Elliot tipped back a drink, draining half of the amber liquid before setting the cut crystal glass on the table between them. "I'd cleared my schedule for the honeymoon. When we split I gave her the tickets since the whole thing was my fault anyway. She and her 'BFF' are skiing in the Alps as we speak. I might as well be doing something productive with my time off."

Clearly, Elliot wouldn't want sympathy. Another drink maybe. He looked like hell, dark circles under his eyes. From lack of sleep most likely. But that didn't explain the nearly shaved head.

"Dude, what happened to you?" Rowan asked, pointing to the short cut.

Elliot's curly mop had become a signature with his fans who collected magazine covers. There were even billboards and posters…. All their pals from the military academy—the ones who'd dubbed themselves the Alpha Brotherhood—never passed up an opportunity to rib Elliot about the underwear ad.

Elliot scratched a hand over his shorn hair. "I had a wreck during a training run. Bit of a fire involved. Singed my hair."

Holy hell. "You caught on fire?"

Elliot grinned. "Just my hair."

"How did I miss hearing about that?"

"No need. It's not a big deal."

Rowan shook his head. "You are one seriously messed-up dude."

But then all his former classmates were messed up in some form. Came with the territory. The things that had landed them in that reform school left them with baggage long after graduation.

"You're the one who hangs out in war-torn villages passing out vaccinations and blankets for fun."

"I'm not trailed by groupies." He shuddered.

"They're harmless most of the time."

Except when they weren't. The very reason he'd consulted with Elliot about the best way to protect Mari and Issa. "I can't thank you enough, brother, for overseeing the security detail. They earned their pay tonight."

"Child's play. So to speak." Elliot lifted his glass again, draining the rest with a wince. "What's up with your papa-and-the-princess deal?"

"The kid needed my help. So I helped."

"You've always been the saint. But that doesn't explain the princess."

Rowan ignored the last part of Elliot's question. "What's so saintly about helping out a kid when I have unlimited funds and Interpol agents at my disposal? Saintly is when something's difficult to do."

"And the woman—the princess?" his half-drunk buddy persisted. "She had a reputation for being very difficult on the subject of Dr. Rowan Boothe."

Like the time she'd written an entire journal piece pointing out potential flaws in his diagnostics program. Sure, he'd made adjustments after reading the piece, but holy hell, it would have been nice—and more expedient—if she'd come to him first. "Mari needs my help, too. That's all it is."

Elliot laughed. "You are so damn delusional."

A truth. And an uncomfortable one.

Beyond their cabana tent, a couple strolled arm-in-arm along the shoreline, sidestepping as a jogger sprinted past with a loping dog.

"If you were a good friend you would let me continue with my denial."

"Maybe I'm wrong." Elliot lifted the decanter and refilled his glass. "It's not denial if you acknowledge said problem."

"I am aware of that fact." His unrelenting desire for Mari was a longtime, ongoing issue he was doing his damnedest to address.

"What do you intend to do about your crush on the princess?"

"Crush? Good God, man. I'm not in junior high."

"Glad you know that. What's your plan?"

"I'm figuring that out as I go." And even if he had one, he wasn't comfortable discussing details of his— feelings?—his attraction.

"What happens if this relationship goes south? Her father has a lot of influence. Even though you're not in his country, his region still neighbors your backyard. That could be...uncomfortable."

Rowan hadn't considered that angle and he should have. Which said a lot for how much Mari messed with his mind. "Let me get this straight, Starc. *You* are doling out relationship advice?"

"I'm a top-notch source when it comes to all the wrong things to do in a long-term relationship." He lifted his glass in toast. "Here's to three broken engagements and counting."

"Who said I'm looking for long-term?"

Elliot leveled an entirely sober stare his way, holding for three crashes of the waves before he said, "You truly are delusional, dude."

"That's not advice."

"It is if you really think about it."

He'd had enough of this discussion about Mari and the possibility of a train wreck of epic proportions. Rowan shoved off the lounger, his shoes sinking in the sand. "Good night."

"Hit a sore spot, did I?" Still, Starc pushed.

"I appreciate your…concern. And your help." He clapped Elliot on the shoulder before sweeping aside the canvas curtain. "I need to return to the hotel."

He'd been gone long enough. As much as he trusted Elliot's choice of guards, he still preferred to keep close.

Wind rolled in off the water, tearing at his open shirt collar as he made his way back up the beach toward the resort. Lights winked from trees. Fake snow speckled windows. Less than two weeks left until Christmas. He would spend the day at his house by the clinic, working any emergency-room walk-ins as he did every year. What plans did Mari have? Would she go to her family?

His parents holed up on Christmas, and frankly, he preferred it that way. Too many painful memories for all of them.

He shut off those thoughts as he entered the resort again. Better to focus on the present. One day at a time. That's the way he'd learned to deal with the crap that had gone down. And right now, his present was filled with Mari and Issa.

Potted palms, carved masks and mounted animal heads passed in a blur as he made his way back to his suite. He nodded to the pair of guards outside the door before stepping inside.

Dimmed lights from the wet bar bathed the sitting

area in an amber glow. Silence echoed as he padded his way to Mari's room. No sounds came from her room this time, no conversation with her royal dad.

The door to Mari's room was ajar and he nudged it open slowly, pushing back thoughts of invading her privacy. This was about safety and checking on the baby.

Not an insane desire to see what Mari looked like sleeping.

To appease his conscience, he checked the baby first and found the chubby infant sleeping, sucking on her tiny fist as she dreamed. Whatever came of his situation with Mari, they'd done right by this baby. They'd kept at least one child safe.

One day at a time. One life saved at a time. It's how he lived. How he atoned for the unforgivable in his past.

Did Issa's mother regret abandoning her child? The note said she wanted her baby in the care of someone like him. But there was no way she could have known the full extent of the resources he had at his disposal with Interpol. If so, she wouldn't have been as quick to abandon her child to him because he could and would find the mother. It wasn't a matter of if. Only a matter of when.

He wouldn't give up. This child's future depended on finding answers.

All the more reason to tread carefully with Mari. He knew what he wanted, but he'd failed to take into consideration how much of a help she would be. How much it would touch his soul seeing her care for the baby. From her initial reaction to the baby, he'd expected her to be awkward with the child, all technical and analytical. But she had an instinct for children, a tenderness in her heart that overcame any awkwardness. A softness that crept over her features.

Watching her sleep now, he could almost forget the way Mari had cut him down to size on more than one occasion in the past. Her hair was down and loose on her pillow, black satin against the white Egyptian cotton pillowcase. Moonlight kissed the curve of her neck, her chest rising and falling slowly.

He could see a strap of creamy satin along her shoulder. Her nightgown? His body tightened and he considered scooping her up and carrying her to his room. To hell with waiting. He could persuade her.

But just as he started to reach for her, his mind snagged on the memory of her talking about how she felt like she'd been a disappointment to her family. The notion that anyone would think this woman less than amazing floored him. He might not agree with her on everything, but he sure as hell saw her value.

Her brilliance of mind and spirit.

He definitely needed to stick to his original plan. He would wait. He couldn't stop thinking about that snippet of her phone conversation with her father. He understood that feeling of inadequacy all too well. She deserved better.

Rather than some half-assed seduction, he needed a plan. A magnificent plan to romance a magnificent woman. The work would be well worth the payoff for both of them.

He backed away from her bed and reached for his cell phone to check in with Salvatore. Pausing at the door, he took in the sight of her, imprinting on his brain the image of Mari sleeping even though that vision ensured *he* wouldn't be sleeping tonight.

Mari's dreams filled with Rowan, filled with his blue eyes stroking her. With his hands caressing her as they floated together in the surf, away from work and responsibilities. She'd never felt so free, so languid, his kisses and touches melting her bones. Her mind filled with his husky whispers of how much he wanted her. Even the sound of his voice stoked her passion higher, hotter, until she ached to wrap her legs around his waist and be filled with his strength.

She couldn't get enough of him. Years of sparring over their work, and even the weather if the subject came up... Now all those frustrating encounters exploded into a deep need, an explosive passion for a man she could have vowed she didn't even like.

Although like had nothing to do with this raw arousal—she felt a need that left her hot and moist between the legs until she squirmed in her bed.

Her bed.

Slowly, her dream world faded as reality interjected itself with tiny details, like the slither of sheets against her skin. The give of the pillow as her head thrashed back and forth. The sound of the ocean outside the window—and the faint rumble of Rowan's voice beyond her door.

She sat upright quickly.

Rowan.

No wonder she'd been dreaming of him. His voice had been filtering into her dream until he took it over. She clutched the puffy comforter to her chest and listened, although the words were indistinguishable. From the periodic silences, he must be talking to someone on the phone.

Mari eased from the bed, careful not to wake the baby. She pulled her robe from over a cane rocking chair and slipped her arms into the cool satin. Her one decadent pleasure—sexy peignoir sets. They made her feel like a silver-screen star from the forties, complete with furry kitten-heel slippers, not so high as to trip her up, but still ultrafeminine.

Would Rowan think them sexy or silly if he noticed them? God, he was filling up her mind and making her care about things—superficial things—that shouldn't matter. Even more distressing, he made her want to climb back into that dream world and forget about everything else.

Her entire focus should be on securing Issa's future. Mari leaned over the lace bassinet to check the infant's breathing. She pressed a kiss to two fingers and skimmed them over Issa's brow, affection clutching her heart. How could one little scrap of humanity become so precious so fast?

Rowan's voice filtered through the door again and piqued her curiosity. Who could he be talking with so late at night? Common sense said it had to be important, maybe even about the baby.

Her throat tightened at the thought of news about Issa's family, and she wasn't sure if the prospect made her happy or sad. She grasped the baby monitor receiver in her hand.

Quietly, she opened the door, careful not to disturb his phone conversation. And yes, she welcomed the opportunity to look at Rowan for a moment, a double-edged pleasure with the heat of her dream still so fresh in her mind. He stood with his back to her, phone pressed to his ear as he faced the picture window, shutters open to reveal the moonlit shoreline.

She couldn't have stopped herself if she tried. And she didn't try. Her gaze skated straight down to his butt. A fine butt, the kind that filled out jeans just right and begged a woman to tuck her hand into his back pocket.

Why hadn't she noticed that about him before? Perhaps because he usually wore his doctor's coat or a suit.

The rest of him, though, was wonderfully familiar. What a time to realize she'd stored so much more about him in her memory than just the sexy glide of his blond hair swept back from his face, his piercing blue eyes, his strong body.

Her fingers itched to scale the expanse of his chest, hard muscled in a way that spoke of real work more than gym time with a personal trainer. Her body responded with a will of its own, her breasts beading in response to just the sight of him, the promise of pleasure in that strong, big body of his.

Were the calluses on his hand imagined in her dream or real? Right now it seemed the most important thing in the world to know, to find out from the ultimate test— his hands on her bare flesh.

His back still to her, he nodded and hmmed at something in the conversation, the broad column of his neck exposed, then he disconnected his call.

Anticipation coursed through her, but she schooled her face to show nothing as he turned.

He showed no surprise at seeing her, his moves smooth and confident. He placed his phone on the wet bar, his eyes sweeping over all of her. His gaze lingered on her shoes and he smiled, then his gaze stroked back up to her face again. "Mari, how long have you been awake?"

"Only a few minutes. Just long enough to hear you 'hmm' and 'uh-huh' a couple of times." She wrapped her arms around her waist, hugging the robe closed and making sure her tingling breasts didn't advertise her arousal. "If I may ask, who were you talking to so late?"

"Checking on our security and following up a lead on the baby."

She stood up straighter and joined him by the window, her heart hammering in her ears. "Did you find her family?"

"Sorry." He cupped her shoulder in a warm grasp, squeezing comfortingly. "Not yet. But we're working on it."

She forced herself to swallow and moisten her suddenly dry mouth. "Who is this 'we' you keep mentioning?"

"I'm a wealthy man now. Wealthy people have connections. I'm using them." His hand slid away, calluses snagging on her satin robe.

Calluses.

The thought of those fingers rasping along her skin made her shiver with want. God, she wasn't used to being this controlled by her body. She was a cerebral person, a thinker, a scientist. She needed to find level ground again, although it was a struggle.

Reining herself in, she eyed Rowan, assessing him. Her instincts told her he was holding something back about his conversation, but she couldn't decipher what that might be. She searched his face, really searched, and what a time to realize she'd never looked deeper than the surface of Rowan before. She'd known his history—a reformed bad boy, the saintly doctor saving the world and soaking up glory like a halo, while she was a person who preferred the shadows.

She'd only stepped into the spotlight now for the baby. And that made her wonder if his halo time had another purpose for him—using that notoriety for his causes. The possibility that she could have been mistaken about his ego, his swagger, gave her pause.

Of course she could just be seeking justification for how his kisses turned her inside out.

Then his hand slid down her arm until he linked fingers with her and tugged her toward the sofa. Her stomach leaped into her throat, but she didn't stop him, curious to see where this would lead. And reluctant to let go of his hand.

He sat, drawing her to sit beside him. Silently. Just staring back at her, his thumb stroking across the inside of her wrist.

Did he expect her to jump him? She'd already told him she wouldn't make the leap into bed with him. Had a part of her secretly hoped he would argue?

Still, he didn't speak or move.

She searched for something to say, anything to fill the empty space between them—and take her mind off the tantalizing feel of his callused thumb rubbing along her speeding pulse. "Do you really think Issa's family will be found?"

"I believe that every possible resource is being devoted to finding out who she is and where she came from."

The clean fresh scent of his aftershave rode every breath she took. She needed to focus on Issa first and foremost.

"Tomorrow—or rather, later this morning—we need to get serious about going public with the press. No more playing at dinner, pretend photos and controlled press releases. I need to use my notoriety to help her."

He squeezed her wrist lightly. "You don't have to put yourself in the line of fire so aggressively."

"Isn't that why you asked me to help you? To add oomph to the search?" His answer became too important to her.

"I could have handled the baby alone." He held her gaze, with undeniable truthfulness in his eyes. "If we're honest here, I wanted to spend more time with you."

Her tummy flipped and another of those tempting Rowan-scented breaths filled her. "You used the baby for selfish reasons? To get closer to me?"

"When you put it like that, it sounds so harsh."

"What *did* you mean then?"

He linked their fingers again, lifting their twined grasp and resting it against his chest. "Having you here does help with the baby's care and with finding the baby's family. But it also helps me get to know you better."

"Do you want to know me better or kiss me?"

His heart thudded against her hand as he leaned even closer, just shy of their lips touching. "Is there a problem with my wanting both?"

"You do understand that nothing is simple with me." Her breath mingled with his.

"Because of who you are? Yes, I realize exactly who you are."

And just that fast, reality iced over her. She could never forget who she was…her father's daughter. A princess. The next in the royal line since she had no siblings, no aunts or uncles. As much as she wanted to believe Rowan's interest in her was genuine, she'd been used and misunderstood too many times in the past.

She angled away from him. "I know you think I'm a spoiled princess."

"Sometimes we say things in anger that we don't mean. I apologize for that." He stretched his arm along the back of the sofa without touching her this time.

"What *do* you think of me?" The opinion of others hadn't mattered to her before…. Okay, that was a lie.

Her parents' opinion mattered. She'd cared what her first lover thought of her only to find he'd used her to get into her father's inner circle.

"Mari, I think you're smart and beautiful."

She grinned. "Organized and uptight."

He smiled back. "Productive, with restrained passions."

"I *am* a spoiled princess," she admitted, unable to resist the draw of his smile, wanting to believe what she saw in his eyes. "I've had every luxury, security, opportunity imaginable. I've had all the things this baby needs, things her mother is so desperate to give her she would give her away to a stranger. I feel awful and guilty for just wanting to be normal."

"Normal life?" He shook his head, the leather sofa creaking as he leaned back and away. "I had that so-called normal life and I still screwed up."

She'd read the press about him, the way he'd turned his life around after a drunk-driving accident as a teen. He was the poster boy for second chances, devoting his life to making amends.

Her negative reports on his program weren't always popular. Some cynics in the medical community had even suggested she had an ax to grind, insinuating he might have spurned her at some point. That assumption stung her pride more than a little.

Still, she couldn't deny the good he'd done with his clinic. The world needed more people like Dr. Rowan Boothe.

"You screwed up as a teenager, but you set yourself on the right path again once you went to that military high school."

"That doesn't erase my mistake. Nothing can." He plowed a hand through his hair. "It frustrates the hell out of me that the press wants to spin it into some kind of feel-good story. So yeah, I get your irritation with the whole media spin."

"But your story gives people hope that they can turn their lives around."

He mumbled a curse.

"What? Don't just go Grinchy on me." She tapped his elbow. "Talk. Like you did at dinner."

"Go Grinchy?" He cocked an eyebrow. "Is that really a word?"

"Of course it is. I loved that movie as a child. I watched a lot of Christmas movies flying across the ocean to spend Christmas with one parent or the other. So, back to the whole Grinchy face. What gives?"

"If you want to change my mood, then let's talk about something else." His arm slid from the back of the sofa until his hand cupped her shoulder. "What else did you enjoy about Christmas when you were a kid?"

"You're not going to distract me." With his words or his touch.

"Says who?" Subtly but deliberately, he pulled her closer.

And angled his mouth over hers.

Seven

Stunned still, Mari froze for an instant. Then all the simmering passion from her dream earlier came roaring to the surface. She looped her arms around Rowan's neck and inched closer to him on the sofa. The satin of her peignoir set made her glide across the leather smoother, easier, until she melted against him, opened her mouth and took him as boldly as he took her.

The sweep of his tongue carried the minty taste of toothpaste, the intoxicating warmth of pure him. His hands roved along her back, up and down her spine in a hypnotizing seduction. He teased his fingers up into her hair, massaging her scalp until her body relaxed, muscle by tense muscle, releasing tensions she hadn't even realized existed. Then he stirred a different sort of tension, a coiling of desire in her belly that pulled tighter and tighter until she arched against him.

Her breasts pressed to his chest, the hard wall of him

putting delicious pressure against her tender, oversensitized flesh.

He reclined with her onto the couch, tucking her beneath him with a possessive growl. She nipped his bottom lip and purred right back. The contrast of cool butter-soft leather beneath her and hot, hard male over her sent her senses on overload.

The feel of his muscled body stretching out over her, blanketing her, made her blood pulse faster, thicker, through her veins. She plucked at the leather string holding back his hair, pulled it loose and glory, glory, his hair slipped free around her fingers. She combed her hands through the coarse strands, just long enough to tickle her face as he kissed.

And this man sure did know how to kiss.

Not just with his mouth and his bold tongue, but he used his hands to stroke her, his body molding to hers. His knee slid between her legs. The thick pressure of his thigh against the core of her sent delicious shivers sparkling upward. All those sensations circled and tightened in her belly with a new intensity.

Her hands learned the planes and lines of him, along his broad shoulders, down his back to the firm butt she'd been checking out not too long ago. Every nerve ending tingled to life, urging her to take more—more of him and more of the moment.

She wanted all of him. Now.

Hooking a leg around his calf, she linked them, bringing him closer still. Her hips rocked against his, the thick length of his arousal pressing against her stomach with delicious promise of what they could have together. Soon. Although not soon enough. Urgency throbbed through her, pulsing into a delicious ache between her legs.

He swept aside her hair and kissed along the sensitive curve of her neck, nipping ever so lightly against her pulse. She hummed her approval and scratched gently over his back, along his shoulders, then down again to yank at his shirt. She couldn't get rid of their clothes fast enough. If she gave herself too long to think, too many practical reasons to stop would start marching through her mind—

A cool whoosh of air swept over her. She opened her eyes to see Rowan standing beside the sofa. Well, not standing exactly, but halfway bent over, his hands on his legs as he hauled in ragged breath after breath. His arousal was unmistakable, so why was he pulling away?

"What? Where?" She tried again to form a coherent sentence. "Where are you going?"

He stared at her in the moonlight, his chest rising and falling hard, like he'd run for miles. His expression was closed. His eyes inscrutable.

"Good night, Mariama."

Her brain couldn't make his words match up with what she was feeling. Something didn't add up. "Good night? That's it?"

"I need to stop now." He tucked his shirt in as he backed away. "Things are getting too intense."

She refused to acknowledge the twinge of hurt she felt at his words. She wasn't opening her emotions to this man.

"Yeah, I noticed." She brazened it out, still committed to re-creating the amazing feelings from her dream. "That intensity we were experiencing about twenty seconds ago was a good thing."

"It will be good, Mari. When you're ready."

Damn, but he confused her. She hated feeling like

the student in need of remedial help. The one who didn't "get" it.

"Um, hello, Rowan. I'm ready now."

"I just need for you to be sure." He backed away another step, his hair tousled from her hungry fingers. "See if you feel the same in the morning. Good night, Mariama."

He pivoted into his room and closed the door behind him.

Mari sagged back on the sofa, befuddled as hell. What was his game here? He bound her to him by enlisting her help with the baby. He clearly wanted her. Yet, he'd walked away.

She wasn't innocent. She'd been with men—two. The first was a one-night stand that had her clamping her legs shut for years to come after she'd learned he'd only wanted access to her family. Then one long-term deal with a man who'd been as introverted as her. Their relationship had dissolved for lack of attention, fading into nothing more than convenient sex. And then not so convenient. Still, the breakup had been messy, her former lover not taking well to having his ego stung over being dumped. He'd been a real jerk.

Whereas Rowan was being a total gentleman. Not pushing. Not taking advantage.

And he was driving her absolutely batty.

Holding back had threatened to drive Rowan over the edge all night long.

At least now he could move forward with the day. The salty morning breeze drifted through the open shutters as he tucked his polo shirt into his jeans, already anticipating seeing Mari. Soon. He'd never wanted a woman this much. Walking away from her last night

had been almost impossible. But he was making progress. She wanted him and he needed this to be very,
very reciprocal.

So he needed to move on with his plan to romance
her. Neither of them had a presentation at the conference
today. He suspected it wouldn't take much persuasion
to convince her to skip out on sitting through boring
slide presentations and rubber chicken.

During his sleepless night, he'd racked his brain for
the best way to sweep her off her feet. She wasn't the
most conventional of women. He'd decided to hedge his
bets by going all out. He'd started off with the traditional stuff, a flower left on her pillow while she'd been
in the shower. He'd also ordered her favorite breakfast
delivered to her room. He planned to end the day with
a beachside dinner and concert.

All traditional "dating" fare.

The afternoon's agenda, however, was a bit of a long
shot. But then he figured it was best to hedge his bets
with her. She'd seemed surprised by the breakfast, and
he could have sworn she was at least a little charmed
by his invitation to spend the day together. Although
he still detected a hint of wariness.

But reminding her of how they could appease the
press into leaving her alone by feeding them a story per-
suaded her. For now, at least. He just prayed the press
conference went smoothly.

Rowan opened his bedroom door and found Mari
already waiting for him in the sitting area with Issa
cradled in her arms. She stood by the stroller, cooing
to the baby and adjusting a pink bootie, her face soft-
ening with affection.

Mari wore a long silky sheath dress that glided across
subtle curves as she swayed back and forth. And the

pink tropical flower he'd left on her pillow was now tucked behind her ear. He stood captivated by her grace as she soothed the infant to sleep. Minutes—or maybe more—later, she leaned to place the baby in the stroller.

She glanced to the side, meeting his gaze with a smile. "Where are we going?"

Had she known he was there the whole time? Did she also know how damn difficult it had been to walk away from her last night? "It's a surprise."

"That makes me a little nervous." She straightened, gripping the stroller. "I'm not good at pulling off anything impetuous."

"We have a baby with us." He rested a hand on top of hers. "How dangerous could my plan be?"

Her pupils widened in response before her gaze skittered away. "Okay, fair enough." She pulled her hand from his and touched the exotic bloom tucked in her hair. "And thank you for the flower."

Ducking his head, he kissed her ear, right beside the flower, breathing in the heady perfume of her, even more tantalizing than the petals. "I'll be thinking of how you taste all day long."

He sketched a quick kiss along her regally high cheekbone before pulling back. Gesturing toward the private elevator, he followed her, taking in the swish of her curls spiraling just past her shoulders. What a time to realize how rarely he saw her with her hair down. She usually kept it pulled back in a reserved bun.

Except for last night when she'd gone to bed. And now.

It was all he could do to keep himself from walking up behind her, sliding his arms around her and pulling her flush against him. The thought of her bottom nestled against him, his face in the sweet curve of her neck… damn. He swallowed hard. Just damn.

He followed her into the elevator and thankfully the glide down went quickly, before he had too much time in the cubicle breathing in the scent of her. The elevator doors opened with a whoosh as hefty as his exhale.

His relief was short-lived. A pack of reporters waited just outside the resort entrance, ready for them to give their first official press conference. He'd expected it, of course. He'd even set this particular one up. But having Mari and the baby here put him on edge. Even knowing Elliot Starc's detail of bodyguards were strategically placed didn't give him total peace. He wondered what would.

Mari pushed the stroller while he palmed her back, guiding her through the lobby. Camera phones snap-snap-snapped as he ushered Mari and Issa across the marble floor. Gawkers whispered as they watched from beside towering columns and sprawling potted ferns.

The doorman waved them through the electric doors and out into chaos. Rowan felt Mari's spine stiffen. Protectiveness pumped through him anew.

He ducked his head toward her. "Are you sure you're okay with this? We can go back to the suite, dine on the balcony, spend our day off in a decadent haze of food and sunshine."

She shook her head tightly. "We proceed as planned. For Issa, I will do anything to get the word out about her story, whatever it takes to be sure she has a real family who loves her and appreciates what a gift she is."

Her ferocity couldn't be denied—and it stirred the hell out of him. Before he did something crazy like kiss her until they both couldn't think, he turned to the reporters gathered on the resort's stone steps.

"No questions today, just a statement," he said firmly with a smile. "Dr. Mandara and I have had our disagreements in the past, but we share a common goal in our desire...to help people in need. This is the holiday season and a defenseless child landed in our radar, this little girl. How could we look away? We're working together to care for this baby until her family can be found. If even Mari and I can work together, then maybe there's hope...."

He winked wryly and laughter rippled through the crowd.

Once they quieted, he continued, "That's all for now. We have a baby, a conference agenda and holiday shopping to juggle. Thank you and Merry Christmas, everyone."

Their bodyguards emerged from the crowd on cue and created a circular wall around them as they walked from the resort to the shopping strip.

Mari glanced up at him, her sandals slapping the wooden boardwalk leading to the stores and stalls of the shoreline marketplace. "Are we truly going shopping? I thought men hated shopping."

"It's better than hanging out inside eating conference food. I hope you don't mind. If you'd rather go back..."

"Bite your tongue." She hip-bumped him as he strode beside her.

"Onward then." He slipped his arm around her shoulders, tucking her to him as they walked.

She glanced up at him. "Thank you."

If he dipped his head, he could kiss her, but even though he'd set up this press coverage, he balked at that much exposure. "Thanks for what?"

"For the press conference, and taking the weight of that worry off me. You handled the media so perfectly.

I'm envious of your ease, though." She scrunched her elegant nose. "I wish I had that skill. Running from them hasn't worked out that well for me."

"I just hope the statement and all of those photos will help Issa."

"Why wouldn't it?"

Helping Interpol gain access to crooks around the world had given him insights into just how selfish, how Machiavellian, people could be. "Think of all the crack-pots who will call claiming to know something just to attach themselves to a high-profile happening or hoping to gain access to you even for a short while knowing that DNA tests will later prove them to be frauds."

"God, I never thought of that," she gasped, her eyes wide and horrified.

He squeezed her shoulder reassuringly, all too aware of how perfectly she fit to his side. "The police are going to be busy sifting through the false leads that come through."

"That's why you wanted to wait a day to officially announce we're fostering her...." she whispered softly to herself as they passed a cluster of street carolers.

"Why did you think I waited?" He saw a whisper of chagrin shimmer in her golden eyes. "Did you think I was buying time to hit on you?"

She lifted a dark eyebrow. "Were you?"

"Maybe." Definitely.

She looked away, sighing. "Honestly, I'm not sure what I thought. Since I stumbled into your suite with that room-service cart, things have been...crazy. I've barely had time to think, things are happening so fast. I just hate to believe anyone would take advantage of this precious baby's situation for attention or reward money."

The reality of just how far people would go made his

jaw flex. "We'll wade through them. No one gains access to this child or you until they've been completely vetted. We will weed through the false claims and selfish agendas. Meanwhile, she's safe with us. She turns toward your voice already."

"You're nice to say that, but she's probably just in search of her next bottle."

"Believe what you want. I know differently." He'd seen scores of mothers and children file through his clinic—biological and adoptive. Bonds formed with or without a blood connection.

"Are you arguing with me? I thought we were supposed to be getting along now. Isn't that what you said at the press conference?"

"I'm teasing you. Flirting. There's a difference." Unable to resist, he pressed a kiss to her forehead.

"Oh."

"Relax. I'm not going to hit on you here." There were far too many cameras for him to be too overt. "Although a longer kiss would certainly give the press something to go wild about. Feed them tidbits and they'll quit digging for other items."

Furrows dug into her forehead. "But it feels too much like letting them win."

"I consider it controlling the PR rather than letting it control me." He guided her by her shoulders, turning toward a reporter with a smile before walking on. "Think about all the positive publicity you're racking up for your father."

"This may have started out to be about keeping the press off my back, but now it's more about the baby."

He agreed with her on that account. But the worry on her face reminded him to stay on track with his plan.

"This conversation is getting entirely too serious for a day of fun and relaxation."

"Of course..." She swiped her hand over her forehead, squeezing her eyes closed for an instant before opening them again and smiling. "Who are you shopping for today? For your family?"

"In a sense."

He stopped in front of a toy store.

Her grin widened, her kissable lips glistening with a hint of gloss. "Are we shopping for Issa?"

"For the kids at my clinic."

Toy shopping with Rowan and Issa, like they were a family, tore at Mari's heart throughout the day. The man who'd left a flower on her pillow and chosen her favorite breakfast was charming. But the man who went shopping for the little patients at his free clinic?

That man was damn near irresistible.

Riding the elevator back up to their suite, she grabbed the brass bar for balance. Her unsteady feet had nothing to do with exhaustion or the jerk of the elevator—and everything to do with the man standing beside her.

Her mind swirled with memories of their utterly carefree day. The outing had been everything she could have hoped for and more. Sure, the paparazzi had followed them, lurking, but Rowan had controlled them, fielding their questions while feeding them enough tidbits to keep them from working themselves into a frenzy. Best of all, Issa had gotten her press coverage. Hopefully the right people would see it.

As much as Mari's stomach clenched at the thought of saying goodbye to the baby, she wanted what was best for the child. She wanted Issa to feel—and be—loved unreservedly. Every child deserved that. And

Rowan was doing everything possible to help this child he'd never met, just like he did the patients at his clinic, even down to the smallest detail.

Such as their shopping spree.

It would have been easier to write it off as a show for the press or a trick to win her over. But he had a list of children's names with notes beside them. Not that she could read his stereotypically wretched doctor's scrawl. But from the way he consulted the list and made choices, he'd clearly made a list of kids' names and preferences. The bodyguards had been kept busy stowing packages in the back of a limo trailing them from store to store.

And he hadn't left Issa off his list. The baby now had a new toy in her stroller, a plush zebra, the black-and-white stripes captivating the infant. The vendor had stitched the baby's name in pink on the toy.

Issa.

The one part of her prior life the little one carried with her—a name. Used for both boys and girls, meaning savior. Appropriate this time of year... Her feet kicked. Could the name be too coincidental? Could whoever left the baby have made up the name to go with the season—while leading authorities astray?

She leaned in to stroke the baby's impossibly soft cheek. Issa's lashes swept open and she stared up at Mari for a frozen moment, wide dark eyes looking up with such complete trust Mari melted. What happened if family came forward and they didn't love her as she deserved?

Those thoughts threatened to steal Mari's joy and she shoved them aside as the elevator doors whooshed open. She refused to let anything rob her of this perfect day and the promise of more. More time with Issa. More time with Rowan.

More kisses?

More of everything?

He'd walked away last night because he thought she wasn't ready. Maybe he was right. Although the fact that he cared about her needs, her well-being, made it all the more difficult to keep him at arm's length. And she couldn't even begin to imagine how his plans for seducing her fit into this whole charade with the baby.

Questions churned in her mind, threatening to steal the joy from the day. In a rare impulsive move, she decided to simply go with the flow. She would quit worrying about when or if they would sleep together and just enjoy being with Rowan. Enjoy the flirting.

Revel in the chemistry they shared rather than wearing herself out denying its existence.

Butterflies stirred in her stomach. She pushed the stroller into their suite just as Rowan's arm shot out to stop her.

"Someone's here," he warned a second before a woman shot up from the sofa.

A woman?

The butterflies slowed and something cold settled in her stomach. Dread?

A redhead with a freckled nose and chic clothes squealed, "Rowan!"

The farm-fresh bombshell sprinted across the room and wrapped her arms around Rowan's neck.

Dread quickly shifted to something darker.

Jealousy.

Eight

Rowan braced his feet as the auburn-haired whirl-wind hit him full force. He'd spoken with his business partner and the partner's wife, Hillary, about the current situation. But he'd assured them Elliot Starc had things under control. Apparently his friends weren't taking him at his word.

Who else was waiting in the suite to blindside him? So much for romance tonight.

"Hillary." Rowan hugged his friend fast before pulling away. "Not that I'm unhappy to see you, but what are you doing here tonight?"

She patted his face. "You should know that word spreads fast among the Brotherhood and everyone available is eager to help." She glanced over her shoulder at Mari and the baby. "And of course, we're insanely curious about your new situation."

Mari looked back and forth between them, a look of confusion on her face. "The Brotherhood?"

"A nickname for some of my high school class-mates," Rowan explained. "We used to call ourselves the Alpha Brotherhood."

They still did, actually, after a few drinks over a game of cards. The name had started as a joke between them, a way of thumbing their noses at the frat-boy types, and after a while, the label stuck.

Hillary thrust a hand toward Mari. "Hi, I'm Hillary Donavan. I'm married to Rowan's former classmate and present business partner, Troy."

Mari's eyebrows arched upward. "Oh, your husband is the computer mogul."

Hillary took over pushing the stroller and preceded them into the suite as if it was her hotel penthouse. "You can go ahead and say it. My husband is the Robin Hood Hacker."

"I wasn't…" Mari stuttered, following the baby buggy deeper into the room. "I wouldn't…uh…"

"It's okay," Hillary said with a calm smile that had smoothed awkward moments in her days as an event planner for high-powered D.C. gatherings. "You can relax. Everyone knows my husband's history."

Mari smiled apologetically, leaning into the stroller to pull the sleeping baby out and cradle her protectively in her arms. "I'm not particularly good with chitchat."

"That's all right. I talk plenty for two people." She cupped the back of the infant's head. "What an ador-able baby. Issa, right?"

"Yes." Rowan pushed the stroller to a corner, light-weight gauzy pink blanket trailing out the side. "Did you see the gossip rags or did the Brotherhood tell you that, too?"

Hillary made herself at home on the leather sofa. "Actually, I'm here to help. Troy and Rowan are more than just business partners on that computer diagnostics project you so disapprove of—" Hillary winked to take the sting out the dig "—they're also longtime friends. I have some last-minute Christmas shopping to do for those tough-to-buy-for people in my life, and voilà. Coming here seemed the perfect thing to do."

The pieces came together in Rowan's mind, Hillary's appearance now making perfect sense. While the Brotherhood kept their Interpol work under wraps, Hillary knew about her husband's freelance agent work and Salvatore had even taken her into the fold for occasional missions. Now she was here. He should have thought of it himself, if his brain hadn't been scrambled by a certain sexy research scientist.

Hillary would make the perfect bodyguard for Mari and Issa. No one would question her presence and she added a layer of protection to this high-profile situation.

Although sometimes the whole Interpol connection also came with dangers. God, he was in the middle of an impossible juggling act.

The baby started fussing and Rowan extended his arms to take her. Mari hesitated, tucking the baby closer. Rowan lifted an eyebrow in surprise.

"Mari? I can take her." He lifted the baby from Mari's arms. "You two keep talking."

"Wow." Hillary laughed. "You sure handle that tiny tyke well. No wonder you're dubbed one of the world's hottest bachelors. Snap a photo of you now and you'll need your own bodyguard."

Mari's smile went tight and Rowan wondered... Holy hell, she couldn't be jealous. Could she? Was that the same look he'd seen drifting through her eyes when Hillary had hugged him earlier? He wanted her to desire him, but he also wanted—needed—for her to trust him.

"Enough, Hillary. You were talking about Troy's computer search…."

"Right—" she turned back to Mari "—and you're taking care of the baby, Rowan. So vamoose. Go fill out your list for Santa. I've got this."

Rowan cocked an eyebrow over being so summarily dismissed. And putting Issa in the bassinet in another room would give him the perfect excuse to slip away and call Troy.

Not to mention time to regroup for the next phase of winning over Mari. He'd made progress with her today.

Now he just had to figure out how to persuade his friends to give him enough space to take that romancing to the next level.

Mari sank to the edge of the sofa. Her head was spinning at how fast things were changing around her. Not to mention how fast this woman was talking.

"Hold on a moment, please." Mari raised a hand. "What were you saying about computer searches into Issa's past?"

Hillary dropped into the wide rattan chair beside her. "No worries. It's all totally legal computer work. I promise. Troy walks on the right side of the law these days. And yes, it's okay to talk about it. I know about my husband's past, and I assume you know about Rowan's. But they've both changed. They're genuinely trying to make amends in more ways than most could imagine."

Mari blinked in the wake of Hurricane Hillary, confused. Why would Rowan have needed to make amends for anything? Sure, he'd led a troubled life as a teen, but his entire adult life had been a walking advertisement for charity work. Even if she disputed some of his methods, she couldn't deny his philanthropic spirit. "I've read the stories of his good deeds."

"There's so much more to Rowan than those stories."

She knew that already. The press adored him and his work, and she had to admit his clinic had helped many. She just wished they could come to an agreement on how to make his work—the computerized side and even the personal side—more effective. If she could solve that problem, who knew how many more small clinics in stretched-thin outposts of the world would benefit from Rowan's model of aid?

"Hillary, why are you telling me this?"

"The competitive animosity between the two of you is not a secret." She tipped her head to the side, twirling a strand of red hair contemplatively. "So I find it strange that you're here."

"I'm here for the baby."

"Really?" Hillary crossed her legs, her eyes glimmering with humor and skepticism. No getting anything past this woman. "There are a million ways the two of you could care for this child other than sharing a suite."

Mari bristled, already feeling overwhelmed by this confident whirlwind who looked like a Ralph Lauren model in skinny jeans and a poet's shirt.

Smoothing her hands over her sack dress, Mari sat up stiffly, channeling every regal cell in her body. "This is quite a personal conversation to be having with someone I only just met."

"You're right. I apologize if I've overstepped." She held up a hand, diamond wedding band set winking in the sunlight. "I've become much more extroverted since marrying Troy. I just wanted you to know Rowan's a better man than people think. A better man than he knows."

Great. Someone else pointing out the perfection of Dr. Rowan Boothe. As if Mari didn't already know. God, how she resented the feelings of insecurity pumping through her. She wanted to be the siren in the peignoir, the confident woman certain that Rowan wanted her with every fiber of his soul. And yes, she knew that was melodramatic and totally unscientific.

Forcing her thoughts to slow and line up logically, she realized that Rowan's eyes had followed her all day long—no skinny jeans needed. And Hillary was right. He and Mari both could have figured out a dozen different ways to care for this baby and stir publicity without sharing a suite. She was here because she wanted to be and Rowan wanted her here, as well.

No more flirting. No more games. No more holding back. She burned to sleep with Rowan.

The next time she had him alone, she intended to see the seduction through to its full, satisfying conclusion.

Finally, Rowan closed his suite door after dinner with Hillary, Troy and Elliot. He plowed his hands through his hair as Mari settled the baby for the night in his room.

He appreeiated the help of his friends—but by the end of supper he had never been happier to see them all head to their own suites. Troy and Hillary were staying in the suite across the hall. Elliot Starc was a floor below, monitoring the surveillance vans outside the resort.

Rowan was more than a little surprised that his friends felt such a need to rally around him just because another orphan had landed on his doorstep. Issa wasn't the first—and she certainly wouldn't be the last—child in need of his patronage.

He suspected his friends' increased interest had something to do with Mari's involvement. No doubt he hadn't been as successful as he would have liked at hiding his attraction to her all these years. They were here out of curiosity as well as genuine caring, stepping up on a personal level, even if Mari didn't know the full weight of what they brought to the table for security and he wasn't in a position to tell her.

Now that a story had broken about an orphan at Christmastime, the attention was swelling by the second. Holiday mayhem made it tougher than ever to record all the comings and goings at the resort. Bogus leads were also coming in by the hundreds. So far no sign of a valid tip. Hillary and Troy were rechecking the police work through computer traces, using Interpol databases.

Intellectually, he understood these things took time and persistence, but thinking about the kid's future, worrying about her, made this more personal than analytical.

Somewhere out there, the baby's family had to be seeing the news reports. Even if they didn't want to claim her, surely someone would step forward with information. Even if the answer came in the form of official surrender of parental rights, at least they would know.

He understood full well how family ties didn't always turn out to be as ideal as one would hope. Memories of his brother's death, of his parents' grief and denial burned through him. He charged across the sitting area to the bar. He started to reach for the scotch and stopped himself. After the way his brother died...

Hell, no.

He opted for a mug of fresh local ginger tea and

one of the Christmas sugar cookies instead and leaned against the bar, staring out over the water as he bit the frosted tree cookie in half. Tomorrow, he and Mari both had conference presentations, then this weekend, the closing dinner and ball. Time was ticking away for all of them. He had to make the most of every moment. Tomorrow, he'd arranged for a spa appointment for Mari after her last presentation. Surely she would appreciate some privacy after all the scrutiny....

The door from Rowan's room opened. Mari slid through and closed it quietly after her. "Baby's sleeping soundly. I would have taken her tonight, you know."

"Fair is fair," he said. "We struck a bargain."

"You're a stubborn man. But then I understand that trait well."

Walking toward him, her silvery-gray sheath dress gliding over her sleek figure, she set the nursery monitor on the edge of the bar. Christmas tunes played softly over the airwaves—jazz versions, soft and soothing. Mari had fallen into the habit of setting her iPhone beside the monitor and using the music to reassure herself the listening device was still on.

She poured herself a mug of steaming ginger tea as well, adding milk and honey. Cupping the thick pottery in both hands, she drank half then cradled the mug to her with a sigh.

He skimmed his knuckles along her patrician cheekbones. "Are you okay?"

Nodding, she set aside her glass. "I just didn't expect the press coverage to be so...comprehensive."

Was it his imagination or did she lean into his touch.

"You're a princess. What you do makes the news." Although even he was surprised at just how intense the media attention had become.

The hotel staff had closed off access to their floor aside from them and the Donavans, a measure taken after a reporter was injured on a window-washing unit trying to get a bonus photo. Rowan rubbed at a kink in the back of his neck, stress-induced from worrying his tail off about all the possible holes in the security. He wasn't sure he felt comfortable taking Mari and Issa out of the hotel again, even with guards.

"But I wanted to bring positive coverage for Issa. Not all of these cranks…"

And she didn't know the half of it. Troy had informed him about a handful of the more colorful leads the police hadn't bothered mentioning. A woman claiming to be Mari's illegitimate half sister had called to say the baby belonged to her. Another call had come from an area prison with someone saying their infant daughter resembled Issa and she thought it was her twin, whom they'd thought died at birth.

All of which turned out to be false, but there was no need to make Mari more upset by sharing the details. "My contacts will sift through them."

"Who are these contacts you keep talking about? Like Hillary and her husband?" She picked up the glass again and sipped carefully.

His glass.

His body tightened as her lips pressed to the edge.

He cleared his throat. "I went to a military high school. Makes sense that some of them would end up in law enforcement positions."

"It was a military *reform* school." She eyed him over the rim of the tumbler through long lashes.

"Actually, about half were there because they wanted a future in the military or law enforcement." He rattled off the details, anything to keep from thinking about how badly he wanted to take that glass from her and kiss her until they both forgot about talking and press conferences. "The rest of us were there because we got into trouble."

"Your Alpha Brotherhood group—you trust these friends with Issa's future?"

"Implicitly."

Shaking her head, she looked away. "I wish I could be as sure about whom to trust."

"You're worried."

"Of course."

"Because you care." Visions of her caring for the baby, insisting Issa stay in her room tonight even though it was his turn, taunted him with how attached she was becoming to the little one already. There was so much more to this woman than he'd known or guessed. She was more emotional than she'd ever let on. Which brought him back to the strange notion that she'd been jealous of Hillary.

A notion he needed to dispel. "What did you think of Hillary?"

"She's outspoken and she's a huge fan of yours." She folded her arms over her chest.

"You can't be jealous."

"At first, when she hugged you...I wondered if she was a girlfriend," she admitted. "Then I realized it might not be my right to ask."

"I kissed you. You have a right to question." He met her gaze full-on, no games or hidden agendas. Just pure honesty. "For the record, I'm the monogamous type. When I'm with a woman, I'm sure as hell not kissing other women."

Her eyes flashed with quick relief before she tipped

her head to the side and touched his chest lightly. "What happened last night—"

"What almost happened—"

"Okay, almost happened, along with the parts that did—"

"I understand." He pressed a hand over hers, wanting to reassure her before she had a chance to start second-guessing things and bolting away. "You want to say it can't happen. Not again."

"Hmm…" She frowned, toying with the simple watch on her wrist. "Have you added mind reader to your list of accomplishments now? If so, please do tell me why I would insist on pushing you away."

"Because we have to take care of the baby." He folded her hand in his and kissed her knuckles, then her wrist. "Your devotion to her is a beautiful thing."

"That's a lovely compliment. Thank you. I would say the same about you."

"A compliment?" he bantered back. "I did *not* expect that."

"Why ever not?" She stepped closer until her breasts almost brushed his chest.

The unmistakably seductive move wasn't lost on him. His pulse kicked up a notch as he wondered just how far she would take this.

And how far he should let it go.

"There is the fact that you haven't missed an opportunity to make it clear how much you don't like me or my work."

"That could be a compelling reason to keep my distance from you." She placed her other hand on his chest, tipping her face up to him until their lips were a whisper apart.

"Be on notice…" He took in the deep amber of her

eyes, the flush spreading across her latte-colored, creamy skin. "I plan to romance you, sweep you off your feet even."

"You are—" she paused, leaning into him, returning his intense gaze "—a confusing man. I thought I knew you but now I'm finding I don't understand you at all. But you need to realize that after last night's kiss…"

"It was more than a kiss," he said hoarsely.

"You're absolutely right on that." Her fingers crawled up his chest until she tapped his bottom lip.

He captured her wrist again just over the thin watch. He thought of the bracelets he'd surreptitiously picked up for her at the marketplace, looking forward to the right moment to give them to her. "But I will not make love to you until you ask me. You have to know that."

"You're mighty confident." Her breath carried heat and a hint of the ginger tea.

Who knew tea could be far more intoxicating than any liquor? "Hopeful."

"Good." Her lips moved against his. "Because I'm asking."

And damn straight he didn't intend to walk away from her again.

Nine

Mari arched up onto her toes to meet Rowan's mouth sealing over hers. Pure want flooded through her. Each minute had felt like an hour from the moment she'd decided to act on her desire tonight until the second he'd kissed her.

Finally, she would be with him, see this crazy attraction through. Whether they were arguing or working together, the tension crackled between them. She recognized that now. They'd been moving toward this moment for years.

She nipped his bottom lip. "We have to be quiet so we don't wake the baby."

"Hmm…" His growl rumbled his chest against her. "Sounds challenging."

"Just how challenging can we make it?" She grazed her nails down his back, the fabric of his shirt carrying the warmth and scent of him.

"Is that a dare?"

She tucked her hands into the back pockets of his jeans as she'd dreamed of doing more than once. "Most definitely."

Angling his head to the side, he stared into her eyes. "And you're sure you're ready for this?"

She dug her fingers into his amazing tush. "Could you quit being so damn admirable? I'm very clearly propositioning you. I am an adult, a very smart adult, totally sober, and completely turned on by you. If that's not clear enough for you, then how about this? Take me to bed or to the couch, but take me now."

A slow and sexy smile creased dimples into his sun-bronzed face. "How convenient you feel that way since you absolutely mesmerize me."

Her stomach fluttered at the obvious appreciation in his eyes, his voice. His *touch*. He made her feel like the sensuous woman who wore peignoirs. He made her feel sexy. Sexier than any man ever had, and yes, that was a part of his appeal.

But she couldn't deny she'd always found him attractive. Who wouldn't? He took handsome to a whole new level, in a totally unselfconscious way. The blond streaks in his hair came from the sun—his muscles from hard work.

And those magnificent callused hands... She could lose herself in the pure sensation of his caress.

He inched aside the strap of her silvery-gray dress. She'd chosen the silky fabric for the decadent glide along her skin—yes, she usually preferred shapeless clothes, but the appreciation in Rowan's eyes relayed loud and clear he'd never judged her by what she wore. He saw her. The woman. And he wanted her.

That knowledge sent a fresh thrill up her spine.

He kissed along her bared neck, to her shoulder, his teeth lightly snapping her champagne-colored satin bra strap—another of her hidden decadences, beautiful underwear. Her head fell back, giving him fuller access. But she didn't intend to be passive in this encounter. Not by a long shot. Her hands soaked up the play of his muscles flexing in his arms as she stroked down, down, farther still to his waistband.

She tugged his polo shirt free and her fingers crawled up under the warm cotton to find even hotter skin. She palmed his back, scaled the hard planes of his shoulder blades as a jazz rendering of "The First Noel" piped through the satellite radio. He was her latest fantasies come to life.

Unable to wait a second longer, she yanked the shirt over his head even if that meant he had to draw his mouth away from her neck. She flung aside his polo, the red shirt floating to rest on the leather sofa. Fire heated his eyes to the hottest blue flame. He skimmed off the other strap of her dress until the silk slithered down her body, hooking briefly on her hips before she shimmied it the rest of the way off to pool at her feet. She kicked aside her sandals as she stepped out of the dress.

His gaze swept over her as fully as she took in the bared expanse of his broad chest, the swirls of hair, the sun-bronzed skin. He traced down the strap of her bra, along the lace edging the cups of her bra, slowly, deliberately outlining each breast. Her nipples beaded against the satin, tight and needy. She burned to be closer to him, as close as possible.

Her breath hitched in her throat and she stepped into his arms. The heat of his skin seared her as if he'd stored up the African sun inside him and shared it with her now.

"Here," she insisted, "on the sofa or the floor. I don't care. Just hurry."

"Princess, I have waited too damn long to rush this. I intend to have you completely and fully, in a real bed. I would prefer it was my bed, but there's a baby snoozing in the bassinet in my room. So let's go to yours."

"Fine," she agreed frantically. "Anywhere, the sooner the better." She slipped a finger into the waistband of his jeans and tugged.

"I like a lady who knows what she wants. Hell, I just like you."

His hands went to the front clasp of her bra and plucked it open and away with deft hands. She gasped as the overhead fan swooshed air over her bared flesh. Then he palmed both curves, warming her with a heat that spread into a tingling fire.

Through the haze of passion she realized her hand was still on his buckle. She fumbled with his belt, then the snap of his jeans, his zipper, until she found his arousal hard and straining against her hand. A growl rumbled low in his throat and she reveled in the sound. Drew in the scent of his soap and his sweat, perspiration already beading his brow from his restraint as she learned the feel of him. She stroked the steely length down, up and again.

"We have to be quiet," she reminded him.

"Both of us," he said with a promise in his voice and in his narrowed eyes.

One of his hands slid from her breast down to her panties, dipping inside, gliding between her legs. She was moist and ready for him. If she'd had her way they would be naked and together on the sofa. He was the one who'd insisted on drawing this out, but then they'd always been competitive.

Although right now that competition was delivering a tense and delicious result rather than the frustration of the past. She bit her bottom lip to hold back a whimper of pleasure. He slipped two fingers inside, deeper, stroking and coaxing her into a moist readiness. She gripped his shoulders, her fingernails digging half-moons into his tanned skin. Each glide took her higher until her legs went weak and he locked an arm around her back.

She gasped against his neck, so close to fulfillment. Aching for completion. "Let's take this to the bed."

"Soon, I promise." His late-day beard rasped against her cheek and he whispered in her ear, "But first, I need to protect you."

She gritted her teeth in frustration over the delay. "Rowan, there are guards stationed inside and outside of the hotel. Can we talk about security forces later?"

Cupping her face in his broad palms, he kissed the tip of her nose. "I mean I need to get birth control."

"Oh…" She gasped, surprised that she hadn't thought of it herself. She'd come in here with the intention of seducing him and she hadn't given a thought to the most important element of that union. So much for her genius IQ in the heat of the moment.

"I'll take care of it." He stepped away and disappeared from her room, his jeans slung low on his hips. Lean muscles rippled with every step.

She was an intelligent, modern woman. A scientist. A woman of logic. She liked to believe she would have realized before it was too late…. Before she could complete the thought, Rowan returned. He tossed a box of condoms on the bed.

"My goodness," she said, smiling, "you're an ambitious man."

"I'll take that as another challenge."

"Sounds like one where we're both winners. Now how about getting rid of those jeans."

"Your wish is my command, Princess." He toed off his shoes, no socks on, and peeled down his jeans without once taking his eyes off her.

His erection strained against his boxers and she opened her arms for him to join her. Then he was kissing her again and, oh, my, but that man knew how to kiss. The intensity of him, the way he was so completely focused on her and the moment fulfilled a long-ignored need to be first with a man. How amazing that the man who would view her this way—see only her—would be Rowan.

He reclined with her on the bed, into the thick comforter and stack of tapestry pillows, the crash and recede of the waves outside echoing the throb of her pulse. The sound of the shore, the luxurious suite, the hard-bodied man stretched over her was like a fantasy come true.

Only one thing kept it from being complete—something easily taken care of. She hooked her thumbs into the band of his boxers and inched them down. He smiled against her mouth as his underwear landed on the floor. Finally—thank heavens—finally, they met bare body to bare body, flesh-to-flesh. The rigid length of him pressed against her stomach, heating her with the promise of pleasure to come.

She dragged her foot up the back of his calf, hooking her leg around him, rocking her hips against him. He shifted his attention from her lips to her neck, licking along her collarbone before reaching her breasts—his mouth on one, his hand on the other. He touched and tasted her with an intuition for what she craved and more, finding nuances of sensitive patches of skin she hadn't realized were favored spots.

And she wanted to give him the same bliss.

Her fingers slid between them until her hand found his erection, exploring the length and feel of him. His forehead fell to rest against her collarbone. His husky growl puffed along oversensitized skin as she continued to stroke. Her thumb glided along the tip, smoothing a damp pearl, slickening her caress. Her mind filled with images of all the ways she wanted to love him through the night, with her hands and her mouth, here and in the shower. She whispered those fantasies in his ear and he throbbed in response in her hand.

Groaning, he reached out to snatch up the box of condoms. Rolling to his side, he clasped her wrist and moved her hand away, then sheathed himself. She watched, vowing next time she would do that for him.

Next time? Definitely a next time. And a next night.

Already she was thinking into the future and that was a scary proposition. Better to live in the now and savor this incredible moment. She clasped Rowan's shoulders as he shifted back over her again.

He balanced on his elbows, holding his weight off her. The thick pressure of him between her legs had her wriggling to get closer, draw him in deeper. She swept her other leg up until her ankles hooked around his waist. Her world filled with the sight of his handsome face and broad shoulders blocking out the rest of the world.

He hooked a hand behind her knee. "Your legs drive me crazy. Do you know that?"

"I do now. I also know you're driving me crazy waiting. I want all of you. Now." She dug her heels into his buttocks and urged him to...

Fill her.

Stretch her.

Thrill her.

Her back bowed up to meet him thrust for thrust, hushed sigh for sigh. Perspiration sealed them together, cool sheets slipping and bunching under them. In a smooth sweep, he kicked the comforter and tapestry pillows to the floor.

Tension gathered inside her, tightening in her belly. Her head dug back into the mattress, the scent of them mingling and filling every gasping breath. He touched her with reverence and perception, but she didn't want gentle or reverent. She needed edgy; she needed completion.

She pushed at his shoulder and flipped him to his back, straddling him, taking him faster and harder, his heated gaze and smile of approval all the encouragement she needed. His hands sketched up her stomach to her breasts, circling and plucking at her nipples as she came, intensifying waves of pleasure, harder, straight to the core of her. She rode the sensations, rode him, taking them both to the edge…and into a climax. Mutual. She bit her bottom lip to hold back the sounds swelling inside her as she stayed true to their vow to keep quiet. Rowan's jaw flexed, his groans mingling with her sighs.

Each rolling wave of bliss drew her, pulling her into a whirlpool of total muscle-melting satisfaction. Her arms gave way and she floated to rest on top of him. Rowan's chest pumped beneath her with labored breaths. His arms locked around her, anchoring her to him and to the moment.

Her body trembled in the wake of each aftershock rippling through her.

Exhaustion pulled at her but she knew if she slept, morning would come too fast with too many questions and possibilities that could take this away. So she blinked back sleep, focusing on multicolored lights beyond the window. Yachts, a sailboat, a ferry. She took in the details to stay awake so once her languid body regained strength, she could play out all those fantasies with Rowan.

She wanted everything she could wring from this stolen moment in case this night was all they could have before she retreated to the safety and order of her cold, clinical world.

"Are you asleep?" Mari's soft voice whispered through Rowan's haze as he sprawled beside her.

He'd wanted Mari for years. He'd known they would be good together. But no way in hell could he have predicted just how mind-blowingly incredible making love to this woman would be.

Sleep wasn't even an option with every fiber of him saturated with the satiny feel of her, the floral scent of her, the driving need to have her again and again until...

His mind stopped short of thoughts of the end. "I'm awake. Do you need something?"

Was she about to boot him out of her bed? Out of her life? He knew too well how fast the loyalties of even good people could shift. He grabbed the rumpled sheet free from around his feet and whipped it out until it fanned to rest over them.

She rolled toward him, her fingers toying with the hair on his chest. "I'm good. *This* is good, staying right here, like this. The past couple of days have been so frenzied, it's a relief to be in the moment."

"I hear ya." He kissed the top of her head, thinking of the bracelets he'd bought for her from the market and planning the right time to place them on her elegant arm.

Her fingers slowed and she looked up at him through long sweeping eyelashes. "You're very good with Issa. Have you ever thought about having kids of your own?"

His voice froze in his throat for a second. He'd given up on perfect family life a long time ago when he'd woken in the hospital to learn he and his brother were responsible for a woman losing her baby. Any hope of resurrecting those dreams died the day his brother crashed his truck into the side of a house.

Rowan sketched his fingers along Mari's stomach. He'd built a new kind of family with the Brotherhood and his patients. "I have my kids at the clinic, children that need me and depend on me."

"So you know that it's possible to love children that aren't your blood relation."

Where was she going with this? And then holy hell, it became all too clear. She was thinking about the possibility of keeping Issa beyond this week. "Are you saying that you're becoming attached to the little rug rat?"

"How could I not?" She leaned over him, resting her chin on her folded hands as she looked into his eyes. "I wonder if Issa landed with me for a reason. I've always planned not to get married. I thought that meant no kids for me—I never considered myself very good with them. But with Issa, I know what to do. She even responds to my voice already."

She was right about that. They shared a special bond that had to be reassuring to an infant whose world had been turned upside down by abandonment. But questions about the baby's past *would* be answered soon. He thought of Hillary and Troy working their tails off to find the baby's family. He hated to think of Mari setting herself up for heartache.

She shook her head before he could think of how

to remind her. "I know it's only been a couple of days and she could well have family out there who wants her. Or her mother might change her mind. I just hate the limbo."

He swept her hair from her face and kissed her, hard. "You won't be in limbo for long, I can promise you that." Guilt pinched over how he'd brought her into this, all but forced her to stay with him. "My friends and I won't rest until we find the truth about Issa's past. That's a good thing, you know."

"Of course I do. Let's change the subject." She pulled a wobbly smile. "I think it's amazing the way your friends all came to help you at the drop of a hat."

"It's what we do for each other." Just as he'd done his best to help his buddy Conrad reconcile with his wife earlier this year. He owed Conrad for helping him start the clinic, but he would have helped regardless.

"In spite of your rocky teenage years, you and your friends have all turned into incredible success stories. I may not always agree with some of your projects, but your philanthropic work is undeniable. It's no secret that your other friend, the casino owner—Conrad Hughes— has poured a lot of money into your clinic, as well."

He tensed at her mention of one of his Alpha Brotherhood buddies, wishing he could share more about the other side of his life. Needing to warn her, to ensure she didn't get too close. There weren't many women who could live with the double life he and his friends led with their Interpol work. Mari had enough complicating her life with her heritage. Better to keep the conversation on well-known facts and off anything that could lead to speculation.

"Conrad invested the start-up cash for my clinic. He

deserves the credit. My financial good fortune came later."

"No need to be so modest. Even before your invention of the diagnostics program, you could have had a lucrative practice anywhere and you chose to be here in Africa, earning a fraction of the salary."

He grunted, tunneling his hand under the sheet to cup her butt and hopefully distract her. "I got by then and I get by even better now."

She smiled against his chest. "Right, the billions you made off that diagnostics program we keep arguing about. I could help you make it better."

He smacked her bottom lightly. "Is that really what you want to talk about and risk a heated debate?"

"Why are you so quick to deflect accolades? The press is totally in love with you. You could really spin that, if you wanted."

He grimaced. "No, thanks."

She elbowed up on his chest. "I do understand your reticence. But think about it. You could inspire other kids. Sure you went to a military reform school, but you studied your butt off for scholarships to become a doctor, made a fortune and seem to be doing your level best to give it all away."

"I'm not giving it *all* away," he said gruffly, a sick feeling churning in his gut at the detour this conversation was taking. He avoided that damn press corps for just this reason. He didn't want anyone digging too deeply and he sure as hell didn't want credit for some noble character he didn't possess. "If I donate everything, I'll be broke and no good to anyone. I'm investing wisely."

"While donating heavily of your money and time."

Throwing all his resources into the black hole of guilt

that he'd never fill. Ever. He took a deep breath to keep that dark cavern at bay.

"Stop, okay?" He kissed her to halt her words. "I do what I do because it's the right thing. I have to give back, to make up for my mistakes."

Her forehead furrowed. "For your drunk-driving accident in high school? I would say you've more than made restitution. You could hire other doctors to help you carry the load."

"How can a person ever make restitution for lives lost?" he barked out, more sharply than he'd intended. But now that he'd started, there was no going back. "Do you know why I was sentenced to the military reform school for my last two years of high school?"

"Because you got in a drunk-driving accident and a woman was injured. You made a horrible, horrible mistake, Rowan. No one's denying that. But it's clear to anyone looking that you've turned your life around."

"You've done your homework where my diagnostics model is concerned, but you've obviously never researched the man behind the medicine." He eased Mari off him and sat up, his elbows on his knees as he hung his head, the weight of the memories too damn much. "The woman driving the other car was pregnant. She lost the baby."

"Oh, no, Rowan how tragic for her." Mari's voice filled with sadness and a hint of horror, but her hand fluttered to rest on his back. "And what a heavy burden for you to carry as the driver of the car."

She didn't know the half of it. No one did. To let the full extent of his guilt out would stain his brother's memory. Yet, for some reason he couldn't pinpoint, he found himself confessing all for the first time. To Mari. "But I wasn't driving."

Her hand slid up to rub the back of his neck and she sat up beside him, sheet clasped to her chest. "The news reports all say you were."

"That's what we told the police." He glanced over at her. "My brother and I both filled out formal statements saying I was the driver."

She stared back at him for two crashes of the waves before her eyes went wide with realization. "Your brother was actually the one behind the wheel that night? And he was drunk?"

Rowan nodded tightly. "We were both injured in the car accident, knocked out and rushed to the nearest hospital. When I woke up from surgery for a punctured lung, my mother was with me. My dad was with my brother, who'd broken his nose and fractured his jaw. They wanted us to get our stories straight before we talked to the police."

That night came roaring back to him, the confusion, the pain. The guilt that never went away no matter how many lives he saved at the clinic.

"Did your parents actually tell you to lie for your brother?" Her eyes went wider with horror. Clearly her parents would have never considered such a thing.

Most never would. He understood that, not that it made him feel one bit better about his own role in what had happened. She needed to understand the position they'd all been in, how he'd tried to salvage his brother's life only to make an even bigger mistake. One that cost him...too much.

"We were both drunk that night, but my brother was eighteen years old. I was only sixteen, a minor. The penalty would be less for me, but Dylan could serve hard time in jail. If I confessed to driving the car, Dylan could still have a future, a chance to turn his life around while he was still young."

"So you took the blame for your brother. You allowed yourself to be sentenced to a military reform school because your family pressured you, oh, Rowan..." She swept back his hair, her hands cool against his skin. "I am so sorry."

But he didn't want or deserve her comfort or sympathy. Rather than reject it outright, he linked fingers with her and lowered her arms.

"There was plenty of blame to go around that night. I could have made so many different choices. I could have called a cab at the party or asked someone else to drive us home." The flashing lights outside reminded him of the flash of headlights before the wreck, the blurred cop cars before he'd blacked out, then finally the arrival of the police to arrest him. "I wasn't behind the wheel, but I was guilty of letting my brother have those keys."

His brother had been a charismatic character, everyone believed him when he said he would change, and Rowan had gotten used to following his lead. When Dylan told him he was doing great in rehab, making his meetings, laying off the bottle, Rowan had believed him.

"What about your brother's guilt for what happened that night? Didn't Dylan deserve to pay for what happened to that woman, for you giving up your high school years?"

Trust Mari to see this analytically, to analyze it in clear-cut terms of rights and wrongs. Life didn't work that way. The world was too full of blurred gray territory.

"My brother paid plenty for that night and the decisions I made." If Rowan had made the right choices in the beginning, his brother would still be alive today. "Two years later, Dylan was in another drunk-driving accident. He drove his truck into the side of a house. He died." Rowan drew in a ragged breath, struggling like hell not to shrug off her touch that left him feeling too raw right now. "So you see, my decisions that night cost two lives."

Mari scooted to kneel in front of him, the sheet still clasped to her chest. Her dark hair spiraled around her shoulders in a wild sexy mess, but her amber eyes were no-nonsense. "You were sixteen years old and your parents pressured you to make the wrong decision. They sacrificed you to save your brother. They were wrong to do that."

Memories grated his insides, every word pouring acid on freshly opened wounds. He left the bed, left her, needing to put distance between himself and Mari's insistence.

He stepped over the tapestry pillows and yanked on his boxers. "You're not hearing me, Mari." He snagged his jeans from the floor and jerked them on one leg at a time. "I accept responsibility for my own actions. I wasn't a little kid. Blaming other people for our mistakes is a cop-out."

And the irony of it all, the more he tried to make amends, the more people painted him as some kind of freaking saint. He needed air. Now.

A ringing phone pierced the silence between them.

Not her ringtone. His, piping through the nursery monitor. Damn it. He'd left his cell phone in his room. "I should get that before it wakes the baby."

He hotfooted it out of her room, grateful for the excuse to escape more of her questions. Why the hell couldn't they just make love until the rest of the world faded away?

With each step out the door, he felt the weight of her gaze following him. He would have to give her some kind of closure to her questions, and he would. Once he had himself under control again.

He opened the door leading into his bedroom. His phone rang on the bamboo dresser near the bassinet. He grabbed the cell and took it back into the sitting area, reading the name scrolling across the screen.

Troy Donavan?

Premonition burned over him. His computer pal had to have found something big in order to warrant a call in the middle of the night.

Mari filled the doorway, tan satin sheet wrapped around her, toga-style. "Is something wrong?"

"I don't know yet." He thumbed the talk button on the cell phone. "Yes?"

"Hi, Rowan." Hillary's voice filled his ear. "It's me. Troy's found a trail connecting a worker at the hotel to a hospital record on one of the outlying islands— he's still working the data. But he's certain he's found Issa's mother."

Ten

Mari cradled sleeping Issa in her arms, rocking her for what would be the last time. She stared past the garland-draped minibar to the midday sun marking the passage of the day, sweeping away precious final minutes with this sweet child she'd already grown to love.

Her heart was breaking in two.

She couldn't believe her time with Issa was coming to an end. Before she'd even been able to fully process the fact that she'd actually followed through on the decision to sleep with Rowan, her world had been tossed into utter chaos with one phone call that swept Issa from them forever.

Troy Donavan had tracked various reflections of reflections in surveillance videos, piecing them together with some maze of other cameras in everything from banks to cops' radar to follow a path to a hint of a clue. They'd found the woman who'd walked away from the room-service trolley where Issa had been hidden. They'd gone a step further in the process to be sure. At some point, Mari had lost the thread of how he'd traced the trail back to a midwife on the mainland who'd delivered Issa. She'd been able to identify the mother, proving the baby's identity with footprint records.

The young mother had made her plan meticulously and worked to cover her tracks. She'd uncovered Rowan's schedule to speak at this conference then managed to get hired as a temp in the extra staff brought on for the holiday crowd. That's why she hadn't been on the employee manifest.

It appeared she'd had a mental breakdown shortly after leaving her child and was currently in a hospital. Issa had no grandparents, but she had a great aunt and uncle who wanted her. Deeply. In their fifties, their four sons were all grown but they hadn't hesitated in stepping up to care for their great niece. They owned a small coastal art gallery on the mainland and had plenty of parenting knowledge. They weren't wealthy, but their business and lives were stable.

All signs indicated they could give Issa a wonderful life full of love. Mari should be turning cartwheels over the news. So many orphans in Africa had no one to call their own and here Issa had a great family ready and eager to care for her.

Still, Mari could barely breathe at the prospect of handing over the baby, even though she knew this was the best thing for Issa.

The main door opened and Mari flinched, clutching the tiny girl closer. Rowan entered, lines fanning from his eyes attesting to the sleepless night they'd both endured after the fateful phone call about Issa's identity.

Rowan had scraped his hair back with a thin leather tie, his jeans and button-down shirt still sporting the wrinkles from when she'd tossed them aside in an effort to get him naked. That seemed eons ago now. Those moments after the call when they'd hastily gotten dressed again had passed in a frenzied haze.

"Any news?" she asked, feeling like a wretched person for hoping somehow she could keep Issa. She wasn't in any position to care for a baby. She'd never even given much thought to being a mother. But right now, it was the only thing she could think about. Who knew that a baby could fill a void in her life that she would have never guessed needed filling?

He shook his head and sat on the arm of the sofa near her, his blue eyes locked on the two of them. "Just more verification of what we learned last night. The mother's note was honest. Her husband was a soldier killed in a border dispute. And just more confirmation to what we already knew—she picked up a job doing temp work here, which is why she didn't show up on the initial employee search. The woman you saw that night running from the cart was, in fact, Issa's mother. She has family support back on the mainland. But it appears her husband's death hit her especially hard when she was already suffering from postpartum depression."

That last part hadn't been in the early reports. The whole issue became muddier now that the baby hadn't been left out of selfishness, but rather out of a deep mental illness. "Issa ended up in a room-service cart because of postpartum depression?"

"Approximately one in eight new mothers suffer from it in the States." He pinched the bridge of his nose as if battling a headache. "Even more so here with the rampant poverty and lack of medical care."

Mari's arms twitched protectively around the bundled infant. Would it have made a difference for Issa's mother if the family had been more supportive? Or had they been shut out? So many questions piled on top of each other until she realized she was simply looking for someone to blame, a reason why it would be okay to keep Issa. The scent of baby detergent—specially bought so she could wash the tiny clothes herself—mingled with sweet baby breath. Such a tender, dear bundle...

When Issa squirmed, Mari forced herself to relax—at least outwardly. "I guess I should be grateful she didn't harm her child. What happens now?"

Mari's eyes dropped to the child as Issa fought off sleep, her tiny fingers clenching and unclenching.

"She goes to her family," he said flatly.

"Where were they when Issa's mother felt so desperate?" The question fell from Mari's heart as much as her mouth, the objective scientist part of her nowhere to be found. She had to be certain before she could let go.

Rowan's hand fell to a tiny baby foot encased in a Christmas plaid sleeper. "The aunt and uncle insist they offered help, and that they didn't know how badly their niece was coping."

"Do you believe them?"

"They don't live nearby so it's entirely possible they missed the signs. Issa's only three months old." He patted the baby's chest once before shoving to his feet again, pacing restlessly. "They came for the funeral six weeks ago, left some money, followed up with calls, but she told them she was managing all right."

"And they believed her." How awful did it make her that she was still desperately searching for something to fault them for, some reason why they couldn't be the right people to raise the little angel in her arms.

"From everything our sources can tell, they're good people. Solid income from their tourist shop." He stopped at the window, palming the glass and leaning forward with a weary sigh. "They want custody of Issa and there's no legal or moral reason I can see why they shouldn't have her."

"What about what we want?" she asked quickly, in case she might have second thoughts and hold back the words.

"We don't have any rights to her." He glanced back over his shoulder. "This is the best scenario we could have hoped would play out. That first night when we spoke to the cops, we both never really dreamed this good of a solution could be found for her."

"I realize that… It's just…"

He turned to face her, leaning back and crossing his arms over his chest. "You already love her."

"Of course I care about her."

A sad half smile tipped his mouth. "That's not what I said."

"I've only known her a few days." Mari rolled out the logic as if somehow she could convince herself.

"I've watched enough new mothers in my line of work to know how fast the heart engages."

What did he hope to achieve by this? By stabbing her with his words? "I'm not her mother."

"You have been, though. You've done everything a mother would do to protect her child. It's not surprising you want to keep her."

Mari's throat clogged with emotion. "I'm in no position to take care of a baby. She has relatives who want her and can care for her. I know what I have to do."

"You're giving her the best chance, like a good mother." He cupped the back of her head, comfort in his gaze and in his touch.

She soaked up his supporting strength. "Are you trying to soften me up again?"

"I'm wounded you would think I'm that manipulative." He winked.

"Ha," she choked on a half laugh. "Now you're trying to make me smile so I won't cry."

He massaged her scalp lightly. "It's okay to cry if you need to."

She shook her head. "I think I'll just keep rocking her, maybe sing some Christmas carols until her family arrives. I know she won't remember me, but…"

A buzzer sounded at their suite door a second before Hillary walked in, followed by Troy. Mari sighed in relief over the brief reprieve. The aunt and uncle weren't here yet.

Hillary smiled gently. "The family is on their way up. I thought you would want the warning."

"Thank you for your help tracking them down." Mari could hardly believe she managed to keep her voice flat and unemotional in light of the caldron churning inside her.

Troy sat on the sofa beside his wife, the wiry computer mogul sliding an arm around Hillary's shoulders. "I'm glad we were able to resolve the issue so quickly."

Yet it felt like she'd spent a lifetime with Rowan and the baby.

Hillary settled into her husband's arm. "Mari, did Rowan tell you the tip that helped us put the pieces together came from the press coverage you brought in?"

"No, not that I remember." Although he might have

said something and she missed it. Since she'd heard Issa was leaving, Mari had been in a fog.

"Thanks to the huge interest your name inspired, we were contacted by a nurse whose story sounded legit. We showed her the composite sketch we'd pieced together from the different camera angles." Hillary rambled on, filling the tense silence. "She identified the woman as a patient she'd helped through delivery. From there, the rest of the pieces came together. She never would have heard about this if not for you and Rowan. You orchestrated this perfectly, Mari."

"With your help. Rowan is lucky to have such great friends."

And with those words she realized she didn't have people to reach out to in a crisis. She had work acquaintances, and she had family members she kept at arm's length. She spent her life focused on her lab. She'd sealed herself off from the world, running from meaningful relationships as surely as she ran from the press. Shutting herself away from her parents' disapproval—her father wanting her to assume her role of princess, her mother encouraging her to be a rebellious child embracing a universe beyond. Ultimately she'd disappointed them both. Rowan and this baby were her first deep connections in so long....

And it was tearing her apart to say goodbye to them.

She didn't want this pain. She wanted her safe world back. The quiet and order of her research lab, where she could quantify results and predict outcomes.

The buzzer sounded again and Mari bit her lip to keep from shouting in denial. Damn it, she would stay in control. She would see this through in a calm manner, do nothing to upset Issa.

Even though every cell in her cried out in denial.

* * *

Rowan watched helplessly as Mari passed the baby over to her relatives—a couple he'd made damn sure to investigate to the fullest. He'd relocated orphans countless times in his life and he'd always been careful, felt the weight of responsibility.

Never had that weight felt this heavy on his shoulders.

He studied the couple, in their fifties, the husband in a crisp linen suit, the wife in a colorful dress with a matching headscarf. The aunt took Issa from Mari's arms while the uncle held a diaper bag.

Mari twisted her hands in front of her, clearly resisting the temptation to yank the baby back. "She likes to be held close, but facing outward so she can see what's going on. And you have to burp her after every ounce of formula or she spits up. She likes music—"

Her voice cracked.

The aunt placed a hand on her arm. "Thank you for taking such good care of little Issa, Princess. If we had known about our niece's intentions, we would have volunteered to take Issa immediately. But when a young mother assures you she is fine, who would ever think to step in and offer to take her child? Trust us though, we will shower her with love. We will make sure she always knows you have been her guardian angel…."

With teary eyes, Mari nodded, but said nothing.

Troy stepped into the awkward silence. "My wife and I will escort you to your car through a back entrance to be sure the press doesn't overrun you."

Thank God, Troy quickly ushered them out before this hellish farewell tore them all in half. Rowan stole one last look at the baby's sweet chubby-cheeked face, swallowed hard and turned to Mari. No doubt she needed him more now.

The second the door closed behind the Donavans, Mari's legs folded.

She sank into the rocking chair again, nearly doubled over as she gulped in air. Her lovely face tensed with pain as she bit her lower lip. "Rowan, I don't think," she gasped, "I can't...I can't give my presentation this afternoon."

He understood the feeling. Rowan hooked his arm around her shoulders. "I'll call the conference coordinator. I'll tell them you're sick."

"But I'm never sick." She looked up at him with bemused eyes, bright with unshed tears. "I never bow out at work. What's wrong with me?"

"You're grieving." So was he. Something about this child was different, maybe because of the role she'd played in bringing Mari to him. Maybe because of the Christmas season. Or perhaps simply because the little tyke had slipped past the defenses he worked so hard to keep in place as he faced year after year of treating bone-crushing poverty and sickness. "You're human."

"I only knew her a few days. She's not my child...." Mari pressed a hand to her chest, rubbing a wound no less deep for not being visible. "I shouldn't be this upset."

"You loved her—you still do." He shifted around to kneel in front of her, stroking her face, giving Mari comfort—a welcome distraction when he needed it most. "That's clear to anyone who saw you with her."

"I know, damn it." She blinked back tears. "I don't want to think about it. I don't want to feel any of this. I just need...this."

Mari grabbed his shirt front, twisted her fist in the

fabric and yanked him toward her as she fell into him. Rowan absorbed their fall with his body, his shoulders meeting the thick carpet. Mari blanketed him, her mouth meeting his with a frenzy and intensity there was no denying. She'd found an outlet for her grief and he was damn well ready to help her with that. They both needed this.

Needed an outlet for all the frustrated emotions roaring through the room.

She wriggled her hips erotically against his ready arousal. A moan of pleasure slipped from her lips as she nipped his ear. There was no need to be silent any longer. Their suite was empty. Too empty. Their first encounter had been focused on staying quiet, in control as they discovered each other for the first time.

Tonight, control didn't exist.

He pushed those thoughts away and focused on Mari, on making sure she was every bit as turned on as he was. He gathered the hem of her dress and bunched it until he found the sweet curve of her bottom. He guided her against him, met her with a rolling rhythm of his own, a synchronicity they'd discovered together last night.

Sitting up, increasing the pressure against his erection, she yanked his shirt open, buttons popping free and flying onto the carpet. Her ragged breathing mingled with his. He swept her dress off and away until she wore only a pale green satin bra and underwear. He was quickly realizing her preference for soft, feminine lingerie and he enjoyed peeling it from her. He flung the bra to rest on the bar. Then twisted his fist in her panties until the thin strap along her hip snapped. The last scrap of fabric fell away.

She clasped his head in her hands and drew his face

to her breasts. Her guidance, her demands, made him even harder. He took her in his mouth, enjoying the giving as much as the taking. Her moans and sighs were driving him wild. And yes, he had his own pent-up frustrations to work out, his own regret over seeing Issa leave... He shut down those thoughts, grounding himself in the now.

Arching onto her heels, Mari fumbled with the fly of his pants.

"Condom," he groaned. "In my pocket."

He lifted his butt off the floor and she stroked behind him to pluck the packet free. Thank heaven he'd thought to keep one on him even in a crisis. Because he couldn't stomach the thought of stopping, not even for an instant.

Then he felt her hands on him, soft, stroking. He throbbed at her touch as she sheathed him in the condom, then took him inside her. His head dug back as he linked fingers with her, following the ride where she took him, hard and fast, noisy and needy. The fallout would have to take care of itself, because right now, they were both locked in a desperate drive to block out the pain of loss.

Already, he could feel the building power of his release rolling through him. He gritted his teeth, grinding back the need to come. Reaching between them to ease her over the edge with him. One look at her face, the crescendo of her sweet cries, told him she was meeting him there now. He thrust, again and again until his orgasm throbbed free while hers pulsed around him.

He caught her as she collapsed into his arms. He soaked in the warmth of her skin, the pounding of her heart—hell, everything about her.

The cooling air brought hints of reality slithering

back, the world expanding around them. The roaring in his ears grew louder, threatening this pocket of peace. It was too soon for him to take her again, but that didn't rule out other pleasurable possibilities.

Rowan eased Mari from him and onto her back. He kissed her mouth, her jaw, along her neck, inhaling the floral essence of her. Her hands skimmed up and down his spine as she reclined languidly. Smiling against her skin, he nipped his way lower, nuzzling and stroking one breast then the other.

"Rowan?"

"Shhh…" He blew across her damp nipple. The damp brown tip pebbled even tighter for him and he took her in his mouth, flicking with his tongue.

He sprinkled kisses along the soft underside, then traveled lower, lower still until he parted her legs and stroked between her thighs, drawing a deep sigh from her. He dipped his head and breathed in the essence of her, tasted her. Teased at the tight bundle of nerves until she rambled a litany of need for more. He was more than happy to comply.

A primitive rush of possession surged through him. She was his. He cupped the soft globes of her bottom and brought her closer to him, circled and laved, worked her until her fingers knotted restlessly in his hair. He took her to the edge of completion again, then held back, taking her to the precipice again and again, knowing her orgasm would be all the more powerful with the build.

Her head thrashed against the carpet and she cried out his name as her release gripped her. Her hands flung out, knocking over an end table, sending a lamp crash-ing to the floor.

He watched the flush of completion spread over her

as he slid back up to lay beside her. The evening breeze drifted over them, threatening to bring reality with it.

There was only one way to make it through the rest of this night. Make love to Mari until they both collapsed with exhaustion. Rolling to his knees, he slid his arms under her, lifting as he stood. He secured her against his chest, the soft give of her body against his stirring him.

Her arm draped around his neck, her head lolling against him as she still breathed heavily in the aftermath of her release. He strode across the suite toward his bedroom, his jeans open and riding low on his hips. Hell, he'd never even gotten his pants off.

He lowered Mari to his bed, the sight of her naked body, long legs and subtle curves stirring him impossibly hard again. Shadows played along her dusky skin, inviting him to explore. To lose himself in the oblivion of her body. To forget for a few hours that the emptiness of their suite was so damn tangible… No baby sighs. No iPhone of Christmas lullabies. Gone.

Just like Issa. Their reason for staying together.

Eleven

Mari had spent a restless night in Rowan's arms. As the morning light pierced through the shutters, he'd suggested they get away from the resort and all the memories of Issa that lurked in their suite. She hadn't even hesitated at jumping on board with his plan.

Literally.

Mari stretched out on the bow of the sailboat and stared up at the cloudless sky, frigate birds gliding overhead with their wide wings extended full-out. Waves slapped against the hull, and lines pinged against the mast. Rowan had leased the thirty-three-foot luxury sailboat for the two of them to escape for the day to a deserted shore. No worries about the press spying on them and no reminders of the baby. Nothing to do but to stare into the azure waters, watching fish and loggerhead turtles.

God, how she needed to get away from the reminders. Her time with the baby had touched her heart and made her realize so many things were missing in her life. Love. Family. She'd buried herself in work, retreating into a world that made sense to her after a lifetime of feeling awkward in her own skin. But holding that sweet little girl had made Mari accept she'd turned her back on far too much.

That didn't mean she had any idea how to fix it. Or herself. She watched Rowan guiding the sailboat, open shirt flapping behind him, sun burnishing his blond hair.

Rowan had made love to her—and she to him—until they'd both fallen into an exhausted sleep. They'd slept, woken only long enough to order room service and made love again. She had the feeling Rowan was as confused and empty as she, but she couldn't quite put her finger on why.

For that matter, maybe she was just too lost in her own hurt to understand his.

In the morning, he'd told her to dress for a day on a boat. She hadn't questioned him, grateful for the distraction. Mari had tossed on a sarong, adding dark glasses and an old-school Greta Garbo scarf to make her escape. He'd surprised her with a gift, bracelets she'd admired at the marketplace their first night out with Issa. She stretched her arm out, watching the sun refract off the silver bangles and colorful beads.

Rowan sailed the boat, handling the lines with ease as the hull chopped through the water toward an empty cove, lush mountains jutting in the distance. They'd followed the coast all morning toward a neighboring island with a private harbor. If only the ache in her heart was as easy to leave behind.

She rolled to her tummy and stretched out along her

towel, her well-loved body languid and a bit stiff. Chin on her hands, she gazed out at the rocks jutting from the water along the secluded coastline. She watched the gannets and petrels swoop and dive for fish. Palm trees clustered along the empty shoreline, creating a thick wall of foliage just beyond the white sandy beaches. Peaceful perfection, all familiar and full of childhood memories of vacationing along similar shores with her parents.

A shadow stretched across her, a broad-shouldered shadow. She flipped to her back again, shading her eyes to look up at Rowan. "Shouldn't you be at the helm?"

"We've dropped anchor." He crouched beside her, too handsome for his own good in swim trunks and an open shirt, ocean breeze pulling at his loose hair. "Come with me and have something to drink?"

She clasped his outstretched hand and stood, walking with him, careful to duck and weave past the boom and riggings. The warm hardwood deck heated her bare feet. "You didn't have to be so secretive about our destination."

"I wanted to surprise you." He jumped down to the deck level, grasping her waist and lowering her to join him. He gestured to where he'd poured them two glasses of mango juice secured in the molded surface between the seat cushions, the pitcher tucked securely in an open cooler at his bare feet.

"That's your only reason?"

"I wasn't sure you would agree, and we both needed to get away from the resort." He passed her a glass, nudging her toward the captain's chair behind the wheel. "Besides, my gorgeous, uptight scientist, you need to have fun."

"I have fun." Sitting, she sipped her drink. The sweet

natural sugars sent a jolt of energy through her, his words putting her on the defensive. "My work is fun."

He cocked an eyebrow, shooting just above his sunglasses.

"Okay, my work is rewarding. And I don't recall being all that uptight when I was sitting on the bar last night." She eyed him over the glass.

"Fair enough. I'm taking you out because I want you mellow and softened up so when I try to seduce you later you completely succumb to my charm." He thudded the heel of his palm to his forehead, clearly doing his best to take her mind off things. "Oh, wait, I already seduced you."

"Maybe I seduced you." She tossed aside her sunglasses and pulled off his aviator shades, her bracelets chiming with each movement. She leaned in to kiss him, more than willing to be distracted from the questions piling up in her mind.

Like where they would go from here once the conference was over. Since she didn't have any suggestions in mind, she sure wasn't going to ask for his opinion.

"Whose turn is it, then, to take the initiative?" He pulled her drink from her and stepped closer.

"I've lost count." She let her eyes sweep over him seductively, immersing herself in this game they both played, delaying the inevitable.

"Princess, you do pay the nicest compliments." He stroked her face, along the scarf holding back her hair, tugging it free.

"You say the strangest things." She traced his mouth, the lips that had brought her such pleasure last night.

"We're here to play, not psychoanalyze."

Her own lips twitched with a self-deprecating smile. "Glad to know it, because I stink at reading people."

"Why do you assume that?" His question mingled with the call of birds in the trees and the plop of fish.

"Call it a geek thing."

"You make geek sexy." He nipped her tracing finger, then sucked lightly.

She rolled her eyes. "You are such a…"

"A what?"

"I don't even have words for you."

His eyes went serious for the first time this morning. "Glad to know I mystify you as much as you bemuse me."

"I've always thought of myself as a straightforward person. Some call that boring." She flinched, hating the feeling that word brought, knowing she couldn't—wouldn't—change. "For me, there's comfort in routine."

Those magnificently blue eyes narrowed and darkened. "Tell me who called you boring and I'll—"

She clapped a hand over his mouth, bracelets dangling. "It's okay. But thanks." She pulled her hand away, a rogue wave bobbing the boat beneath her. "I had trouble making friends in school. I didn't fit in for so many reasons—everything from my ridiculous IQ to the whole princess thing. I was either much younger than my classmates or they were sucking up because of my family. There was no sisterhood for me. It was tough for people to see the real me behind all that clutter."

"I wasn't an instant fit at school, either." He shifted to stand beside her, looping an arm around her shoulders bared by the sarong.

She leaned against him, looking out over the azure blue waters. The continent of her birth was such a mixture of lush magnificence and stark poverty. "You don't need to change your history to make me feel better. I'm okay with myself."

"God's honest truth here." He rested his chin on top of her head. "My academy brothers and I were all misfits. The headmaster there did a good job at redirecting us, channeling us, helping us figure out ways to put our lives on the right path again."

"All of you? That's quite a track record."

He went still against her. "Not all of us. Some of us were too far gone to be rehabilitated." His sigh whispered over her, warmer than the sun. "You may have read in the news about Malcolm Douglas's business manager—he was a schoolmate of ours. He lost his way, forgot about rules and integrity. He did some shady stuff to try and wrangle publicity for his client."

"Your friend. Malcolm. Another of your Brotherhood?"

"Malcolm and I aren't as close as I am to the others. But yes, he's a friend." He turned her by her shoulders and stared into her eyes. "We're not perfect, any of us, but the core group of us, we can call on each other for anything, anytime."

"Like how the casino owner friend provided the start-up money for your clinic…"

Rowan had built an incredible support system for himself after his parents failed him. While she'd cut herself off from the world.

"That he did. You wouldn't recognize Conrad from the high school photos. He was gangly and wore glasses back then, but he was a brilliant guy and he knew it. Folks called him Mr. Wall Street, because of his dad and how Conrad used his trust fund to manipulate the stock market to punish sweatshop businesses."

"You all may have been misfits, but it appears you share a need for justice."

"We didn't all get along at first. I was different

from them, though, or so I liked to tell myself. I didn't come from money like most of the guys there—or like you—and I wasn't inordinately talented like Douglas. I thought I was better than those overprivileged brats."

"Yet, Conrad must respect you to have invested so much money to start the clinic."

"If we're going to be honest—" he laughed softly "—I'm where I am today because of a cookie."

"A cookie?" She tipped her head back to the warm sunshine, soaking in the heat of the day and the strength of the man beside her.

"My mom used to send me these care packages full of peanut-butter cookies with M&M's baked into them." His eyes took on a faraway look and a fond smile.

Mari could only think that same mother had sent him to that school in his brother's place. Those cookies must have tasted like dust in light of such a betrayal from the woman who should have protected him. She bit back the urge to call his mother an unflattering name and just listened, ocean wind rustling her hair.

"One day, I was in my bunk, knocking back a couple of those cookies while doing my macro biology homework." He toyed with the end of her scarf. "I looked up to find Conrad staring at those cookies like they were caviar. I knew better than to offer him one. His pride would have made him toss it back in my face."

She linked fingers with him and squeezed as he continued, her cheek against the warm cotton of his shirt, her ear taking in the steady thrum of his heart.

"We were all pretty angry at life in those days. But I had my cookies and letters from Mom to get me through the days when I didn't think I could live with the guilt of what I'd done."

What his family had done. His mother, father and his brother. Why couldn't he see how they'd sacrificed him?

"But back to Conrad. About a week later, I was on my way to the cafeteria and I saw him in the visitation area with his dad. I was jealous as hell since my folks couldn't afford to fly out to visit me—and then I realized he and his dad were fighting."

"About what?" She couldn't help but ask, desperate for this unfiltered look into the teenage Rowan, hungry for insights about what had shaped him into the man he'd become.

"From what Conrad shouted, it was clear his father wanted him to run a scam on Troy's parents and convince them to invest in some bogus company or another. Conrad decked his dad. It took two security guards to pull him off."

Hearing the things that Rowan and his friends had been through as teens, she felt petty for her anger over her own childhood. The grief Rowan and his friends had faced, the storms in their worlds, felt so massive in comparison to her own. She had two parents that loved her, two homes, and yes, she was shuttled back and forth, but in complete luxury.

"And the cookie?"

"I'm getting there." He sketched his fingers up and down her bare arm. "Conrad spent a couple of days in the infirmary—his dad hit him back and dislocated Conrad's shoulder. The cops didn't press charges on the old man because the son threw the first punch. Anyhow, Conrad's first day out of the infirmary, I felt bad for him so I wrapped a cookie in a napkin and put it on his bunk. He didn't say anything, but he didn't toss it back in my face, either." He threw his hands wide. "And here I am today."

Her heart hurt so badly she could barely push words out. "Why are you telling me this?"

"I don't know. I just want you to understand why my work is so important to me, so much so that I couldn't have kept Issa even if her family didn't come through. Because if I start keeping every orphan that tugs at my emotions, I won't be able to sustain all I've fought so hard to build. The clinic…it's everything to me. It helps me fill the hole left by Dylan's death, helps me make up for the lives lost."

She heard him, heard an isolation in his words in spite of all those friends. He'd committed himself to a life of service that left him on a constant, lonely quest. And right then and there, her soul ached for him.

She slid her hand up into his hair, guiding his mouth to hers. He stepped between her knees, and she locked her arms around his neck. Tight. Demanding and taking.

"Now," she whispered against his mouth, fishing in his back pocket for a condom.

He palmed her knees apart and she purred her approval. Her fingers made fast work of his swim trunks, freeing his erection and sheathing him swiftly, surely.

She locked her legs around his waist and drew him in deeper. He drove into her again and again. She angled back, gripping the bar, bracelets sliding down to collect along her hand. He took in the beauty of her, her smooth skin, pert breasts, her head thrown back and hair swaying with every thrust. The boat rocked in a rhythm that matched theirs as his shouts of completion twined and mingled with hers, carried on the breeze.

In that moment she felt connected to him more than physically. She identified with him, overwhelmed by an understanding of him being as alone in the world as her. But also hammered by a powerlessness to change that. His vision and walls were as strong as hers, always had been. Maybe more so.

What a time to figure out she might have sacrificed too much for her work—only realizing that now, as she fell for a man who would sacrifice anything for *his*.

The taste of the sea, sweat and Mari still clinging to his skin, Rowan opened the door to their suite the next morning, praying the return to land and real life wouldn't bring on the crushing sense of loss. He'd hoped to distract her from Issa—and also find some way to carve out a future for them. They were both dedicated to their work. They could share that, even in their disagreements. They could use that as a springboard to work out solutions. Together. His time with her overnight on the sailboat had only affirmed that for him.

He just hoped he'd made a good start in persuading Mari of the same thing.

Guiding her into the suite with a hand low on her spine, he stepped deeper into the room. Only to stop short. His senses went on alert. There was someone here.

Damn it, there was more traffic through this supposedly secure room than through the lobby. Which of course meant it was one of his friends.

Elliot Starc rose from the sofa and from Mari's gasp beside him, clearly she recognized the world-famous race-car driver...and underwear model.

Rowan swallowed a curse. "Good morning, Elliot. Did you get booted out of your own room?"

Laughing, Elliot took Mari's hand lightly and ignored Rowan's question. "Princess, it's an honor to meet you."

"Mr. Starc, you're one of Rowan's Brotherhood friends, I assume."

Elliot's eyebrows shot up. "You told her?"

"We talk." Among other things.

"Well, color me stunned. That baby was lucky to have landed in Rowan's room. Our Interpol connections kept all of you safe while bringing this to a speedy conclusion."

Crap. The mention of Interpol hung in the air, Mari's eyes darting to his.

Oblivious to the gaffe, Elliot continued, "Which brings me to my reason for being here. I've emailed a summary of the existing security detail, but I need to get back to training, get my mind back in the game so I don't set more than my hair on fire."

Rowan pulled a tight smile. "Thanks, buddy."

Mari frowned. "Interpol?"

Elliot turned sharply to Rowan. "You said you told her about the Brotherhood."

"Classmates. I told her we're classmates." He didn't doubt she would keep his secret safe, but knowing wouldn't help her and anything that didn't help was harmful. "You, my friend, made a mighty big assumption for someone who should know better."

"She's a princess. You've been guarding her." Elliot scratched his sheared hair. "I thought… Ah, hell. Just…" Throwing his hands out and swiping the air as if that explained it all, Elliot spun on his heel and walked out the door.

Mari sat hard, sinking like a stone on the edge of the sofa. "You're with Interpol?" She huffed on a long sigh. "Of course you're with Interpol."

"I'm a physician. That's my primary goal, my mission in life." He paused, unable to dodge the truth as he kneeled in front of her. "But yes, I help out Interpol on occasion with freelance work in the area. No one thinks twice about someone like me wandering around wealthy fundraisers or traveling to remote countries."

He could see her closing down, pulling away.

"Mari?"

"It's your job. I understand."

"Are you angry with me for not telling you?"

"Why would you? It's not my secret to know. Your friend…he assumed more about us than he should. But you know I won't say a word. I understand well what it's like to be married to your work."

Her words came out measured and even, her body still, her spine taking on that regal "back off" air that shouted of generations of royalty. "Mari, this doesn't have to mean things change between us. If anything we can work together."

"Work, right…" Her amber eyes flickered with something he couldn't quite pin down.

"Are you all right?"

"I'll be fine. It's all just a lot to process, this today. Issa yesterday."

He cradled her shoulders in his hands. She eased away.

"Mari, it's okay to shout at me if you're mad. Or to cry about Issa. I'm here for you," he said, searching for the right way to approach her.

"Fine. You want me to talk? To yell? You've got it. I would appreciate your acting like we're equal rather than stepping into your benevolent physician shoes because no one would dare to contradict the man who does so much for the world." She shrugged free of his grip.

"Excuse me for trying to be a nice guy." He held up his hands.

"You're always the nice guy." She shot to her feet. "The saint. Giving out comfort, saving the world, using that as a wall between you and other people."

"What the hell are you talking about?" He stood warily, watching her pace.

"There you go. Get mad at me." She stopped in front of him, crossing her arms over her chest. "At least real emotions put us on an even footing. Oh, wait, we're not even. You're the suave doctor/secret agent. I'm the awkward genius who locks herself away in a lab."

"Are we really returning to the old antagonistic back-and-forth way of communicating?" he asked. Her words felt damn unfair when he was working his tail off to help her through a rough time. "I thought we'd moved past that."

"That's not what I'm talking about and you know it. You're a smart man."

"Actually, you're the certified genius here. How about you explain it to me."

"You want me to cry and grieve and open myself up to you." She jabbed his chest with one finger, her voice rising with every word. "But what about you? When do you open up to me? When are you going to give me something besides the saintly work side of your life?"

"I've told you things about my past," he answered defensively.

"To be fair, yes you have," she conceded without backing down. "Some things. Certainly not everything. And when have you let me in? You're fine with things as long as you're the one doling out comfort. But accepting it? No way. Like now. You have every reason to grieve for Issa."

"She's in good hands, well cared for," he said through gritted teeth.

"See? There you go doing just what I said. You want me to cry and be emotional, but you—" she waved a hand "—you're just fine. Did you even allow yourself to grieve for your brother?"

His head snapped back, her words smacking him even as she kept her hands fisted at her sides. "Don't you dare use my brother against me. That has nothing to do with what we're discussing now."

"It has everything to do with what we're talking about. But if I'm mistaken, then explain it to me. Explain what you're feeling."

She waited while he searched for the right words, but everything he'd offered her so far hadn't worked. He didn't have a clue what to say to reassure her. And apparently he waited too long.

"That's what I thought." She shook her head sadly, backing away from him step by step. "I'm returning to my old room. There's no reason for me to be here anymore."

She spun away, the hem of her sarong fluttering as she raced into her room and slammed the door. He could hear her tossing her suitcase on the bed. Heard her muffled sobs. And heard the click of the lock that spoke loud and clear.

He'd blown it. Royally, so to speak. He might be confused about a lot of things. But one was crystal clear.

He was no longer welcome in Mari's life.

Twelve

The conference was over. Her week with Rowan was done.

Mari stood in front of the mirrored vanity and tucked the final pin into her hair, which was swept back in a sleek bun. Tonight's ball signified an official end to their time together. There was no dodging the event without being conspicuous and stirring up more talk in the press.

As if there wasn't enough talk already. At least all reports from the media—and from Rowan's Interpol friends—indicated that Issa was adapting well in her new home after only a couple of days. Something to be eternally grateful for. A blessing in this heartbreaking week.

Her pride demanded she finish with her head held high.

After her confrontation with Rowan, she'd waited the

remainder of her stay, hoping he would fight for her as hard as he fought for his work, for every person who walked through those clinic doors. But she hadn't heard a word from him since she'd stormed from his room and she'd gone back to her simple room a floor below. How easily he'd let her go, and in doing so, broken her heart.

But his ability to disconnect with her also filled her with resolve.

She wouldn't be like him anymore, hiding from the world. She was through staying in the shadows for fear of disappointing people.

Mari smoothed her hands down the shimmering red strapless dress, black swirls through the fabric giving the impression of phantom roses. The dress hugged her upper body, fitted past her hips then swept to the ground with a short train. It was a magnificent gown. She'd never worn anything like it. She would have called it a Cinderella moment except she didn't want to be some delicate princess at the ball. She was a one-day queen, boldly stepping into her own.

Her hands fell to the small tiara, diamonds refracting the vanity lights. Carefully, she tucked the crown—symbolic of so much more—on her head.

Stepping from her room, she checked the halls and, how ironic, for once the corridor was empty. No fans to carefully maneuver. She could make her way to the brass-plated elevator in peace.

Jabbing the elevator button, she curled her toes in her silken ballet slippers. Her stomach churned with nerves over facing the crowd downstairs alone, even more than that, over facing Rowan again. But she powered on, one leather-clad foot at a time. While she was ready to meet the world head-on in her red Vera Wang, she wasn't prepared to do so wearing high heels that would likely send her stumbling down the stairs.

She was bold, but practical.

Finally, the elevator doors slid open, except the elevator wasn't empty. Her stomach dropped in shock faster than a cart on a roller-coaster ride.

"Papa?" She stared at her father, her royal father.

But even more surprising, her mother stood beside him. "Going down, dear?"

Stunned numb, she stepped into the elevator car, brass doors sliding closed behind her.

"Mother, why are you and Papa here? *Together?*" she squeaked as her mom hugged her fast and tight.

The familiar scent of her mom's perfume enveloped her, like a bower of gardenias. And her mom wasn't dressed for a simple visit. Susan Mandara was decked out for the ball in a Christmas-green gown, her blond hair piled on top of her head. Familiar, yet so unusual, since Mari couldn't remember the last time she'd seen Adeen and Susan Mandara standing side by side in anything other than old pictures.

Her father kissed her on the forehead. "Happy Christmas, little princess."

She clutched her daddy's forearms, the same arms that used to toss her high in the air as a child. Always catching her.

Tonight, her father wore a tuxedo with a crimson tribal robe over it, trimmed in gold. As a child, she used to sneak his robes out to wear for dress-up with her parents laughing, her mother affectionately calling him Deen, her nickname for him. She'd forgotten that happy memory until just now.

Her mother smoothed cool hands over her daughter's face. "Your father and I have a child together." She gave

Mari's face a final pat. "Deen and I are bonded for life, *by* life, through you. We came to offer support and help you with all the press scrutiny."

Did they expect her to fail? She couldn't resist saying, "Some of this togetherness would have been welcome when I was younger."

"We've mellowed with age." Susan stroked her daughter's forehead. "I wish we could have given you a simpler path. We certainly wanted to."

If her mother had wanted to keep things simple, marrying a prince was surely a weird way to go about it.

Her father nodded his head. "You look magnificent. You are everything I wanted my princess to grow up to be."

"You're just saying that because I'm decked out in something other than a sack," she teased him, even though her heart ached with the cost of her newfound confidence. "But I can assure you, I still detest ribbon cuttings and state dinners."

"And you still care about the people. You'll make your mark in a different manner than I did. That's good." He held out both elbows as the elevator doors slid open on the ground floor. "Ladies? Shall we?"

Decorations in the hallway had doubled since she went upstairs to change after the final presentation of the day. Mari strode past oil palm trees decorated with bells. Music drifted from the ballroom, a live band played carols on flutes, harps and drums.

The sounds of Christmas. The sounds of home. Tables laden with food. She could almost taste the sweet cookies and the meats marinated in *chakalaka*.

A few steps later, she stood on the marble threshold of the grand ballroom. All eyes turned to her and for a moment her feet stayed rooted to the floor. Cameras clicked and she didn't so much as flinch or cringe. She wasn't sure what to do next as she swept the room with her eyes, taking in the ballroom full of medical professionals decked out in all their finery, with local bigwigs in attendance, as well.

Then her gaze hitched on Rowan, wearing a traditional tuxedo, so handsome he took her breath away.

His hair was swept back, just brushing his collar, his eyes blue flames that singed her even from across the room. She expected him to continue ignoring her. But he surprised her by striding straight toward her. All eyes followed him, and her heart leaped into her throat.

Rowan stopped in front of them and nodded to her father. "Sir, I believe your daughter and I owe the media a dance."

Owe the media?

What about what they owed each other?

And how could he just stand there as if nothing had happened between them, as if they hadn't bared their bodies and souls to each other? She had a gloriously undignified moment of wanting to kick him. But this was her time to shine and she refused to let him wreck it. She stepped into his arms, and he gestured to the band. They segued into a rendition of "Ave Maria," with a soloist singing.

Her heart took hope that he'd chosen the piece for her. He led her to the middle of the dance floor. Other couples melted away and into the crowd, leaving them alone, at the mercy of curious eyes and cameras.

As she allowed herself to be swept into his arms—into the music—she searched for something to say. "I appreciate the lovely song choice."

"It fits," he answered, but his face was still creased in a scowl, his eyes roving over her.

"Don't you like the dress?"

"I like the woman in the dress," he said hoarsely. "If you'd been paying attention, you would have realized my eyes have been saying that for a long time before you changed up your wardrobe."

"So why are you scowling?"

"Because I want this whole farce of a week to be over."

"Oh," she said simply, too aware of his hand on her waist, his other clasping her fingers.

"Do you believe me? About the dress, I mean." His feet moved in synch with hers, their bodies as fluid on the dance floor as they'd been making love.

"We've exchanged jabs in the past, insults even, but you've always been honest."

"Then why are you still sleeping on another floor of the hotel?"

"Oh, Rowan," she said bittersweetly. "Sex isn't the problem between us."

"Remind me what is?"

"The way you close people—me—out. It took me a long time to realize I'm deserving of everything. And so are you."

"I guess there's nothing left to say then."

The music faded away, and with a final sweep across the floor he stopped in front of her parents.

Rowan passed her hand back to her father. "With all due respect, sir, take better care of her."

Her mother smothered a laugh.

Her father arched a royal eyebrow. "I beg your pardon."

"More security detail. She's a princess. She deserves to be cared for and protected like one."

With a final nod, Rowan turned away and melted into the crowd and out of her life.

Five hours later, Mari hugged her pillow to her chest, watching her mom settle into the other double bed in the darkened room. "Mother, aren't we wealthy enough for you to have a suite or at least a room of your own?"

Susan rolled to her side, facing her daughter in the shadowy room lit only by moonlight streaming in. "I honestly thought you would be staying with Dr. Boothe even though this room was still booked in your name. And even with the show of good faith your father and I have given, we're not back to sharing a room."

Curtains rustled with the night ocean breeze and sounds of a steel-drum band playing on the beach for some late-night partiers.

"Rowan and I aren't a couple anymore." Although the haunting beauty of that dance still whispered through her, making her wonder what more she could have done. "It was just a...fling."

The most incredible few days of her life.

"Mari dear, you are not the fling sort," her mother reminded her affectionately. "So why are you walking away from him?"

Tears clogged her throat. "I'm honestly too upset to talk about this." She flipped onto her back, clenching her fists against the memory of his tuxedoed shoulders under her hands.

The covers rustled across the room as her mother sat up. "I made the biggest mistake of my life when I was about your age."

"Marrying my father. Yeah, I got that." Was it in her DNA to fail at relationships? Her parents had both been divorced twice.

"No, marrying the man I loved—your father— was the right move. Thinking I could change him? I screwed up there." She hugged her knees to her chest, her graying blond hair trailing down her back. "Before you think I'm taking all the blame here, he thought I would change, as well. So the divorce truly was a fifty-fifty screw-up on our part. He should have realized my free spirit is what he fell in love with and I should have recognized how drawn I was to his devotion to his country."

What was her mother trying to tell her? She wanted to understand, to step outside of the awkwardness in more ways than just being comfortable in a killer red dress. Except her mom was talking about not changing at all.

"You're going to have to spell it out for me more clearly."

"Your father and I weren't a good couple. We weren't even particularly good at being parents. But, God, you sure turned out amazing," her mother said with an unmistakable pride, soothing years of feeling like a disappointment. "Deen and I did some things right, and maybe if we'd focused more on the things we did right, we might have lasted."

Mari ached to pour out all the details of her fight with Rowan, how she needed him to open up. And how ironic was it that he accused her of not venting her emotions? Her thoughts jumbled together until she blurted out in frustration, "Do you know how difficult it is to love a saint?"

Her mother reached out in the dark, across the divide between their beds. "You love him?"

Mari reached back and clasped her mother's hand.

"Of course I do. I just don't know how to get through to him."

"You two have been a couple for—what?—a week? Seems to me like you're giving up awful fast."

Mari bristled defensively. "I've known him for years. And it's been an intense week."

"And you're giving that up? I'd so hoped you would be smarter than I was." Her mom gave her hand a final squeeze. "Think about it. Good night, Mari."

Long into the night, Mari stared out the window at the shoreline twinkling with lighted palm trees. The rolling waves crashed a steady reminder of her day sailing with Rowan. He'd done so much to comfort her. Not just with words, but with actions, by planning the day away from the hotel and painful memories.

What had she done for him?

Nothing.

She'd simply demanded her expectations for him rather than accepting him as he was. He'd accepted and appreciated her long before a ball gown. Even when he disagreed with her, he'd respected her opinion.

Damn it all, she *was* smarter than this. Of course Rowan had built walls around himself. Every person in his family had let him down—his parents and his brother. None of them had ever put him or his well-being first. Sure, he'd made friends with his schoolmates, but he'd even admitted to feeling different from them.

Now she'd let him down, as well. He'd reached out to her as best he could and she'd told him what he offered wasn't good enough, maybe because she'd been scared of not being enough for him.

But she knew better than that now. A confidence flowed through her like a calming breeze blowing in off the ocean. With that calm came the surety of what to do next.

It was time to fight for the man she loved, a man she loved for his every saintly imperfection.

Rowan had always been glad to return to his clinic on the mainland. He'd spent every Christmas here in surgical scrubs taking care of patients since moving to Africa. He welcomed the work, leaving holiday celebrations to people with families.

Yet, for some reason, the CD of Christmas carols and a pre-lit tree in the corner didn't stir much in the way of festive feelings this year. A few gifts remained for the patients still in the hospital, the other presents having been passed out earlier, each box a reminder of shopping with Mari.

So he buried himself in work.

Phone tucked under his chin, he listened to Elliot's positive update on Issa, followed by a rambling recounting of his Australian Christmas vacation. Rowan cranked back in a chair behind his desk, scanning a computer file record on a new mother and infant due to be discharged first thing in the morning.

One wing of the facility held a thirty-bed hospital unit and the other wing housed a clinic. Not overly large, but all top-of-the-line and designed for efficiency. They doled out anything from vaccinations to prenatal care to HIV/AIDS treatment.

The most gut-wrenching of all? The patients who came for both prenatal care and HIV treatment. There was a desperate need here and he couldn't help everyone, but one at a time, he was doing his damnedest.

The antibacterial scent saturated each breath he took. Two nurses chatted with another doctor at the station across the hall. Other than that, the place was quiet as a church mouse this late at night.

"Elliot, if you've got a point here, make it. I've got a Christmas Eve dinner to eat."

Really, just a plate to warm in the microwave but he wasn't particularly hungry anyhow. Visions of Mari in that red gown, cloaked in total confidence, still haunted his every waking and sleeping thought. He'd meant what he'd said when he told her it didn't matter to him what clothes she wore. But he was damn proud of the peace she seemed to have found with being in the spotlight. Too bad he couldn't really be a part of it.

"Ah, Rowan, I really thought you were smarter than me, brother," Elliot teased over the phone from his Australian holiday. The background echoed with drunken carolers belting out a raucous version of "The Twelve Days of Christmas."

"As I recall, our grades were fairly on par with each other back in the day."

"Sure, but I've had about four concussions since then, not to mention getting set on fire."

A reluctant smile tugged at Rowan. "Your point?"

"Why in the hell did you let that woman go?" Elliot asked, the sounds of laughter and splashing behind him. "You're clearly crazy about her and she's nuts about you. And the chemistry… Every time you looked at each other, it was all I could do not to shout at you two to get a room."

"She doesn't want me in her life." The slice of her rejection still cut so much deeper than any other.

"Did she tell you that?"

"Very clearly," he said tightly, not enjoying in the least reliving the moment. "I think her words were along the lines of 'have a nice life.'"

"You've never been particularly self-aware."

He winced, closing down the computer file on his new maternity patient. "That's what she said."

"So are you going to continue to be a miserable ass or are you going to go out and meet Mari at the clinic gate?"

At the gate? He creaked upright in his chair, swinging his feet to the floor. "What the hell are you talking about? You're in Australia."

But he stormed over to look out his office window anyway.

"Sure, but you tasked me with her security and I figured some follow-up was in order. I've been keeping track of her with a combo of guards and a good old-fashioned GPS on her rental car. If my satellite connection is any good, she should be arriving right about... now."

Rowan spotted an SUV rounding the corner into sight, headlights sweeping the road as the vehicle drove toward the clinic. Could it really be Mari? Here? Suddenly, Elliot's call made perfect sense. He'd been stringing Rowan along on the line until just the right moment.

"And Rowan," Elliot continued, "be sure you're the one to say the whole 'love you' part first since she came to you. Merry Christmas, brother."

Love her?

Of course he loved her. Wanted her. Admired her. Desired her. Always had, and why he hadn't thought to tell her before now was incomprehensible to him. Thank God for his friends, who knew him well enough to boot him in the tail when he needed that nudge most.

Thank God for Mari, who hadn't given up on him. She challenged him. Disagreed with him. But yet here she was, for him.

The line disconnected as he was already out the door and sprinting down the hall, hand over his pager to keep it from dislodging from his scrubs in his haste. His gym shoes squeaked against the tiles as he turned the corner and burst out through the front door, into the starlit night. The brisk wind rippled his surgical scrubs.

The tan SUV parked beside the clinic's ambulance under a sprawling shea butter tree. The vehicle's dome light flicked on, and Merry Christmas to him, he saw Mari's beautiful face inside. She stepped out, one incredibly long leg at a time, wearing flowing silk pants and a tunic. The fabric glided along her skin the way his hands ached to do again.

Her appearance here gave him the first hope in nearly a week that he would get to do just that.

"You came," he said simply.

"Of course. It's Christmas." She walked toward him, the African night sky almost as magnificent as his princess. She wore the bracelets he'd given her, the bangles chiming against each other. Toe-to-toe, she stopped in front of him, the sweet scent and heat of her reaching out to him. "Where else would I be but with the man I l—"

He pressed a finger against her lips. "Wait, hold that thought. I have something I need to say first. I love you, Mariama Mandara. I've wanted you and yes, loved you, for longer than I can remember. And I will do whatever it takes to be worthy of your love in return."

"Ah, Rowan, don't you know? You're already exactly what I need and everything I want. God knows, if you get any more saintly you're likely to be raptured and I would miss you so very much. I love you, too."

Relief flooded him, his heart soaking up every word like the parched ground around him absorbing a rain shower. Unable to wait another second, he hauled her to his chest and kissed her, deeply, intensely, hoping she really understood just how much he meant those words. He loved her. The truth of that sang through him as tangibly as the carols carrying gently through an open window.

Ending the kiss with a nip to his bottom lip, Mari smiled up at him. "I had a far more eloquent speech planned. I even practiced saying it on the way over because I wanted the words to be as special as what we've shared together."

"I hope you trust I love you, too." He only wished he had a more romantic way of telling her.

"I do. You showed me." She tugged the ends of the stethoscope draped around his neck, her bracelets sliding along her arm. "I just needed to stop long enough to listen with my heart. And my heart says we're perfect for each other. That we're meant to be together."

"Then why did we give each other such a hard time all these years?"

"We are both smart, dedicated people with a lot to offer, but we should be challenged. It makes us better at what we do." She tugged his face closer, punctuating the words with a quick kiss. "And if I have my way, I'm going to challenge you every day for the rest of my life."

"You have mesmerized me since the moment I first saw you." Desire and love interlocked inside him, each spiking the other to a higher level.

"That's one of the things I love most about you." She toyed with his hair, which just brushed the collar of his scrubs.

"What would that be?" He looped his arms low around her waist.

"You think my baggy, wrinkled wardrobe is sexy."

"Actually, I think peeling the clothes off of you is life's most perfect pleasure." He brought them closer together, grateful to have her in his arms, determined never to let this woman slip away from him again.

"Well, then, Dr. Boothe, let's find somewhere private to go so you can unwrap your Christmas present."

* * * * *

MAYBE THIS CHRISTMAS...?

ALISON ROBERTS

Alison Roberts is a New Zealander, currently lucky enough to live near a beautiful beach in Auckland. She is also lucky enough to write for both the Mills & Boon Cherish and Medical Romance lines. A primary school teacher in a former life, she is also a qualified paramedic. She loves to travel and dance, drink champagne and spend time with her daughter and her friends.

CHAPTER ONE

'HER name's Sophie Gillespie. She's six months old.'

A surprisingly heavy burden, but perhaps that was because Gemma hadn't thought to bring a pushchair and she'd been holding the baby on her hip for far too long already. The A and E department of the Queen Mary Infirmary in Manchester, England, was heaving and, because it was Christmas Eve, it all seemed rather surreal.

Reams of tired-looking tinsel had been strung in loops along the walls. A bunch of red and green balloons had been tied to the display screen, currently advertising the waiting time as being an hour and a half. And if they were this busy when it wasn't quite seven p.m., Gemma knew that the waiting time would only increase as new cases came in by ambulance and demanded the attention of the doctors and nurses on duty in the department.

'Look…this is an emergency.'

'Uh-huh?'

The middle-aged receptionist looked as if she'd seen it all. And she probably had. There was a group of very drunk teenage girls in naughty elf costumes singing and shouting loudly in a corner of the reception area. One of them was holding a bloodstained cloth to her face. Another was holding a vomit bag. A trio of equally drunk young men was watching the elves with appreciation and trying to outdo each other with wolf whistles. The expressions on the faces of the people between the groups were long-suffering. A woman sitting beside a small, crying boy looked to be at the end of her tether and she was glaring at Gemma, who appeared to be attempting to queue jump.

The receptionist peered over her glasses at Sophie, who wasn't helping. Thanks to the dose of paracetamol she'd given her as she'd left the house, the baby was looking a lot better than she had been. Her face was still flushed and her eyes over-bright but she wasn't crying with that frightening, high-pitched note any more. She was, in fact, smiling at the receptionist.

'She's running a temperature,' Gemma said. 'She's got a rash.'

'It's probably just a virus. Take a seat, please, ma'am. We'll get her seen as soon as possible.'

'What—in a couple of *hours*?'

Gemma could feel the heat radiating off the baby in her arms. She could feel the way Sophie was slumped listlessly against her body. The smile was fading and any moment now Sophie would start crying again. She took a deep breath.

'As soon as possible might be too late,' she snapped. 'She needs to be seen *now*. Please…' she added, trying to keep her voice from wavering. 'I just need to rule out the possibility that it's meningitis.'

'Rule out?' The receptionist peered over her glasses again, this time at Gemma. 'What are you, a doctor?'

'Yes, I am.' Gemma knew her tone lacked conviction. Could she still claim to be a doctor when it had been so long since she'd been anywhere near a patient?

'Not at this hospital you're not.'

Gemma closed her eyes for a heartbeat. 'I used to be.'

'And you're an expert in meningitis, then? What... you're going to tell me you're a paediatrician?'

Like the other woman waiting with a child, the receptionist clearly thought Gemma was trying to queue jump. And now there were people behind her, waiting to check in. One was a man in a dinner suit with a firm hold around the waist of a woman in an elegant black dress who had a halo of silver tinsel on her head.

'Can you hurry up?' the man said loudly. 'My wife needs help here.'

Sophie whimpered and Gemma knew she had to do something fast. Something she had sworn not to do. She took another deep breath and leaned closer to the hole in the bulletproof glass protecting the reception area.

'No, I'm not a paediatrician and I don't work at this hospital.' Her tone of voice was enough to encourage the receptionist to make eye contact. 'But my husband does.' At least, he did, as far as she knew. He could have moved on, though, couldn't he? In more ways than just where he worked. 'And he *is* a paediatrician,' she added, mentally crossing her fingers that this information would be enough to get her seen faster.

'Oh? What's his name, then?'

'Andrew Baxter.'

The woman behind her groaned and clutched her stomach. The man pushed past Gemma.

'For God's sake, I think my wife might be having a miscarriage.'

The receptionist's eyes had widened at Gemma's words. Now they widened even further as her gaze flicked to the next person in the queue and a look of alarm crossed her face. She leapt to her feet, signalling for assistance from other staff members. Moments later, the man and his wife were being ushered through the internal doors. The receptionist gave Gemma an apologetic glance.

'I won't be long. I'll get you seen next and…and I'll find out if your husband's on call.'

No. That was the last thing Gemma wanted.

Oh…Lord. What would Andy think if someone told him that his wife was in Reception? That she was holding a child that she thought might have meningitis?

He'd think it was his worst nightmare. The ghost of a Christmas past that he'd probably spent the last six years trying to forget.

Just like she had.

Dr Andrew Baxter was in his favourite place in the world. The large dayroom at the end of Queen Mary's paediatric ward.

He was admiring the enormous Christmas tree the staff had just finished decorating and he found himself smiling as he thought about the huge sack of gifts hiding in the sluice room that he would be in charge of distributing tomorrow when he was suitably dressed in his Santa costume.

It was hard to believe there had been a time when he hadn't been able to bring himself to come into this area of the ward. Especially at this particular time of year. When he'd been focused purely on the children who were too sick to enjoy this room with its bright decorations and abundance of toys.

Time really did heal, didn't it?

It couldn't wipe out the scars, of course. Andy knew there was a poignant ache behind his smile and he knew that he'd have to field a few significantly sympathetic glances from his colleagues tomorrow, but he could handle it now.

Enjoy it, even. And that was more than he'd ever hoped would be the case.

With it being after seven p.m., the dayroom would normally be empty as children were settled into bed for the night but here, just like in the outside world, Christmas Eve sparkled with a particular kind of magic that meant normal rules became rather flexible.

Four-year-old Ruth, who was recovering from a bone-marrow transplant to treat her leukaemia, was still at risk for infection but her dad, David, had carried her as far as the door so that she could see the tree. They were both wearing gowns and hats and had masks covering their faces but Andy saw the way David whispered in his daughter's ear and then pointed. He could see the way the child's eyes grew wide with wonder and then sense the urgency of the whisper back to her father.

Andy stepped closer.

'Hello, gorgeous.' He smiled at Ruth. 'Do you like our Christmas tree?'

A shy nod but then Ruth buried her face against her father's neck.

'Ruthie's worried that Father Christmas won't come to the hospital.'

'He *always* comes,' Andy said.

His confidence was absolute and why wouldn't it be? He'd been filling the role for years now and knew he could carry it off to perfection. Being tall and broad, it was easy to pad himself out with a couple of pillows so that his body shape was unrecognisable. The latest beard and moustache was a glue-on variety that couldn't be tugged off by a curious child and it was luxuriant enough to disguise him completely once the hat was in place.

Ruth's eyes appeared again and, after a brief glance at Andy, she whispered in her father's ear again. David grinned at Andy.

'She wants to know if he's going to bring her a present.'

'Sure is.' Andy nodded. There would be more than one that had Ruth's name on it. Every child on the ward had a parcel set aside for them from the pile of the donated gifts and parents were invited to put something special into Santa's sack as well. Not that Ruth would be able to join the throng that gathered around the tree for the ceremony but, if her latest test results were good, she should be able to watch from behind the windows and receive her gifts at a safer distance.

'Of course, he can't come to deliver the presents until all the girls and boys are asleep,' Andy added, with a wink at David. 'Might be time for bed?'

Ruth looked at him properly this time. 'But...how does he know I'm in hos—in...hostible?'

Andy knew his face was solemn. 'He just does,' he said calmly. 'Santa's magic. *Christmas* is magic.'

He watched David carry Ruth back to her room, making a mental note to chase up the latest lab results on this patient later tonight. He might put in a quick call to her specialist consultant as well, to discuss what participation might be allowable tomorrow.

Andrew Baxter was a general paediatrician. He was the primary consultant for medical cases that were admitted to the ward and stayed involved if they were referred on to surgeons, but he was also involved in every other case that came through these doors in some way. The 'outside' world was pretty irrelevant these days. This was *his* world. His home.

It didn't matter if the young patients were admitted under an oncologist for cancer treatment or a specialist paediatric cardiologist for heart problems or an orthopaedic surgeon who was dealing with a traumatic injury. Andy was an automatic part of the team. He knew every child who was in here and some of them he knew extremely well because they got admitted more than once or stayed for a long time.

Like John Boy, who was still in the dayroom, circling the tree as he watched the fairy-lights sparkling. Eleven years old, John Boy had a progressive and debilitating syndrome that led to myriad physical challenges and his life expectancy was no more than fifteen to twenty years at best. If the cardiologists couldn't deal with the abnormalities that were causing a degree of heart failure this time, that life expectancy could be drastically reduced.

Of mixed race, with ultra-curly black hair and a wide, white smile, the lad had been fostered out since birth but had spent more of his life in hospital than out of it and he was a firm favourite on this ward. With his frail, twisted body now confined to a wheelchair, John Boy had lost none of his sense of humour and determination to cause mischief.

Right now, he was making some loud and rather disgusting noises, his head hanging almost between his knees. Andy moved swiftly.

'Hey, John Boy! What's going on?'

John Boy groaned impressively and waved his hand feebly. Andy looked down and stepped back hurriedly from the pile of vomit on the floor.

'Oh...*no*...'

A nurse, Carla, was climbing down the ladder she had used to fasten the huge star on the top of the tree.

'Oh *no*,' she echoed, but she was laughing. 'Not

again, John Boy. That plastic vomit joke is getting old, you know?'

Andy nudged the offensive-looking puddle with his foot. Sure enough, the edge lifted cleanly. John Boy was laughing so hard he had to hold onto the side of his wheelchair to stop him falling out and the sound was so contagious everybody in the room was either laughing or smiling. The noise level was almost enough to drown out the sound of Andy's pager.

Still grinning, he walked to the wall phone and took the call. Within seconds his grin was only a memory and the frown on his face was enough to raise Carla's eyebrows. She straightened swiftly from picking up the plastic vomit. She dropped it in John Boy's lap, which caused a new paroxysm of mirth.

'What's up, Andy?'

But he couldn't tell her. He didn't want to tell anyone. It couldn't be true, surely? He kept his eyes focused on John Boy instead. On a patient. An anchor in his real world.

'His lips are getting blue,' he growled. 'Get him back to his room and get some oxygen on, would you, please, Carla?'

He knew they were both staring at him as he left the room. He knew that the tone of his voice had been enough to stop John Boy laughing as if a switch had been flicked off and he hated it that he'd been responsible for that.

But he hadn't been able to prevent that tone. Not

when he was struggling to hold back so many memories. Bad memories.

Oh…God… If this was really happening, why on earth did it have to happen *tonight* of all nights?

The emergency department was packed to the gills.

Andy entered through the internal double doors. Serious cases were filling the resuscitation bays. He could see an elderly man hooked up to monitors, sitting up and struggling to breathe even with the assistance of CPAP. Heart failure secondary to an infarction, probably. Ambulance officers were still hovering in the next bay where a trauma victim was being assessed. One of them was holding a cyclist's helmet, which was in two pieces. The next bay had staff intubating an unconscious man. A woman was standing in the corner of the bay, sobbing.

'I told him not to go up on the roof,' Andy heard her gasp. 'I didn't even *want* a stupid flashing reindeer.'

The cubicles were next and they were also full. One had a very well-dressed woman lying on the bed, a crooked tinsel halo still on her head.

'Can't you do something?' The man with her was glaring at the poor junior registrar. 'She's pregnant, for God's sake…'

So many people who were having their Christmas Eves ruined by illness or accident. This would have been a very depressing place to be except for the numerous staff members. Some of the nurses were wearing Santa hats or had flashing earrings. All of them, even the ones having to deal with life-threatening situations, were doing it with skill and patience and as much good cheer as was possible. Andy caught more than one smile of greeting. These people were his colleagues. The closest thing he had to family, in fact.

He smiled back and reached the central station to find a nurse he'd actually taken out once, a long time ago. Julia had made it very clear that she was disappointed it had never gone any further and she greeted him now with a very warm smile.

'Andy... Merry Christmas, almost.'

'You, too.' Julia's long blonde hair was tied back in a ponytail that had tinsel wound around the top. 'You guys look busy.'

'One of our biggest nights. Have you just come to visit?'

'No, I got paged. A baby...' Andy had to swallow rather hard. 'Query meningitis?'

Julia looked up at the glass board with the spaces for each cubicle had names and details that it was her job tonight to keep updated. 'Doesn't ring a bell...'

'Brought in by a woman called Gemma...Baxter.' The hesitation was momentary but significant. Would Gemma have gone back to her maiden name by now? She couldn't have got married again. Not when they'd never formalised a divorce. Julia didn't seem to notice the surname and Andy hurried on. 'Someone called Janice called it through.'

'Janice?' Julia looked puzzled. 'She's on Reception. In the waiting room.' Julia frowned. 'If she's got a query

meningitis it should have come through as a priority. I
hope she's not waiting for a bed or something. Let me
go and check.'

'That's OK, I'll do that.' He could almost hear the
wheels turning for Julia now. She was staring at him
with an odd expression.

'Did you say her name was *Baxter*? Is she a relative?'

Was she? Did it still count if you were still legally
married to someone even if they'd simply walked out
of your life?

Andy had reached the external set of double doors
that led into the waiting room. He spotted Gemma the
instant he pushed through the doors. It didn't matter
that the place was crowded and it should have been hard
to find anybody—his gaze went unswervingly straight
towards her as if it was some kind of magnetic force.

The impact was enough to stop him in his tracks
for a moment.

His head was telling him that it didn't count. Their
marriage had been over a very long time ago and there
was nothing there for him now.

His heart was telling him something very different.

This was the woman he had vowed to love, honour
and cherish until they were parted by death. He'd meant
every single word of those marriage vows.

For a moment, Andy could ignore everything that
had happened since the day those vows had been spoken. He could forget about the way they'd been driven
apart by forces too overwhelming for either of them

to even begin to fight. He could forget that it had been years since he'd seen Gemma or heard the sound of her voice.

What he couldn't forget was what had drawn them together in the first place. That absolute surety that they were perfect for each other.

True soul mates.

For just that blink of time that pure feeling, one far too big to be enclosed by a tiny word like love, shone out of the dark corner of his heart that had been locked and abandoned for so long.

And…and that glow *hurt*, dammit.

Sophie was starting to grizzle again.

Gemma bounced her gently and started walking in a small circle, away from the queue waiting to see the receptionist. What was going on? She'd been told to wait but she'd expected to at least be shown through to a cubicle in the department. With the drama of the staff rushing to attend to the woman having a threatened miscarriage she seemed to have been forgotten.

Had they rung Andy? Was he on call or…even worse, had they rung him at home and made him feel obliged to come in on Christmas Eve and sort out a ghost from his past?

Oh…Lord. He probably had a new partner by now. He might even have his own kids. Except, if that was the case, why hadn't he contacted her to ask for a divorce? She'd had no contact at all. For four years. Ever since she'd packed that bag and—

'Gemma?'

The voice was angry. And it was male, but even before Gemma whirled to face the speaker she knew it wasn't Andy.

'Simon! What are you doing here?'

Not only was it Simon, he had the children in tow. All of them. Seven-year-old Hazel, five-year-old Jamie and the twins, Chloe and Ben, who were three and a half.

'Go on,' she heard him snap. 'There she is.'

Hazel, bless her, was hanging onto a twin with each hand and hauling them forward. No easy task because they were clearly exhausted. What were they doing out of bed? They'd been asleep when Gemma had left the house and they were in their pyjamas and rubbing bleary eyes now, as though they hadn't woken up properly. Ben was clutching his favourite soft toy as if afraid someone was about to rip it out of his arms.

A sudden fear gripped Gemma. They were sick. With whatever Sophie had wrong with her.

But why was Simon here? OK, he'd arrived at the house a few minutes before the babysitter had been due and she'd had to rush off with Sophie but…but Hazel's bottom lip was wobbling and she was like another little mother to these children and *never* cried.

'Oh…hon come here.' Gemma balanced Sophie with one arm and held the other one out to gather Hazel and the twins close. 'It's all right…'

'No, it's not.' Simon had a hand on Jamie's shoulder,

pushing the small boy towards her. 'Your babysitter decided not to show.'

'What? Oh, no...'

'She rang. Had a car accident or some such excuse.'

'Oh, my God! Is she all right?'

'She sounded fine.' Simon shook his head. 'Look, I'm sorry, Gemma but, you know...I had no idea what I was signing up for here.'

'No.' Of course he hadn't. This had been a blind date that an old friend had insisted on setting her up with. Just a glass of wine, she'd said. At your local. Just see if you like him. He's gorgeous. And rich. And *single*.

There was no denying that Simon was good looking. Blond, blue-eyed and extremely well dressed, too. And...smooth was the first thought that had come to mind when she'd let him into the house. But definitely not her type. He'd been horrified when she'd said she had to get Sophie to the hospital and could he please wait until the babysitter arrived.

And...

'How did you get them here?'

'I drove, of course. You practically live in the next county.'

Hardly. The house was rural, certainly, but on the very edge of the city, which made Queen Mary's the closest hospital, otherwise Gemma would have gone somewhere else.

'What about the car seats?'

'Ooh, look...' Jamie was pointing to the area of the

waiting room set up to cater for children. 'There's toys.'
He trotted off.

'He didn't use them,' Hazel said. 'I told him and
he...' Her breath hitched. 'He told me to shut up.'

Gemma's jaw dropped. She stared at Simon, who
simply shrugged.

'Look, I could've left them in the house. If Jane had
told me anything more than that you were a cute, single chick who was desperate for a date, I wouldn't have
come near you with a bargepole. I don't *do* kids.'

Chloe chose that moment to hold her arms up, asking to be cuddled. When it didn't happen instantly, she
burst into tears. Sophie's grizzles turned into a full-
blown wail. Ben sat down on the floor and buried his
face against the well-worn fluff of his toy. Simon looked
at them all for a second, shook his head in disbelief,
turned on his heel and walked out.

Gemma had no idea what to do first. Hazel was
pressed against her, her skinny little body shaking with
repressed sobs. Gemma didn't need to look down. She
knew that there would be tears streaming down Hazel's
cheeks. Both Chloe and Sophie were howling and...
Where on earth had Jamie got to?

Wildly, Gemma scanned the waiting room as she
tried to tamp down the escalating tension from the
sounds of miserable children all around her. The action came to a juddering halt, however, when her gaze
collided with a person who'd been standing there watching the whole, horrible scene with Simon.

A man who had shaggy brown hair instead of

groomed blond waves. Brown eyes, not blue. Who couldn't be considered well dressed with his crooked tie and shirtsleeves that were trying to come down from where they'd been rolled up. But her type?

Oh…yes. The archetype, in fact. Because this was Andy. The man she'd fallen in love with. The man she'd known would be the only one for her for the rest of her life. For just an instant, Gemma could forget that this was the man whose life she'd done her best to ruin because the first wave of emotion to hit her was one of…

Relief.

Thank *God*. No matter what happened in this next micro-chapter of her life, she could deal with it if she had Andy nearby.

Her touchstone.

The rock that had been missing from her life for so long. Yes, she'd learned to stand on her own two feet but the ground had never felt solid enough to trust. To put roots into.

The blessed relief that felt like a homecoming twisted almost instantly into something else, however. Fear?

He hadn't said her name but he looked as angry as Simon had been when he'd stormed into the waiting room of Queen Mary's.

Or…maybe it wasn't anger. She'd seen that kind of look before, during a fight. Partly anger but also pain. And bewilderment. The result of being attacked when you didn't know quite what it was about and why you deserved it in the first place.

Gemma didn't know what to say. Maybe Andy didn't either. He was looking at the baby in her arms.

'I'll take her,' he said. 'You bring the others and follow me.'

CHAPTER TWO

THANK heavens there was a sick baby to assess.

It was another blessing that Andy had had plenty of practice in using a professional mode to override personal pain. This might be the best test yet, mind you.

Gemma's baby?

She had found someone to take his place in her life and she'd had his *baby*? A baby he now had cradled in his own arms as he led the way from the waiting room into the business area of the emergency department. Gemma was a good few steps behind him. He hadn't waited quite long enough for her to scoop up the youngest girl and send the oldest one to fetch the boy called Jamie from the playpen.

Jamie?

Something was struggling to escape from the part of his brain he was overriding but Andy didn't dare release the circuit breaker he'd had to slam on within seconds of walking into that waiting room.

That first glimpse of Gemma had hit him like an emotional sledgehammer. The power of that initial, soul-deep response had had the potential to destroy him utterly if he hadn't been able to shut it down fast. Fortunately, some automatic survival instinct had kicked in and extinguished that blinding glow. Shutting off his emotional response had left him with a lens focused on physical attributes and…astonishingly, it could have been yesterday that he'd last seen her.

OK, her hair was longer. Those luxuriant brown waves had barely touched her shoulders back then and they were in a loose plait that hung down to the middle of her back now. Same colour, though, and even in the artificial glare of the neon strip lighting in here it was alive with sparks of russet and deep gold. She'd filled out a little, too, but that only made her look more like the woman he'd fallen in love with instead of the pale shadow that had slipped out of his life four years ago.

How much worse was it going to be when he was close enough to see her eyes? Nobody else in the world had Gemma's eyes. They might share that glowing hazel shade but he'd never seen anyone with the unusual gold rims around the irises and the matching chips in their depths.

So far, by concentrating on the small people around her, Andy had managed to avoid more than a grazing glance. He was still avoiding direct eye contact as he walked briskly ahead of her.

He was getting close to the triage desk now and Julia was watching his approach. Or rather she was staring at the small train of followers he knew he had. Gemma must look like the old woman from the shoe, he thought grimly. So many children she didn't know what to do.

The irony would be unbearable if he let himself go there.

'Space?' he queried crisply. 'Query meningitis here.'

'Um…' Julia gave her head a tiny shake and turned it to glance over her shoulder at the board. 'Resus One's just been cleared…but—'

'Thanks.' Andy didn't give her time to say that it probably needed to be kept clear for a more urgent case. The privacy and space of one of the larger areas would be ideal to contain this unacceptably large group. It wasn't until he led them all into the space he realised that isolating himself from the hubbub of the cubicles would only intensify the undercurrents happening here but, by then, it was too late.

A nurse had just finished smoothing a clean sheet onto the bed. Andy laid the baby down gently. Her wails had diminished as he'd carried her here but the volume got turned up as he put her down and she was rubbing her eyes with small, tight fists. Was the light hurting her? Andy angled the lamp away.

'What's going on?' he asked. It was quite easy to ask the question without looking directly at Gemma. Right now she was just another parent of a sick child.

'Fever, irritability, refusing food.' Gemma's voice was strained. 'She vomited once and her cry sounded…' her voice wavered '…kind of high-pitched.'

Andy focused on the baby. He slid one hand behind her head. Lifting it gently, he was relieved to see her neck flex. If this was a case of meningitis, it was at an early stage but he could feel the heat from the skin beneath wisps of golden hair darkened by perspiration.

'Let's get her undressed,' he told the nurse. 'I'd like some baseline vital signs, too, thanks.'

Hard to assess a rate of breathing when a baby was this distressed, of course. And the bulging fontanelle could be the result of the effort of crying rather than anything more sinister. Andy straightened for a moment, frowning, as he tried to take in an overall impression.

It didn't help that there were so many other children in here. The small girl in Gemma's arms was still whimpering and the older boy was whining.

'But *why* can't I go and play with the toys?'

'Shh, Jamie.' The older girl gave him a shove. 'Sophie's *sick*. She might be going to *die*.'

Andy's eyebrows reversed direction and shot up. The matter-of-fact tone of the child was shocking. He heard Gemma gasp and it was impossible to prevent his gaze going straight to her face.

She was looking straight back at him.

He could see a mirror of his own shock at Sophie's statement. And see a flash of despair in Gemma's eyes.

And he could see something else. A plea? No, it was more like an entire library of unspoken words. Instant understanding and...trust that what was known wouldn't be used for harm.

And there was that glow again, dammit. Rays of intense light and warmth seeping out from the mental lid he'd slammed over the hole in his heart. Andy struggled to push the lid more firmly into place. To find something to screw it down with.

She's moved on, a small voice reminded Andy. *She's got children. Another man's children.*

It was Gemma who dragged her gaze clear.

'She's *not* going to die, Hazel.' But was there an edge of desperation in Gemma's voice?

'She's here so that we can look after her,' Andy added in his most reassuring adult-to-child tone. 'And make sure that she doesn't...' The stare he was receiving from Jamie was disconcerting. 'That nothing bad happens.'

The nurse was pulling Sophie's arms from the sleeves of a soft, hand-knitted cardigan. Sophie was not co-operating. She was flexing her arms tightly and kicking out with her feet. Nothing floppy about her, Andy thought. It was a good sign that she was so upset. It wouldn't be much fun for anybody if a lumbar puncture was needed to confirm the possibility of meningitis, though. He certainly wouldn't be doing a procedure like that with an audience of young children, especially when one of them was calmly expecting a catastrophe.

Hazel was giving him a stare as direct as Jamie's had been. She looked far older than her years and there was something familiar about that serious scrutiny. The penny finally dropped.

Hazel? Jamie? There was no way he could ignore the pull into the forbidden area now. Not that he was going to raise that lid, even a millimetre, but he could tread—carefully—around its perimeter. Andy directed a cautious glance at Gemma.

'These are your sister's children? Laura and Evan's kids?'

He didn't need to see her nodding. Of course they were. Four years was a long time in a child's life. The last time he'd seen Hazel she'd been a three-year-old. James had been a baby not much older than Sophie and...and Laura had been pregnant with twins, hadn't she?

The nurse had succeeded in undressing Sophie now, removing sheepskin bootees and peeling away the soft stretchy suit to leave her in just a singlet and nappy. Sophie was still protesting the procedure and she was starting to sound exhausted on top of being so unhappy. Gemma stepped closer. She tried to reach out a hand to touch the baby but the child she was holding wrapped her arms more tightly around her neck.

'No-o-o... Don't put me down, Aunty Gemma.'

Hazel was peering under the bed. 'You come out of there, Ben. Right *now*.'

'And Sophie?' Andy couldn't stem a wash of relief so strong it made his chest feel too tight to take a new breath. 'She's Laura's baby?'

'She was.' Gemma managed to secure her burden with one arm and touch Sophie's head with her other hand. She looked up at Andy. 'She's mine now. They all are.'

Andy said nothing. He knew his question was written all over his face.

'They were bringing Sophie home from the hospital,' Gemma said quietly. 'There was a head-on collision with a truck at the intersection where their lane joins the main road. A car came out of the lane without giving way and Evan swerved and that put them over the centre line. They…they both died at the scene.' She pressed her lips together hard and squeezed her eyes shut for a heartbeat.

'Oh, my God,' Andy breathed. Laura had been his sister-in-law. Bright and bubbly and so full of life. Gemma had been more than a big sister to her. She had been her mother as well. The news must have been unbelievably devastating. 'Gemma…I'm so sorry.'

Gemma opened her eyes again, avoiding his gaze. Because accepting sympathy might undo her in front of the children? Her voice was stronger. Artificially bright. 'Luckily the car seat saved Sophie from any injury.'

'And you were here in Manchester?' Andy still couldn't get his head around it. How long had she been here and why hadn't he known anything about it? It felt…wrong.

'No. I was in Sydney. Australia.'

Of course she had been. In the place she'd taken off to four years ago. The point on the globe where she could be as far as possible away from him. Andy could feel his own lips tightening. Could feel himself stepping back from that dangerous, personal ground.

'But you came back. To look after the kids.'

'Of course.'

Two tiny words that said *so* much. Andy knew exactly why Gemma had come back. But the simple statement prised open a completely separate can of worms at the same time. She could abandon her career and traverse the globe to care for children for her sister's sake?

She hadn't been able to do even half of that for him, had she?

There was anger trapped amongst the pain and grief in that no-go area. Plenty of it. Especially now that he had successfully extinguished that glow. He turned back to his patient.

'Let's get her singlet off as well. I want to check for any sign of a rash.'

Gemma wasn't sure who she felt the most sorry for.

Sophie? A tiny baby who was not only feeling sick but had to be frightened by the bright lights and strange environment and unfamiliar people pulling her clothes off and poking at her.

Hazel? A child who was disturbingly solemn these days. It was scary the way she seemed to be braced for fate to wipe another member of her family from the face of the earth.

The twins, who were so tired they didn't know what to do with themselves?

Herself?

Oh, yes...it would be all too easy to make it about herself at this particular moment.

Not because she was half out of her mind with worry. Or that her arms were beginning to ache unbearably from holding the heavy weight of three-year-old Chloe who was slumped and almost asleep, with her head buried against Gemma's shoulder, but still making sad, whimpering sounds.

No. The real pain was coming from watching Andy. Seeing the changes that four years had etched into his face. The fine lines that had deepened around his eyes. The flecks of silver amongst the warm brown hair at his temples. The five-o'clock shadow that looked...coarser than she remembered.

Or maybe it wasn't the changes that were making her feel like this. Maybe it was the things that *hadn't* changed that were squeezing her heart until it ached harder than her arms.

That crease of genuine concern between his eyebrows. The confident but gentle movements of his hands as they touched the baby, seeking answers to so many questions. The way she could almost see his mind working with that absolute thoroughness and speed and intelligence she knew he possessed.

'She's got a bit of a rash on her trunk but that could be a heat rash from running a fever. This could be petechiae around her eyes, though.' Andy was bent over the baby, cupping her head reassuringly with one hand, using a single finger of his other hand to press an area close to her eyes, checking to see if the tiny spots would vanish with pressure. He glanced up at Gemma. 'Has she been vomiting at all?'

'Just the once. After a feed. She refused her bottle after that.'

Andy's nod was thoughtful. 'Could have been enough

to push her venous pressure up and cause these.' But he was frowning. 'We'll have to keep an eye on them.'

He took his stethoscope out to listen to the tiny chest but paused for a moment when Sophie stretched out her hand. He gave her a finger to clutch. Gemma watched those tiny starfish fingers curl around Andy's finger and she could actually feel how warm and strong it must seem. Something curled inside her at the same time. The memory of what it was like to touch Andy? To feel his strength and his warmth and the steady, comforting beat of his heart?

It was so, so easy to remember how much she had loved this man.

How much she *still* loved him.

That's why you set him free, her mind whispered. *You have no claim on him any more. He wouldn't want you to have one.*

His voice was soft enough to bring a lump to her throat.

'It's all right, chicken,' he told Sophie. 'You'll get a proper cuddle soon, I promise.'

He might well give her that cuddle himself, Gemma thought, and the fresh shaft of misery told her exactly who it was that she felt most sorry for here.

Andy.

No wonder she had felt that edge of anger when she'd told him she'd come rushing back from Australia to step into the terrible gap left by her sister's death.

Andy had been the one who'd wanted a big family. For Gemma it had come well down the list of any priorities. A list that had always been headed by her determination to achieve a stellar career.

The irony of what she was throwing in his face to-night was undeserved. Cruel, even.

Andy was the one with the stellar career now. The grapevine that existed in the medical world easily extended as far as Australia and she'd heard about his growing reputation as a leader in his field.

And her career?

Snuffed out. For the last six months and for as far as she could see into the future, she would be a stay-at-home mum.

To a ridiculous number of children. The big family Andy had always wanted and she had refused to consider. In those days, she hadn't even wanted one child, had she?

Sophie's exhausted cries had settled into the occasional miserable hiccup as Andy completed his initial examination, which included peering into her ears with an otoscope.

'I don't think it's meningitis,' he told Gemma finally.

'Oh...thank God for that.' The tight knot in Gemma's stomach eased just a little, knowing that Sophie might not have to go through an invasive procedure like a lumbar puncture.

Andy could see the relief in Gemma's eyes but he couldn't smile at her. He knew she wasn't going to be happy with what he was about to say.

'I'm going to take some bloods.'

Sure enough, the fear was there again. Enough to

show Andy that Gemma was totally committed to this family of orphans. Their welfare was *her* welfare.

'Her right eardrum is pretty inflamed,' he continued, 'and otitis media could well be enough to explain her symptoms but I'm concerned about that rash. We've had a local outbreak of measles recently and one or two of those children have had some unpleasant complications.'

Gemma was listening carefully. So was Hazel.

'Kirsty's got measles,' she said.

'Who's Kirsty?' Andy's voice was deceptively calm. 'A friend of yours?'

Hazel nodded. 'She comes to play at my house sometimes.'

Andy's glance held Gemma. 'Have the other children been vaccinated?'

'I...don't know, sorry.'

'We can find out. But not tonight, obviously.' Andy straightened. He could see the nurse preparing a tray for taking blood samples from Sophie but it wasn't something he wanted the other children to watch. He'd ask Gemma to take them all into the relatives' room for a few minutes.

She could take them all home. Even Sophie. He could issue instructions to keep them quarantined at home until the results came in and that way he'd be doing his duty in not risking the spread of a potentially dangerous illness. Gemma was more than capable of watching for any signs of deterioration in the baby's condition but... if he sent them home, would he see any of them again?

Did he want to?

Andy didn't know the answer to that so he wasn't willing to take the risk of losing what little control he had over the situation. And even the possibility of a potentially serious illness like measles made it perfectly justifiable to keep Sophie here until they were confident of the diagnosis.

To keep them all here, for that matter.

Quarantined, in fact.

'I'll be back in a minute,' he excused himself. 'I've got a phone call I need to make.'

Thirty minutes later, Gemma found herself in a single room at the end of the paediatric ward. Already containing two single beds and armchairs suitable for parents to crash in, the staff had squeezed in two extra cots and a bassinette.

'Just for a while,' Andy told her. 'Until we get the results back on those blood tests and we can rule out measles.'

Sophie was sound asleep in the bassinette with a dose of paracetamol and antibiotics on board. The twins were eyeing the cots dubiously. Jamie and Hazel were eyeing the hospital-issue pyjamas a nurse had provided.

'I want to go home,' Hazel whispered sadly.

'I know, hon, but we can't. Not yet.'

'But it's Christmas Eve.'

Gemma couldn't say anything. The true irony of this situation was pressing down on her. An unbearable weight that made it impossible to look directly at Andy.

She heard him clear his throat. An uncomfortable sound.

'Will you be all right getting the kids settled? I... have a patient in the PICU I really need to follow up on.'

'Of course. Thanks for all your help.'

'I'll come back later.'

Gemma said nothing. She couldn't because the lump in her throat was too huge.

It was Christmas Eve and Andy was going to the paediatric intensive care unit.

The place it had all begun, ten years ago.

CHAPTER THREE

Christmas: ten years ago

'IT's a big ask, Gemma. I know that.'

The PICU consultant was dressed in a dinner suit, complete with a black velvet bow-tie. He was running late for a Christmas Eve function. Gemma already felt guilty for calling him in but she'd had no choice, had she? Her senior registrar and the consultant on duty were caught up dealing with a six-month-old baby in heart failure and a new admission with a severe asthma attack.

The deterioration in five-year-old Jessica's condition had been inevitable but the decision to withdraw treatment and end the child's suffering had certainly not been one a junior doctor could make.

'You don't have to do it immediately,' her consultant continued. 'Any time tonight is all right. Wait until you've got the support you need. I'm sorry…but I really can't stay. This function is a huge deal for my daughter. She's leading in the carol choir doing a solo of "Once in Royal David's City" and if I don't make it my name will be mud and tomorrow's...'

'Christmas.' Gemma nodded. She managed a smile. 'Family time that shouldn't be spoiled if it can be helped.'

'You've got it.' The older man sighed. 'If there was any chance of improving the outcome by heroic measures right now I'd stay, of course. But we'd only be prolonging the inevitable.'

'I know.'

They'd all known that almost as soon as Jessica had been admitted. The battle against cancer had been going on for half the little girl's life and she'd seemed to be in remission but any infection in someone with a compromised immune system was potentially catastrophic.

Over the last few days they had been fighting multi-organ failure and the decision that had been made over the last hour had been much bigger than whether or not to begin dialysis to cope with her kidneys shutting down.

Gemma had to swallow the lump in her throat. 'I just don't understand why her mother won't come back in.'

'She's a foster-mother, Gemma,' he reminded her. 'She loves Jessica dearly but she's got six other children at home and...it's Christmas Eve. She was in here for most of the day and she's said her goodbyes. It's not as if Jessica's going to wake up. You'll take her off the life support and she'll just stop breathing. It probably won't take very long.' The consultant glanced at his watch as he reached for a pen. 'I'll write it up. As I said, I know it's a big ask. No one will blame you if you're not up for it but I know how much time you've spent with her since her admission and I thought...'

Gemma took a shaky inward breath. Yes, she'd spent a lot of time with Jessica. Too much, probably, especially before she'd been sedated and put on life support. Certainly enough time to have fallen in love with the child and, if the closest thing to a mother she had couldn't be here at the end then someone who loved her was surely next best.

'I can do it,' she whispered. 'But...not just yet.'

'Take all the time you need.' The consultant signed his name on the order and turned to leave. He paused to offer Gemma a sympathetic smile. 'You're one of the best junior doctors I've ever had the pleasure of working with,' he said, 'but this isn't a time for being brave and trying to cope on your own. Every person who works in here will understand how tough this is. Take your pick but find someone to lean on, OK?'

Gemma couldn't speak. She could only nod.

It was the way she was standing that caught his attention.

She looked as though she was gathering resolution to dive into a pool of icy water. Or knock on a door when she knew that somebody she really didn't want to see was going to answer the summons. What was going on in that closed room of the PICU? Andrew Baxter had to focus to tune back into what his registrar was saying.

'So we'll keep up the inotropic support overnight.

Keep an eye on all the parameters, especially urine output. If it hasn't picked up by morning we'll be looking
at some more invasive treatment for the heart failure.'
The registrar yawned. 'Call me if anything changes
but, in the meantime, I'm going to get my head down
for a bit.' His smile was cheerful. 'You get to stay up
and mind the shop. One of the perks of being the new
kid on the block.'

'I don't mind.' Andy returned the smile, aware of
the woman still standing as still as a statue outside that
room. He hesitated only briefly after his companion left.

'Hey.' His greeting was quiet. 'Do you...um...need
any help?'

She looked up at him and Andy was struck by two
things. The first, and most obvious, was the level of
distress in her eyes. The second was the eyes themselves. He'd never seen anything like them. Flecks of
gold in the rich hazel depths and an extraordinary rim
of the same gold around the edges of the irises. He
couldn't help holding the eye contact for longer than
he should with someone he'd never met but she didn't
seem to mind. One side of her mouth curved upwards
in a wry smile.

'Got a bit of courage to spare?'

Andy could feel himself standing a little bit taller.
Feeling more confident than he knew he had a right to.
'You bet,' he said. 'How much would you like?'

'Buckets,' she said, a tiny wobble in her voice. 'Have
you ever had to turn off someone's life support?'

Andy blew out a slow breath. 'Hardly. I'm a baby

doctor. I started in the August intake and I've only just begun my second rotation.'

'Me, too.'

'And your team has left you to deal with this on your own?' Andy was horrified.

She shook her head. 'I get to choose a support person. My registrar is busy with the other consultant on the asthma case that came in a little while ago and the other registrar on duty is in with a baby. I think it's a cardiac case.'

Andy nodded. 'It is. I'm on a cardiology run. Six-month-old that's come in with heart failure. I'll probably be here all night, monitoring him. At the moment they're trying to decide whether to take him up to the cath lab for a procedure. I got sent out to check availability.'

'Sounds full on.'

'It won't be. If we're not going to the cath lab immediately I'll be floating around here pretty much for hours.' Andy tried to sound casual but her words were echoing in his head. She was allowed to choose a support person. The desire to *be* that person came from nowhere but it was disturbingly strong. It was emotional support she needed, not medical expertise, and surely he would understand how she would be feeling better than anyone else around here. They were both baby doctors and he knew how nervous he'd be in her position. How hard something like this would be.

Andy gave her an encouraging smile. 'I could be your support person.'

* * *

Gemma could feel her eyes widening.

She didn't even know this guy's name and he was being so...*nice*.

Genuine, too. He had dark brown eyes that radiated warmth. And understanding. Well, that made sense. He was at the same stage of his career as she was with hers and he'd never been in this position. Maybe, like her, he still hadn't even seen someone actually die. Gemma could be quite sure that anyone else here in the PICU had seen it before. It didn't mean that they wouldn't be able to support her but they might have forgotten just how scary it was that first time. Not knowing how it might hit you. How unprofessional you might end up looking...

Gemma didn't want to look unprofessional. Not in front of people who were more senior to herself and might judge her for it.

Kind eyes was smiling at her. 'Sorry—I haven't even introduced myself. Andrew Baxter. Andy...' He held out his hand.

Gemma automatically took the hand. It was warm and big and gave hers a friendly squeeze rather than a formal shake. He let go almost immediately but she could still feel the warmth. And the strength.

'I'm Gemma,' she told him.

'Hello, Gemma.' Andy's smile faded and he looked suddenly sombre. 'Would you like me to check with my consultant about whether it's OK for me to hang out with you for a while?'

Gemma found herself nodding. 'I'll ask whether

someone more senior has to be there. But there's no rush,' she added hurriedly. 'I wanted to just sit with Jessie for a bit first.'

He held her gaze for a moment, a question in his eyes. And then he nodded as though he approved of the plan.

'I'll come and find you,' he promised.

It was remarkably private in one of these areas of the PICU when the curtains were drawn over the big windows and the door was closed.

Remarkably quiet, too, with just the gentle hiss of the ventilator and muted beeping from the bank of monitoring equipment.

The nurse had given Gemma a concerned look before she'd left her alone in there with Jessica.

'Are you sure you don't want me to stay?'

Gemma shook her head and offered a faint smile. 'Thanks, but I need to do this in my own time,' she said. 'And…I think one of the other house officers is going to come and keep me company for a bit.'

The door opened quietly a few minutes later and then closed again. Andy moved with unusual grace for a big man as he positioned a chair and then sat down so that he was looking across the bed at Gemma.

Except he wasn't looking at Gemma. His gaze was fixed on Jessica's pale little face. He reached out and made her hand disappear beneath his.

'Hello, there, Jessie,' he whispered. 'I'm Andy. I'm Gemma's friend.'

Gemma liked that. She certainly needed a friend right now.

For several minutes they simply sat there in silence.

'Do you think she's aware of anything?' Gemma asked softly.

'I had a look at her chart on the way in,' Andy responded. 'She's well sedated so I'm sure she's not in any pain.'

'But nobody really knows, do they? Whether there's an awareness of...something.'

'Something like whether there's somebody there that cares about you?'

'Mmm.' Gemma took hold of Jessie's other hand as she looked up. Away from the harsh strip lighting of the main area of the PICU, Andy's face looked softer. His dark hair was just as tousled, the strong planes of his cheeks and jaw a little less craggy and his eyes were even warmer.

But what was really appealing was that he seemed to get what she was doing in here. Why it was important. His posture was also relaxed enough to suggest he wasn't going to put any pressure on her to hurry what had to be done.

'I saw she had a guardian listed as next of kin rather than family but...' Andy shook his head. 'I still don't understand why it's just us in here.'

'She's fostered,' Gemma told him. 'She was in foster-care even before she was diagnosed with a brain tumour over two years ago and she's had major medical issues ever since. There are very few foster-parents out there who would be prepared to cope with that.' She knew

she was sounding a bit defensive but she knew how
hard it could be.

'And the woman who's been doing it has a bunch of
other kids who need her tonight. She's been in here half
the day and…she couldn't face this.'

'But you can.' The statement was quiet and had a
strong undercurrent of admiration.

Gemma's breath came out in a short huff. 'I don't
know about that. It's…' For some strange reason she
found herself on the verge of dumping her whole life
history onto someone who was a stranger to her, which
was pretty weird when she was such a fiercely private
person. 'It's complicated.'

Andy said nothing for another minute or so. Then he
cleared his throat. 'So…where did you do your training?'

'Birmingham.' Gemma felt herself frowning. What
on earth did this have to do with anything? Then she
got it. Andy wanted to give her some time to get used
to him. To trust him? Given that she'd learned not to
trust people very early in life it was a strategy she could
appreciate. Oddly, it felt redundant. How could she not
instinctively trust someone who had such kind eyes?

Her abrupt response was still hanging in the air.
Gemma cleared her throat. 'How 'bout you? Where
did you train?'

'Cambridge.'

'Nice.'

Andy nodded. 'What made you choose Birmingham?'

'I lived there. With my younger sister.' Gemma

paused for a heartbeat. Reminded herself that Andy was trying to build trust here and it couldn't hurt to help. 'She was still at school,' she added, 'and I didn't want to move her.'

Andy's eyebrows rose. 'There was just the two of you?'

It was Gemma's turn to nod. And then she took a deep breath. Maybe she needed to accelerate this 'getting to know you' phase because she really did need a friend here. Someone she could trust. Someone who knew they could trust her. Or maybe it had already been accelerated because of an instant connection that somehow disengaged all her normal protective mechanisms.

'We were foster-kids,' she told him quietly. 'I got guardianship of Laura as soon as I turned eighteen. She was thirteen then.'

She could feel the way his gaze was fixed on her even though she was keeping her head bowed, watching as she rubbed the back of Jessie's hand with her thumb.

'Wow... That's not something siblings often do for each other. Laura's very lucky to have you for a sister.'

'No. I'm the lucky one. Laura's an amazing person. One of those naturally happy people, you know? She can make everyone around her feel better just by being there.'

'You're both lucky, then,' Andy said. 'Me, I'm an only child. I dreamt of having a sibling. Lots of them, in fact. I couldn't think of anything better than having a really big family but it never happened.' He shrugged, as though excusing Gemma from feeling sorry for him.

'Guess it'll be up to me to change the next Baxter generation.'

'You want lots of kids?'

'At least half a dozen.' Andy grinned. 'What about you?'

Gemma shook her head sharply.

'You don't want kids?'

'Sure. One or two. But that's so far into the future it doesn't register yet.' She could feel her spine straighten a little. 'I haven't worked as hard as I have not to make sure I get my career exactly where I want it before I take time off to have a baby.'

'Going to be rich and famous, huh?'

'That's the plan.' Oh, help…that had sounded shallow hadn't it? 'Secure, anyway,' Gemma added. 'And… respected, I guess.'

Andy nodded as though he understood where she was coming from. 'How old were you when you went into foster-care?'

'I was eight. Laura was only three. Luckily we got sent places together. Probably because I kicked up such a fuss if they made noises about separating us and also because I was prepared to take care of Laura myself.' She looked up then and offered a smile. 'I was quite likely to bite anybody that tried to take over.'

Andy grinned. 'I can believe that.' Then his face sobered again. He looked at Jessie and then back at Gemma. He didn't say anything but she knew he was joining the dots. She didn't need to spell out the complexities of why she felt a bond with this child and why it was important for her to be here with her at the end of her short life.

'You're quite something, aren't you?' he said finally.

A warm glow unfurled somewhere deep inside Gemma but outwardly all she did was shrug. 'I wouldn't say that.'

'I would. You completed your medical degree. It was hard enough for me and I had family support and no responsibilities. I've still got a pretty impressive student debt.'

'Tell me about it.' But Gemma didn't want to go there. She'd shared more than enough of her difficult background. Any more and they'd need to bring in the violins and that was definitely not an atmosphere that was going to help get her into the right space for what had to come. The task she still wasn't quite ready for. Time to change the subject and get to know her new friend a little better. 'What made you choose to go into medicine?'

'I think I always wanted to be a doctor. My dad's a GP in Norwich.'

'Family tradition?'

Andy grinned. 'Familiar, anyway. I just grew up knowing that the only thing I wanted to be was a doctor. Maybe I was too lazy to think of anything else I wanted to be.' His gaze was interested. 'How 'bout you?'

'Laura had to have her appendix out when she was seven and the surgeon was the loveliest woman, who arranged permission for me to stay in the hospital with her for a couple of days. I fell in love with both the surgeon and the hospital. Plus, I had to choose a career that would enable me to always be able to take care of my sister.'

'So you're going into surgery for a speciality?'

Gemma smiled. 'Haven't thought about that too much yet. I'm concentrating on surviving the next couple of years.'

'Me, too. I figure that it could be a process of elimination. It's a good thing we get all these rotations. I'll cross off the ones that don't feel right along the way.' He looked at Jessie and sighed. 'Might have to cross off PICU. It's pretty intense, isn't it?'

'But awesome when the outcome is good. What's happening with that baby that came in under your team?'

'He's been off colour for a few days but his mother brought him in because he was so breathless he couldn't finish his bottle. We started diuretics in ED but his blood gases showed metabolic acidosis.'

'Has he got a congenital abnormality?'

Andy shook his head. 'Echocardiography was normal. The likely scenario is an infection of some kind. Viral or bacterial.'

'Will he make it?'

Andy looked grim. 'About thirty per cent of kids that are like this die or require transplantation in the first year after the infection. His parents are distraught. It's their first baby.'

His empathy for those parents was transparent and Gemma felt a flash of sympathy. Maybe it was a haz-

ard of the job for junior doctors that they became too
emotionally involved with their cases. Andy wasn't only
prepared to care about his own case, he was now in,
boots and all, to Gemma's.

He not only had kind eyes, this man. He had a huge
heart.

'They're not bad odds,' she offered. 'Worth fighting
for, that's for sure.'

'Mmm. Speaking of which, I'd better go and check
on things. Like his urine output.' Andy got to his feet.
'Will you be OK for a bit?'

Gemma nodded. 'I…might take her lines out.'

'But you won't do anything else? Until I get back?'

He looked so anxious. So concerned. For *her*.

Gemma felt something very big squeeze in her chest
as she smiled at him. 'No. I won't do anything until
you get back.'

By the time Andy got back to Jessica's room, he
could see that things had changed. Gemma had taken
off all the cardiac monitoring patches and the ECG
machine was silent. The IV lines were out as well, including the central line that had been in place beneath
a tiny collar bone. No blood pressure or heart rate or
other vital signs were being recorded now. The screens
on the monitors were blank, which accentuated the soft
lighting. The only thing left to remove was the breathing tube. The only sound in the room was the gentle
hiss of mechanically moving air.

Gemma had not only removed the invasive lines, she

had covered the wounds with sticky dots and cleaned away any trace of blood.

'She hardly bled at all,' she told Andy. 'Her blood pressure must be really low.'

'Would you like me to remove the ET tube?'

He was watching Gemma's face carefully. He saw the fear in her eyes that was quickly shuttered by their lids. She had amazing eyelashes, a part of his brain registered. Thick and dark, like her hair, and he was sure she wasn't wearing any make-up. Right now, her lips were unnaturally pale. It was the tiny tremble in her lips that really undid Andy, though. He stepped closer and put his arm around her shoulders.

'Let's do it together.'

So they did. Gemma peeled away the tape securing the tube in place with as much care as if Jessica had been awake and feeling the unpleasant sensation. It was Andy who slipped the tube out and turned off the hiss of the ventilator.

For a long, long moment, they simply stood there. One of Gemma's hands was holding Jessie's. The other had somehow found its way into Andy's and he gripped it firmly.

They watched as the little girl struggled to take a breath on her own. Her face was still. Peaceful, even, but the small chest rose and fell slowly.

Andy could actually hear Gemma swallow. Her voice sounded thick. So quiet he had to lean closer to hear the words.

'How long do you think…?'

'I don't know.'

They watched for another breath. And another.

'Do you think…?' Gemma had to swallow again. Andy could see a tear trickling down the side of her nose. 'Do you think it would be OK to hold her?'

Andy felt dangerously close to tears himself. 'Of course it would.'

He guided Gemma to one of the comfortable chairs that were always in these rooms for exhausted parents. He gathered Jessica's limp body into his arms and gently transferred her into Gemma's. She eased the little girl's head into the crook of her elbow and stroked away a few strands of hair.

'It's OK, hon,' she whispered. 'We're here. You're not alone.'

God…this was hard. Much harder than Andy had expected it to be. He had to look away and try to breathe past the painful lump in his throat.

He heard Gemma start to hum. Shakily at first, with no discernible tune, but then the sound grew stronger and he recognised it.

'The "Skye Boat Song",' he whispered.

Gemma looked up and her smile was poignant. 'It was Laura's favourite,' she said very softly. 'It always helped her get to sleep, no matter what was happening around us.'

The tight feeling in Andy's chest got bigger. What kind of childhood had Gemma had? She had an inner strength that shone through, despite the vulnerability he was witnessing in having to deal with this heart-breaking event.

She was, quite simply…astonishing.

Jessica's breathing pattern had changed. She would take a deep breath and then several shallow ones and then there would be a pause before the next deep breath. Cheyne Stokes breathing, it was called. A sign that death was close.

Andy kept an eye on the clock in case Gemma didn't remember to record the time of death. He moved closer too, perching a hip on the arm of the chair so that he could put a hand on Gemma's shoulder and let her know that he was connected here.

He could look down. At a brave young woman holding a child as if she was hers. As if she was loved and would be mourned when she was gone.

Jessica was gone a short time later but neither of them moved for several minutes and they both had tears running freely.

It was hours later that Andy saw Gemma again. Waiting for a lift. The doors opened just as he got close so he got into the lift with her. He hadn't intended to but she'd looked wrecked the last time he'd seen her in the PICU and he had to make sure she was OK.

It was Gemma who spoke first as the doors of the lift closed.

'Thank you,' she said quietly. 'For…before. I couldn't have done that without you.'

'Yes, you could.' Andy was embarrassed by her gratitude. He looked down and nudged something with his foot. What was it? He stooped and picked it up.

'What's that?'

'A bit of rubbish.'

Gemma looked at the sprig of green plastic with tiny white balls. 'It's mistletoe,' she said. Her breath was a huff. 'I'd almost forgotten but it's Christmas Day now, isn't it?'

'It is indeed.' Andy turned his head to smile at her. 'Merry Christmas, Gemma.'

She held his gaze and Andy knew in that moment that he was going to see her again. That something had started tonight that he wouldn't be able to stop. Wouldn't want to stop. He raised the twig of mistletoe above their heads as the lift slowed.

He only meant to give her a peck on the cheek but she moved her head as the doors opened and her lips brushed his.

For a heartbeat, she stood very still.

As stunned as he was?

'Um...Merry Christmas, Andy,' she whispered. 'See you around.' And then she was gone.

'Yes,' Andy told the silent corridor before he pushed the button to go back to the floor he needed. 'You certainly will.'

CHAPTER FOUR

THE children weren't at all happy about having to go to sleep in a strange room on Christmas Eve.

'No!' Ben shouted when Gemma tried to lift him into the cot. 'No, no, *n-o-o...*'

'Shh,' Gemma commanded. 'Don't wake Sophie up.' Or disturb any of the other sick children in this ward, she thought. It was a privilege to be keeping all these children together right now, she knew that. Of course she would have been allowed to stay with Sophie but if the others had been banned, she had nobody to step in and help out at such short notice and she would have had to leave the baby alone.

With her spirits sinking a little further, Gemma remembered she hadn't even texted the babysitter she had arranged for tonight to see if she was all right after her car accident.

Ben curled into a mutinous ball on the floor, having squirmed out of her arms. He also began crying. So did Chloe.

'I want Mummy,' she sobbed.

Even though the door to the room was firmly closed,

Gemma could hear the faint wail of another miserable child somewhere. Set off by Ben and Chloe?

'Come on, guys,' she pleaded. 'It's not for long. Here...' She crouched on the floor and held out her arms. 'Cuddles?'

Chloe stuck out a quivering bottom lip. 'You're... not...Mummy.'

Oh...*God*...

Gemma felt like crying herself. She wasn't Mummy. She wasn't even a beloved aunty, was she? She'd fled from being involved in the lives of these children four years ago before the twins had even been born so she'd been no better than a complete stranger to them when she'd rushed back into their world six months ago.

It had seemed like she'd been making progress. The children had gradually got used to her and she'd done her best to make them feel loved and as secure as possible. But Chloe's whimpered words had taken her straight back to square one.

Or maybe not quite.

Hazel heaved a world-weary sigh that should only have been able to come from someone with several decades more life experience than a seven-year-old.

'Aunty Gemma is our mummy now, Chloe.'

Chloe eyed her older sister. Big, blue eyes swam with tears. She turned back to Gemma, sticking her thumb into her mouth. Thinking mode.

The nurses had provided a box of toys in the room and Jamie was sitting in the corner, doing a big-piece jigsaw puzzle of a squirrel. He looked up at Chloe.

'I love Aunty Gemma,' he said. 'She's a good mummy.'

The matter-of-fact words were sweet praise indeed. Gemma had to blink hard. The smile she gave Chloe was distinctly wobbly.

Chloe gave an enormous sniffle, pulled her thumb from her mouth with a popping sound and then held her arms wide to launch herself at Gemma.

Ben wanted in on the cuddle, of course, and Gemma suddenly had her arms overloaded with a warm tangle of chunky, three-year-old limbs and sweet-smelling, still baby-soft hair. She even got a sticky kiss from Chloe.

'Bed now?' Gemma suggested hopefully a minute or two later.

'Will you tell us a story?'

'Of course I will.'

But with Ben in one cot, Chloe shook her head firmly when Gemma went to lift her into the other cot.

'Want Ben,' she said. 'Same bed.'

'Hmm.' Gemma was dubious. 'It would be a bit of a squash, wouldn't it?'

But Ben, bless him, wriggled to one side. 'Lotsa room,' he declared. 'Digger's not big.'

'Digger' was Ben's favourite toy—a soft, brightly coloured bulldozer. Thank goodness it hadn't been left behind when Simon had brought the children in because Ben would never get to sleep without it. Chloe was the same about Raggy Doll.

Gemma's heart sank. Where *was* Raggy Doll?

Chloe didn't seem to have noticed yet that her cuddly was missing.

'I think sleeping with Ben is a great idea.' Gemma lifted Chloe into the cot. 'You can snuggle up like kittens in a basket.'

'I want a kitten,' Chloe said wistfully. 'Is Santa going to bring me one?'

'Maybe.' Gemma knew about the Christmas wish. She had a very cute, soft toy kitten wrapped and ready to go under the tree. Hopefully that would defer the longing for the real thing. 'Jamie? Can you find a story in the box, please? Then you could come and sit on my knee and listen too.'

Had the nurse deliberately put a story about Christmas in the box for the children? Gemma wasn't sure if it was going to be helpful to remind them about how much their own Christmas was being disrupted this year but the two older children listened with rapt attention to a tale of siblings who thought Christmas was boring until they both became involved in the magic of a pantomime performance. The twins were asleep by the time Gemma was halfway through the story and Jamie was struggling to keep his eyes open by the end.

'I want to go to a pantomime,' Hazel said as Gemma lifted Jamie into a bed. 'Mummy always said she'd take us. "Next year."'

'I'll take you,' Gemma promised, tucking Jamie in. 'Your mummy and I saw *Cinderella* when she was about your age. It was her favourite game for ages afterwards, playing pantomines.'

'I want to see *Jack and the Beanstalk*,' Jamie mumbled drowsily. 'Like in the story.'

ALISON ROBERTS 61

And with that, he was asleep. Hazel, however, looked far from tired.

'When will you take us?' she demanded.

It was on the tip of Gemma's tongue to say 'Next year', which was only logical. It was far too late to arrange anything for this Christmas season. But then she looked into her niece's wide, blue eyes and she could see something that just shouldn't be there. An understanding that life did not necessarily deliver what you most wanted. That dreams weren't worth having because they were most likely not going to come true.

If she said 'Next year', Hazel would hear an echo of her mother's voice and maybe she would try and protect her heart from yet more pain by assuming it wasn't going to happen. Terrible accidents happened all the time, didn't they? 'Next year' her aunt might not be here any more.

'I think…' Gemma was speaking cautiously because she wasn't a hundred per cent sure '…that some pantomines go at least until the end of December. If we can find one that does and I can find someone to look after Sophie, I'll take you all.' She offered Hazel a hopeful smile. 'I'll go on the internet on my phone and see what I can find out.'

To Gemma's surprise, she discovered there was a lot of entertainment for children available in and around the city. Why had it not occurred to her to look into this before?

'*The Wind in the Willows* is on for another couple of weeks,' she told Hazel. 'That would be fun.'

'Mmm.' Hazel had a fingertip against her teeth.

'Don't bite your nails, hon.'

She checked her phone again. 'Oh...*Jack and the Beanstalk* is on until the end of December. Shall I see if I can book some tickets?'

''Kay.'

'You're still biting.'

'Can't help it.'

Gemma sighed. The bad habit had only started in the last six months and it was always worse if Hazel was upset or worried about something. She closed her phone for the moment and went to give the little girl a hug.

'Sophie's going to be fine,' she told her. 'Try not to worry so much.'

'But it's not Sophie that I'm worried about.'

'What is it?'

Hazel kept her chin lowered. 'We're supposed to leave Santa a snack. We always put a glass of milk and a chocolate biscuit beside the fireplace. Sometimes he's not so hungry because all the boys and girls give him snacks but he always drinks some of the milk and takes a big bite out of the biccie.'

Hazel gave a huge sniff as she turned to stare at her little brother. Jamie was as soundly asleep as the twins but Hazel lowered her voice anyway.

'I know it's your mummy and daddy that give you most of the presents,' she whispered, 'but there's always a special one that they don't know about. It's wrapped in special paper and it doesn't have a label. *That's* the one that Santa brings.'

Another little piece broke off Gemma's heart as she thought of the family traditions Laura and Evan had been creating for their children. The kind that would get carried on for generations.

She hadn't known and it was too late to find different, special paper and leave those gifts without a label. Worse, she'd labelled more than one already as having been given by Father Christmas.

Oh…help…

'If he sees that we don't care enough to leave him something to eat and drink, he might think we don't even believe in him and he won't leave the special present,' Hazel continued sadly. 'And then it won't be really Christmas, will it?'

'Oh…hon…'

How could she fix this? Take a label off some of the gifts? Suggest that Santa had liked their Christmas paper enough to use it again on *his* special gifts?

But it was only a small part of the real problem here, wasn't it?

The bigger issue was that it wasn't going to be really Christmas because Christmas was all about family.

These children had been precious to their parents, who had created the best possible environment in which to raise them. It wasn't just the gorgeous, semi-rural property with the good school available nearby. It was more the loving environment. Parents that could weave positive family values and unique traditions into the upbringing of their children and celebrate them with joy on occasions like birthdays and Christmas.

That was what was missing from their lives now. The absolute security of that love and the demonstration of it through little things like the details of what happened on Christmas Eve.

Gemma was at a loss but she had to try and make this better somehow.

'I love you,' she said, pulling Hazel into her arms for a cuddle. 'I'm not going anywhere. I will always be here for all of you and I will always love you.' She took a deep breath. 'Christmas *is* different this year and I'm really, really sorry about that, but it's still Christmas and we'll make it special because we love each other and we'll be together.' She tightened her hold into an extra squeeze and kissed the top of Hazel's head. 'We'll do it together, OK? Make it really special for everybody.'

Hazel wrapped her arms around Gemma's neck. 'You're nice, Aunty Gemma,' she whispered. 'I love you, too.'

For the second time that evening Gemma felt herself far too close to tears. Partly, it was from relief that she had managed to slot into the lives of her nieces and nephews and earn their trust.

Their love was a huge bonus.

Sophie was stirring as Gemma blinked back her tears. A whimper became a cry that threatened to wake the other children. Gemma hurried to lift her from the bassinette.

'I can hold her,' Hazel offered.

Gemma shook her head, bouncing the baby gently in her arms. 'It's late, sweetheart, and you need to try and get some rest, too.' Tension was rising at the same pace as Sophie's volume. Chloe stirred and whimpered in the cot.

Gemma thought quickly. 'I'll take Sophie for a bit of a walk and see if I can get a bottle heated for her. She's probably hungry by now.' She eyed Hazel anxiously. 'I won't be far away. Just out in the corridor.'

'I'll be OK.' Hazel nodded.

'Look…there's a button beside the bed, on the end of that cord thing. If you push that, a nurse will come. Why don't you curl up on the bed and try and go to sleep?'

"Kay.' Hazel came close enough to drop a kiss onto the back of her smallest sister's head. 'Shh…' she told the baby. 'It's OK. Aunty Gemma's looking after you. She's looking after all of us.'

Hazel's words echoed in Gemma's mind as she slipped out of the room and closed the door behind her. The ward corridor was dim but she could see the lighted area of the nurses' station and wondered if it would be acceptable to walk that far. Or were they being strictly quarantined until blood tests revealed whether Sophie might have a contagious disease like measles?

A smaller, bobbing light came towards her. The nurse was pointing the torch at the floor but raised it to illuminate Sophie's face.

'Problems?'

'The other children are asleep so I didn't want her to wake them. Sometimes walking up and down and singing is enough to get her to settle again but I think she might be hungry.'

'Might be a good time to change her nappy. We can take her temperature and check on what's happening with that rash, too. Then I can see about a bottle for you.'

'Thank you.' Gemma eyed the door of the private room they had been assigned. 'Are we still being quarantined? Do we need to do the nappy in there?'

The nurse also eyed the door. There were several children asleep in there and Sophie's cries stepped up a level in volume again. She shook her head.

'We can use the treatment room,' she said. 'It's not as though you're going to come anywhere near any other children at this time of night.'

She led the way. 'I'm Lisa Jones, by the way. Night shift nurse manager.'

'I'm Gemma Ba—' Gemma caught herself but Lisa smiled.

'Baxter, yes?' Even in the dim periphery of the torchlight Gemma could see the curiosity in Lisa's glance. 'None of us knew that Andy was still married.' Her smile widened. 'It explains why so many women got so disappointed by never getting past first base.'

For Gemma, it raised more questions rather than provided any kind of explanation. Had Andy avoided having any kind of meaningful relationship with another woman?

Why?

And why on earth did it give her a frisson of...what... *relief*?

'We've been separated for some time,' she informed

Lisa, her voice tight enough to let the nurse know that the topic of conversation was not welcome. 'I've been working in Australia.'

The lights in the treatment room were overly bright. Sophie's increasing distress made further personal conversation impossible, which was fine by Gemma. She'd had no intention of gossiping about her personal life but Lisa had nodded at her statement as though she knew already.

And why wouldn't she? The kind of tragedy and its aftermath that she and Andy had been through would have been hot news on any hospital grapevine. She had to assume everybody knew virtually everything around here.

Was that the explanation for Andy's apparently monastic existence in the last few years? Had he simply been successful in keeping his private life private? Or did he have the same problem she knew she would always face—of knowing that any relationship she might find could never adequately take the place of what was missing from her life? And, therefore, what was the point of even going there?

No. Sadly, Gemma was quite sure that wouldn't be what, if anything, was holding Andy back. She had been the one who had failed to live up to being a good partner in their marriage. It would be easy for Andy to find more than a replacement to fill that gap in his life. He would have no trouble finding a vastly improved model.

The casually uttered words of the nurse went round

and round in the back of Gemma's mind as she watched Lisa remove Sophie's nappy and expertly assess her skin for any sign of a rash.

So *many* women?

So disappointed?

'Her skin's looking good,' Lisa declared. 'Let's get some fresh pants on her and take her temp.'

Sophie's temperature had come down a little.

'That's excellent,' Lisa told the baby. 'We'll get you dressed again, give you a bit more paracetamol and then you can have some supper. Maybe that will stop you howling, yes?'

But Sophie stopped crying even before the formula was prepared and heated for her. She stopped when she'd been buttoned back into her stretchy suit and Gemma had picked her up for a cuddle. Rubbing her face in the dip beneath Gemma's collarbone, the ear-splitting shrieks subsided with remarkable speed, although she could still feel the tiny body in her arms jerking with deep, gulping breaths.

'Ohh...' Lisa smiled at them. 'Look at that. She just wanted her mummy.'

Gemma opened her mouth to deny the title and say she was only her aunt but then she closed it again.

She *was* Sophie's mummy now, wasn't she? She always would be. Maybe her bond with her, her sister's last child, would be the strongest because Sophie would have no memories of anyone else being there for her.

And at this moment the sweetness of being able to

comfort this tiny person was overwhelming. The best feeling in the world?

Holding the bottle as Sophie sucked on it was just as good. Something in the way she held eye contact with Gemma as she drank tugged on a very deep place in her heart. The tiny hand curled over her big finger on top of the bottle added another poignant beat every time it squeezed rhythmically. Like a kitten kneading its mother's stomach.

Another nurse came into the central station as Gemma sat there, feeding Sophie. Her face was creased with concern.

'Lisa? Ruth's awake and complaining of a tummy-ache. Should I give her something?'

'What's her temperature?'

'Normal. Everything seems fine…but…'

'I'll come and see her. Did you check on John Boy?'

'His sats are down. Jules is watching him and she put his oxygen flow up to six litres. He's awake, too, I'm afraid. He's not complaining of anything, as usual, but I think he might need some additional pain relief. Should we page Andy?'

'Give me a minute or two to double-check. We don't want to pull him away from the PICU unless we have to.'

'John Boy?' Gemma queried as Lisa draped a stethoscope around her neck and picked up a chart. 'Is that really his name?'

Lisa grinned. 'Maybe somebody was a fan of *The Waltons*, way back.' Her smile faded. 'Or maybe it was just because he was one of far too many children before he went into foster-care. He's a neat kid. Has some pretty serious heart failure to contend with at the moment.' She picked up another chart.

'And Ruthie's battling leukaemia. We need to keep a close eye on any symptoms in case it's infection or rejection after her bone-marrow transplant. I'll need to check them both and maybe drag Andy back from the PICU. Not that he'll mind,' she added. 'They're both favourites with him.' She paused by the door to glance back at Gemma. 'Will you be OK?'

Gemma nodded. The bottle was almost empty. 'I'll take Sophie back to the room. She'll probably be asleep again by the time I get there.'

She could hear the muted sounds of increased activity in the ward as she walked slowly back to the room. Maybe Lisa shouldn't have been giving her any details of her patients' histories but that kind of confidentiality was more relaxed on a paediatric ward and she was a doctor herself. She certainly couldn't accuse any of the people she'd met so far of being unprofessional. Young lives were at stake here and the staff were clearly dedicated.

Including Andy, obviously. Both these sick children were favourites? And he wouldn't mind a late-night call to pull him back to the ward?

Gemma's steps slowed to the point where she actually stopped and turned for a long look down the ward corridor. She could see doors that were open and hear the squeak of a trolley being moved.

Right at the end of the corridor she could see small flashes of red and green and blue. There must be a Christmas tree in the dayroom, she decided. Of course there would be. She might have been away from dealing with patients for a long time but she remembered the extra lengths medical staff went to in order to make a day like Christmas special for anyone unfortunate enough to be confined in a hospital. That kind of effort always reached its peak when children were involved.

Rapid footsteps sounded and Gemma saw a nurse hurrying into the nurses' station. She could hear the low buzz of an urgent conversation, which was probably summoning Andy back to the ward.

To his world, in fact.

And suddenly Gemma understood.

She looked down at the baby in her arms and remembered that feeling she'd had when she'd picked her up and Sophie had stopped crying.

She'd never understood how Andy could have chosen to go into paediatrics after what had happened. It had felt like he was rubbing salt into her wounds. Like he was telling the world it didn't matter and that he could move on.

But did he get that same kind of feeling from comforting these sick children? And their families? How much would it be magnified by being able to save their lives or at least improve them, instead of only offering the comfort of cleanliness and warmth and food?

She got it.

Finally. Too late, of course, but Gemma felt humbled by the knowledge.

She tiptoed back into the room to find that Hazel had fallen asleep as well. She and Sophie were the only ones awake now and Sophie's eyelids were showing no sign of drooping. She grinned up at Gemma, who found herself smiling back.

She began to walk between the door and window. Back and forth. Humming softly to the tune of a song she knew would only soothe the other children and was therefore very unlikely to wake them. A tune that was automatic enough to allow her thoughts to continue tumbling unchecked.

Dear Lord...was that the *'Skye Boat Song'* he could hear?

It stopped Andy in his tracks outside the room that Gemma and the children were in. The door was slightly ajar, which was how he could hear the sound. The curtains on the corridor side of the room had not been completely closed either, so Andy could see inside.

He couldn't stop for more than a few seconds because he was needed elsewhere. The nursing staff was worried about Ruth. And John Boy. Neither problem sounded serious but he needed to check to reassure himself as much as his colleagues.

A few seconds was enough to take in the picture,

though. Hazel was asleep on one of the beds, curled up with a blanket carefully draped over her. Jamie was asleep on the other bed, flat on his back and looking angelic with his blond curls and an amused tilt to the corners of his mouth. An opened story book lay on the floor near his bed.

The twins were in the same cot, a tangle of limbs in fluffy pyjamas that made them look like puppies in a box. A brightly coloured toy had been pushed to one end and was threatening to fall through the bars.

And there was Gemma. Walking slowly back and forth with her head bent low enough for her cheek to be resting gently on the baby's head.

It was the picture of a mother caring for her children. Andy could imagine the lilt of her voice as she'd read them a story. See her drawing up the blanket to tuck it around Hazel. Soon she would probably rescue the falling toy and put it back beside Ben and maybe she would smooth strands of hair off his forehead and give him a kiss.

The tenderness of the picture made Andy's heart ache. The yearning sensation stayed with him as he moved on to deal with his young patients.

It was still with him a little while later when he'd checked both Ruth and John Boy and charted extra medications to help them both get a good night's sleep.

He could feel the pull back to that room at the end of the corridor and it was so strong it hurt.

Or maybe it was something else that was causing the pain.

Trying to get his head straight, Andy walked in the opposite direction from the room that held Gemma and all the Gillespie children in it. He found himself in the ward's dayroom, staring at the coloured flashes coming from the lights on the Christmas tree.

Christmas was such a part of his and Gemma's story, wasn't it?

That first Christmas, ten years ago, had been when he'd met the woman he'd known was going to be the love of his life.

What if someone had asked him, a few weeks later, what he saw for his future? OK, maybe it had been later than that that the dream had taken firm shape but the longing had always been there, hadn't it?

A variation on the picture he'd been caught by when he'd come back into the ward a short time ago.

A loving family with Gemma at its heart.

Oh...how he wanted to go back to that room. But he couldn't make his feet move. What if she was still singing to get Sophie back to sleep?

The song she had sung to her little sister so many years ago to help her sleep no matter what had been happening around them.

The song she had sung to a dying child who'd had nobody around to love them at the end.

The song she had sung to Max.

The lights on the Christmas tree seemed to intensify and grow spikes of colour that blurred until Andy could blink the extra moisture away.

Christmas...

Family...
Gemma...
...Heartache.

CHAPTER FIVE

Christmas: eight years ago

THE cafeteria on the first floor of Queen Mary's hospital was even more crowded and noisy than usual.

The vast room was still decorated with huge, rainbow-hued paper bells and chains thanks to the staff party that had been hosted in here last night. The festive spirit seemed to have lingered as well judging by the peals of laughter amongst the hubbub of conversation, clash of cutlery on china and pagers and mobile phones going off. The faint strains of a Christmas carol could be heard coming from a CD player near the cash register.

Gemma eyed the food selection dubiously. 'Have you got any sushi left?'

'Long gone. Sorry, love. You're a bit late for lunch.'

'Tell me about it.' Gemma heaved a sigh. 'I'll have some macaroni cheese, thanks.'

'Good choice.' The kitchen hand nodded. 'You need a bit of meat on your bones, you do.'

As she pushed her tray further along the counter,

Gemma's smile had nothing to do with the gelatinous heap of hot food on her plate. She was happy because she knew that somewhere in this crowded space Andy was waiting for her. And, if the Christmas fairies were kind, they might get a whole thirty minutes of each other's company.

It should have been almost impossible to spot a single person quickly amongst the hordes but Gemma simply stood still near the till, holding her tray. She closed her eyes for a moment, listening to the sound of a choir singing 'Oh, Come, All Ye Faithful' from the CD player and then opened her eyes and let something she couldn't name direct her gaze.

'Joyful and triumphant...' the choir sang, and they were right because it had worked.

It always worked.

Andy broke off the conversation he was having with someone at an adjoining table and his gaze zeroed in to meet Gemma's. He waved and smiled and Gemma let out the breath she hadn't noticed she was holding.

How long would it last? she wondered as she got closer. It had been two years since she'd met Andy in the PICU that night. Over a year since they'd moved in together and yet her stomach still did that odd little flip when she saw him smile at her. A flip that sent waves of something rippling through her body. Something strong and safe that had become her touchstone in a world that was often exhausting and challenging and difficult. Something that was also thrilling because it reminded her of what the world was like when it was just the two of them and they had a whole night to be together. Something that was joyous, too, because it held a promise of how good the future might be.

'Good grief, what *is* that?'

'Macaroni cheese. Want some?' Gemma held up a loaded fork and laughed as Andy's eyes widened in mock horror.

'I'm OK, thanks. Up to coffee already, see? I had a turkey roll. With stuffing and cranberry sauce. Probably leftovers from the supper last night but it was still great.'

'Didn't see any of them. Anyway...' Gemma wolfed the forkful. 'I'm starving and carb loading is a good idea because I'll need the energy to cope with the marathon that will probably be the rest of my shift.'

'How's it going in babyland?'

'Flat out. You'd think people would time getting pregnant a bit better, wouldn't you?' Gemma spoke around another forkful of cheesy pasta. 'Two Caesars, a forceps and a breech. And that was all by elevenses.'

'Well, I've had two heart attacks, an amputated finger, critical asthma and unexplained abdominal pain.'

Gemma grinned. 'You're looking surprisingly well, in that case. Good job on the finger, too. Can't see a scar, even.'

It was an old joke but Andy had no trouble smiling back. For a heartbeat the cacophony of sounds, the harsh lighting and even the competing smells of various foodstuffs faded away. He could even forget about that awful stuff

Gemma was eating. His outward breath was a sigh of pure contentment.

He could lose himself in her eyes like this every time. Especially when she smiled. It made him feel…good.

Really good. As if he was in exactly the right place in his life. With exactly the right person.

'Still OK for tonight?' It wasn't beyond the realms of possibility that Gemma would have put her hand up for an extra shift if things were desperate.

'Can't wait.' Gemma ate another mouthful and chased a drop of cheese sauce from her lips with her tongue.

Andy's gut tightened pleasurably. He couldn't wait either.

'How good is it that we've both got Christmas Eve off duty?'

'I know. Sometimes I wonder why we bothered moving in together when we only see each other in here or when we bump into each other in some corridor.'

'Because we've both got horrendous student debts and two can live as cheaply as one.'

They both smiled. They both knew the real reason why they had moved in together and it wasn't simply to save money. It had been the logical next step in a relationship that had the potential to last for ever.

'Speaking of debt,' Andy said, 'I've checked online and the bank holidays mean we've got a few days' grace to pay the power bill. That means you've got a bit extra for the groceries.'

'Hooray.' Gemma's eyes lit up. 'Chocolate.'

'I was thinking maybe a bottle of wine? For tonight?'

'Mmm. Chocolate *and* wine. Heaven.'

'Maybe some food, too?'

'Hmm.' Still eating, Gemma pulled a notebook and pen from her pocket. 'I'd better write a list. You're on a late day, aren't you?'

'Yeah…sorry. Won't finish till eight p.m. at the earliest. Supermarkets will be shut by then, otherwise I'd come and help you shop.'

Gemma shook her head. 'How often do we get an evening with neither of us rostered on? I don't want to waste it in the aisles of a supermarket.' She glanced at Andy as he drained his coffee cup. 'We're out of coffee at home, aren't we?'

'Yep. And milk and bread. And I used the last of the shampoo this morning.'

Gemma scribbled the items on the list. 'I'll get some bacon and eggs for Christmas breakfast. It's good that we're working tomorrow, isn't it? We should get a nice Christmas lunch and that'll save us buying our own turkey.'

'The perks of being a junior doctor,' Andy agreed wryly. 'Overworked and underpaid but…hey…we get a free Christmas lunch.'

'At least you don't have to dress up in a Santa suit. You should see the party they're organising in the paediatric ward.'

'I did. I went up to check on that kid that came into A and E last night. The one that got hit by the car that lost control on the ice?'

'Oh…how's she doing?'

'Fractured pelvis and ribs but it was the head injury I was really worried about. CT was clear. Just bad concussion.' Andy knew he was sounding pleased. It had been a full-on resuscitation that he'd run by himself. He *was* pleased with the outcome.

Gemma looked up from her expanding list. She smiled. 'You're loving Emergency, aren't you?'

'Who wouldn't? You get a bit of everything. Neonates to geriatrics. Superficial to critical. Medical, surgical and trauma. It's a roller-coaster.'

'You want to choose it for a specialty?'

'You know? I think I might.' The thought of taking another step into shaping the future into exactly what he wanted it to look like was a great feeling. It would be perfect if Gemma could find that kind of satisfaction as well. They were due to nominate the specialty they would become a registrar in for the coming year but Gemma was using her head rather than her heart to try and make the decisions that would shape the rest of her career.

She wanted something that would have a research component that could take that career to medical-rock-star level. So far, the real contenders were either oncology or anaesthetics with a sub-specialty of pain control.

'You're going to cross O&G off your list, aren't you?'

Gemma nodded emphatically. 'It's not for me. All those *babies*…'

She was pulling an overly dramatic face but her final word seemed to hang in the air and suddenly a charged silence fell between them. A kitchen hand pushed a trolley past their table. She gathered up Andy's plate and cup and stacked them. She eyed Gemma's unfinished plate.

'You all done with that?'

'What? Oh...yes. I've had enough.'

Clearly, Gemma had lost the voracious appetite she'd arrived with. They both watched her plate being scraped and stacked and the cutlery being dropped into a bucket of sudsy water. Then they looked at each other and Andy raised his eyebrows in a silent question.

Gemma shook her head and looked away again.

Oh...*hell*...

He reached out to give Gemma's hand a reassuring squeeze. 'It's only been a couple of days, babe. You're on the Pill and the percentage failure rate is ridiculously small. Stop stressing.'

'One per cent isn't ridiculously small, you know. Not if it happens to be you.'

'Try to think of it as a ninety-nine per cent chance of there being nothing to worry about.'

The sound of pagers going off was just part of the background noise in the busy cafeteria full of medics but this time it was close enough to make them both reach for the devices clipped to their belts.

'It's me.' Gemma sighed. 'Probably another Caesar, the rate we're going today. Nobody wants to wait and have their baby on Christmas Day.'

'I'll come with you. I was due back downstairs about five minutes ago, I think.'

Saying nothing as they edged their way between tables was fine but the silence was noticeable as soon as they left the cafeteria. A short walk took them to the bank of lifts where they had to part company. Gemma had to wait for a lift while Andy took the stairs down to the ground level. It wasn't much of a wait. The light glowed and a pinging sound announced the arrival of the lift.

'See you tonight.' Gemma's smile was a bit tight and Andy could see the shadow of anxiety in her eyes.

To hell with hospital etiquette, he decided, bending his head to brush her lips with his own.

'Stop worrying,' he said softly. 'Doctor's orders.'

Stop worrying?

Fat chance. But it was possible to shove the worry into a parking lot at the back of her brain. It was something that junior doctors got very practised at. All that worry over the last couple of years...

Could they handle the responsibility of being *real* doctors with lives affected by their decisions?

Could they cope with the exhaustion of long hours and having every job that more senior staff couldn't be bothered doing thrown their way?

Could they even begin to make a dent in the massive amount of debt they'd accumulated in their training?

You had to be dedicated to a career in medicine, that was for sure. But that was part of what had drawn Gemma and Andy together in the first place. They might have come into medicine from different directions but the determination to excel in a career they were both in love with was something they shared. Maybe that was why the relationship worked so well even when it was hard to find any quality time together to nurture it. They both understood the pressures and made allowances for it. Most of the time, anyway.

Gemma filled her trolley at the supermarket rapidly but she was being careful of what she pulled from the shelves and freezers. Only the essentials and the least expensive options. Except she had leeway to be just a little bit extravagant today, didn't she? It was Christmas and although they'd made a pact not to spend anything on buying presents for each other, it would be a gift in itself to have a special evening together. A nice dinner by candlelight. Wine. An early night...

A smile tugged at Gemma's lips as she chose Andy's favourite red wine and then went to find some steak to go with it. Maybe it was partly due to the pressure and small amount of time they had together at home that meant their love-making had never lost the magic of that first time, only a few days after their first meeting. If anything, it had got better and better as they learned more about each other and had fallen in love and chosen to make a commitment.

That love was growing stronger as time went by as well. Just thinking about Andy as she manoeuvred the trolley through crowded aisles gave Gemma the kind of warm internal glow that only her little sister had ever evoked in her before. The kind that made you want to cherish and nurture someone. The kind of giving that actually meant you could receive more than you gave.

Passing a Christmas confectionery stand, Gemma added a couple of candy canes, a big bag of cheesy ring snacks and the ultimate treat of her favourite brand of Swiss chocolate that came in the shape of gold-wrapped reindeer with red ribbons and bells around their necks. Andy wouldn't be as excited about the chocolate as she was and, still feeling the glow, Gemma wanted to find something special just for him. She headed for the toiletries section with the intention of at least checking out the price of aftershave or something. They needed shampoo, anyway, didn't they?

She walked past the over-the-counter medications first and the slim, blue and white boxes on the bottom shelf seemed to be glowing. The price on the home pregnancy test kits was high but Gemma stopped in her tracks. She even picked a box up.

It would be the best Christmas gift for both of them, wouldn't it? To find that they weren't in that unlucky one per cent? To know that the future was still wide open and full of promise?

After a long moment she reluctantly returned the box to the shelf. She could do a test for free at work and what possible difference could waiting a day or two make? What if the news was what she so desperately didn't want it to be and Christmas was ruined for both of them? Gemma turned and fled the aisle, any thoughts of aftershave or even shampoo forgotten.

Her mobile was ringing as she headed out into the freezing, dark evening, laden with shopping bags. She had to put down two of the bags to reach her phone but she couldn't ignore the call. What if it was Andy, saying he was going to have to work later than expected? It would be an awful waste if she'd spent so much on a special dinner and then it was ruined by having to be kept warm for too long.

But it wasn't Andy.

'Laura!' Gemma forgot about how cold it was, standing out here. 'Hey, hon…how *are* you? Merry almost Christmas. Did you get my card?'

Her little sister was laughing. 'Good and yes and same to you…'

'Did you get some time off work? Are you going to be able to come up?'

'Yes, but—'

'Oh…' Gemma couldn't help interrupting. 'It'll be so good to see you. It's been way too long.'

'I know. Gem?'

Gemma caught her breath. 'What?'

'I've got something to tell you.'

Gemma was still holding that breath. 'Oh, my God, you're not pregnant, are you?'

'*No…*' Laura was laughing again. 'At least, not yet.'

'What does that mean? You're *planning* to be pregnant?' Gemma had to shake her head. This was more than ironic.

'Ev's asked me to marry him, Gem. We're *engaged*. I've got a ring and everything.'

'Oh…' Gemma was lost for words. Laura sounded *so* happy. She was only twenty-two but her boyfriend Evan had been in her life for longer than Andy had been in hers. A builder with a solid future ahead of him, Evan had met Laura when he'd gone into the kitchen shop she worked in. 'That's fantastic, hon. I'm so happy for you.'

'That's not even the best bit. You know how Evan's always had a dream of finding some ramshackle old barn and converting it into a dream house? Well, he's found one on the internet and…you'll never guess.'

Gemma's heart skipped a beat. 'Don't tell me it's in Australia or somewhere.'

'No, silly. It's in spitting distance of you. Outskirts of Manchester. We've put an offer in. We should know whether we've got it or not by the time we come up to see you for New Year…' Laura's excitement was almost palpable. 'I can't wait… Will you help me plan my wedding?'

'Of course I will.'

'It'll be your turn next. We can make an extra scrapbook of ideas for you.'

It was Gemma's turn to laugh. 'As if… It'll be ten years before I've got time to even think about a wedding.' After all, why would you go to the expense of having a wedding unless you were ready to settle down and start a family?

'And keep your fingers crossed for us about the barn. How good would it be if we got it? There's even room for a pony for the kids. Hey...is it snowing up your way?'

Gemma looked around. The freezing sleet had, indeed, turned to fluffy white flakes while she'd been standing here, talking. 'Sure is, and I'm freezing. I need to get my groceries home and get some dinner on. Love you. I'll call you tomorrow.'

'Love you, too. Say hi to Andy for me.'

The snow was beginning to settle as Gemma reached the iron railing that marked her destination. She glanced below street level at the two-metre square of concrete that was the garden their basement bedsit looked out on.

A converted semi-rural barn? Settling down to make babies and even planning ahead for the pets those children would have?

Did she feel envious of her little sister?

Maybe a little but only because Laura was achieving her dream. They wanted very different things from life and Gemma still had a mountain to climb before she reached hers. There was a touch of sadness there too, letting go of the responsibility she'd had since childhood of protecting the person she loved most in the world. She could turn over that responsibility to Evan now, with the absolute confidence that he would step up to the mark.

Mixed in with both those realisations was also a definite fizzle of excitement. Background parental-type anxiety about Laura had always been there and had sometimes distracted her from her own goals.

That distraction was gone. She could focus on climbing her personal mountain now and eventually, like Laura, she would achieve everything she'd always dreamed of.

Andy spotted the tree branch beside a rubbish skip near the bus stop.

It must have broken off a good-sized Christmas tree a few days ago, he decided, because it was a bit wilted and had a ragged strip of bark at its base. Still…it was a good three feet high and not that lopsided. If he held it at an angle it looked like a small Christmas tree.

Just the right size for a very small apartment.

His feet crunched in a thin layer of snow when he got off the bus. A white Christmas this year, then. The best kind. Even a thin layer smoothed out the rough edges and made everything look a bit softer and prettier. The bare concrete yard beside the steps down to his front door looked positively festive with the glow of light coming through the gap where the curtain was frayed.

The smell of hot food as he went inside was mouth-watering. Gemma's face when she saw what he was carrying was priceless.

'For me? You shouldn't have…' She was laughing as Andy propped the branch against the end of the couch and swept her into a hug.

'Nothing's too much trouble for the woman I love,' he said. 'I had to put up with several people who didn't want to be close to a prickly pine tree on the bus but I just said, "Merry Christmas to you, too". And I smiled a lot.'

Gemma was smiling now. Right into his eyes. And then she gave him a kiss that was a promise of things to come. 'It's gorgeous,' she told him. 'And I know just what we can use to decorate it.'

They propped the branch up with medical textbooks from their bookshelf. Gemma ripped open the bag of cheesy rings and held one up. 'Perfect, yes?'

'Mmm.' Andy snatched the ring and ate it.

'No-o-o...' Gemma held the bag out of reach. 'Look.' She took a ring out and poked the end of a branch through its centre. The lurid yellow coating of the snack food stood out against the dark green of the pine needles.

By the time the bag was empty their fingers had a thick yellow coating as well but the small tree looked as though it was covered with oddly shaped golden lights. Gemma put her head on one side as she considered the final result. Grinning, she went to fetch something from a grocery bag beside the kitchen bench.

Using a knife, she poked a hole into the bottom of the gold-wrapped chocolate reindeer and then poked the uppermost point of the tree inside. The heavy ornament tipped sideways at a drunken angle but it didn't fall off. Gemma nodded with satisfaction.

'Perfect,' she declared. 'All it needs now is a pile of gifts underneath.' She caught her bottom lip between her teeth, turning to Andy. 'I haven't got a gift for you, babe, I'm sorry.'

'We made a pact, remember? But...I do have a gift for you...kind of.'

Gemma thumped his shoulder. 'How could you? What about the pact? Now I feel *really* awful.'

'I didn't spend any money on it,' Andy said. 'I nicked it from work. And…you might not like it, anyway.'

'Show me.'

Andy felt in the pocket of the coat he'd dropped over the end of the couch when the tree decoration had got properly under way. He held up the slim, rectangular box with some trepidation. It wasn't much of a gift.

'Peace of mind?' he offered softly.

The laughter and lightness was sucked out of the room so fast Andy cursed himself for even having the idea in the first place, but Gemma, her face completely neutral, took the box and disappeared into the tiny bathroom of the apartment.

She didn't come out.

Andy waited for two minutes and then paced back and forth for another three. These tests only took a minute to cook, didn't they? He knocked on the door.

'You OK?'

He got no answer. Unsure whether to burst in on her, Andy leaned his forehead on the door and that was when he heard it.

A stifled sob.

He threw the door open. Gemma was sitting on the toilet lid, staring at the stick she held in one hand. Her other hand was cradling her forehead. She had tears coursing down her face.

Andy dropped to his knees in front of her and reached

to spread his hands and hold as much of Gemma as he could grasp.

'It's OK,' he told her. 'We'll cope.'

But Gemma shook her head, shaking with sobs. Andy waited and finally, she started to force some words out.

'I thought...you know...I thought if the worst happened, it wasn't that big a deal... Lots of people have terminations because...they can't afford a baby...or it's just totally the wrong time in their lives...'

The chill that ran down Andy's spine made it hard to stay silent and keep listening but Gemma wasn't finished yet.

'But then it hit me...you know? This is a *baby*, Andy. *Our* baby...and I just can't...'

'No...of course you can't.' His relief was astonishingly strong. Andy stood up, gathering Gemma in his arms. Holding her tight.

'It's over,' Gemma sobbed against his chest. 'My career. All those dreams...'

'No,' he said fiercely. 'They're not over. I won't let that happen, Gem. We're in this together. We'll make it work.'

'But...*how*?'

'I don't know yet.' Andy took a deep breath, thinking fast. 'We're going to be specialist registrars. We'll have more defined hours. We can juggle shifts and use the hospital day-care facilities. I'll make sure I do half the chores. My parents would help us with a deposit for a bigger apartment. A house, even.'

'But you swore you would never accept financial help from your family. You wanted to make it on your own.'

'This is more important. We all have to compromise sometimes in life. It'll be temporary. Just like how hard it might be for the first year or so of having a baby. It's temporary. You have to look at the bigger picture.'

Gemma seemed calmer now. 'What's that?'

'Us.' Andy pulled back far enough to meet Gemma's gaze. 'I love you,' he said softly. 'I want to be with you for the rest of my life. I want us to have a family together. Maybe we're getting pushed into it a bit faster than would have been ideal but…God, Gemma. I love you *so* much…'

'I love you, too.'

'Marry me.' The words came from nowhere but the moment they left his lips Andy knew they were exactly what he wanted to say. What he wanted to happen, with all his heart. Gemma was staring at him, open-mouthed. 'Please?' he added.

She was still staring. He could almost see the whirl of her thoughts. The fear of how hard it would be now to achieve the career she wanted so much. Trying to process the concept of marriage and family when it had been the last thing she'd wanted. What had she always said? That she'd spent virtually her whole life being a parent to her younger sister and it would be a very long time before she wanted to go there again. But mixed in with the negative, difficult thoughts Andy could also see something glowing. Her trust in him.

Her love.

'I could go down on one knee,' he offered with a crooked smile.

Gemma's lips twitched. 'I think you already did that when I was sitting on the loo.' She bit her lip. 'Oh, my God, Andy. You just proposed to me in the *bathroom*.'

'Easily fixed.' Andy led her back into their small living area. The chocolate reindeer on the top of their joke of a Christmas tree was hanging upside down now.

But it gave Andy inspiration.

'Don't move,' he told Gemma.

It was there somewhere, he knew it was. In a box at the back of the crowded wardrobe in the bedroom. Amongst a collection of old snapshots and Scout badges and odd treasures that marked important milestones in his life. When he found it, he went back to Gemma and held it aloft triumphantly.

'Remember this?'

Gemma smiled but her eyes filled with tears again as she nodded.

Andy kept hold of the piece of plastic mistletoe. He moved his hand so that it was above Gemma's head. And then he kissed her. Maybe he couldn't put how much he loved her into the right words but he could *show* her.

Her eyes were still closed when he finally broke the tender kiss. When she opened them, they were as misty as her smile.

'Yes,' she whispered. 'I'd love to marry you.' Her smile wobbled. 'Laura's coming next week to talk about *her* wedding. She's the one who actually wants to have a baby soon. She's not going to believe this. I don't think I believe it.'

Andy kissed her again. He believed it. He knew it wasn't going to be easy but the confidence that they would make it through and that it was the right thing to do was growing. He just needed to convince Gemma.

'Let's have dinner,' he suggested. 'Don't know about you, but I'm absolutely *starving*.' He rescued the upside-down reindeer and gave it to Gemma. 'Dessert.' He grinned.

She smiled back and that was the moment Andy knew that everything would be all right. They could do this.

Together.

CHAPTER SIX

THE yearning wouldn't go away.

If anything, standing in front of the ward Christmas tree and letting memories from the past out of their locked cage had made it worse.

Andy could feel that moment when he'd proposed to Gemma as if it had just happened. The confidence of his love for her that he'd been so sure would carry them through anything life could throw at them. The excitement at the thought of being a father, which had been so unexpected because he'd known that Gemma would have resisted starting a family for as long as possible. The sheer joy of her acceptance of his proposal… Knowing that he'd won. He'd found the holy grail of winning a partner for life.

Something that huge and that real couldn't have simply faded into nothingness, could it?

Bled to death in the wake of the trauma of Gemma leaving him?

No.

Those few minutes in front of the Christmas tree

had let Andy know without a shadow of a doubt that it was all still there.

On his side, at least.

But what about Gemma? There'd been that moment earlier this evening when he'd thought he could see something that suggested it hadn't changed for her either. Not below the surface.

That look in her eyes when Hazel had dropped the verbal bombshell that Sophie might be going to die.

He hadn't imagined that link. The kind of connection that only came from knowing somebody else almost as well as you knew yourself.

If it had just been the knowledge it would have little more than a shared memory but there had been something much bigger in that shared glance. An expectation of trust, because that was what was being offered.

And somehow, putting those components together had added up to much, much more than he would have expected the total to be. The combination of a shared past and continued trust could only be fused by love.

Yes. If he chose to interpret that moment with an open mind—or rather heart—he might believe that beneath the landslide of rubble they'd piled onto their relationship and tried to bury it with there was still a rock-solid foundation. It was possible that Gemma still loved him.

As much as he still loved her?

Could he go there with some emotional rescue dogs and sniff out some signs of life beneath that rubble?

Did he want to?

Maybe he didn't but maybe he had no choice.

He'd never moved on, had he? He'd tried. God knew, he'd tried so many times but the initial flash of attraction he might have discovered with other women soon flickered out. As much as he desperately wanted to find them, the channels that created the kind of connection he'd had with Gemma didn't seem to exist with anybody else.

Without any conscious decision, Andy found his feet moving him back towards Gemma's room. The route took him past the nurses' station.

'Andy?' Lisa was sitting at the desk beside the phone. She looked up, about to say something, but then frowned. 'You OK?'

Oh...help. Did his disturbed emotional state show on his face that clearly? 'I'm fine,' he said. 'What's up?'

'Two things. You remember Chantelle Simms?'

'Of course. Three-year-old with severe abdominal pain and diarrhoea. No fever, nothing showing on a scan and normal bloods. We discharged her this morning.'

'Yes, well, she's just been brought back into Emergency. Screaming with pain and the mother is beside herself. They're having trouble calming either of them down but when they have, they're going to send her back up.'

Andy was frowning now. 'What on earth did we miss? She seemed absolutely fine when we sent her home this morning. And her mum was so relieved that they didn't have to stay in for Christmas. What was the mum's name again?'

'Deirdre.'

'Hmm.' Something was nagging at the back of Andy's mind. She'd been a young, single mother. So worried about her daughter.

'She's all I have in the world, Dr Baxter. I couldn't bear it if something happened to her.'

There'd been tears. Uncontrolled sobbing, in fact, that had needed a fair bit of reassurance and shoulder patting.

A perfectly normal parental reaction to having a child who was clearly unwell. But…

'The other thing…' Lisa was reaching for a piece of paper. 'Results on the Gillespie baby have come through. Looks like it's not measles or meningitis or anything nasty.'

Andy scanned the results himself. 'Thank goodness for that. I guess the ear infection is definitely the culprit.'

'Her temperature was well down when I checked her vital signs a wee while ago. Will you discharge her?'

Andy glanced at his watch. 'It's after midnight,' he observed. 'It would be a bit rough to send Gemma home with five kids to try and settle again.'

'Mmm.' Lisa's tone was neutral but her gaze was steady. Curious.

'She might want to go, of course.' Andy did his best to keep his own tone just as neutral. 'I'll give her the option.' He turned away, before Lisa could try and read anything more into the situation. 'Give me a call as soon as Chantelle and her mum arrive on the ward.'

* * *

There was a brief period of absolute peace when Gemma had finally settled Sophie back into the bassinette. For a long minute or two she simply stood there in the midst of this little tribe of sleeping children and listened to the sound of their breathing.

Feeling the tension of this extraordinarily difficult night ebbing to a point where it could become quite manageable.

And then there was a soft tap at the door and it opened and there was Andy.

'Hi...' His smile seemed tentative in the half-light and his voice was too quiet to read anything into his tone. 'How's it going?'

Gemma knew her own smile was also tentative but she was struggling here. With an echo of that relief that Andy's presence had brought with it from the moment she'd first seen him again in Queen Mary's waiting room. With the yearning for it to be more than what it could possibly be now. With...*missing* him so much.

It shouldn't be this hard, she told herself in those split seconds of trying to pull herself together enough to give him a coherent response and not just burst into tears and throw herself into his arms or something.

Missing Andy was just a part of life for her now, wasn't it?

In the beginning, she had missed him in the way you might miss a limb that had been torn off in a dreadful accident. An unbearably painful injury and, even though you knew the limb was no longer there, you could *feel* it. And you'd go to do things that required its presence, forgetting for a split second that it was no longer available. And with the realisation of the way things really were now would come a fresh wave of that excruciating pain.

But nobody could live like that for ever and, as trite as it sounded, time was a great healer. Well, a pretty good one, anyway. Protective mechanisms like blocking emails, not picking up those early phone calls and deleting the voice mail before listening had also helped.

And, at some point, it had become the safe and sensible thing to continue to do. Contacting Andy would be to invite news that he'd moved on. That he had found someone who could give him all the things that she hadn't been able to. That might have been the object of the exercise, of course, but Gemma wasn't ready to hear about it.

Maybe she never would be.

Because, while she thought she'd become used to missing Andy, she'd been wrong.

And being this close, where she could see him and hear him and even touch him, but what they'd once had was gone.

And…oh, God…she missed that *so* much and there was no way she could tell him that because he'd moved on with his life. He had a career he clearly loved and he was admired and respected by his colleagues. He might have someone else in his private life. He seemed to have found peace, at least, and he didn't deserve her coming back and damaging the good space he was in.

'It's all good,' she heard herself whispering finally, in response to Andy's query. 'They're all asleep.'

Andy was looking around the room. Slowly. His gaze rested on each child and lingered longest on Sophie. He looked about to speak but then beckoned Gemma. She followed him out of the room.

'Don't want to wake anybody,' Andy said. 'Unless you do?'

Gemma blinked. 'Why would I want to do that?'

'We've got the lab results back. There's no reason to keep Sophie or any of the other children in any kind of quarantine. It's not measles.'

'Thank goodness.'

'And it's certainly not...anything else that's serious.' Andy's hesitation might not have been noticeable to anybody else but it shouted a single word to Gemma.

Her indrawn breath was a gulp. She had to look away. To break that connection that had the potential to open such deep, deep wounds.

'So...' Andy cleared his throat. 'If you wanted, you could take all the children home, but...'

Gemma's gaze flew back to meet his. There was a 'but'? A potential complication for Sophie?

'I thought you might like to let them sleep until morning. It would be a shame to start Christmas Day with overtired and unhappy children, wouldn't it?'

'Would that be OK?'

Andy nodded. 'I have a feeling that both I and my registrar will be far too busy to sign the discharge papers before morning.'

'Oh...' The decision was a no-brainer. 'Thanks, Andy.'

'No problem.' He cleared his throat again and glanced at his watch. 'I'm going to hang around for a bit because there's a re-admission coming up from Emergency soon.' His tone was both confident and casual but the glance he sent Gemma held a question that he seemed unsure of even asking. 'Would you...like a coffee?'

What Gemma really needed was a few hours' sleep so that she would be able to take care of the children in the morning so a stimulant like coffee would not be a good idea.

But that wasn't what Andy was offering, was it?

He was asking if she'd like the chance to talk. To him. Alone? Her heart gave a thump and picked up speed. This was unexpected. She'd had no way of preparing for such a conversation. Did Andy want to know something in particular or did he feel the need to go over old, painful ground? And, if he did, could she bring herself to refuse?

There were things she would like to know herself. Like whether there *was* someone special in his life that his colleagues didn't know about.

Like how he was feeling seeing her again like this. Had he missed her the way she'd missed him? Was he aware of the sheet of seemingly unbreakable glass between them that could move and reshape itself to provide a barrier for even physical touch?

'I'd l—' The word died on Gemma's lips. *Like* wasn't

really an appropriate expectation in accepting this invitation. *Love* even less so. 'Um...yes,' she said quietly instead.

'Come with me.' Andy turned. 'I'll ask Lisa to get one of the nurses to keep an eye on the children. We can make a drink in the kitchen and then take it into my office.'

He'd done it now.

Engineered a situation that could well make everything far harder than it needed to be.

He'd taken Gemma away from the children. Removed himself from any distraction or the chaperonage of colleagues.

He'd brought her into a private space. Not even a neutral space. This was his office. More than a home away from home because the apartment he lived in was merely a space to exist when he was away from work.

This office was his real home because home was where the heart was. It was here that he kept his favourite books and CDs and...oh, yeah...

How could he have forgotten that photo on his desk? The one of he and Gemma in the park that day. Standing in several inches of snow, kissing beneath the frosted branches of an old, weeping elm tree. A photo that had been taken on a day's leave that they had laughingly deemed their honeymoon. When they'd gone to Cambridge to tell his parents that a new generation of the Baxter family was on its way.

Maybe Gemma couldn't see the photograph from

where she was sitting in the leather armchair reserved for visitors. Andy pulled the chair from behind his desk, both to sit without the barrier of furniture between them but also to distract Gemma from spotting the photograph.

He really didn't want her to see it. She'd moved on with her life, having chosen to leave him behind. He didn't want her to know that he hadn't managed to do the same. He didn't want to make himself so vulnerable all over again.

'So...' Andy took a sip of his coffee, watching Gemma over the rim of the mug. 'Here we are, then.'

'Mmm.' Gemma was staring at the liquid in her mug as though trying to decide whether she wanted to drink it or not. Her body language suggested she felt as awkward as Andy suddenly did.

The silence that fell seemed impossible to break but then Gemma raised her chin for just an instant to meet his eyes before she looked down again.

'Sorry,' she said.

Why was she sorry? Because seeing him again was the last thing she had wanted?

Andy felt his breath leave his chest in a sigh. If someone had asked him that morning, he might have said that seeing Gemma was the last thing *he* would want, but, now that it had happened, he knew it would have been a lie. A huge lie.

'I'm not,' he said quietly. 'It's good to see you, Gem.'

Her face lifted sharply, revealing a startled gaze instead of an apologetic one. She hadn't expected him to say that but something was shining through the surprise. Hope?

'You're looking good,' Andy added with a smile.

Gemma gave an incredulous huff. 'Are you kidding? I'm like the walking dead. I've never been as tired as I've been in the last six months. Not even when we were doing a hundred-plus hours a week as junior doctors.'

'Running on adrenaline,' Andy sympathised. 'It catches up with you eventually.'

His gaze held hers for a heartbeat longer. Did she remember the rare occasions that their days off had coincided back then? They'd have such big plans to make the most of the day but, so often, they would end up on the couch, wrapped in each other's arms. Sound asleep. A tangle of limbs like the twins in their shared cot down the corridor.

Andy could actually remember the feel of being that close to Gemma. Hearing the sound of her soft breathing. Feeling the steady thump of her heart. Being aware of the solid security of knowing that he was not, and never would be, alone in the world.

He had to look away but his traitorous glance slid towards that photograph on his desk.

'Yeah...I'm a wreck,' Gemma was saying. 'Haven't been near a hairdresser since I got back. Can't even remember where I left my mascara.'

'You don't need it.' Andy could hear the raw edge in his voice but couldn't stop the words from emerging. 'You never did.'

Another silence fell, just as awkward as the last one.

Andy had to break it this time because he could feel Gemma waiting. Poised, as if she didn't know what direction to jump. He was being given the choice here, but he was nowhere near ready to take the unexpected route that was becoming so visible.

So tempting.

And then Andy saw Gemma's gaze rake his desk and get caught by the photograph. Something like panic pushed him forward. He found a bright, casual tone to use.

'What's it like, living in Sydney?' he asked.

The disappointment was absolutely crushing.

It was the kind of question you might ask a complete stranger. Virtually the complete opposite of the last words he'd spoken—telling her that she didn't need to wear mascara.

Reminding her that he'd always thought she was beautiful, even first thing in the morning or after a solid night on call when she'd had no sleep and had felt like a zombie. And…he had *that* photograph on his desk. A reminder of just how close they had once been there in front of him. Every day. Why?

And why had he said something that had brought them so close again and then pushed her away so abruptly by saying something so impersonal?

He needs time, she reminded herself. We both do. Time to get used to breathing the same air again.

'Sydney's great,' she said. 'Gorgeous city.'

'What part do you live in?'

'I had an apartment close to where I worked at Sydney Harbour Hospital.' Gemma emphasised the past tense. 'Top floor of a block and I had a balcony that looked over the Harbour Bridge and the Opera House. Pretty much like a postcard.'

She couldn't read any expression on Andy's face and Gemma knew he had to work hard to appear that impassive. Especially when she'd never had any trouble reading the tiny changes that could happen around his eyes and mouth. She realised she could still read the impassiveness just as easily. He didn't like what he was hearing.

Sure enough, his voice was tightly controlled when he spoke again.

'And the job? Was that perfect, too?'

There was anger behind those words. Hurt. Fair enough. Gemma closed her eyes for a moment.

'I became a consultant radiologist a year ago. Specialising in MRI and ultrasound.'

'Any particular interests?' Andy sounded genuinely interested now. This was safe ground. A professional discussion rather than personal.

'Image-guided procedures,' Gemma responded.

'Like biopsies?'

'And surgeries. I especially like being involved in spinal and neurological cases.'

Andy looked impressed. 'Sounds fascinating. Full on, I bet.'

'Yes. It was.'

He raised an eyebrow. 'Past tense?'

Gemma shrugged. 'For the foreseeable future. And at the rate the technologies change, I doubt that I'll ever catch up again.'

And it didn't matter, she wanted to add. There *were* more important things in life than a high-powered career. She'd learned that the hard way, being thrown in at the deep end as the only living relative for five young orphans. Andy had known it all along, hadn't he?

But how could she tell him that?

If it hadn't taken her so long to learn, they would probably still be together. As an intact family, even.

No...she couldn't go there.

And...it was too late now, anyway.

Wasn't it?

Andy couldn't interpret the look he was getting from Gemma.

Did she think he wouldn't understand how important her career was to her? He almost snorted aloud. It had always been more important than anything else in her life. Including him. He might not like that about her but he'd always understood.

'You could probably get a job here,' he told her. 'There's always a shortage of specialist skills like you have. Part time,' he added, seeing her incredulous expression. 'When you've got childcare organised.'

Gemma was still staring at him. She looked totally lost for words.

'Is...um...money a problem?' How sad that he felt

so uncomfortable asking such a personal question but, if that was what was holding her back, he could help.

Gemma shook her head. 'Not at all. Both Laura and Evan had good life insurance cover. The house is safe and the children will always be well provided for. Financially, I probably never need to work again.'

'But you want to.'

Gemma looked away. 'It's not an option right now. I'm not even thinking about it.'

Really? She'd become the thing she'd sworn she never would be. A full-time stay-at-home mother. And she was OK with that?

The idea was confusing enough to make Andy head for safe territory.

'Is the house the same one? The barn conversion?'

'Yes. Evan made such a fabulous job of it. It's an amazing family home.'

'I remember. He sourced those old beams and stained-glass windows. I helped him shift all those stone slabs for doing the kitchen floor.' Andy smiled ruefully. 'Don't think my back has ever been quite the same.'

'They did heaps more while I've been away, too. Added on a new wing after the twins came along. And Laura somehow found time to create a huge garden. You could just about stock a supermarket from the vegetable patch and orchard.'

'There was a lot of land to play with, that's for sure.'

'A lot of it is in paddocks. There's a few pet sheep and Hazel's got a pony. Lots of hens, too. Laura sold eggs to the neighbours.'

'Sounds...idyllic.'

Andy could have kicked himself as the word came out. The situation was so far from idyllic...for everybody involved. The children had lost their parents. Gemma had lost her sister and brother-in-law and she'd had to leave the career she loved so much. And maybe she'd had to leave more than her career behind in Sydney. The man he'd heard berating her in the reception area had clearly been expecting to go on a date with Gemma but did that necessarily mean she hadn't left someone special behind in Australia?

'Sorry,' he muttered. 'I didn't mean that to sound...I don't know...flippant.'

'It's OK. It *is* idyllic. It was Laura's dream home and lifestyle and I intend to keep it alive for her children, no matter what.'

'Family,' Andy murmured. 'That's what it's all about, isn't it?'

'Yes.'

He could see Gemma swallow hard and take a deep breath. Open her mouth to say something that was obviously difficult.

'What about you, Andy? Are you...? I mean, is there someone...um... Have you got...?'

What? A substitute for the family he could have had with her? Andy waited for her to finish the question, his heart sinking. He didn't want to talk about himself. There was nothing to tell Gemma but too much he wanted to say.

And maybe he could talk to her now. Really talk.

They were closed off from the world here and he could feel the strangeness of being alone with Gemma again wearing off. Every time his eyes met hers, he could feel barriers cracking. Chunks of them falling away, even. Could he tell her the truth? And, if he did, where would that lead them?

But neither of them got the chance to say anything else. A knock on the door heralded the appearance of a nurse.

'Lisa said to tell you that Chantelle's arrived on the ward. Her mother's refusing to let your registrar admit her. She wants you.' From somewhere down the corridor came the faint wail of a frightened child.

'I'll be right there.' Andy pushed himself to his feet. The spell was broken and the outside world had intruded, and maybe that was for the best. He left his coffee where it was on the desk. He'd only taken that one sip and it would be stone cold by the time he got back.

Gemma hadn't drunk hers either.

'Stay here and finish your coffee if you like,' he told her. 'I'll come back and…maybe we could talk some more.'

Gemma gave him another one of those surprised looks. 'If you want to,' she said. Her unfinished question was still hanging in the air.

'I do,' Andy said quietly.

But Gemma didn't seem to be listening to him any more. The silent question on her face was directed at the nurse.

'It's not one of yours crying, don't worry,' the nurse reassured her.

But Gemma was on her feet now and Andy could feel the tension in her body. She was clearly still listening to the baby cry and needed to make sure it wasn't one of her own.

She was scared, Andy realised. Terrified that something horrible was going to happen to one of those precious kids.

Of course she was.

He had to reach out and touch her. To offer his own reassurance. To let her know that he understood.

Really understood.

And when Gemma tilted her chin and met his gaze, he could see that his message was being received with all the nuances that came from their past.

Just like him, she was listening to that cry and thinking about Max.

CHAPTER SEVEN

Christmas: six years ago

'CALL for you, Gemma. Outside line.'

'Thank you.' Gemma dumped the armload of patient notes she was carrying on the desk and reached for the phone. 'Hi hon, how's it going?'

There was surprised laughter on the line. 'How did you know it was me?'

Gemma groaned. 'I didn't. And I didn't think it *was* you, Laura. I thought it was Andy. He was going to call and let me know how Max is.'

'Is he sick?'

'Bit sniffly and grumpy this morning. Probably just a cold coming on but he had me up a few times in the night.'

'Oh, no…poor you. That's all you need when you've got to get up and go to work.'

'Worse for Andy if he's been unsettled all day. There's no guarantee he'll get any sleep on night shift.'

'Poor him, too. Can't believe he has to do a night shift on Christmas Eve.'

'We figured it's a small price to pay for having been able to juggle our rosters so well. Things will get easier in the new year once Max starts day care for more than one day a week.'

'And you've definitely got tomorrow off? You're not going to get called in at the last minute or something?'

'No way. Not when we're going to see your new kitchen in action for the first time. That Aga is going to cook the perfect turkey or there'll be some serious questions being asked.'

Laura laughed. 'Fingers crossed. I'm doing my best. Oh…I can't wait, Gem. Max and Hazel are old enough to know what's going on now. They'll be able to *play* together. It's going to be a real, family Christmas. Dream-come-true stuff…'

'You're not going to start crying on me, are you?'

The sniff was noisy enough to make Gemma wince. 'No-o-o… I'm just…so happy.'

'I will be, too, as soon as I get away from here. I've got a full ward round to get done first, though, so I'll have to go.'

'OK…but…'

'But?' There was an urgency in Laura's tone that made Gemma pause. 'What's wrong?'

'I'm not supposed to tell you yet but…I'm going to *burst* if I don't.'

'Don't do that. It would be messy and I have no idea how to cook turkeys.' Gemma heard another sniff. And then a very happy sigh. Where had she heard that before?

'Oh, my God, Laura…are you *pregnant* again?'

'I think I might be. I *hope* so.'

'Fingers crossed, then.' Gemma closed her eyes as she shook her head. 'Rather you than me.'

'Maybe it'll be a boy this time. So Max won't have to play with girls all his life.'

'Good thinking.'

'You could always have another one…' Laura suggested breathlessly. 'Remember how fun it was when we both had babies at the same time?'

'Fun? Are you kidding? It was a logistical nightmare. One that's only just starting to get manageable. No…' Gemma glanced at her watch. 'I've got to go, Laura. I'll see you in the morning.'

'Are you mad at me?'

'No, of course not. I'm delighted for you. I'm delighted that you're going to provide a whole bunch of cousins for Max so I won't have to feel guilty about him being an only child. But I *have* to go. Now. Love you. 'Bye.'

Gemma eyed the phone after she'd hung up on Laura. She got as far as dialling the outside line, intending to call Andy and see how things were going at home. But what if he'd just got Max down for his nap and was finally grabbing the hour or two's sleep he must desperately need? Gemma put the phone down again. With a resigned sigh she picked up the big stack of patient notes and headed out into the ward.

There were fourteen patients to check on. Some would need physical examinations and some would need results chased up and possibly further investigations ordered. She might even have to call the consultant in if there was anything she was really concerned about. All these patients and probably a few family members would need a chance to talk to their doctor. If she was really, really lucky, she would be able to get through it all in four hours or so.

And then she could go home to the two men in her life and start Christmas.

How good was that going to be?

There were no flowers allowed in the respiratory ward Gemma was working in at the moment so the staff had made up for a year's worth of lacking colour by going to town with non-allergenic Christmas decorations. Tinsel and banners and multicoloured baubles were tied to every handle, strung across doorways and decorated bed ends and trolleys. With a smile, Gemma broke off a piece of bright green tinsel and tied it around the short ponytail taming her hair.

Then she went to collect her junior houseman and a nurse from the staff kitchen. If Andy called she would interrupt the round for a couple of minutes. If he didn't, that meant everything was fine and she'd wait until she got home to catch up.

Gemma and Andy were still living in a basement flat but this one had two bedrooms, a bigger living area and even two chairs and a microscopic patch of grass outside. It also cost nearly twice as much as their first flat had but, with them both working full time finally, it was getting much easier to manage the finances. They were at last saving for a deposit on a house of their own and the plan was for them to have moved by next Christmas.

It was nearly six p.m. by the time Gemma arrived home. Andy was due to start his night shift at nine p.m. so they would have a good couple of hours together before he had to head off.

'Hi, honey…I'm home,' she called as she closed the front door behind her. It was a standing joke but, in the silence that followed her greeting, Gemma bit her lip. It didn't always produce a smile. Maybe Andy had had a rough day, in which case the sing-song announcement of her arrival to take over the parenting duties could be met with some built-up resentment. It was something she'd had to work on herself in those early days when she'd had the lion's share of caring for Max.

The tiny hallway of the flat was no more than a place to hang coats and keys. It finished with a bathroom at the end. A door to the left led to the main bedroom. The second bedroom opened off that and would probably get turned into a walk-in wardrobe by a future owner. A door to the right led to the open-plan living room and kitchen with the door that opened to the tiny, below street level courtyard.

At this time of the evening Max would be due for his bath but the door to the bathroom was closed so that obviously wasn't happening. Gemma could feel a knot of tension in her stomach now. Playing with Max in the bath was such a treat it was the reward for anything not so good that had happened during the day.

The time afterwards, with Max in his fluffy pyjamas, smelling sweetly of baby powder and ready for cuddles and bedtime, was the best of family time. It was when they both knew that the struggle was worth it. That the bond they all had was precious.

Maybe Andy was still feeding Max his dinner but it was too quiet for that to be happening. Max loved his food. He was always messy and noisy, especially when he had his favourite wooden spoon to bang on the tray of his high chair.

And why hadn't the lights been turned on? It was pitch black outside now. And freezing. But the shiver that ran through Gemma as she flung her coat onto a hook didn't feel like it was caused by the cold. The door to the living room was slightly ajar so it made no sound as Gemma pushed it open.

There was a source of light after all. The twinkling lights on the Christmas tree shone green and red and blue in turn. A real Christmas tree this year, albeit an artificial one. Yesterday they had taken far too many photographs of Max sitting beneath it wearing a Santa hat and looking impossibly cute amongst the brightly wrapped parcels.

It took less than the time to draw a breath to see what was going on. Andy was sound asleep on the couch, one arm trailing to leave an upturned palm on the rug, the fingers curled gently. Right beside that hand was the baby monitor so that he would hear the moment Max woke up from his nap.

Gemma's heart sank. Andy must have been desperate to let Max have such a late nap and it meant that she would be lucky to get him back to bed this side of midnight after he'd had his dinner and bath. She couldn't berate Andy for it, though. They did what they had to do as far as coping with parenting and they had a pact to support each other a hundred per cent.

Gemma flicked on a lamp and then the kitchen light. She filled the jug and plugged it in. Andy was going to need a bucket of coffee before setting off to work.

Neither the light nor the sound of her moving around woke Andy up so Gemma went and knelt beside the couch, intending to wake him with a kiss on his cheek.

She simply knelt there for a long moment, however. Andy looked *so* tired. He hadn't shaved today and his jaw was dark enough to make the rest of face look pale. Even in sleep, she could see the weary furrows etched into his forehead and around his eyes and Gemma felt guilty. If she hadn't been so hell-bent on keeping her career on track, she could have made life so much easier for both of them for this early stage of family life but no...she'd worked until she'd been eight and a half months pregnant and then she'd gone back to work when Max had been only six weeks old.

And Andy had kept his promise of making parenthood an equally shared venture. Done more than his share quite often, in fact, and had never argued over some of the big issues, like stopping breastfeeding so they could share night feeds and remove a looming hassle from her return to work.

Yep. He was a hero, all right. Gemma lifted her hand

and gently brushed a lock of unruly hair back from Andy's forehead. The sudden rush of tenderness almost brought tears to her eyes. While having a baby and now a boisterous toddler in their lives had covered a lot of the romance with things like dirty nappies and broken sleep, the underlying love they had for each other had become stronger because of it. Right then, Gemma vowed to try and make life just a bit easier for Andy. Or, at least, to show him, more often, how much she cared about him.

The touch of her hand had been enough to jump-start Andy's journey to consciousness. With his eyes still firmly closed, his lips curled in a smile and his hand came up from the floor to catch Gemma's. He pulled her closer, turning his head and she willingly bent down to kiss his lips.

'Mmm…you're home early…' he murmured.

'Hardly. It's half past six.'

Andy's eyes shot open. *'What?'*

Gemma froze at his horrified tone. 'How long have you been asleep?'

'I put Max down for his nap after lunch.' Andy was pulling himself into a sitting position. With a groan he covered his face with his hands and massaged his forehead. 'It would have been about one o'clock.'

He'd been asleep for five and half hours? Gemma still felt frozen. Oh…God…she was too scared to go and check. Memories of Max as a tiny baby, so soundly asleep that you couldn't see whether he was breathing or not, came back to haunt her. But sixteen months was way too late to be worrying about cot death, wasn't it?

As if to reassure her, there was a crackle from the baby monitor. A snuffling sound and then a grunt. Gemma was half way to being on her feet when a new sound was transmitted.

It was a child's cry but it was not a sound she had ever heard Max making before. Or any child, for that matter. It was a weird, high-pitched keening that made her blood run cold.

Andy was on his feet now as well. Gemma saw the Adam's apple in his throat move as he swallowed hard. His face went white.

With a muttered oath he overtook Gemma as they both rushed into their son's bedroom.

This was a nightmare.

He was supposed to be in the emergency department of the Queen Mary Infirmary as a senior registrar on night duty, not as the parent of a seriously sick child.

Somebody's cellphone was ringing with the tune of 'Jingle Bells'. A young female member of the domestic staff went past with a mop and bucket and a headband sporting reindeer antlers with flashing lights on the top. The nurse doing triage was wearing a Santa hat identical to the one they'd been taking photos of Max wearing last night.

How could anyone be thinking of Christmas right now?

It had ceased to be of any relevance whatsoever from

the moment they had turned the light on in Max's bedroom and seen his flushed, feverish-looking face. The fontanelle on the top of his head had been bulging and tense but what had terrified both Andy and Gemma most had been finding the rash on his abdomen and chest. Just a few spots but they had been bright red and refused to blanch with pressure.

There had been no time to wait for an ambulance and neither of them had seemed to notice that they were breaking the law by having Max wrapped in a blanket in Gemma's arms instead of being in his car seat as they'd rushed him to hospital.

Arriving here—to the expertise and technology geared to save lives should have been a comfort but it only marked the real beginning of the nightmare. Gemma had tears streaming down her face as she helped two nurses hold Max as still as possible, curled up on his side so that the senior ED consultant could perform a lumbar puncture. It was an agonisingly slow wait for the drops of clear fluid to be collected into several different tubes.

Finally, it was over, and Gemma was allowed to pick Max up and cuddle him for a minute.

'We'll get IV access and start the antibiotics now,' the consultant said. 'I'll get a bed organised in the PICU.' He picked up a chart. 'Run through it again for me. He was symptom-free yesterday?'

Gemma rocked Max, who was looking drowsy now. 'He had an unsettled night but he wasn't running a temperature. I thought he might be getting a new tooth or something.'

'And this morning?'

'He was just a bit...irritable. A slight sniffle, that's all. Like the very start of a head cold.'

'He was rubbing his ear at lunchtime,' Andy added. 'He's had ear infections before so I assumed that's what it was. I gave him some paracetamol and he settled for a nap without a fuss.'

'And he slept for five and a half hours.' The consultant's tone held a grim edge. 'How long does he normally nap?'

'An hour. An hour and a half if we're lucky.' It was Gemma who answered. Andy could feel her gaze on him. He swallowed hard.

'I fell asleep as well,' he admitted. 'I have to, when I'm working nights and looking after Max during the day. I didn't think to set an alarm because...'

Because he'd never needed to. He'd had the monitor right beside him and he knew he'd wake at the first squeak. Maybe Max had made a sound at some stage but he'd slipped into such a deep sleep by then it had simply become part of a dream. This was his fault. He should have spotted the signs. Had Max in here with some powerful antibiotics running through his veins hours ago.

Because every minute counted in the war against bacterial meningitis.

'When did he last pass any urine?'

'I changed his nappy before lunch.'

'It's still dry now,' Gemma added quietly.

The consultant had finished scribbling his notes. He turned to his registrar, who was still filling in the forms for the CSF and blood samples collected. 'Make sure you've covered microscopy, culture, protein and glucose analysis. And put a rush on getting the results.'

'Will do.'

'Go up to PICU with the Baxters. I'll come up as soon as I've got a minute. Make sure that plasma and urine electrolytes are carefully monitored and fluids restricted until we see some signs of recovery.'

Recovery.

That was the magic word.

The only gift that mattered this Christmas. Gemma had heard the word as well. Huge eyes in a pale face searched out and locked on his. Andy took a step closer and put his arm around both Gemma and Max. He might be powerless in protecting his family from what was happening but at least he could hold them close.

'We'll start a standard combination antibiotic regime immediately,' the consultant was telling them both. 'And then we'll transfer you upstairs.' He paused and Andy knew that this was the moment to offer a family reassurance if there was any to be had.

'We'd better start both of you on prophylactic antibiotics as well.' The consultant's voice was sympathetic. 'I'm really sorry, but this looks like a clear case of meningococcal disease.'

Recovery was looking further away instead of closer

as the hours ticked past and Christmas Eve became Christmas Day.

'He's in septic shock,' the PICU consultant told them. 'We're going to intubate and get him onto a ventilator.'

The rash was rapidly evolving. Instead of the tiny red pinpricks on Max's chest and abdomen, he now had a rash over his entire body. And it wasn't just little spots. They seemed to be joining together in places to make ugly, dark stains on his skin that looked like inkblots.

He wasn't just put on the ventilator. Their precious little boy had to have a nasogastric tube placed. And a urinary catheter. A larger-bore IV line was inserted as well so that therapy to control his blood pressure and electrolyte abnormalities could be administered.

'Order some fresh frozen plasma, too,' the consultant told his registrar. 'It's highly likely we've got coagulation issues happening.'

For any parents this was terrifying. For Gemma and Andy, who could understand all the terminology and the reasons that particular tests were being ordered or procedures were being done, it was even worse. They knew exactly how dangerous an illness this was. They knew what needed to be done and could have done it themselve...on someone else's child.

But this was their son. Their only child. And even if there hadn't been rules about treating close relatives yourselves, the emotional involvement rendered them incapable of being relied on for objective analysis or the ability to perform invasive procedures.

For a short time, after the initial rush to get ventilation started and new drugs including narcotic pain relief on board, there was a lull in the number of people hovering over Max and disturbing his body with different procedures or tests.

Andy and Gemma could sit beside the bed, holding each other's hands tightly. Almost too scared to breathe.

For a long time neither of them spoke. It was Andy who broke the silence.

'I'm sorry, Gem.'

'What for?'

'I fell asleep. I should have spotted this so much earlier.'

The extra squeeze on his hand was comforting. 'You can't blame yourself. You were exhausted. You have to nap when Maxie's asleep. If he didn't wake up, then of course you wouldn't have either.'

'I know, but—'

'If we're going to go down the "Who can we blame?" track, what about me? I knew he was sniffly this morning and I still went off to work. I'm the mother who wouldn't stay at home full time, which was why you were exhausted in the first place. It's my fault as much as yours.'

'It's nobody's fault,' Andy had to admit. 'It's...' His throat was closing. Clogging with tears that were too deep to come out. 'It's bloody awful, that's what.'

'He can fight this. I remember a case when I was doing Paeds. A nine-month-old girl who had it as badly as this. Full septic shock and organ failure and she was on ventilation for ten days. She ended up having to have surgical debridement of the skin on her fingers and toes but she survived. Nothing got...got amputated...'

Gemma's voice disintegrated into a choked sob and she lowered her head and began sobbing silently, her pain and fear almost palpable things. Andy put his arm around her shoulders and drew her close enough for her head to rest on his chest. The position they still slept in by choice. He rubbed her back gently in big circles.

A nurse came close. 'Your sister's here,' she said. 'Laura Gillespie? I've put her in the relatives' room. Do you want to go and see her?'

Andy's hold on Gemma tightened. They couldn't leave Max by himself even if he was unconscious. He didn't want Gemma out of reach either. He had to hold them all close together. As a family.

But Laura was family, too. A combination of both sister and child to Gemma after she'd practically raised her. She was also the mother of Max's best friend and cousin, Hazel. They couldn't shut her out.

'Bring her in,' he suggested. 'And...she and her family had better start the prophylactic antibiotics, too. They've spent time with us over the last few days.'

They were supposed to be spending the day together tomorrow. Celebrating Christmas.

Laura came in, wearing a gown and mask. She stopped abruptly when she got close to the bed and uttered a soft cry of horror.

It had the effect of showing both Andy and Gemma the scene through fresh eyes.

Max's tiny, naked body lay on the top of the bed,

criss-crossed by the wires connecting electrodes to
the monitoring equipment. Numerous IV ports were
splashes of colour amongst the clear tubing and white
tape. He had tubes in his nose and his mouth and a
blood-pressure cuff, which looked far too big, covering an upper arm.

The most shocking thing, however, was the discol-
ouration of his skin. The mottling of the dreadful rash
as it spread and intensified.

Laura couldn't cope. Her voice was anguished as she
excused herself only minutes later.

'I'll be right outside. Come and get me if...'

Andy nodded. He would go and get her if there was
something she could do to help. Or if things got any
worse.

Things did get worse within the next couple of hours
despite treatment that was as aggressive as this awful
disease. Constant monitoring and adjustments to the
drug regime were made but Max's blood pressure continued to drop. His renal function declined and it became harder to keep oxygen saturation levels up to an
acceptable range.

Worst of all, his little feet and hands were showing
marked changes in their colour. The inkblots expanded
and darkened until the skin looked almost black. The
medical team fought a valiant battle but somewhere just
before dawn they knew they had lost. The tubes and
wires were taken off and the parents were left alone with
their child for the final minutes of his life.

The first stages of grief were a curious phenomenon for Gemma. It was Andy who cried first—great racking sobs of unbearable pain—but she felt completely numb. As though she was sleepwalking through a nightmare that would have to end at some point but not yet.

She held her son as he took his last breath and she had Andy holding them both. It was almost a rerun of the night they'd first met and yet it couldn't have been more different. They hadn't even known each other then and now they had a bond that was so strong it seemed as if nothing could ever break it.

Even this?

Andy didn't seem to think so. When they finally had to leave Max behind, he put his arms around Gemma and held her so tightly she couldn't breathe.

'We'll get through this,' he promised, in a broken whisper. 'Somehow, we're going to get through this together.'

Laura had been distraught. They'd had to call Evan and tell him to come and get her in his work van because there was no way she could drive herself home. She had wanted Gemma and Andy to come with her but couldn't persuade them.

'We need time together,' Gemma told her sister. 'In our own home.'

Only maybe that hadn't been the best idea because walking into the house and feeling how empty it was without Max destroyed Andy all over again and he sat on the couch, his head in his hands, sobbing.

Still Gemma couldn't cry. She knew it would come

and when it did she would fall into a pit of grief that would be terrifying in its depth but she was still in that protective, trance-like state.

She walked around the apartment, touching things. The floppy-eared rabbit toy that had been such a favourite. Why hadn't they remembered to take that to the hospital with them? The presents were still under the tree. They were all for Max. What should she do with them now? Brushing loose strands of hair back from her face, she felt the length of that stupid green tinsel still tied to her ponytail. She pulled it free and let it drift to the floor.

The kitchen was a mess. Dishes from lunch sat in the sink and the tray of the highchair was covered with what looked like dried-up custard. There were things all over the table, too. Paper and scissors and glue.

Andy had been making a card. He'd printed out one of the photos of Max they'd taken yesterday and had made a Christmas card. Inside, in wobbly writing that was supposed to look like a toddler had written it were the words:

Merry Christmas. I love you Mummy. From Max.

There was something else on the table beside the card. Without thinking, Gemma picked it up and carried it through to the living room. And it was then that the words on the home-made card sank in.

The moment the wall of grief hit her.

Andy was on his feet in an instant. Holding her in his arms. Sinking with her to the floor as they started to face the unthinkable.

It was a long, long time later that Andy noticed Gemma's clenched fist.

'What have you got?'

Gemma uncurled her fingers. She was holding a shared memento that somehow managed to never get lost and to make an appearance every Christmas.

The sad little piece of plastic mistletoe that she'd found in the lift the first night they'd met. The one Andy had held above her head after he'd proposed to her when she'd found out she was pregnant.

There would be no kiss this year. Instead, they simply clung to each other and cried.

CHAPTER EIGHT

THE reassurance that it hadn't been one of 'her' children crying hadn't been enough.

Gemma abandoned her own cup of coffee and went back to their room to find that they were, indeed, all fast asleep.

What was it about sleeping children that tugged so hard at the heartstrings? Maybe it was that perfect skin and a baby's cupid bow of a mouth that took years to change shape. The spread-eagled position that advertised utter relaxation. Or was it the innocence of such young faces that had yet to face the harsh realities of the world?

Except that these children had already faced too much. Sophie knew nothing about it, of course, and even the twins were young enough to have accepted the massive change in their lives but Jamie, and especially Hazel, would always be aware of that sad gap left by having their own parents torn away. And, while Gemma was doing her best to fill the gap, she could never replace a father completely.

Standing there in the semi-darkness, letting her

gaze travel from one child to the next and back again, Gemma was overwhelmed by how protective she felt. How much she loved these children. And by the joy of remembering the cuddles and kisses she had received as she'd settled them down tonight. The words the children had said.

I love Aunty Gemma. She's a good mummy.

You're nice, Aunty Gemma. I love you, too.

It's OK. Aunty Gemma's looking after you. She's looking after all of us.

She was. She always would. Always. Oh…help. She had tears running down her cheeks again. Just as well she had lost her mascara but she must still look a mess. With a sniff and a quick scrub at her cheeks Gemma started moving again. Not into the children's room but down towards the bathroom so that she could wash her face and try and make herself look a bit more respectable.

Because it wasn't just the nurse's reassurance about the children that hadn't been enough. The conversation with Andy felt like it had only just begun. That it had been interrupted at a crucial moment even. Andy had invited her to stay and finish her coffee. He'd said he'd come back and that he wanted to talk some more.

Gemma wanted that, too. *So* much.

Despite it being in the early hours of the morning, Gemma found she wasn't alone in the bathroom. While she was splashing her face with some cold water at the basin, a toilet flushed and then the door banged as a young woman came out in a hurry.

'Oh, God, I needed that!' she exclaimed, heading for the basin beside Gemma. 'I've been hanging on for *hours*.'

Gemma glanced sideways as she reached for some paper towels. The woman looked barely more than a teenager. She was wearing leggings and layers of clothing on her upper body but she was painfully thin. She had dark hair that reached her waist and an abundance of silver jewellery that rattled as she moved her hands and dug in an oversized shoulder-bag.

'Rough night, huh?' she said sympathetically.

'Oh, man…you've got no idea.' The girl didn't look at Gemma. She had pulled a mascara wand from the bag that was balanced precariously on the edge of the basin. She leaned forward to peer at herself in the mirror. 'How awful is it to have to come into a *hospital* on Christmas Eve? We'll be in here for Christmas *Day*.'

The words struck an odd note because attending to her eyelashes seemed to be the most important thing on this girl's mind. Gemma took another glance at her own blotchy face, dismissed the reflection and screwed up the paper towels to drop them into the bin.

'They make it special,' she told the girl. 'Everybody knows how tough it is on kids to be in here for Christmas. And on their parents,' she added kindly. 'In fact, it's probably tougher on you than it is on your baby.'

It would have to be a baby she was in with, wouldn't it? She was so young.

'Tell me about it.' The girl was fishing in her bag

again. This time it was for lip gloss. 'We've got the loveliest doctor, though. How 'bout you?'

Did she mean Andy? Was this the mother of his latest admission? And she was in here, trying to make herself look as attractive as possible?

Was that why *she* was beginning to feel judgmental? That there was something about this young woman she really didn't like?

'We're doing fine,' she said coolly, already moving away. 'We'll be going home tomorrow.'

'Lucky you. We'll probably be here for ages. Oh... damn...' A careless nudge as she leaned closer to the mirror had dislodged the bag and sent it flying to the floor. A heap of objects escaped to scatter themselves on the floor.

A small bottle rolled rapidly enough to knock Gemma's foot. She bent down and picked it up to hand it back but all those years of medical training made her glance automatically at the label as she did so.

A well-known brand of laxatives. Well...that might go some way to explaining why this girl was so thin. The bottle was snatched out of her hand with a haste that suggested Gemma was correct in thinking the medication might be being abused.

'Gotta run,' the girl said. 'Catch ya later.'

There wasn't much Andy could do for the three-year-old girl who'd been readmitted tonight, of all nights. The morphine she'd been given for the severe abdominal pain had worked its magic and the child was now comfortably asleep. A new raft of investigations would need to be ordered but that was a task for the morning and most of those tests would have to wait in any case. Only absolute emergencies could be dealt with on Christmas Day.

With some relief, Andy headed back to his office. Would Gemma still be there?

He hoped so.

Or did he? He'd been on the point of confessing how empty his life was without her. Feeling closer to her with every passing minute.

Would the barriers be back in place by now?

Gemma wasn't sitting in the armchair. She was standing beside his desk, staring at that photograph. She jumped when she heard him approach and when her gaze met his, she looked…guilty.

What for?

Nosing around in personal things or because the photograph reminded her of what they'd once had? What she'd thrown away?

Andy's breath came out in a sigh. Yes…the barriers were there again.

'How's it going?' he asked. 'That coffee was probably undrinkable.'

'I forgot about it. I went to check on the children.'

'They OK?'

'Sound asleep.'

'That's good. They'll be fine in the morning and ready to enjoy their Christmas Day.'

'I hope so.' Gemma was biting her bottom lip, a sure

sign that she wasn't feeling comfortable. 'How's your patient?'

'Also asleep.' Andy shook his head. 'I have to confess I have no idea what's going on there. We've done a raft of tests, including a CT, and everything's normal. Her mother's convinced she's got appendicitis. Wanted me to call in a surgeon immediately. She said she had her appendix out a couple of years ago and she reckons Chantelle's got exactly the same symptoms. Plus, she looked it up on the internet.'

'Oh...' Gemma's lips had an amused curve to them. 'Can't argue with the internet, can you?'

Andy smiled. 'Not easily, no.'

Gemma was watching him. The guilty expression had long since vanished. Right now she was looking as if she was concentrating hard on something.

'Chantelle's mother,' she said. 'Does she look about nineteen, long dark hair and a ton of jewellery?'

'That's her. Why?'

'I met her in the bathroom.'

Andy nodded. 'Yeah...she dashed off to the loo when I was examining Chantelle.'

'Does she...I mean...does something strike you as being a bit off key with her?'

Andy frowned. 'She's very young. Needs more reassurance than Chantelle, that's for sure.'

'Hmm.'

The sound that Gemma made took Andy back through the years. Right back to when they had both been junior doctors, in fact, and had spent hours discussing their cases and bouncing ideas around. Sparking off each other like that had been something they'd both loved. It had invariably pushed them both to think harder and perform better. And he recognised that sound. Gemma had thought of something he probably hadn't. The old response came automatically to his lips.

'OK, Einstein. Spill.'

Gemma's lips twitched but then her face became serious. 'Has Munchausen's by proxy occurred to you?'

Andy blinked. 'No. Should it?'

'Difficulty coming up with any kind of definitive diagnosis? A caregiver who's had the same symptoms as the child within the previous five years?'

'Mmm. It's not a conclusion I'd be happy jumping to.' He stared at Gemma, narrowing his eyes. 'You sound a bit too sure of yourself. Did Deidre say something in the bathroom?'

'No. It was more what she wasn't saying.'

'What do you mean?'

'She was busy fixing her make-up. Saying how awful it was to be stuck in hospital. Only she didn't sound that cut up about it, you know? And she didn't even mention her baby. And...'

'And?'

'And it might be nothing but she knocked her bag over and I picked up a bottle of pills. Laxatives.'

Andy could almost hear the penny dropping. 'Oh, hell,' he groaned. 'That would do it. Diarrhoea. Violent abdominal cramps. Normal test results.' He ran his hands through his hair, wondering how he was going to deal with this.

'Have you got access to Chantelle's previous health records?'

'Not yet. She only came in the first time a couple of days ago and they've moved recently from up north. We've requested information but…well, it is Christmas. Silly season.'

'Might be worth having a chat to someone. Maybe looking at the mother's records, too. It's another sign, isn't it? Moving around and going to new hospitals or doctors.'

Andy nodded. 'No time like the present. If I get any red flags, I could at least talk to Deirdre about it. Get those laxatives off her before she makes the poor kid suffer any more, if that is what's happening.'

He caught Gemma's gaze. They were both confident they were on the right track. They both knew that if they *were* right, mother and child would need a lot of help and it would be far better to step in now before any real harm was done.

'I'll come and find you,' Andy said. 'And let you know what they say.'

It was over an hour later when Andy eased open the door of the children's room. Gemma had been dozing in the armchair but came awake instantly when she'd sensed the movement.

The only light came from the nightlights plugged in

low to the floor in both the room and the corridor outside, but Gemma could see how tense Andy was.

Or maybe it was more that she could sense it. The same way she'd picked up the silent opening of the door when she'd been more than half-asleep.

Gemma uncurled her legs and got to her feet. As she got closer to Andy she could see how still he was holding himself. How wary the expression in his eyes was. He wasn't at all sure he wanted to be here, was he? The tension felt like nervousness. Borderline fear, even?

It was instantly contagious. They'd always been able to connect effortlessly. To gauge and respond to each other on both intellectual and emotional levels.

Andy was here because something had changed. He wanted—or needed—time with *her*. A heartbeat later, his words confirmed the impression.

'I need some fresh air,' Andy muttered quietly. 'Want to come with me?'

Did she?

Gemma could feel her heart rate accelerating. Her mouth felt dry. A short time ago, in his office, she had sensed them getting closer and had been so disappointed when Andy had pushed her away with the impersonal questions about her life in Sydney.

The opposite was happening here.

And that was making Gemma feel very, very nervous.

It was Christmas Eve, for heaven's sake. A time of year that bound them together with memories that were very painful. It could be the worst time to try and reconnect on a deeper level.

Or...it might be the only time when emotions could be strong enough to break down barriers.

Andy was holding out his hand and suddenly Gemma had her answer.

Of course she wanted to go with him. She *had* to.

No words were needed on her part. Gemma simply put her hand in Andy's.

He led them at a fast pace along the corridor, out of the ward and up a stairwell.

'Don't worry. I've told Lisa to page me if any of the children wake up.'

Up and up the stairs they went until they came to a heavy metal fire door. Gemma knew exactly where they were going. It was the place they'd often headed for as young doctors, when the only time they'd seemed to get alone together had been moments they'd been able to escape from work and come here.

On to the roof of Queen Mary Infirmary.

The air was fresh all right.

Freezing, in fact, but Gemma wasn't about to complain. It wasn't bothering her yet because she was so aware of the warmth of Andy's hand.

He was still holding it. Up all those stairs and even when he'd pushed open the heavy door to the roof space. Now, as the blast of icy air hit, he increased the pressure of his grip.

'Can you stand it?'

Gemma could only nod. Oh...yes...

'It's pretty cold,' Andy added as he led them on a route that had once been so well trodden. Round the back of the structure that held the workings of the nearest set of lifts. Into a sheltered corner well away from the heli-pad. A private place that had a great view over the city of Manchester. The blinking light of a plane coming in to land could be seen beneath the heavy, low-slung clouds.

'Santa's sleigh, you reckon?' Gemma smiled but couldn't repress a small shiver.

Andy didn't smile at her weak joke. 'I just need a minute,' he apologised. 'Head-clearing stuff. The cold is…cleansing or something, I guess.'

'Oh…' Gemma understood instantly. 'We were right, then.'

'*You* were.' But something made Andy pause and take a slow, inward breath.

'We' was more accurate. He'd been reminded at the time of the way they'd once sparked off each other professionally and come up with things that had been more than the sum of different ideas. Something that had pushed them both into being better doctors. Better people even?

It had been the same as parenting together.

The same as making love.

They had always been a perfect team. Two halves of a whole that was impossible to achieve alone. Or with anybody else.

God…how could he have forgotten how powerful that was? How much…*less* his life was without it?

Feeling it again now was terrifying. How the hell was he going to say goodbye to her tomorrow and watch her walk out of his life again?

Andy cleared his throat and deliberately avoided catching Gemma's gaze. Avoided saying anything remotely personal. The only thing he couldn't bring himself to do was break the handclasp. He needed that touch. That warmth. To feel that connection for just a little longer.

'First hospital I rang where she was last living was able to fill me in. Mind you, it wouldn't have mattered what hospital I rang. She's well known in the system up there. Had a perfectly normal appendix removed the year before she had a baby and someone finally flagged the possibility of Munchausen's.

'Maybe that procedure was major enough to keep her happy for a while. Or maybe becoming a mother changed something. This is the first time Chantelle's been the patient instead of Deirdre.'

'Thank goodness it's been caught early. I've heard of cases that went on for years and years before the truth came out.'

'Mmm. This could have gone the same way if I didn't have so much faith in your instincts. She denied it all fiercely at first. Until I called her bluff and said there was an easy blood test I could do to check for something like laxatives in Chantelle's blood and then she knew she was busted and it all came out along with a lot of tears.'

* * *

Gemma squeezed his hand. It would have been an emotional and difficult conversation to have had. And he still had faith in her instincts? For some reason, it felt like a much bigger compliment than telling her she had never needed to wear mascara. It felt like the way they'd once been together. A perfect team.

'I've referred her to the psych team and Social Services will be notified tomorrow.' Andy stopped talking and heaved a sigh as he closed his eyes. 'It wasn't pleasant. We do everything we can to keep parents and their kids together. Goes against the grain to start something that might break them up.'

He opened his eyes and looked straight at Gemma.

'Enough about me. You OK, Gem?'

His tone was so gentle. So caring. His face got a bit blurry as tears stung her eyes.

'He's always there, isn't he?' Andy went on in that same, soft voice. 'When you hear a baby cry in the distance. Or when you have to deal with someone who has a kid and they don't know how lucky they are.'

Gemma nodded. Yes. The memories of Max were always there.

'It doesn't hurt so much these days, though, does it?'

Gemma shook her head. It was true. Time might not heal things like that completely but the pain was…encapsulated somehow now.

'I find I can remember the good bits now and it doesn't automatically undo me,' Andy said. 'Do you?'

Gemma nodded again. Her voice seemed to have deserted her. Because she was afraid that by speaking she might break the spell that Andy's words were casting?

'Is there one thing that stands out for you?' Andy's question was gentle. She didn't have to go there if she didn't want to. 'A favourite memory?'

Gemma didn't have to take any time to think about the answer to that question.

'Holding him that first time,' she whispered. 'Feeling like...a mother.'

It wasn't the whole answer. Or the whole memory. Because a huge part of what had created the magic of that moment had been seeing Andy's big hands cradling his newborn son with such exquisitely gentle care and reverence. The way she had felt overwhelmed with love.

For both Andy and Max.

Andy was nodding. It felt like he was stroking the top of her head. 'For me, too. That extraordinary feeling of being more than a couple. Being...a family. Nothing prepares you for how different it feels. And you'd never really know if you hadn't been there yourself, would you?'

Gemma swallowed. Hard. 'No.'

Andy had harnessed that knowledge. Used it to become the kind of doctor who could relate to children and their parents. She had no doubt that his caring extended to the whole family of any of his young patients. It was far more than she had been brave enough to do.

His words were making her remember more than the magic of a new family being created. They had taken her back to older memories. To when they *were* just a couple. To when that had seemed too good to be improved on.

She needed to say something else. To try and move the conversation on. Could she do it without breaking the spell that seemed to have caught them both?

'The first time Max smiled,' she offered softly. 'That's a special memory. He...he looked so like you.'

A miniature version of the smile she loved so much. Had loved since the first time she'd seen it. When she'd been standing outside the door of little Jessica's room in the PICU, too scared to go inside and begin what she knew she had to do. When he'd offered to be her support person and he'd smiled in a way that made her feel more courageous all by itself. Not alone any more. Brave enough to cope with anything.

'I still remember how jealous I was when he spoke his first words. You remember what they were?'

Of course she did.

'Mum, mum, mum.'

Gemma's indrawn breath was a gulp. At the same moment her body decided to let her know how cold it really was out here by shuddering dramatically.

'Oh...Gem...' Andy pulled her close.

Gemma could feel herself snuggling closer to Andy and she didn't feel cold any more. How could she with his arms around her like this? So close she could feel the steady thump of his heart?

For a long moment they stood there in silence. Gemma could feel when Andy's head tipped so that his cheek was resting on the top of her head. It felt so familiar. So good.

As if she'd come home after far too long away.

'I'm so sorry.' Andy's voice was a rumble against her ear. 'I didn't mean to stir it all up again...'

'It's...OK...' Gemma sniffed and took a deep breath as she raised her face from the warmth and comfort of Andy's chest. 'Really,' she added, seeing the concern on his face. 'It's part of my life and I couldn't forget Max even if I wanted to. Which I don't. Ever. And...if I try and share those memories with anyone else, they...'

'They don't share them,' Andy continued for her. 'They can't possibly understand.'

No. The only people in the world who could still share Max were his parents. His mother and father. Andy and herself.

There was no way she could break the eye contact. It was intense and it held shared memories that were deeper than the 'snapshot' moments they'd had with their baby.

They were the memories of how much of a team they'd been. Andy had been the husband that most women would dream of. Rarely complaining about having to take his turn cooking or doing dishes. Happy to do the supermarket run and put the rubbish out and even clean the loo. They might have both felt they were doing more than their share at times but that's what it had taken to be young parents together so they had done it. Together. And it would have been enough if Max hadn't got sick.

It hadn't just been sharing all those household duties. They had both worked irregular and long hours, slotting in extra study when they'd been able to, juggling the days and nights so that Max would have one parent with him for as much time as was humanly possible.

Gemma remembered Andy bringing her a cup of coffee at some horribly early hour after they'd both been up half the night with a teething baby. She remembered him sitting on the side of her bed, stroking her hair until she woke up enough to drink it and then get ready for a day at work. She remembered the guilt she'd felt, knowing that Andy would probably get no sleep during the day and would then have to front up for a night shift and he'd make damn sure he was awake enough to do his job well.

Had she really secretly blamed him for falling asleep for so long on the day that Max died?

Oh…God…

Still the eye contact went on. She could see that a million thoughts were racing through Andy's mind as well.

Was he thinking the same thing? That, once, they had been such a great team? An amazing little family?

How could she have walked away from that?

Gemma's lips trembled. She willed herself not to cry but it was hard.

She had hurt them both so badly. The kind of hurt that could never be undone or even repaired. She had destroyed everything they'd tried to cling to in the wake of losing their child.

They couldn't go back.

Except...the way Andy was *looking* at her now...

It made Gemma think that some things hadn't changed at all. They'd been covered up, yes, but the love that had brought them together all those years ago was still there.

Was it possible she could ask Andy to forgive her?

Gemma's eyes had always been the most astonishing Andy had ever seen. It had been the colour that had struck him first, of course. Those gold flecks and the perfect, matching halos around the edge of the irises. But it hadn't taken very long to get caught by so much more.

They said that the eyes were the windows to the soul and, sure, Gemma had stained-glass beauties instead of plain glass but it was the light that shone through that made them so extraordinarily beautiful as far as he was concerned.

She'd asked him for some spare courage in that first exchange of words but he'd known she hadn't really needed it. The more he'd learned about her the more he'd realised how right he'd been.

Gemma had been courageous her entire life. She'd been a protector and mother figure for her baby sister. She'd fought for the chance to use her intelligence and perseverance to succeed in her dream career. She'd stepped up to the plate when she'd been faced with an unexpected pregnancy and she had loved Max as much as he had.

She still hurt, as much as he did. He could see it in her eyes now.

He couldn't look away. Because he could see more than the pain of the poignant memories they shared.

He could see the connection they'd always had.

The love?

Was it possible that Gemma…? The thought dissolved as the emotional response to what he could see tipped Andy into a place he hadn't been in for many, many years.

A place where passion ruled and everything else in the world ceased to exist.

The only muscles that moved in his body were the tiny ones that controlled his eyes but he felt them as his gaze finally left Gemma's and dropped to her mouth.

Maybe it was the trembling of her lips that tipped him over the edge of control. He was holding the woman he'd loved so much in his arms. He could feel the shape of her. The warmth of her body despite the sub-zero temperatures. His own heart was speeding up to match the thump of her pulse against his chest.

What man could have resisted that tremble? He needed to make it go away so that Gemma wouldn't be so unhappy. His hands were already in use, holding her against him, so the only part of his body that he had available was his mouth. Without thinking, Andy lowered his head and covered her lips with his own.

A light touch. Meant to be comforting. Broken almost as soon as it was made.

But then Andy raised his gaze to her eyes again.

And the world stopped.

They were both in that space now. Nothing else existed. It was just the two of them and the pull between them was a force that was overwhelming.

This time Gemma moved at the same time Andy did. Their mouths met with a pressure that was almost painful. Andy had to let go of Gemma's body and cradle her head to protect it, but he still felt the thump as her back came up against the wall. He felt her hands gripping his arms and then sliding up, touching the sides of his face before her fingers were buried in his hair.

It wasn't enough. It didn't matter how many times he changed the angle of the kiss or how hard he pressed or how often his tongue danced with Gemma's.

It just wasn't enough.

Maybe nothing could be.

They were both completely out of breath when they finally pulled apart. They stood there, shocked at what had just happened.

The evidence of the passion that they still shared.

As if driven by shared frustration, they both moved again but this time they both jerked back the instant before their lips touched.

There was confusion mixed with desire now.

Should they be giving in to this?

Could they go far enough to satisfy that desire?

And, if they did, would there be any point given that the way they'd parted had destroyed any possibility of a future relationship because a relationship had to be built on trust? It wasn't that he wouldn't *want* to trust

her again. He just *couldn't*. That self-protection mechanism was too strong.

Andy could feel his physical response to Gemma
closing down. Getting locked away. When their eye
contact broke, they both moved apart. Turned away
from each other.

What had just happened there?

Gemma barely heard Andy mutter something about
needing to get back inside before they both froze to
death.

Whatever it was that had just happened, it was over.

But there was no denying that it *had* happened. Dear
Lord... She didn't even know whether Andy was single any more. Maybe he wasn't and that was why he'd
pulled down the shutters and turned away.

Had it just been a response to being so close? Sharing
memories that were theirs alone?

A blast from the past?

Andy wasn't even touching her now. There would be
no hand-holding on the way back to the ward. He wasn't
looking at her either as he held open the fire door for her
to go back inside. He was staring up at the night sky.

'Santa's sleigh seems to be caught in a holding pattern,' he said. 'Let's hope he gets to land before morning.'

Gemma's quick smile was automatic but she said
nothing.

Her brain was too busy thinking about something
very different.

Another Christmas. The last one they had shared.

The final blow to their marriage that was now the barrier that could keep them apart for ever.

The year they'd lost Max had been the ultimate Christmas from hell. But that last one hadn't been so far behind, had it?

CHAPTER NINE

Christmas: four years ago

'So YOU'RE not working on Christmas Day this year, then?'

'No.' Gemma was glad the room she was in was too dark for her consultant to read the expression on her face. She knew it would be one of utter dread.

'Got family stuff on?'

'Mmm.' The oppressive weight of that dread intensified. She had known it would be like this. Why…oh, *why* had she let Laura bully her into it?

'Please, Gemma. I want this to be a real Christmas. A family one. You and Andy can't go through the rest of your lives avoiding every celebration that involves kids. It's not fair. On me or Ev or the children…' She'd been crying by now. *'Most of all it's not fair on you. You've got to start…I don't know…living again. Not just working. I know how hard it is but…please, Gem. Just try? Ev's already talked to Andy and he said he'll come. Please…'*

The radiology consultant cleared his throat. 'Anyway...let's get this tutorial out of the way, shall we? Tell me about case nine.'

The only source of light in this room was coming from the glass screens that had X-ray images clipped onto them.

'There's a focal shadow in the right lower lobe. Suggestive of pneumonia.'

'Differential diagnoses?'

'Carcinoma and lymphoma.'

'Good. Case ten?'

Gemma didn't have to look at the image for more than a few seconds. 'Classic evidence of left ventricular failure.'

'Such as?'

'Cardiomegaly, upper lobe and pulmonary vein diversion and...' Gemma had to grin. 'I can see sternotomy wires so it's highly likely this patient has had coronary bypass surgery.'

The older man chuckled. 'I don't think I've got anything in this lot that's going to trip you up. You pass, Gemma. Tutorials are over. You're perfectly competent in X-ray interpretation and you know when you need to call in a second opinion. Now...you going to come to the departmental Christmas party after work today?'

'No.'

There was a tiny silence in the dark. 'Nobody would ever call you a party animal, Gemma, but couldn't you make an exception just this once?'

Oh...great... There seemed to be a conspiracy going on, courtesy of the festive season. Did everybody see it as the perfect time to give her a bit of a push? Propel her back into the land of the living and the happy? Make everything all right again?

Fix things between Andy and herself even?

Gemma let her breath out in a long sigh. She hadn't even seen Andy that morning because he'd got up well before her. She'd known there was something he wanted to say to her because she'd sensed him standing there at the bedroom door, looking at her.

And she'd pretended to be still deeply asleep.

He'd simply let himself quietly out of the apartment without saying goodbye. Without even pausing long enough to have breakfast.

She would have to go and see him now. She'd been putting it off all day, letting her job fill her head. Telling herself she was too busy to think about anything else. Too busy to even answer when he'd texted her. Three times.

Staying inside her comfort zone. Not thinking about her reluctant agreement to visit Andy on the paediatric ward before she went home. A concession that had been dragged out of her at the end of their last, awful argument.

'It's where I work, Gem. Everybody's partners come to the Christmas party. I'm not even asking you to come to that, but, for God's sake, couldn't you just show your face on the ward? The staff up there think my wife is just a figment of my imagination. Sometimes it feels that way to me, too.'

'You know what they say...' The radiology consultant was on his feet, flicking off the X-ray screens. Any moment now he would turn on the main light and Gemma would have to be careful what showed on her face. 'All work and no play...'

'Yeah...yeah...' Gemma smiled to keep her tone light. 'The paper I want to get finished is interesting enough to count as play. I've got all the stats. I just need to write up the discussion bit.'

'The one about the false negatives in head injury with CT scans read by ED staff?'

'That's the one.'

'Sounds like work to me.'

Gemma shrugged. All work and no play was fine by her. It was pretty much what had kept her sane for the last two years.

Had her permit for staying in that safe place run out? Was that why she was aware of the increasing pressure to start behaving differently?

Was there more to Laura's passionate plea for a family Christmas than met the eye? When had Evan talked to Andy about it? Maybe he'd had a heart-to-heart with Laura as well. Maybe they'd all decided that if she could be surrounded by children and happy times she might decide that she was ready to try again.

The sensation of dread was suffocating now. Was that what Andy wanted to talk to her about?

Having another baby?

No. She wasn't going there. She couldn't. She couldn't even bring herself to talk about it.

'Well…have a great Christmas anyway.' The consultant was heading home. 'See you in the new year.'

'You, too.' Gemma could feel how tight her smile was. Every cell in her body seemed to be holding itself rigid.

Of course there was a conspiracy. Laura was pregnant again, wasn't she? And it wasn't enough to highlight the lack in Gemma and Andy's lives by simply having another baby. This time she was pregnant with *twins*.

The pressure was building. Something was going to snap and Gemma knew it was going to hurt someone. Herself? Of course. But what about the other people in her life?

Laura and Evan.

Cute three-year-old Hazel and her baby brother, Jamie.

Andy…

And hadn't she already hurt Andy enough?

Oh, yes…more than enough.

It was probably the understatement of the century that she hadn't been easy to live with for the past two years. She'd been perfectly well aware of how much it had hurt Andy to be shut out but she hadn't been capable of engaging with anyone on more than a professional level. The rest of her had become numb within days of losing Max. In the beginning she'd been grateful for that numbness. Clung to it, in fact, when anything threatened to penetrate. And then, when she'd been ready to try and feel again, she hadn't known how and that had been frightening. It had been so much easier to retreat back into the safe, numb space.

But the safety barriers of that comfort zone seemed to be crumbling and, yes, it was because it was Christmas. She'd been given a free pass to avoid all the emotional connotations last year but nothing came without a price tag eventually, did it?

She was going to have to pay this time.

And Gemma knew she was going to be dipping into an account that was still overdrawn.

'Hey, Dr Andy. D'ya know what day it is tomorrow?'

'Sure do, John Boy.' Andy dropped to a couch to put him at eye level with the seven-year-old boy he'd come to know very well during his time as a paediatric registrar. 'It's Christmas.'

John Boy's smile was enough to make you think that life was wonderful. This admission had been to try and correct a badly deformed bone in his lower leg to preserve his ability to walk a little longer. He had a complicated external fixation device from knee to ankle but he was up on crutches already and into mischief all over the ward. He got away with all sorts of things, from small misdemeanours like raiding the fridge in the staffroom to major naughtiness like going AWOL from the ward and ending up somewhere like the hospital laundry. It wasn't just because he'd spent his short life either in hospital or foster-care. It was because of that smile.

The one that said that, yes, life was full of hard stuff

but you could find good stuff, too, and if you didn't make the most of it, you were pretty stupid.

It was being around kids like John Boy that had given Andy a way forward in life.

If only Gemma could meet him. Or any of the other children that came through these doors on a regular basis. Or their families, who managed to stick together during the hard times and gain strength from each other.

'I'm gonna get presents.' John Boy's smile was still lighting up his small, dark face. 'I always do when I'm in here for Christmas. Santa comes.'

'I heard that.' More than heard it. He was lined up to don the costume and do it himself this year. He'd have to disguise his voice when he was handing out the gifts to the children. John Boy was probably too smart to get fooled for a moment but he'd probably go along with the pretence simply because it was fun. Andy hoped the gifts with this boy's name on them were special ones this year because he gave so much to others without even realising it.

'I'm gonna tell that new kid that came in today. He was crying.'

'Paul? He's not feeling so good today, John Boy. Why don't you just say hi and give him a smile?'

'Okey-dokey.' John Boy concentrated hard and moved his crutches. The short conversation had been enough to make him breathless so he waited for a moment before pushing his body into motion. 'See ya, Dr Andy.'

'See ya, John Boy.'

Andy watched the lad's slow movement down the corridor. He saw a nurse spot John Boy and smile as if her day had just brightened out of sight. He wished Gemma was here. If only she could receive that gift of knowing how good life could still be in the face of the difficult stuff. But how could she receive anything emotional like that when she'd shut herself off so completely?

Andy was at his wits' end. He'd tried everything he could think of. At first it had been easy to know what to do because they had both been so shattered by their grief. All they had been able to do had been to hold onto each other and cry.

He'd reached a point, after a few months of that desperately sad place, where he'd had to move forward to save himself. Gemma had agreed that it was the right thing to do but had simply refused to come with him. Worse than that. She had moved in the opposite direction. Andy had faced the tough stuff head on. It was hard to be around children and he couldn't let it grow into something that would destroy too much of him so he'd chosen paediatrics for his specialty.

Gemma had chosen not only to avoid children but to avoid people as much as she could. She'd chosen radiology as a specialty and spent most of her working life shut into a dark room, analysing the images that the technicians obtained from patients.

She'd hurled herself into postgraduate study as well so that when they were home together she was invariably on the computer or buried in a textbook. The care they had taken of each other in the early days after that dreadful Christmas had morphed into a relationship that felt like housemates. Polite housemates who had sex occasionally, sure, but something huge was missing. And it was something that had been there before they'd had Max so his absence from their lives wasn't enough to explain that massive hole.

Trying to push at all only led to fights but Andy was getting desperate. So was Laura.

'We've got to do something, Andy. I think she's lost and if we don't reach out and grab her, she'll disappear for ever. It's Christmas. The perfect time. Maybe the last chance we'll get.'

An hour or two with her sister's family for Christmas dinner wasn't going to be enough for Andy, however. He was desperate to get their professional lives to connect again, too. So he'd pushed and forced her to agree to come to the paediatric departmental party today.

And then he'd had second thoughts that morning when he'd stood there, watching her sleep. Feeling the gulf between them but knowing how much he still loved her. Wondering if she really *was* asleep or just avoiding him…again. He'd tried texting her a few times today, too. He just wanted to talk. If it was too much for her, she didn't have to go to the stupid party. They could go somewhere by themselves. Maybe, if he could show her that he was trying to understand, at least it could open the door to some real communication.

'You still here, Andy? Thought you'd be at the party by now.'

'I'll head off soon.' He'd give Gemma another ten minutes and if she hadn't arrived by then he'd go past Radiology and see if she was still at work. She'd said she'd text him but maybe things were really busy. Perhaps that was why she hadn't answered any of his messages. Why she hadn't turned up to visit his ward.

He used the ten minutes to wander around, seeing what everybody was up to. A Christmas movie was playing in the dayroom for the children who were well enough to be out of bed. A nurse who had angel wings pinned to the back of her uniform and a tinsel halo on her head was handing out ice-block treats. John Boy was using his like a sword to play with another small boy in a wheelchair. The Christmas tree had its lights flashing and there were spraypainted snowflakes on the windows.

A nurse was holding the door of a storage area open for a man Andy recognised as a patient's father. He grinned and took an armload of carrier bags into the private space. The nurse picked up one of the rolls of Christmas wrapping paper he'd dropped and handed it in before closing the door. She grinned at Andy, putting her finger to her lips.

Christmas carols were playing at the nurses' station and being sung along to with varying degrees of tunefulness. A tired-looking mother paused to listen and miraculously the crying baby in her arms became quiet. Her companion, probably her husband, was holding a toddler on his hip. The two parents exchanged a smile of pure relief as the baby settled.

Andy smiled, too.

And then he turned and his smile faded. Gemma was standing there, staring at the couple. At the baby the woman was holding?

No. It was the toddler that had caught her attention. Less than two years old, the little boy was wearing a Santa hat. Like Max had been in that last photograph of him that had ever been taken.

Oh…help.

'Gemma.' Andy pasted his smile back in place. 'I was just coming to find you.'

He could see how carefully she was holding herself. When he put his arm around her shoulders, he could feel a tension that made his heart plummet. She felt brittle enough to snap at any moment. She'd kept her promise but right now Andy wished she hadn't. It had been a bad idea to push her into this.

'You know what?' He began leading her out of the ward. 'I don't think I want to hang around here any longer today. Let me grab my jacket and we could head out for a drink. Dinner, maybe.'

'I…I'd rather just go home. I want to finish that paper I'm writing up for *Radiology Today*.' Gemma was walking just slightly ahead of Andy, taking her shoulders out of range for his arm. She was talking quickly. Sounding too bright. 'You know, the one about the false negatives for CT interpretation by ED staff?'

She was running again, Andy thought sadly. Avoiding anything that could be deemed too personal. Anything that required an emotional response.

He couldn't live like this any longer. He knew the Gemma he loved was still there somewhere but he was too bone tired of trying to coax her back.

'It's almost Christmas,' he said. 'It's time to stop thinking about work for a few days.' Taking a longer step, he got close enough to put his hand on Gemma's shoulder. 'It's the time people like to be with the people they care about. That's all I'm asking for...a bit of time with you. Is that too much to ask?'

'Of course not. Sorry.' Gemma's pace slowed. 'It's just...' She stopped and turned, looking up at him. 'It's Christmas, Andy. I can't...' She caught her bottom lip between her teeth. 'It's too...soon.'

The pain in her eyes cut into Andy. A rare glimpse of the real Gemma. But how long could he keep comforting her? Telling her that things would come right in time and that she would find a way through this? She thought she'd found the answer in burying herself in her career but she was so wrong. Not that he could suggest anything else. He'd tried to get her to go to professional counselling. He'd even once suggested that she might need antidepressant medication and that had led to a row that had lasted for weeks. She could cope, she'd yelled at him, but only if she was allowed to cope in her own way.

'Just leave me alone. Why can't you leave me the hell alone?'

Laura could be right. Gemma was lost and something had to be done.

'It's been two years, Gem,' he said quietly. 'We *have* to move on.'

Her eyes widened with shock. '*We* have to move on? You did that a long time ago, Andy. This isn't *your* problem.'

'What do you mean?' They weren't far away from the office Andy shared with the other departmental registrars. He walked to the door and opened it, then turned and stared at Gemma.

This was it. They couldn't shove it all under the carpet any more. They had to confront this issue before it destroyed them, no matter how painful that might be.

Andy looked so *angry*.

Or was that desperate?

Gemma couldn't find any of that comforting numbness to pull around her as she forced her feet to move and take her into the office. She knew she couldn't brush this off by dismissing the conversation because she had something really important that had to be done. Like writing some totally irrelevant professional article.

This was what was important.

Their relationship.

Their future.

She was being dragged out of whatever safe place she had managed to create for herself, whether she was ready or not.

Because Andy couldn't wait any longer.

And fair enough.

Two years? It really had been that long, hadn't it?

Nothing like having an anniversary that coincided with something like Christmas to make sure you could never forget.

Gemma stopped as soon as Andy closed the office door behind her. The other registrars were not here. They were probably at the staff Christmas party. Someone had strung tinsel around the room and there was a miniature fir tree on one of the desks, decorated with boiled sweets tied to the branches. A gift from a patient? Christmas cards, some home-made, with children's drawings were pinned to the notice-board.

The room was small but Andy put as much distance between them as he could before turning to face her.

That hurt.

Were things really so bad that he didn't even want to be within touching distance right now?

'I don't know what to do, Gemma.' Andy's voice was low. And raw. 'I've been careful not to try and push you. I've given you all the support and space I know how to give. So has Laura. And Evan. We've *all* done everything we could to help you get through losing Max. You've got the career you always wanted but...' He pushed both his hands through his hair, making it stand up in spikes before holding his hands up in a gesture of surrender.

'But it's *all* you seem to want now. Your career. You don't have time for me. Or for your family. You won't have anything to do with children if you can help it. You won't even have anything to do with Christmas. And

Christmas comes around every year, Gemma.' Andy's voice was getting louder.

'Whether you're ready for it or not, it comes and you have to *deal* with it. You can't hide for ever.'

'I'm not hiding. I said I'd go to Laura's this year. I've...I've got presents for the kids. I'm *trying*, Andy.'

'You've refused to go to any Christmas parties here. You flat out refused to have a single decoration at home, let alone a Christmas tree.'

'You can't turn around without bumping into a Christmas tree around here.' Gemma waved her hand at the small version on the desk to emphasise her point. 'We don't *need* one at home.'

'I think we do.' Andy's voice was so controlled now. So vehement. Gemma had never heard him sound like this and it frightened her. 'I think it would be a symbol. That we've got past a tragedy. That we've still got some kind of future.'

Oh...God... Was this an ultimatum?

Andy was rubbing his forehead now. Clearly, he was finding this difficult but he couldn't stop. Something had been unleashed that couldn't be caught and locked away again. When he looked back at Gemma, his face was anguished.

'I just don't understand,' he said. 'Why can't you get past it? You never even wanted a baby in the first place.'

Something cold trickled down Gemma's spine. She couldn't deny that, could she? She couldn't say that things had changed the moment she'd held Max in her arms for the first time or that being a family had meant as much to her as it did to Andy.

She hadn't wanted to be pregnant. She'd wanted her career. To outward appearances, she had spent the last two years simply proving that. Looking as though she was relieved not to have the constraints of being a mother holding her back. Spending every waking hour working.

She'd thought Andy had understood that it was the only way she'd been able to get through each day. He'd done the same thing, hadn't he? Thrown himself into his work? He'd tried to be interested in the specialty she'd chosen but she hadn't been able to return that interest. Why hadn't she seen just how far it was pushing them apart?

Maybe she had but she'd put off trying to do anything about it because it was too hard. Too painful.

This was too painful. He was reminding her of something she'd felt ashamed of even thinking after Max's birth.

It reminded her of something else that had haunted her ever since.

'And you only married me because I was pregnant.'

A stunned silence fell. Andy looked as though she'd given him a physical blow. As though he had to stay very still for a moment to work out exactly where he'd been injured. When he spoke again, his voice was soft. Almost defeated.

'So why am I still here, Gem? For God's sake... I *love* you. All I want is for you to be happy because it's becoming very obvious that nobody around you is going to be happy unless you are.'

'It's...harder for me.'

'What is?'

The numb place had vanished completely. Gemma felt like she had in those awful days before she'd discovered it. Her heart was breaking all over again.

'I...' I miss my baby, she wanted to cry. I miss holding him and hearing him laugh. I see his smile every time *you* smile. I feel so empty. Like there's nothing left...just a big, black hole...

The words wouldn't come out. Gemma was too scared to break the dam because she knew the flood would drown her.

'You think it's been *easy* for me?' Andy sounded incredulous. 'To get over losing our child?'

Gemma stared back at him helplessly. Of course he'd coped better than she had. 'You *work* with children,' she whispered.

'And you think it's been *easy*? That it doesn't remind me of Max and break my heart every time something goes wrong?' Gemma could see his Adam's apple bob as he swallowed hard.

'I love kids. I always have. The *easy* thing to do would have been to avoid them. Like you did. But I knew that would have ended up being only half a life so I took the hard road and jumped in the deep end. I didn't know whether I'd sink or swim but I did know that I understand how parents feel and that I'd do whatever it took to win the battle to save a child's life.'

Maybe that explained why Andy had gone off to work day after day, looking so grim. He'd had to find the strength to face his demons and he'd never told her because…because he'd been trying to protect her? Knowing she was facing her own demons in her own way? Oh…dear Lord…

'It's who I am now,' Andy continued. 'Who I'll be for the rest of my life.' His breath came out in a huff. 'Maybe it was meant to happen so that I would be this person. So I could spend my working life doing the best I can to keep families together. It doesn't mean I don't still want to have my *own* family. Can't you understand that?'

Gemma nodded, very slowly. Of course she could understand it. She'd always known that Andy wanted to have a family of his own. She'd watched the way he'd been drawn further into her sister's family over the last months. How much he loved being with Hazel and little Jamie. He didn't know about the twins yet but she could imagine the look on his face when he was given the news.

The longing she would see there.

She couldn't do it. She couldn't face being pregnant again and giving birth and holding an infant with the knowledge that it could all be ripped away. There wasn't enough of her heart left as it was. If any more got ripped out, it wouldn't be able to sustain life even.

Andy was walking towards her. He took her hands in his.

'I love you, Gem,' he said quietly.

'I…I love you, too,' she whispered.

'Then help me. Help *us*. We can't live like this for ever. It's been two years of hell. Isn't that long enough?'

Gemma could only nod. She had done this. Put Andy through months and months of hell because she hadn't been brave enough to even try putting her feet in the water, let alone jumping in at any deep end. This *was* all her fault. But she couldn't fix it, could she? Not if it meant having another baby.

Andy pulled her close and held her tightly. So tightly she couldn't breathe but that was OK. She didn't want to breathe because if she did, she'd have to think. And all she could think about was how she was destroying the person she loved most in the world.

'I need a drink,' she heard him say above her head. 'Come with me?'

Gemma shook her head this time. Somehow she found her voice and the words that might give her a brief reprieve.

'I think I need a bit of time on my own. To…think. Why don't you go to your Christmas party for a while and have a drink there?'

The pressure around her body eased a little too quickly. Andy knew he was being pushed away. He stepped back and Gemma knew he was watching her but she kept her head down. She couldn't face meeting his eyes just yet. Not with this new knowledge of how much she had failed their marriage. Would continue to fail it. After a long, silent moment Andy turned away and left, leaving only the echo of a sad sigh.

* * *

The apartment felt cold and empty.

Gemma couldn't stay there. Why on earth hadn't they moved somewhere else after Max had died? Made a fresh start?

Because she hadn't suggested it? They'd all been tiptoeing around her. Trying to protect her. Letting her build her defensive walls and use her career like a statement of denial about how deeply she'd been hurt.

She couldn't deny anything now.

And she couldn't stay here.

Gemma had no idea what she should do. She knew Andy loved her. If she told him she could never face the prospect of having another baby, he would take that on board and live with it.

And it would always be there as an undercurrent in their marriage. A resentment that would simmer away in dark corners ready to explode if tension built from any cause.

It was blindingly simple really.

Andy wanted a family. She didn't. *Couldn't.*

And, because she loved Andy with all the heart she had left, she had to set him free to get what he wanted from his life.

It might destroy her but she was broken anyway, wasn't she? At least Andy had the guts to face life and put the pieces back together again. To *live*. All she was doing was surviving.

But the decision was too big. Too terrifying. Maybe what she needed to do was give them both some space so that, when they saw each other again, they could talk about it.

Yes. That was the first step. Gemma pulled a suitcase from the storeroom that had once been a nursery. Mechanically, she began opening drawers and pulling out items that she might need for a few days. Underwear and tights. Nightwear and jeans. She moved to the wardrobe and pulled things off random hangers without even thinking, rolling the items of clothing and stuffing them into the suitcase.

Where would she go?

The obvious answer was to Laura and Evan's house but how would that help? Laura was just as worried about her as Andy was. She would want to see their marriage survive and she would try and convince Gemma that another baby was exactly what was needed. Of course she would. She was probably glowing with her own new pregnancy already.

And it was *Christmas*.

And Jamie was almost the same age as Max had been when…when…

Gemma almost couldn't see what she was stuffing into a toilet bag in the bathroom.

She was falling again.

Falling apart.

She couldn't go to Laura's. She'd leave the gifts for Andy to take. She would text Laura to say she was sorry but she needed some time on her own and then she'd turn her phone off so she couldn't receive a response.

She couldn't stay here.

She could go to a hotel but that wouldn't be far enough. If she was within reach of Andy she could never do what she had to do.

Set him free. Give him a 'get out of hell' card.

He could find someone else. Someone who would be able to be the mother to the children he wanted.

Could she stand seeing that happen? No. Even being in another city in England would be too close. She had to get further away. Maybe as far as the other side of the world?

Where was her passport?

It took some hunting down. It was in a desk drawer, along with all sorts of other bits and pieces. Lanyards with name tags from various conferences she and Andy had attended over the last couple of years. Some keys, the usefulness of which had been long forgotten. An old phone charger. Paper clips and even bits of rubbish.

No.

Gemma stared at the item in her hand. It wasn't rubbish exactly but why had this been shoved in a drawer and not thrown out when it had last been seen two years ago?

It was that piece of plastic mistletoe.

It was also the final straw because Gemma couldn't even remember when Andy had last kissed her.

She dropped the piece of mistletoe and picked up her passport. And her suitcase.

And left.

CHAPTER TEN

IT WAS almost dawn.

Christmas Day.

Gemma hadn't seen Andy since she'd followed him down from the roof of the Queen Mary Infirmary.

'I have to duck home for a bit. I need to collect the Santa suit I'll be wearing in the morning.'

'You're the ward Santa this year?'

'It'll be my fifth time. It's become a tradition.'

The image stayed with Gemma as she returned to the children's room and settled herself in the armchair in the hope of catching at least a little sleep. She could picture Andy in the dayroom. Beside that Christmas tree. Handing out gifts to the small patients he spent his life caring for.

Five times? That meant the first time he'd played the role would have been the year that she'd walked out. He'd never mentioned that he was going to do it.

Why? Because he'd known that she wouldn't understand how he was even able to think of doing it?

How hard would it have been for him that first time? Even on its own, it would have been heart-breaking

for a father who'd lost his own son but that year he
would have still been reeling from going home to find
an empty house the night before.

She'd tried to write Andy a note before she'd left but
words had failed her. In the end, the scrap of tearstained
paper had held only four words.

'I'm sorry. For everything.'

She'd left it on top of the desk. With her vision
blurred by tears she had picked up the nearest available object to attract attention to the piece of paper in
the centre of a bare desktop. And the way she'd been
feeling, it had seemed appropriate to use that piece of
plastic mistletoe.

Gemma heard a snuffle from one of the children and
echoed it softly herself. Sleep was not going to release
her any time soon, she realised. Her mind was too full.
Of memories. Of Andy. Of that kiss on the rooftop with
the lights of Santa's sleigh scribing slow circuits in the
sky above them.

Her love for Andy hadn't diminished one little bit.
Had she done the right thing by setting him free? If
he hadn't moved on and found someone else to be the
mother of his children, surely the answer was no. And,
if the answer *was* no, did that mean there was still a
chance for her to be with him?

The way he'd kissed her. Where would that kiss have
gone if they hadn't been on a hospital roof in freezing
weather?

A smile was competing with the threat of tears now.
Gemma knew exactly where that kiss would have gone.

Other emotions were colliding inside her. Echoes of grief that had to come from those shared memories of Max. Guilt at the way she had been so self-obsessed with that grief. Had she really thought that her way of coping had been the right way? That Andy had found it all so much easier?

Sitting here in the dark, surrounded by sleeping children, Gemma was at last in a space where she could see a much bigger picture. It wasn't simply that there were more important things in life than a brilliant career. It was a combination of wisdom gained from isolation. From the devastating loss of a sister she had only stayed in touch with via phone and email for years. From having to step up to become a mother for her nieces and nephews.

Running away and burying herself in her career had been a successful device in hiding from the pain of losing Max but it was only now that she could see the full extent of the collateral damage.

She'd lost the place she thought of as her home.

She'd lost her family. Watching the precious early years of these children growing up.

She'd lost Andy.

Love. That's what she'd taken out of her life. People and places that she loved and people that she could be loved by.

Emotional safety was a very lonely place.

So lonely that a tiny whimper from Sophie had Gemma on her feet almost eagerly. She laid a gentle hand on the baby's forehead. Her temperature had obviously dropped and her skin felt soft and dry and healthy. Sophie stirred, bringing a small fist up to her mouth. The vigorous sucking noises made Gemma smile.

'You're getting ready to be hungry, darling, aren't you?' she whispered. Reaching into the bassinette, she picked up the bundle of baby and blanket, tucking it into her arms. 'Come on. We'll tiptoe down to the kitchen and see what we can find.'

The ward was beginning to stir. People arriving early for the day shift were quietly preparing to take over from the weary night staff. Fixing a bottle of formula for Sophie, Gemma was greeted by one of the day staff. A nurse called Carla.

'You'll stay for the Christmas breakfast, won't you?' she asked. 'The night nurses have labelled some spare gifts for the children.'

Could she stay and watch Andy do his thing as Santa? Heaven help her, but she wanted to so much. If she gave in to that desire, though, would it make it that much harder to walk away? It was what she would have to so. Or was it?

That kiss on the roof had done more than awaken too many memories of what being so close to Andy was like. It had planted a seed of hope.

Carla misinterpreted the hesitation she could see on Gemma's face.

'I could get one of the registrars to sign Sophie's discharge form but I'd rather Andy signed you off and... he's going to be a bit busy for a while. He got held up checking our little bone-marrow-transplant girl so he won't have much time to get changed when he gets back. Santa's supposed to make his big entrance at the end of breakfast-time.'

Gemma opened the microwave to rescue the bottle of warm milk. Sophie reached out for it and whimpered.

'I'll see how we go,' she told Carla. She smiled. 'It's never a quick job getting my lot organised.'

'I'm sure they'd want to stay.' Carla's gaze was frankly curious. 'I hear that Andy's their uncle?'

Gemma's nod was wary. The children didn't know that Andy was still their uncle. On paper, anyway. But of course they'd want to stay.

As much as she did?

Back in the room, Gemma settled into the armchair to feed Sophie, grateful that she still had some time before the other children were likely to wake up. She had to decide what the best thing to do for the children was and she couldn't let that decision be influenced by all the memories and feelings that had been stirred into life for her again. What if the children found out about Andy's relationship to them but he wanted nothing more to do with them? They had suffered the loss of too many adults in their lives already.

The last of the bottle had been hungrily guzzled and Gemma was holding Sophie up against her shoulder to burp her when Hazel woke up. There was enough light in the room for her to see the way her niece's eyes snapped open fully as she registered her unfamiliar surroundings. She heard the sharp, fearful intake of breath.

'It's OK, hon,' she said softly. 'You're safe. Everything's fine.'

Hazel's gasp turned into a sigh of relief as she scrambled into a sitting position.

'I need to wee,' she informed Gemma.

'Can you wait for a sec?' Gemma made faster circles on Sophie's back and patted it a few times. 'Soph will get grumpy if she doesn't have a burp.' She sniffed. 'And I think she's overdue for a nappy change, too, but I can do that after I show you where the bathroom is.'

'I can go to the loo by myself,' Hazel said with some indignation. 'I'm *seven*.'

'I know. I just thought…being in a strange place…'

'I can manage.' But Hazel hesitated when she got to the door. 'Which way do I go?'

'Left.' Gemma tilted her head for emphasis because both her hands were full of baby. 'If you can't see a door that has a sign saying "Bathroom", just go a bit further and you'll find a nurse you can ask. They're all very nice.'

Hazel nodded, went outside the door and looked up and down the corridor. She couldn't see anybody in either direction.

Which way was left again?

Andy eyed the big, plastic rubbish sack on the chair. He needed to go and find a spare pillow or two to stuff under the red jacket of the Santa suit the sack contained. And was that special glue still in the smaller bag containing the fake beard? It had taken some time to find that glue again. Why on earth had he put it in his desk drawer?

Andy opened the sack, lifting out the red hat with white trim on the top to have a look but then he paused, hat in hand, turning his head very slowly. An odd prickle on the back of his neck suggested he wasn't alone.

Glancing over his shoulder, he found his instincts hadn't deceived him. A small girl was standing, framed by the office doorway. She was wearing hospital-issue pyjamas but she wasn't a patient.

'Hazel.' A beat of alarm pulsed through Andy. Had Gemma sent her oldest niece to find him? Why couldn't she come herself? 'What's up, chicken?'

Hazel's bottom lip quivered. 'I went to find the loo,' she said, 'and...I got lost.'

'Oh, no...' Andy's smile was sympathetic. He dropped the hat he was still holding onto the top of the bag and held his hand out towards Hazel. He could fix this. He could show her where the toilet was.

But, with a sob, Hazel launched herself at him and Andy found himself scooping the small girl into his arms to give her a cuddle.

'Hey...it's not that bad. You didn't really get lost cos you found me.'

'That's not why I'm crying,' Hazel sobbed.

'What is it, then?' Andy wasn't used to holding distressed children. He might be in the same room but there were always parents or nurses to do the cuddling. He'd almost forgotten what it was like to have small arms entwined around his neck as though he was some kind of giant lifesaver.

'It's…' Hazel unfurled one arm to point at the Santa hat that had slid from the top of the sack to land on the floor. 'It's *Christmas*.'

Andy nodded. 'So it is. But…it's supposed to be a happy day, you know.'

'Not…not when you don't have a mummy or daddy any more.'

'No.' Andy closed his eyes for a moment and held Hazel closer. This was the first Christmas for these children since they had become orphans. As the oldest, Hazel would have the clearest memories of their parents and she would be missing them most. 'I'm sorry about that, chicken. It's really sad, isn't it?'

'Mmm.' Hazel snuffled and then sniffed loudly.

'Would you like a tissue?'

'No…' She ducked her head and wiped her nose on her pyjama sleeve. 'S'okay.'

'But you'd like to go to the toilet?'

'Yes.'

'Come on, then.' Andy put her down. Hazel's fingers caught on his name badge as he lowered her to the floor. Then she took his hand and let him lead her out into the corridor and down towards the bathroom.

'My last name is Gillespie,' she told him.

'I know.'

'Your name's on your badge.'

'It is.'

'Why have you got the same name as Aunty Gemma?'

'Because…' Oh, help. Andy's respect for children meant that he always tried to be as honest as he could within the limits of their understanding. How much did Hazel know? Or remember? 'Gemma's got the same name as me because we got married.'

'When?'

'A long time ago. Before you were born even. Here's the bathroom. I'll wait out here for you and make sure you don't get lost going back to your room.'

Hazel was back in a commendably short time. She slipped her hand into Andy's without hesitation and the trusting gesture was heart-melting.

'Gemma's Mummy's sister,' she told Andy.

'I know.'

'Are you mummy's brother, then?'

'Kind of. I married your mummy's sister so that made me something called a brother-in-law to your mummy.'

Hazel looked confused.

'I'm…I was your uncle,' he added.

Hazel looked even more confused. 'Why did you stop being my uncle?'

'I…didn't.' Whatever had melted inside him moments before had congealed into something hard now. He'd missed these children far more than he'd realised. They had been part of his family. The closest thing he'd had to children of his own after losing Max.

'So I can still call you "Uncle"?'

'Sure.'

Hazel tried it out. 'Uncle…Andy…'

Could she remember using the name? He could remember. He could actually hear an echo of a three-year-old's gleeful shriek as he came through the front door of that wonderful old, converted barn.

'If you're still our uncle, how come you never come to visit us, then?'

A fair question but he couldn't tell a seven-year-old it was because it had been simply too painful. That the children were part of Gemma and if she didn't want him in her life any more, he'd felt that maybe he had no right to keep any part of her family.

'I don't know, chicken. I'm sorry. I should have.'

If he'd kept up contact with Gemma's family, he would have known about the tragedy. He could have been there for Gemma. He might have been able to re-establish contact with her and not have had to live with the awful silence of the last four years. But that was exactly why he'd let the contact lapse in the first place.

It had been Gemma's choice to leave and she'd ignored his attempts to track her down by phone. She hadn't wanted to live with him any more. Not even in the same country. She hadn't wanted to talk to him. She'd wanted space and he'd given it to her. And the weeks had turned into months and he had kept putting off making contact that would probably deal another blow of rejection. And then the months had turned into years. How on earth had he let that happen?

'So why did you stop being married to Aunty

Gemma?' Hazel asked as they neared the door to her room.

Tricky question. How could Andy answer that without getting into a complicated discussion about divorce laws?

'We haven't stopped being married, exactly,' he said awkwardly. 'We just haven't been living together.'

'Why not? Aunty Gemma's nice.' Hazel stopped outside the door to their room and gave Andy a very steady glance. 'Aunty Gemma's our mummy now.'

'I know. You're very lucky. She *is* nice.'

Hazel opened the door. Jamie was getting dressed. The twins were standing up in the cot, blinking sleepily. Chloe had her thumb in her mouth. Ben was holding Digger under his arm.

Gemma was changing Sophie's nappy. 'You've been gone a long time, hon,' she said, without looking up. 'I was getting worried.' Sticking the last piece of tape into place, she looked up to see Andy standing beside Hazel and she stilled.

'Oh…hi…'

'Hey…' Andy responded.

They both seemed to be at a complete loss for words. Standing there staring at each other like embarrassed teenagers on a first date. Was Gemma's head suddenly filled with that kiss? Like his was?

Hazel looked at Gemma and then at Andy. Then at Gemma again.

'Uncle Andy says you're still married.'

'O…' Gemma bit her lip. 'That's…true, I guess.'

'And you're our mummy now.'

'Also true.'

Hazel nodded as though she had finally sorted out something important in her mind. She turned back and looked up at Andy.

'That means you're our daddy now, doesn't it?'

Oh...no...

Gemma saw the way the colour drained out of Andy's face. He looked around at all the children in the room and then opened his mouth to say something but didn't get the chance because a nurse appeared beside him.

'I just came to see if you guys needed a hand with anything in here,' the nurse said cheerfully.

Andy muttered something completely unintelligible, stepped back, turned and strode away.

Gemma could feel every step of his increasing the distance between them and something finally snapped. She couldn't let him walk out like this. Not after the bombshell that Hazel had just dropped.

'Yes,' she told the nurse. She handed Sophie over. 'Please watch the children for a few minutes. I have to...'

She didn't know quite *what* she had to do.

She just knew she had to do *something* and it could possibly be the most important thing she was ever going to do in her life.

Right at this moment, it felt like her life depended on it.

Her sentence didn't need to be finished in any case because she was already outside the room. She could

see Andy at some distance down the corridor. Already
past where his office was. Where was he going?

Gemma started running.

'Andy….*wait for me…*'

CHAPTER ELEVEN

ANDY was heading for the stairs.

An escape route. To the roof, maybe, for some more fresh air?

He heard the sound of Gemma's voice behind him.

'Andy....*please* wait.'

No. Not the roof. Not when the last time he'd been there was still so fresh in his memory. He could feel that kiss, all over again, in every cell of his body.

He could feel the desire.

And the confusion.

The wanting to open himself up to Gemma again.

The fear that came with knowing how much pain that could cause. Was he strong enough to go through that again? Did he want to even go there?

He didn't really have a choice. Not when he could sense the speed and urgency with which Gemma was approaching him. When he could hear the desperate plea in her voice.

Andy stopped and turned to face Gemma.

She almost skidded to a halt just a few feet away from him. She must have run all the way from the children's room because she needed to catch her breath for a moment. At least it gave Andy the chance to say something first, instead of waiting for the axe to fall.

'I'm sorry,' he said. 'I shouldn't have said anything to Hazel. But she noticed that our names were still the same. We *are* still married…legally, anyway…and…I like to be honest with kids if I can be.'

Gemma nodded. She opened her mouth and then closed it again. She took in a great gulp of air.

'Why?' The word came out in a kind of croak.

Andy raised his eyebrows. 'Don't you think it's a good thing to be honest?'

Gemma shook her head with a sharp movement. 'No…*why* are we still married?'

Here it came, Andy thought. The axe. There was no reason for them to still be married so Gemma was about to ask him to set divorce proceedings in place.

Her eyes were searching his face. 'I've been waiting to hear from you. I thought you would have found someone else long before this. Someone who could give you the baby you wanted. Someone who…who could make you happy.'

Her voice broke.

Andy stared at her. Behind them, kitchen staff were pushing the breakfast trolleys into the ward and the smell of bacon and eggs and other breakfast treats filled the air. The trolleys had strings of bells attached to them and the kitchen staff were singing 'Jingle Bells' with great enthusiasm for so early in the morning.

Andy barely heard them and was only vaguely aware

of the smell of hot food. His focus was on Gemma. On what she was saying, of course, but more the look on her face.

'Was that really what you thought would happen when you left?'

Gemma nodded. She had a tear rolling down the side of her nose. 'You wanted to start again. You wanted a Christmas tree and...and you wanted a baby. I couldn't give you anything you wanted but...I wanted you to be happy because...because I love you so-much.'

Love?

Not *loved*?

Andy shook his head. He let his breath out in a huff that was almost laughter. 'How the hell did you expect me to be *happy* when I didn't have you?'

'Because...you weren't happy with me.'

The statement was so simple.

But so huge.

'I'm sorry.' The words came from somewhere very deep inside Andy. A space he had tried to stay away from for a very long time. 'I've wanted to say it a million times but I thought it was far too late.'

'What are *you* sorry for? It's me that messed things up in the end.'

'I'm sorry I couldn't help you. I knew you were hurting but there seemed to be nothing I could do that would help. In the end, I guess I gave up trying.'

'You were hurting just as much. *I'm* sorry.' Gemma sniffed and rubbed at her nose. 'I know I made it harder for you...'

'I think we made it harder for each other, even if it was the last thing we wanted to do.'

'But you tried to help me. I just made your life hell. You *said* that.'

He had. He couldn't deny it. The echo was right there.

It's been two years of hell...

'I'm sorry. I—'

'I couldn't understand,' Gemma cut in, 'the way you were dealing with it all. I couldn't see what you got out of being near other children. Maybe I never would have if I hadn't been thrown into being a mother figure.'

Andy felt his lips twist at the irony of the cards fate had chosen to deal. 'It was the last thing you ever wanted to be, wasn't it? A stay-at-home mum to a big bunch of kids?'

Gemma's voice was soft. 'Losing someone as precious as a person is a very fast way of learning what's really important in life. I should have learned that way back when we lost Max. Maybe I would have if I hadn't been so completely numb for so long.'

'I'm so sorry you had to learn it the way you did. Laura was very special.'

Gemma's nod was jerky. 'She was. But she's not the only person I love that I lost.'

'No. Evan was great, too.'

'I wasn't talking about Ev either.'

The way Gemma was looking at him was...heartbreaking. He'd never seen her looking so forlorn. So vulnerable.

And then it hit him.

She was talking about *him*.

Andy could feel that glow again. The one he'd felt when he'd gone into the reception area in the emergency department and seen her again for the first time in so long. Shafts of it were coming from beneath the lid he'd slammed over the hole it lived in. If he let it out, was it possible that the light would be bright enough to blind him to the pain?

Was it really true that she'd left him because she wanted him to be happy? And she thought he'd be happier *without* her?

How stupid was that?

If Gemma kept looking at him like that, the glow couldn't do anything but get stronger. It was so strong already that it was pushing up that lid without any conscious effort on his part.

Andy took a deep, deep breath.

'You haven't lost me, Gem,' he said quietly.

'You haven't found someone else?'

'I tried,' Andy admitted. He gave his head a small, sad shake. 'But they weren't you.'

Somehow, without either of them taking a noticeable step, they had come closer together. Within touching distance but only their eyes were holding each other's.

'I can't ask you to take on a ready-made family.' Gemma's smile wobbled. 'I've got five kids. *Five.*'

'They're already part of my family,' Andy said. 'They always have been. I've just been...absent from *their* lives.'

'You and me both.'

'You've made up for it now.'

'I'm trying. But I don't want to put any pressure on you. We don't have to rush anything, Andy.' Gemma's smile was still wobbling. 'It's enough to know that you don't hate me. That…there might still be a chance…'

'Hate you? As if I could.' Andy was watching her lips. They'd been trembling like that up on the roof, hadn't they? He'd cured that by kissing her.

He could do it again.

He moved closer.

'Andy?' The call was urgent. 'Thank goodness…I've found you.' Carla sounded anxious. 'Breakfast is nearly finished. Why aren't you in the Santa suit?'

The dayroom was packed as full as a can of sardines.

Beds lined the walls for the children who weren't mobile. There were wheelchairs tucked into corners, adults holding small children in their arms and a group of children, nurses and parents sitting cross-legged on the floor.

Christmas music was playing, the lights on the Christmas tree were sparkling and Santa was sitting in all his red and white glory on a throne that looked suspiciously like an adult-sized wheelchair covered by an old red velvet curtain.

Gemma was standing just inside the door. She had Sophie in her arms, who was sleeping like a little angel. Hazel was pressed to one side and she had a twin clutching each of her legs. Jamie had edged closer to the chil-

dren sitting on the carpet. Gemma was very proud
of how well her little family was behaving. And she
was selfishly delighted as well because it gave her the
chance to simply stand there and enjoy looking at Andy.

She was loving seeing how much pleasure he was
getting playing his part in giving so many children a
happy day. And every so often, when he was waiting for
a new parcel to appear from the sack or another child
to come and share centre stage, his gaze would stray
toward the door.

To where Gemma was standing.

As if he wanted to reassure himself that she was
still here.

That he hadn't imagined the urgent, whispered exchange of plans for the rest of today as Carla had su-
pervised his attention to important Christmas duties.

He would go home with Gemma and the children
after he was finished here. They could all have some
time together. All of them.

And later, when the children were in bed, they would
be able to talk.

Really talk.

The way they had all those years ago? Before they
had carried such a burden of grief? Before they had
been tired and stressed new parents even?

The way they had when they had been starting out
perhaps. So very much in love, with a future in which
almost anything had seemed possible.

They were both older and wiser now.

If they still loved each other enough, surely anything *was* possible.

Every time Andy's gaze found hers, Gemma found herself feeling more and more hopeful.

The touch of eye contact was like a physical caress that became steadily easier. More familiar. Touching a little deeper every time. Trusting a little more every time. How crazy was it that they could be so far apart in a crowded room and be getting closer with every passing minute?

It was magic.

Christmas magic.

'Ho, ho, ho,' Santa boomed. 'Do I have another present in my sack?'

A young nurse wearing a very cute elf costume reached into the sack and produced both a parcel and a very wide smile.

'It's for John Boy,' she announced.

Santa peered over his gold-rimmed spectacles. 'Is there a John Boy here?'

'It's *me*.' John Boy looked around the whole room to make sure everybody had heard the exciting news and his smile was enough to create a ripple of laughter.

The parcel for John Boy was the largest one yet and he couldn't wait to rip the wrapping paper off.

'It's a box of magic tricks,' he said in awe.

'Better than jokes.' Santa nodded. 'You won't find any plastic vomit in there, lad.'

John Boy grinned. 'How do you know about that?'

Santa wasn't disconcerted in the least. The fluffy

beard moved as he grinned and he tapped the side of his nose with a white-gloved hand. The lights on the tree made his spectacles shine as he looked up. Gemma was close enough to see the crinkles at the corners of his eyes as he smiled at her.

He'd been about to kiss her before, when Carla had interrupted them, but it didn't matter. There would be plenty of time for that later.

Nothing needed to be rushed.

As corny as she knew it was to even think it, Gemma couldn't help reminding herself that today was the first day of the rest of her life.

Of their lives.

And it was Christmas. Having Andy back in her life would be the most priceless gift she could ever receive.

Her eyes were misty as she led the twins up to receive the gifts Santa's elf had found near the bottom of the sack with their names on.

How priceless a gift would it be to these children if they could have Andy as a father?

The sack seemed to be bottomless.

Gift after gift had been distributed. There was a sea of wrapping paper on the floor. His elf had trotted back and forth to give parcels to the children in their beds and she'd even put on a special elf mask to give Ruthie her present on the other side of the glass windows where she was standing with her parents to watch. The extras in attendance, like siblings of patients and all the

Gillespie children, had been given small presents to let them feel included.

Surely, surely it was almost over.

He could take off this astonishingly hot outfit and he could leave work. He could go with Gemma and the children and find the time and space they needed to... to put things right?

To start again?

Andy had no idea what the immediate future held. What he did know was that he was feeling more alive than he had done for years. Bursting with it, in fact. He couldn't wait to step into that future.

Because Gemma would be there.

And the children.

His family.

The elf produced yet another parcel. It looked like a late entry. The size and shape suggested a very generic bar of chocolate.

'It's for Gemma.' Even the elf was losing a little of her enthusiasm.

John Boy hadn't pushed his wheelchair very far away after receiving his gift. He was inspecting a black bag and a plastic egg that were clearly the components of a magic trick but he looked up at the announcement.

'Who's Gemma?'

Carla had taken Sophie, and Gemma was picking her way towards him through the crowd, looking embarrassed at being included.

Andy smiled. 'Gemma's...'

What could he say? There were more people than

John Boy who seemed to be interested in his response. Carla's eyebrows were very high. His elf had her mouth open.

Who was Gemma indeed? Could he call her his wife? No. It was too soon. It would be making assumptions that he had no right to make no matter how much he might want to believe in them.

But then his gaze caught Gemma's as she came closer.

And he knew. He just knew that everything was going to be all right. He could see a reflection of love that was every bit as strong as the love he was feeling for her.

'Gemma's my wife,' he told John Boy.

It felt *so* good to say that.

So right.

Gemma seemed to think so, too, because she was smiling. And crying? She certainly wasn't looking where she was going, which was probably why she tripped on the footplate of John Boy's wheelchair.

Andy leapt off the Christmas throne to catch her before she fell.

John Boy was grinning from ear to ear.

'That makes her Mrs Santa,' he said loudly.

The world seemed to stop spinning for a moment. Was it really all right for this to be happening so fast? So publicly?

'Hmm...' Andy needed to let Gemma know she wasn't under pressure here. 'I guess it might.'

Gemma was laughing.

'I think it does,' she said.

Andy caught his breath. 'Do you want to be Mrs Santa?'

She was looking up at him, those amazing eyes dancing with joy. 'If you're Santa, then yes…of course I want to be Mrs Santa.'

'That's good.' Andy finally remembered to use his Santa voice again. 'Because I have a present for you.'

'It's chocolate,' John Boy said.

'Maybe I have another present for Gemma,' Santa said.

'What is it?'

The question came from John Boy but when Andy hesitated he could suddenly feel way too many pairs of eyes on him.

'Where is it?' John Boy demanded.

'In my pocket,' Andy admitted. He was talking to Gemma now. Only Gemma. He dropped his voice to a whisper that none of the children could overhear. 'I found it in the desk drawer this morning when I was looking for the beard glue.'

Gemma knew what it was.

He'd kept it? After all these years?

That scrappy little piece of plastic mistletoe?

Yes. There it was. He was holding it above her head.

And Santa was kissing her. Amongst the tickle of all that white fluff, she could feel the warmth of Andy's lips. The strength of his love.

The promise of the future.

'Eww.' John Boy was joyously disgusted by the display.

But everyone else seemed to think it was a bonus gift. Gemma could hear clapping. Cheers even.

Nothing to compare with what she could see in Andy's eyes, though.

The joy.

The hope.

'Let's go home,' Andy said softly. 'I have a sleigh that's not far away.'

Gemma held his gaze. 'Does it have room for a few kids?'

'It was made for kids. And you. Especially you.'

'Oi...' John Boy's voice was stern. 'You're not going to start that kissing stuff again, are you?'

Gemma and Andy looked at each other. And smiled.

Of course they were. But not yet. Not here.

'Yes, please, Santa,' Gemma whispered. 'Let's go home.'

* * * * *

THE SHERIFF'S
DOORSTEP BABY

TERESA CARPENTER

For my nieces Amanda, Ashley, Sammy, Erika,
Michelle, Gabrielle and Rachel.
You are everything a heroine should be:
beautiful, smart, talented and loving.
I'm proud of you all.

Teresa Carpenter believes that with love and family anything is possible. She writes in a Southern California coastal city surrounded by her large family. Teresa loves writing about babies and grandmas. Her books have rated as Top Picks by *RT Book Reviews* and have been nominated Best Romance of the Year on some review sites. If she's not at a family event, she's reading or writing her next grand romance.

PROLOGUE

"Daddy! Daddy! You're here."

"Mama! Hi! Over here."

Arms flung wide, ten-year-old Michelle Ross twirled in a wide circle, her long blond curls and wide pink skirt flowing out around her. She determinedly ignored the excited calls of her friends as their parents arrived to visit.

For the first time ever she felt beautiful.

She loved Princess Camp, even if her dad didn't come to parents' day. He said he would, but he promised lots of things that didn't happen. Duty first.

She begged and begged Daddy to be able to come. And of course, he said no. And continued to say no until Aunt Yvonne finally stepped in to plead Michelle's case. She had to behave all of June and July—which had been torture—but come August she'd been off to camp. And all that boring good behavior paid off.

She shared a cabin with Elle and Amanda. They instantly became BFFs and did everything together. And Michelle loved it all, even the etiquette classes. A princess needed to know how to conduct herself!

"Michelle, these are my parents." Dragging a dark-haired man by his hand, Elle proudly presented her father. "Daddy, Mama, Michelle is in my cabin. She's Beauty. I'm Belle and Amanda is Rapunzel. We're going to do a dance for the talent show. Sleeping Beauty had the gift of song, so Michelle's going to sing."

"Hello, Michelle." Elle's father greeted her and shook her hand. "What a lovely young woman you are. I can see why you're Beauty."

She giggled and dropped into a shallow curtsy. "It's so nice to meet you."

"What lovely manners," Elle's mother said with a kind smile.

"The pleasure is all ours." Her dad tugged on Elle's dark red ponytail. "I can't wait to see you girls dance. And to hear you sing, Michelle."

"The talent show isn't until after dinner," Elle advised him. "Come on. I want to show you my cabin, and the pool, and the gazebo."

He laughed indulgently. "We're coming, Elle. But what about your friend?"

"Oh. Michelle's waiting for her dad. Right?"

"Yes—" Michelle nodded and put hope into her voice "—he should be along anytime."

Elle's mom looked down the empty drive and frowned. "I don't like leaving you alone out here."

"I have to stay in the courtyard," Michelle reassured her. "I'll be fine."

"Elle, I think we should ask your friend to keep us company until her dad comes along."

"Yeah." Elle grabbed Michelle's hand, swung it back

and forth. "Come with us. Your dad can find us when he gets here."

"Maybe." Michelle bit her lip. She should wait for Daddy. She was excited to show her dad around camp, to tell him what she'd learned, and how much she loved her time here. More than anything she wanted him to hear her sing and to impress on him that she should come back next year. But the truth was he probably wouldn't even show. He meant his promises when he made them, yet the need to protect and serve took first place every time.

But Elle's daddy thought Michelle was pretty and she wanted to go with them.

"I guess I can look around with you until he gets here."

"Yippee!" Elle smiled and together they skipped ahead.

They showed Elle's parents the cabin and the pool. And when they headed back to the main cabin, The Castle, Michelle looked around hopefully and glanced toward the parking lot, but saw no sign of her dad.

She got ready for the talent show with Elle and Amanda and pretended not to be nervous as she checked the audience repeatedly for her father.

"Come on, Michelle." Amanda grabbed her hand and tugged her away from the wings. "It's our turn."

Michelle frantically searched the crowd one last time but there was no denying the inevitable. Another promise broken. Daddy wouldn't see her sing. She sighed her disappointment and followed her friends onstage.

CHAPTER ONE

HANDS braced on his hips, Sheriff Nate Connor stood looking down at the strange beauty sleeping on his couch. Rolled up in his fleece throw, purple-and-pink-striped socks peeked out from one end and sunshine-yellow hair cascaded from the other.

With a muffled curse he holstered the nine millimeter he'd palmed when he found his front door unlocked. Not that he'd really expected to need it, but a soldier was always prepared. Even in River Run, where the population was less than five thousand.

Luck and skill had kept him from shooting himself when he tripped over the guitar case negligently left in the entry hall.

He considered reaching for his handcuffs, but the woman wasn't a complete stranger. He'd seen sufficient pictures here in this house and on his predecessor's desk to recognize the pretty flow of hair. He was enough of a lawman to figure out she was his new landlord.

And they'd met briefly at her father's funeral seven months ago.

Yeah, he knew who sleeping beauty was. The question was why?

Why was she here and why did she think she could make herself at home on his couch?

He'd had his own plans for that couch. Today was supposed to have been his first day off in over a month. The storm changed that. An overnight delivery truck had skidded on ice and ended up on its side in the pass, blocking traffic in both directions. By the time they got it cleared up, they were in the middle of a full-blown blizzard, and he'd given up any hope of regaining his day off.

A surge of wind knocking branches against the house punctuated the thought.

After a ten-hour day, he'd planned to come home, heat up a frozen dinner and watch the game he'd recorded earlier.

Plans delayed by his uninvited guest's possession of said couch.

A soft snore came from the fleece-wrapped bundle. Nate's dark brows slammed together in a scowl. Now that was irritating. Not because the sound annoyed him, but because it didn't. It had been cute.

He had no room in his life for soft and cute, no patience for trespassing blondes interrupting the last of his day off.

In the past seven months he'd heard nothing from Michelle Ross. Now she slept tucked up on his couch. She may own the place but he had a contract stating it was his for the next four months. He didn't know what brought her to town, but she wasn't staying here.

A matter he meant to take up with her right now.

"Ms. Ross."

No response.

"Ms. Ross." Advancing on the couch, he repeated the demand for her attention, and then again, louder each time. She stirred and then settled against the cushions, sighing as she pulled the throw tighter around herself.

Finally he leaned down and shook her shoulder. "Come on, beauty, wake up."

She stirred and mumbled something.

Instinctively, he leaned closer to hear what she said.

But suddenly she turned and her lips brushed his. That's when her eyes opened. Lovely eyes that brought the green of spring to a late-winter's storm. And that thought distracted him long enough for her to wrap her arms around his neck and draw him down for a deeper kiss.

Questions of who and why and what disappeared in a rush of sensation. She felt warm and soft, and tasted oh, so sweet. This was what home should feel like, what a welcome should taste like.

Nate threaded his hands in all that hair and sank into the moment. After the day he'd had, he let the heat of the kiss sweep him away.

Michelle dreamed of a man on a white horse riding through the forest. Tall and strong, he carried a sword and sought a beautiful princess, ready to save her from all her woes. Michelle was both the princess and not. She liked the safety the knight represented, but it never came free and she wanted to save herself.

Only fools and optimists believed in love. Which left her out. She was nobody's fool. And she'd given up on optimism early in life. She preferred to control her own destiny than hope for the best.

Now the knight was on top of her, holding her gently, his hands fisted in her hair, broad shoulders blocking out the world. He smelled like the fleece that held her in warmth and comfort, of the woods and man. But he was heat and power and his lips were on hers and she didn't care if there was a price. Safe had never felt so good.

She arched into the kiss, opening her lips at the demand of his, welcoming him in, savoring the spicy taste of the man who held her so securely.

His hand moved in a sweeping caress from her head to her waist, where skin met skin. The shock of his cold fingers reached beyond Michelle's lethargy.

Her eyes flew open and she realized this was no dream, no Prince Charming of childish imaginings, but a flesh-and-blood man with a bold kiss and cold hands.

She broke off the kiss, planted both palms flat against his chest and pushed. "Back up, buddy!"

For a moment, just a heartbeat, he held the embrace, and then he released her and surged to his feet.

"Hell. I must be more tired than I thought." He scrubbed both hands over a face a shade too ordinary to be considered handsome. Straight dark eyebrows topped fierce gray eyes. Cut military-short, his hair was a tawny blend of brown, blond and red. Temper, or maybe it was passion, brought a ruddy hue to his cheeks.

The khaki uniform so like her father's had her narrowing her eyes on him as she swung her feet to the floor and sat up. Pain throbbed in her ankle, but she ignored it.

"Who are you and what are you doing in my house?" she demanded. "Besides accosting me?"

"You mean my home?" His hands went to his hips, and he met her glare for glare. "And you kissed me."

She raised brows at him. "A neat trick for someone asleep. I inherited this house from my father."

"And I rented it from him."

That surprised her. "He didn't tell me anything about renting the house. When did that happen?"

"Ben rented me a room when I first moved to town and I continued to rent the place when he moved in with his lady friend almost a year ago."

"Dad had a girlfriend?" She'd been dreaming of princesses and white knights, but clearly she'd fallen down the rabbit hole. As far as she knew, Dad had never had a lady friend.

"I remember you now, from my father's funeral." Usually great with names, she reached for his and came up short. The funeral had been hard for her. She took a stab. "Gabe?"

"Nate." He corrected. "Nate Connor."

"Well, Nate, it seems you took over Dad's job, and you took over his house."

His expression frosted over. "What are you implying?"

"Nothing nefarious." She waved off his paranoia. "I'm just saying this is my house."

She'd only come back to River Run to sell the house so she could move to Los Angeles and pursue her songwriting career.

She'd escaped this town when she graduated from

high school—couldn't leave the little burg fast enough—and nothing had changed since. With her dad's passing the small town had even less going for it now than it had when she was a kid.

So no, she hadn't crept through Dead Man's Pass praying to a deity she hadn't spoken to in way too long to be kicked out of her own home.

"It's your house, but it's rented to me. I have a contract if you'd like to see it." Nate crossed his arms over his chest, causing his biceps to pop. "You didn't talk to your dad much, did you?"

The truth she'd come to acknowledge since her dad's passing hit her hard. Hearing the censure from the current sheriff didn't help.

"You don't know anything about my relationship with my father." Anger had her pushing to her feet. The ankle she'd injured walking up the snow-covered path from the car to the front door protested at the sudden motion, at the sudden weight, and gave out on her.

He caught her before she could fall, putting those impressive biceps to work, his grip under her elbows easily holding her weight off the sore foot.

"Are you okay?" Exasperation sat alongside concern in the question.

"Fine." She attempted to shrug off his touch, but he held firm until she was seated once again. "I tripped on something on the way up the walk."

He frowned. "I'll check it out tomorrow. Do you need ice for your ankle?"

It irked to hear him playing host in her house. She

shook her head. "I'm fine. How long did you know my dad?"

"Three years," he said as he shrugged out of his jacket and hung it on the newel post.

She waited, hearing the cry of a kitten in the lull, but that was all he shared. Great. Her father had been the same all her life, bound by duty, determined to steal all the joy from her life. Now it seemed there'd been more to him than she remembered, but the bearer of the news was no more talkative than her father had been.

"Not very long," she challenged.

"Not compared to twenty-five years, no. But I talked to him, worked with him, spent time with him. You let a complete stranger make funeral arrangements."

Shame burned in her. That had been the lowest time in her life. A bad week capped off by the loss of her father. Yeah, she should have come home and taken care of the details of Dad's funeral, but she'd been trying to save her job, trying to hold together the fraying edges of her life.

In the end she'd only been delaying the inevitable.

"I thanked you for your help." She tried to find a smile and a little of her patented charm to ease the way with him. She'd learned early in life that a pretty girl had power, and she wielded the tool of her looks like any other talent.

But she was too weary, too annoyed with him and the crying of his cat, to bother. Or maybe she was too unsettled by the taste of him still in her mouth to summon a smile.

And what had that been about anyway? She was supposed to have kissed him in her sleep? Right.

So okay, she'd been kissing the knight in her dream. Coincidence. By no means did that translate into smooching a stranger in her sleep.

"Huh." He dismissed her claim of gratitude. "Where are you staying?"

She frowned. "What do you mean? This is my home, I'm staying here."

"I have a contract that says you're not."

"You can't throw me out of my own house." Dread tightened like a fist in her gut. She couldn't afford to pay for alternative accommodations.

"This badge says I can."

"Please." She gestured to her swollen foot. "I couldn't leave if I wanted. I can't drive."

He drew a set of keys from his pants pocket. "I can take you wherever you need to go."

Sleet blew against the window as the wind roared, a timely reminder of the harsh weather.

"I'm not leaving." Defiant, she crossed her arms over her chest and made a show of settling back into the couch. The tension from the long trip was back as she faced being expelled from her own home, the stress aggravated by the cries of distress from the kitten deep in the house.

"Oh, you are."

She shook her head, holding up a staying hand. "Before we continue this argument, can you go feed your cat? The distressful cries are driving me crazy."

"What are you talking about? I don't have a cat."

She blinked in surprise. "Well, then one is trying to get in. Don't you hear that? It's been crying for the last five minutes."

This should be interesting. Would the big bad sheriff help the stray or leave it to fend for itself in the storm he was so ready to toss her out into?

He cocked his head as he listened. The roaring wind covered the sound for a moment and then the plaintive wail came again, weaker now. Poor kitty.

"That's not a cat." Suddenly his expression changed, became harder—something she couldn't have imagined—and determined. Urgent now he moved to the front door, flung it open, and charged coatless into the blizzard. "It's a—"

The wind grabbed his last word and garbled it, but it sounded like he'd said *baby.* Unbelieving, she hobbled over to the door, righted her suitcase, which had fallen, and set it and her guitar case against the wall.

Using the door for support, she peered into the darkness and screamed when Nate loomed up in front of her. He carried a baby seat. The howling she'd mistaken for a cat's yowls had turned to faint whimpers.

"My God. Hurry," she urged him. "A baby! What if I hadn't heard him crying?" She slowly followed Nate to the couch, where he set the carrier down. "Poor thing, he's shivering. And look how red his skin is."

"Hypothermia. Get him out of the seat and his clothes," Nate ordered. "Put him inside your shirt and wrap up in the fleece. Don't rub his skin. I'll get the fire going."

Michelle sat down and pulled a damp blue blanket

away to get at the straps holding the baby in the seat. Quiet now, eyes closed, the infant shook so hard the seat moved. A dingy white cap covered the child's head, but he wore no socks and his thin outfit offered little protection against the elements, including his own blanket.

Next she unbuttoned her pink-and-purple plaid flannel shirt and pulled her T-shirt from her jeans. Her heart broke as she lifted the tiny body, quickly stripped him down to his diaper and then cuddled him to her chest under her shirt. Teeth chattering at the chill he brought with him, she wrapped them both in the warm fleece blanket.

"His hands and feet are freezing cold," she reported, happy to see the fire going. Already the room felt warmer. "How could anyone leave a baby out in a storm like that? It's inhumane."

"Yes, it is." Ice dripped from the words as Nate came to stand over her. "It's neglect and child endangerment. I hope you have a good lawyer."

CHAPTER TWO

"THAT'S not funny." Glaring up into the sheriff's cold gray eyes, Michelle carefully shifted the baby so his nose wasn't pressed into her.

"It's not meant to be." He tapped his badge. "I don't joke about the law."

"And I don't abandon defenseless babies."

"No, you just break into houses."

"It's my house," she reminded him through gritted teeth. "So there's no reason I wouldn't have brought the baby inside."

"You knew it was a boy," he said, arms braced across his broad chest.

"A guess from the blue blanket. And it hasn't been substantiated yet. You called him a boy, too."

"He arrived at the same time you did."

"You don't know what time I got here." She narrowed her eyes at him. "Seems to me he arrived at the same time you did."

How dare he accuse her of such an atrocious act? She fully admitted she looked out for number one. You had to put yourself first when no one else did. But she had a soft spot for kids, got along with them better than a lot of adults.

She narrowed her eyes at him. "And as you're so quick to claim, it's your doorstep." She made a point of pulling open the neck of her shirt and looking from the baby to the man. "I think he has your eyes."

His frown turned ferocious. "That's not my kid."

"Are you sure?" she persisted just to aggravate him. "He looks about three or four months old. Think back about a year, something will come to you."

"There is no possibility the child is mine."

"How can you be so sure? A lot of men have vague memories when it comes to things like this."

"I know."

"Oh, right." She rolled her eyes at his arrogance. *"You know."*

"I haven't been with a woman since I moved to River Run." Acknowledgment of what he'd revealed came sharp on the heels of his outburst. "Ah, hell."

"Why?" The word burst from her. Shocked, she ran her gaze over him. "You're not bad-looking and your body is smoking hot."

"I have my reasons, which are none of your business." The grimness of his tone warned her the topic was closed.

"Okay." She valued her own privacy too much to disrespect other people's rights to the same. "We've established he's not mine and not yours, so who is he? Was the seat all that was with him? Was there a diaper bag? Maybe there's a note."

"I'll check." Happy for action, he headed for the door.

While he was gone she went through the seat. She found a pacifier and a soggy piece of paper. She was trying to shake it open when Nate returned with a diaper bag.

"What's that?" he demanded.

"It was in the seat." She handed the paper to him. "I think it's the note we're looking for."

Sitting beside her, he carefully unfolded the paper and spread the note. He took up a good portion of the couch and Michelle would have moved away from the large bulk of him, but she wanted to see the note.

Plus he was warm. And he smelled good.

So instead of sensibly moving away, she scooted closer and peered over his large arm. Pretending not to notice his big hands and the thick width of his wrist, she read the note.

Nate,
This is your cosin Jack. I never wanted a kid. Im too old and I cant take care of him and work. I gotta work to stay outta the joint. Jack talked good about you. He was good to me so Im giving his kid to you. If you don't want him giv him to somebody to giv him a good home.

"Well, I'm off the hook. Too bad for you," Michelle muttered. The letter offended her. She knew desperation, knew self-absorption, and she could never abandon a child. She suddenly had new respect for her father, who'd at least accepted the responsibility of raising her.

"Joint?" she sneered.

"She means jail."

"I know what joint means. She's barely literate, but that's no excuse for abandoning her baby. How could she give her son away? What about your cousin Jack? Where is he?"

"Dead."

Oh, man. "I'm sorry. What happened?"

"He was killed in a bar fight five months ago."

"Oh."

"Don't say it like that." The eyes he turned on her were grieving. "Like he was a lowlife drunk. Jack was a nice guy, but he was troubled. He should never have followed me into the service. Some men aren't meant to be killers. A stint on the front line messed him up good, and then they sent him home. But the damage was done. He began drinking, had a hard time keeping a job."

Nate rubbed a hand over the back of his neck. "He was excited about the baby. Becoming a father was the first thing he cared about in a long time. And then he was gone. He didn't even get to see his son."

"I'm sorry," she said again, with more feeling this time. It was a sad story. She looked down at the lump of the baby under her shirt and thought he had a hard time ahead of him. She didn't remember her mother, she'd died when Michelle was two, but she had been loved, coddled during those first formative years. Little Jack didn't even have that.

When she looked up, she found the sheriff watching her.

"You need to call Child Services."

"Why?"

Her eyebrows lifted, giving away her surprise. "So they can come get Jack, of course."

He shook his head. "They'd only try to locate his next of kin, and that's me, so there's no need to call them."

"But you aren't equipped to take care of him."

"No," he said grimly, "but it looks like I have little choice."

"So what does that mean? What are you going to do?"

He shrugged. "Raise him."

She blinked at him. "Just like that?"

"Yeah."

"Wow." What did it say about him that he hadn't even hesitated? That he was honorable? Responsible? Both fit with him being a sheriff. "You're not even going to think about it?"

"My uncle took me in, taught me what it meant to be a man. Jack was like a brother to me. Of course I'm going to take care of his kid."

"That's huge. There aren't many men I know who would just take a baby in like that."

"Then they aren't men."

That was a pretty tough stance. But after a moment's thought, Michelle nodded. He was right. One thing she could say about her dad, he'd never tried to give her away.

"Do you have to start tonight? Couldn't you call Child Services to take him until you move into your new place and get all the gear you'll need?" How could she work on the house with a baby around? They required care and feeding, and quiet.

His hands went to his hips and he shook his head, his expression forbidding.

"Ms. Ross, if anyone is leaving tonight, it's you. As it is, you'll be leaving first thing in the morning. Because this is my place for the next four months."

"But I need to sell the house. And I need to make improvements."

"Not my problem."

"But it's my house."

"And I have a lease. We've been over this."

"But—"

He held up a hand. "There are rental laws. Read them. Then we'll talk."

Michelle wanted to bite the offending hand. Arrogant jerk. It wasn't her fault her father rented the place without letting her know. She had the right to move on with her life and selling this house was a big part of that.

But she was smart enough to know pressing the issue wouldn't gain her any points, so she retreated.

She nodded at the note. "What about the mother? She didn't sign the note. Do you know her?"

"I met her. Wasn't impressed." The very flatness of his tone spoke volumes. "She has a criminal record so she won't get another chance to hurt Jack."

"Understand I have no sympathy for the woman, but it's possible she knocked. We were arguing and the storm is loud."

"Then she should have knocked harder—" there was no give in his response "—waited for me to open the door and talked to me."

"You might have said no."

"That's no excuse."

"No, but it's a possibility she wasn't willing to risk. Wait…" Michelle suddenly noticed something was different. "He's stopped shivering. I heard that's bad."

"Maybe not." His calm response took the edge off her panic. "If he were still in the cold, yes. But he's been warming up. The need to shiver is gone. Is he still breathing?"

She froze, worried for a moment he'd stopped, but she felt the soft heat of his breath against her chest.

"Yeah." She glanced down at her misshaped T-shirt. "I'd feel better if I could see him."

Nate stepped over, grabbed the neck of her undershirt in both hands and effortlessly tore an eight-inch rip down the front. Michelle gasped, shocked by his outrageous action.

"Hey!" she protested, glowering at him.

"You said you wanted to see the baby. Now you can."

Yeah, and the swell of her breasts and the pink lace of her bra. She pulled her flannel shirt closed over herself and the baby.

"I thought the point was to keep the baby warm."

"Right. And skin-to-skin is the best way. Warm fluids would be good, too."

She nodded toward the diaper bag. "There's probably stuff to make a bottle in there. Do you think you can handle it or should we trade places?"

"If I'm going to raise him, I may as well learn how to feed him now." He grabbed a bottle and a tin of formula from the diaper bag and headed for the kitchen.

Michelle frowned after him. Most people would

probably find that admirable. She just found it annoying. It was just as much a fault to have to do everything yourself as to want everyone else to do it for you.

Then again she may just be reacting to her disappointment in not getting to see the baby pressed to Nate's bare chest.

She imagined it would be a pretty impressive sight.

Thinking about it, she decided, no, her annoyance had nothing to do with being denied an erotic peek and everything to do with Sheriff Nate Connor being an arrogant pain in the butt.

In the kitchen Nate leaned against the counter and curled his shaking hands into fists.

How righteous he sounded when he told her he'd be raising Jack. Little did she know the internal fight he went through.

What did he know about raising a kid? Nothing. Sure his uncle had taken him in, but he'd been a stupid teenager and Uncle Stan already had a kid, so taking on Nate had been nothing new. And the Lord knew Nate was already messed up so there was little Uncle Stan could do to damage him.

Not so with Jack. He was an infant with his whole life spread out before him. The damage Nate could do encompassed everything from the baby's health to his spiritual upraising. Nate groaned. Hell, he couldn't remember the last time he went to church, the last time he'd done more than take the Lord's name in vain.

New rule—no cursing.

Because he was a father now, no matter how freaked

the notion made him. Because he was no coward and no quitter. He owed Uncle Stan and Jack, so Nate reached for the can of formula and began to read.

He would learn and he would adjust. And he and baby Jack would be just fine.

The baby stirred against Michelle and she looked down into frowning gray eyes. Jack was awake.

"Hey, little guy, how are you doing?" She smiled in relief and to assure him she was a friend. His color had improved and she cuddled him close and rubbed a finger over the downy softness of wispy wheat-colored hair. "Are you feeling better?"

He blinked at her, which she took as a yes.

"Bad news, buddy, your mom, the lowlife witch—" Michelle's sweet tone never changed as she dealt the insult "—dropped you on Cousin Nate's doorstep in the middle of the biggest storm of the season."

He stared at her with sober eyes, taking in every word she spoke.

"Hopefully, your daddy was smarter than your mommy." She nodded at the alertness in his gaze. "The good news is your cousin Nate says he's going to raise you." Chewing the inside of her cheek, she sighed. "Actually, I'm not going to lie to you. It's a good news-bad news thing. He'll be a rock for you, but he'll have impossible expectations. At least that's how it was with my dad."

His little face crumpled and he began to whimper.

"Oh, shoot." Michelle gently bounced Jack, trying to

calm him. "No, baby, don't cry. Shh. Maybe I'm wrong. Maybe Nate is different."

"Different from what?" a deep voice demanded.

Flinching internally, she carefully controlled her expression when she met Nate's challenging gaze.

"I was warning him how difficult it can be to live with a sheriff."

He lifted one dark brow, silent reproach in the gesture. "Thanks for undermining me before I've even met the kid."

"The truth is the truth."

"Being sheriff is what I do." He handed her the full bottle. "It's not who I am."

"I was raised by a lawman." The warm bottle felt good in her hand. She checked the temperature of the formula on her wrist. Perfect, of course. She fed it to Jack, who latched onto the nipple and sucked, his little hands coming up to rest on the bottle. "I know what wearing that uniform means. Long hours, community service, duty first. Family a far and distant second."

"You don't know anything about me. I won't be judged by the actions of another."

"Fine. Prove me wrong."

"I would." Nate settled into the corner of the couch. "But you won't be around to see. You just want to sell this house and head back to the city."

He was right. And she wouldn't apologize for wanting to move forward with her life. "I'm not going back to San Francisco. I'm moving to Los Angeles."

"Really?" He lifted one dark brow. "Following some guy south?"

She snorted. As if she'd move across town for some guy. "My agent thinks it'll be better for my songwriting career. And now who's judging?"

"I'm just calling it as I see it."

"There's nothing in this town for me anymore."

"You've never believed there was anything here for you," he said.

Michelle glanced up from the sweet baby to study the stoic sheriff. How did he know her so well when they'd only met briefly at the funeral before today? She didn't think Dad had been the type to talk about his absent daughter. Maybe she'd been wrong about that.

"You were wrong then and you're wrong now."

"Wrong?" Could he read minds now?

"About what the town has to offer."

"I don't have anything in common with the people here. I want more."

"More what?"

The same question her dad had always had for her. She didn't know! She just knew this town lacked what she needed.

"More everything. More music, more options, more money, more entertainment, more men, more people who want more."

And Dad had never understood, never accepted how important music was to her, that songwriting wasn't just a dream but what drove her.

"Shallow. I guess you're right after all. River Run has character, people with heart and integrity who care about their neighbors, where life is more important than entertainment and meeting strangers in the street."

No surprise, Sheriff Nate Connor didn't understand, either. Why that hurt she couldn't say.

She ran the back of her finger over baby Jack's powder-soft cheek, wishing him a better life in River Run than she'd had. "He's asleep again."

"Good. Hypothermia is hard on the system."

"Is the storm going to get better or worse tomorrow?"

"Why? You have somewhere you gotta be?" he mocked her.

"Just answer the question."

"Worse. This was only supposed to be a light snow flurry, but a massive cold front pushed down from Alaska causing blizzard conditions. It's supposed to get worse before it gets better. We've battened down the town and advised people to stay inside except for emergencies."

Nodding, she tucked the fleece-wrapped baby in the crook of the couch and set his bottle on the oak coffee table.

"Then I should get at least one of my other suitcases tonight." She reached for her shoes.

Nate didn't move. "You're not going out in the storm. Didn't you hear me say I advised the townspeople to stay inside?"

"This is an emergency."

"You're safe and sound inside a warm house. There's food and water, and a flushing toilet. How is this an emergency?"

His long-suffering expression made her grit her teeth.

"I need clothes. I have a change of underwear in my overnight case, but not clothes." She tugged at her

ripped T-shirt. "And the ones I have on came into contact with a Neanderthal."

"You can borrow something of mine." He shrugged
off her sarcasm. "Nobody is going back out into the
storm."

Shooting daggers at him, because she'd hoped he'd
offer to get the cases for her, she made her way around
the table to the middle of the room. Her ankle throbbed
but held her weight.

"Ten minutes ago you were ready to send me on my
way."

"That was before I'd been back outside. The storm
has worsened."

"All the more reason to go now. I'm going to get my
suitcase and you can't stop me."

He laughed. And pushed to his feet with a lithe grace
that spoke of muscle and discipline and the easy strength
to make her do anything he wanted her to.

Aggravating man.

"You don't scare me." Still she couldn't prevent
taking an instinctive step back. And immediately felt
her ankle turn. Pain streaked through her foot and she
started to fall.

She screamed.

The baby cried.

And the lights went out.

CHAPTER THREE

"I've got you." Nate caught a bundle of soft female curves in his arms. She smelled of something fruity, clean and tart…and good enough to eat.

Too bad she was prickly as a porcupine. Because it looked as if he was stuck with her for a couple of days.

"I'm fine." She twisted against him, seeking release. "You've made your point. I'm not going outside."

"Stay still." He shifted his hold from her arms to her waist, practically spanning the narrow width with his hands. She was tinier than he'd thought. "You're going to hurt yourself worse than you already have."

"The baby is crying."

"We'll get to Jack in a minute." For some reason Nate couldn't let Michelle go. She'd untucked her shirt when she stuck the baby under the hem and the thumb of his right hand rested on the silky warmth of her skin. It wasn't personal, he assured himself. It wasn't Michelle he wanted.

It just felt so good to hold a woman in his arms.

But he had enough common sense to know the landlord who wanted to sell his house out from under him was not the place to kick-start his libido.

He had no choice but to let her stay for a couple of days, but after that she'd be gone. Either to a place in town or preferably back to the city to stay until his lease ended and she could return to do her thing without his bumping into her.

She stopped struggling, going totally still. The lights were out but the fire gave off enough light for him to realize the dark shook her.

He could handle a woman's tears. When your mother cried at the drop of a hat, you learned to cope or became an emotional wreck yourself. Still the long day—days— and the baby must have him off his game, because he really didn't want to see the tears sparkling in Michelle's emerald-bright eyes fall. Already he knew enough about her to know she'd hate putting on a tearful display for him.

"What's wrong, Michelle? Are you afraid of the dark?"

Anger instantly sparked, wiping the distress from her face, replacing it with haughty distain.

"Of course not." Her chin lifted and instead of pulling away from him she stepped forward until her pink flannel shirt brushed against the khaki of his uniform. "I'm at my best in the dark."

His body reacted with a rush. Holy sh— Moly.

Ding! Ding! Ding! Round one to Michelle.

A warrior knew the advantages of a timely retreat. He quickly released her and took two steps back, narrowly missing the coffee table and a fall of his own.

She flipped her hair and flashed him a glance of triumph as she moved to pick up the baby and coo at him.

Not a tear in sight, and she seemed to have forgotten her missing suitcases.

Mission accomplished. So it hadn't been a total defeat.

"Good. Then keep an eye on Jack. I'm going to go get some flashlights and candles. Plus I have to make some calls. I may be a few minutes."

"Okay." But she couldn't prevent a flinch of uncertainty.

"Don't let the fire go out."

"Don't worry."

"I'll be as fast as I can and we'll get some light in here."

"Thanks. I think the dark upsets Jack."

Nate stared down at Jack held snuggly in her arms and an unexpected rush of emotion swelled up in him. The baby had Nate's uncle's eyes, the resemblance especially strong with Jack scowling like he was doing now.

How Nate had loved that old man.

Funny, he'd always thought of Uncle Stan as old, but hell, at forty-two his uncle had only been ten years older than Nate was now when he took in a wild fourteen-year-old.

He'd been in a bad place but Uncle Stan took no guff from him. There'd been no bluff in the man, but he'd cared. He'd been as free with his affections as he'd been with his disciplines. Nate had needed both.

He'd learned how a real man acted.

How proud Uncle Stan would be of baby Jack. Though it hurt Nate to admit it, he was glad his uncle hadn't seen Jack Sr.'s spiral into drunken obscureness.

He wouldn't have blamed Nate—Stan believed a man was responsible for his own choices—but it would have killed him to see Jack's pain, and the weakness that took him over.

The baby, the continuance of the Connor family, would have thrilled Uncle Stan. Michelle was surprised by Nate's willingness to take the baby on, but Nate owed Uncle Stan and Jack too much, loved them too much, to shame them by turning away baby Jack.

Which meant for the time being he needed Michelle. At least for tonight; beyond that, he'd see.

"Right." He mocked her claim that Jack was the one afraid of the dark.

She hit him with a scorching glare, but all she said, was "Food would be good, too."

Her bravado and the underlying vulnerability got to him. He called himself a chump but once he'd gathered the flashlights, candles and a battery lantern he returned to the living room.

He lit candles and placed them on the mantel, handed her a flashlight and set the blazing lantern on the coffee table. But it was her smile that lit up the room.

"Double chump," he muttered as he escaped to the kitchen. The phones were out, too, so he used his cell to call the county supervisor's office to get the status of the utilities. He learned the storm had taken out several major hubs. And then the line went dead as his phone beeped and informed him he was out of service.

"Great."

The need to fix the problems pressed at him, but there was literally nothing he could do except prepare for the cold night ahead. The loss of electricity meant they'd have no working heater.

He grabbed a box from the utility room and piled in his stash from the refrigerator and cupboard, tossed in utensils and topped it with plates, mugs, a pan and napkins. Next he used the flashlight he'd kept to find two sleeping bags in the attached garage.

Why he bothered to go to so much trouble for a woman so self-absorbed she rarely contacted the father who obviously adored her, Nate didn't know. And sure she was watching the baby, but she hadn't even offered to help. No doubt she expected to be waited on hand and foot. Well, that wouldn't wash here. He expected people to pull their own weight and since her temporary stay was on his dime, she'd just have to meet his expectations.

He frowned, remembering what he'd overheard her telling Jack. That kids of sheriffs had to live with high expectations and little freedom. It made him recall the early days with his uncle Stan. That's exactly how he'd felt. The restrictions had chafed badly, but it had also felt good to know someone cared about where he was and what he was doing. To have someone who checked up on him and made sure he had something to eat.

It took two trips to get everything to the living room and Michelle was sitting on the hearth pawing through the food box when he came back with the sleeping bags.

"Big boy, you are my hero." The sultry look of anticipation on her face made him wish she were gazing at him instead of the stew she was transferring from plastic container to cast-iron pot. "I'm starved, and this smells really good."

When she put her finger in her mouth to clean off a smudge of gravy, he had to disguise a groan with a cough.

That brought her attention up from the food.

"You're not catching a cold, are you?"

Was that real concern in her voice?

"Because you're a parent now, you have to take better care of yourself."

Nate rolled his eyes. He should have known better.

"Thanks for your concern." The sarcasm slid off his tongue before he could rein it in. Damn, now he'd have to put up with the sulks for an hour while she pouted around. He moderated his tone. "But I'm fine."

Unoffended, she flashed him a dimpled grin. "I'm just saying. No more wandering around in the cold without a jacket."

Surprised by her easy response, Nate felt some of the tension in his shoulders lessen. Maybe the woman had a few redeeming qualities.

"Yes, Mother."

"Oh." Her green eyes widened and then narrowed dangerously. "You didn't go there."

He had. And her huff made him add, "You want a cap and slippers to go with that advice?"

"You're going to pay for that, buster." She promised retribution. "Now you get to play chef."

She pushed the heavy pot into the flames of the fire. And to punctuate her point she stood, dusted off her curvy butt and hobbled back to the couch, where she claimed her seat in the corner. Arms crossed over her chest plumped up her breasts, pushing pink lace and considerable cleavage into view.

"I like it steaming hot," she said with a slow lick of her lips.

Oh, devious, devious woman. The wanton knew exactly how to make a man pay. And it had nothing to do with cooking supper.

Determined to keep his composure, he put his back to the tempting sight of the contrary female.

"You're fickle, Ms. Ross. First I'm your hero, then I'm a sorry fellow tasked with heating your stew."

He glanced over his shoulder, taking in the cozy scene backlit by the encompassing darkness. Baby sleeping, a tiny blanket-wrapped bundle; smug woman, pretty in pink flannel. As she caught his gaze, she flipped her hair in a gesture no doubt learned in the cradle. The long tresses looked like flowing gold in the firelight.

"Cooked steaming hot," he emphasized.

She lifted a brow. "I wasn't talking about the stew."

Michelle bit back a laugh. She swore the man almost swallowed his tongue.

Served him right. Calling her *mother*. The nerve.

Stew was good, though. As if on cue, her stomach growled. Not loud enough to be heard, thank goodness, but a definite reminder it had been close to nine hours since she last ate.

"But it'll do for now," she purred, taking satisfaction in seeing his shoulders brace as if ready for a fight. Better prepare, big boy, she was here to fight for her inheritance, and she wouldn't let a massive he-man stand in her way.

Flirting came as natural to her as breathing. And if a little harmless seduction threw him off his stride, good. It might get her what she wanted and no way would she fall for River Run's newest lawman.

"You'll mind your manners if you want a serving," he calmly responded.

Ah. A challenge.

"You'd really deny an injured woman a simple meal?" she chastised in a wounded voice, soft and just a little accusatory.

He just shook his head without turning and dished up two bowls of the savory stew. Then he opened a foil-wrapped loaf of bread and cut two big slices, putting one in each of the bowls. Walking over, he handed one of the bowls to her.

"Thank you." She reached eagerly for the meal, too hungry to pretend otherwise. The first bite tasted divine and she moaned in pleasure. "Excellent. Did you make this?"

"No," he said from the brown corduroy recliner next to her. "A friend cooked it for me." He eyed her over his steaming bowl. "You're going to be trouble."

It wasn't a question, but she nodded. She didn't usually reveal her weaknesses, especially to strong competitors, but weariness and desperation drove her to the point of honesty.

"I need to stay here," she said bravely.

"And if I say no?"

She chewed carefully, the yummy stew suddenly sitting heavy in her stomach. "You can't."

"We both know I should."

"I don't know that," she denied. "I think we can help each other out here."

That stopped him midbite. He lifted one dark eyebrow. "How's that?"

"I need a place to stay." She choked out the words, then cleared her throat and put determination in the rest. "And you need help with little Jack."

"Hmm. Seems I could hire someone who won't cause trouble to do that."

"But you don't have to pay me." Hmm. "Much."

He laughed. A hearty, rusty-sounding bark that came from deep inside him and startled the baby awake.

Michelle immediately reached for the baby, her first instinct to soothe and settle him, and then her healthy sense of self-preservation kicked in. So instead she cooed to little Jack on her way to handing him to Nate.

Let him see what he'd be dealing with without in-house assistance.

"Here you go." She held the crying child out to Nate.

"Humph." He set his bowl on the coffee table and took the squalling baby into his arms.

The trick worked because the baby continued to cry no matter what Nate did to soothe him. Then she felt bad because Jack refused to be mollified. Nate patted him, talked to him, put him over his shoulder and held him in his lap. Actually he was very good with the baby, holding him well and confidently.

But nothing made Jack happy.

Once she finished eating she set her dishes aside and took him so Nate could finish his meal.

She thought she'd be able calm the child, even hummed a little song for him, which seemed to be working and then it wasn't. Instead he worked himself into a full screaming fit. So much for her plan. And her ego.

"I changed his diaper," she said even as she checked him again to make sure he was still dry. "And he just had a bottle. I don't know why he's so upset."

"Maybe he's still hungry," Nate offered. "Do you think he'd like some stew?"

"He's too small to eat that. Or any solids. How old did you say he was?"

"Four months."

Did that mean Jack could have food? She wasn't sure. "I don't know. I had a coworker with a new baby. I think she started feeding her little girl about this age. But if so, it was only soft cereal or pureed fruits and vegetables."

"Yeah, well, we don't have any of that. I'm going to give him a little of the broth."

Michelle hesitated, still unsure, but the frantic crying wore at her nerves. At this point she was willing to give it a try. She gratefully released the baby into Nate's care.

"Be careful," she urged him. "Make sure you don't get any chunks of food. And don't give him too much. It's rich and his system won't be used to it."

"Let's see if he even likes it." Nate dipped the tip of his spoon in the thick broth and brought it to the shrieking baby's mouth, touching the tiny tongue with a small taste. For a moment there was no change, but Nate tried it again. This time the crying stuttered as Jack worked his tongue against his lips, but his little body still shuddered with the force of his sobs.

"That's promising." Nate fed him another small sip.

"Not too fast," she cautioned as blessed silence surrounded them.

"He likes it."

"I'm sure he does. It's got more flavor than anything else he's ever eaten."

"It shut him up." Nate sent her a superior look as he continued to feed the baby. "You can't argue with the results."

"I can if he gets sick later," she shot back. "I think that's enough."

"Okay. One more." He talked to the baby, explained this was the last bite, but he could have another bottle later. And Nate continued to talk to Jack after he lifted him to his shoulder, telling him about the storm and how Jack had to do his part to help them all have a good night under the trying circumstances.

He talked until Jack fell asleep.

"Good job." She applauded. "Hopefully he's out for a while."

"I guess it's too much to hope he's out for the night?"

"Afraid so. Speaking of which, who gets him for the night? Are you ready to agree to my terms?"

He sighed, the baby lifting and falling with the movement of his broad chest. "Trouble with a capital *T.*"

She grinned at the resignation in his voice. "Just saying. Life will be so much easier with me around."

"Huk."

What kind of noise was that?

"You okay?" She couldn't tell if he was choking or trying not to laugh. Maybe a little of both?

He reprimanded her with the flash of diamond-sharp eyes as he fought to get himself under control.

"Witch. Lucky for me I don't need to make a decision tonight." He nodded at a couple of sleeping bags she hadn't noticed before. "We'll be sleeping together down here next to the fire."

CHAPTER FOUR

MICHELLE'S spine snapped straight. "What do you mean sleep together? Why do we have to sleep down here?"

"The heater is electric," Nate stated calmly. "That means there's no heat upstairs."

"Surely we'd be warm enough under our blankets? I don't remember sleeping down here as a kid."

"Your dad told me he changed from gas to electric some years ago. Probably felt it was safer." He stood and set the baby in the seat. "But if you want to try finding enough blankets to huddle under, be my guest. Jack and I are sleeping down here next to the fire."

As if he cared less what she chose to do, he gathered the dirty dishes and pot of stew and carried it all into the kitchen.

Obviously no help would be coming from that direction. Michelle bit her lip and eyed the distance to the stairs. The twelve feet seemed daunting enough considering her foot had given out when she'd barely passed the coffee table before the lights went out. Add in the stairs and the walk down the hall while carrying her overnight bag and gathering extra blankets along the way, and she saw the impossibility of the challenge.

"I'll sleep on the couch," she announced when Nate returned to the room.

"Suit yourself." He offered no argument. But he stood and surveyed her with his hands braced on his hips. "It'll be a little lumpy once I remove the mattress from the Hide-A-Bed, but you can keep the cushions."

Though it seemed an obvious question, she didn't ask why he didn't just pull out the Hide-A-Bed and use it as is. He'd already stated his intent to be close to the fire.

Plus she didn't want to share a bed with Nate Connor. He was too big, too gruff, too dominating to share such a small space with. There'd be no getting away from him.

She could still feel the imprint of his body on hers, remember the taste of him on her tongue. The memories made sharing a bed with him too tempting and way too dangerous.

Nope, not going there. The couch made total sense. She wouldn't have to walk up the stairs. She'd be near the fire. And she'd have the necessary distance from the sexy but aggravating sheriff.

Her game plan set, she glanced up to see Nate zipping the two sleeping bags together.

"Hey, I need one of those over here."

"Nope," he said without looking up. "I'm too big to share one sleeping bag with the baby."

Measuring the width of his shoulders, she really couldn't argue with the statement. "Then he can sleep with me."

"Nope." He finished with the bags and draped them over the back of the chair. Next he picked up the heavy coffee table and easily moved it across the room, opening up the space in front of the fire. Then he turned toward the couch. "I'm going to need you to move."

"Why not?" She held out a hand, silently asking for assistance in rising.

"Because you're going to get cold and end up down on the mattress with us." He grasped her hand and pulled her to her feet.

She practically flew off the couch, ending up way too close to him. She looked into his eyes, pretended to be unaffected by the show of strength. The man was solid as a rock and warm as sun-baked stone.

"That seems easy to predict since you won't give me a sleeping bag." Making no attempt to move out of his way, she lazily twirled a strand of hair around her finger. "I'm disappointed in you, Nate. Trying to maneuver me into sleeping with you on our first date."

A ferocious scowl crashed over his brow, making him look like an angry lion.

"Woman, are you crazy? We're snowed in. We are not, nor will we ever be, dating."

"Really?" she challenged in a totally reasonable tone. "I cooked for you. You revealed your sexual history. And we necked on the couch. Sounds like a date to me."

His glower intensified through her recitation. "You *are* insane."

"Maybe." She shrugged, pleased at riling him. "But I'm not easy. You're going to have to work harder than that to get me between the sleeping bags."

He cringed.

Not a great reaction for her ego, but she didn't let it

show. And it had been a bad pun. "Can you at least find me some blankets?"

He wanted to say no, his reluctance was written all over him. But he picked up a flashlight and turned for the stairs. The noise announcing his annoyance would have been a huff coming from a woman, but it was too low and rough to be considered anything other than a growl.

Rather than take the chance that his temper would have him tossing the cushions beyond her reach, she removed them and set them beside the couch. She tried to pull out the bed but couldn't get good purchase with her bad foot.

Jack stirred so she lifted him, sat and hummed softly until he settled into sleep again.

Nate returned with a large navy blue comforter and a couple of pillows. He dropped everything on the far side of the room and came to stand over her.

"How's he doing?" For all their differences, Jack represented neutral ground.

"He's restless," she said quietly, hoping not to disturb the sleeping baby. "I'm sure he misses his mom."

"He's going to have to get over that." Nate's tone was grim.

"So you don't think she'll be back? She may not be much of a mother, but she's all he's ever known."

"If she has any smarts at all, she better not show up here. If I see her again, I'll press charges for child endangerment. Which reminds me, I need you to write out a statement."

Michelle shrank from the idea. It spoke of an involvement she preferred to stay away from. But Jack's welfare demanded she do the right thing.

"Can it wait until the morning? I'm wiped."

He gave one short nod. "I guess. Let's get these beds put together."

He made short work of it, easily pulling out the Hide-A-Bed and stripping off the mattress then folding it back up and putting the cushions back in place.

Considering his grouchiness she watched in wonder as he brought over the comforter, draped it in half over the couch and tossed a pillow on the end away from the fire. Next he placed the mattress vertically in front of the fire and spread out the doubled-up sleeping bags.

When the beds were done, he came for Jack.

"I'm sure you remember where the bathroom is," he mentioned as he rose from placing the baby between the sleeping bags.

She nodded but lost track of the comment when he stripped off his shirt, giving her the view she'd missed earlier. She'd been right—he was ripped. *Impressive* was too mild a word for how fine he looked.

She was so distracted she failed to notice his hands move toward his belt buckle.

"Weren't you headed to the bathroom?" he demanded.

"What?" She took in his stance and grinned. "Don't mind me. I'm not shy," she assured him. "But since you appear to be, I'll respect your sensibilities."

Picking up her suitcase, she limped toward the hall. A sigh sounded behind her, and then a large hand took the case from her and Nate disappeared down the hall, his broad shoulders shadowed against the light he carried. He turned through a door and the light dimmed.

Her hero yet again. How could she have forgotten a light?

The man had such a protective streak she was no longer surprised he'd taken on Jack so easily. He returned so quickly she had no time to step out of his way. Suddenly she found herself pressed up against all that gorgeous skin.

Oh, my. Warm and hard, he felt so good she wanted to melt into all that masculine heat. He must have taken time somewhere along the line to wash up because he smelled yummy. She recognized the smell of his soap from the throw she'd been wrapped up in earlier. It was even better on his heated skin.

"Mmm. You do smell good." She restrained the urge to lick the hard pecs in front of her. Instead she lifted her gaze to his. "Almost good enough to make me forget my vow to never get involved with a man in law enforcement."

"You tempt me, Ms. Ross." Long-fingered hands wrapped around her waist and lifted her into the air. He turned so they traded places, and then he let her feet touch the ground. But rather than release her, he bent over her, his lips just an inch away from hers. His minty breath was an enticing invitation that whispered over her skin. She was about to meet him halfway, when he shifted his head to speak in her ear. "But it's best if we don't complicate this relationship more than necessary."

"Complicated doesn't scare me," she bluffed.

Okay, that felt a little too real. Maybe she needed to dial it back a bit.

Why encourage him when she agreed with his decree? Starting something with anyone in River Run smacked of stupidity. Starting something with the sheriff would be a mistake of major proportions.

He lifted a dark brow as he straightened. "That's because you don't stick around for the complications."

"Ouch!" She flinched, exaggerating her hurt to hide the pain. "That's just mean."

"Sometimes the truth hurts."

"Indeed. But I have to wonder. Is your fear of complications responsible for your long dry spell? Are you a simple man, Sheriff?"

"Give the lady a prize." He mocked her. "I spend my days solving problems and keeping order. When I get home, I want peace and quiet, not to juggle the needs and demands of three different women and their well-meaning friends and relatives."

"Ah." She nodded sagely but made no effort to hide the glee in her eyes. "Now I understand. A virile, strong-bodied man like you comes to town unattached. The matchmakers probably swarmed all over you."

She tapped her finger against her lips as she contemplated him. "Which means one of two things happened. Either you accepted their cleverly casual offers for a home-cooked meal and found yourself set up with a number of lovely companions eager to follow up with a date. And you made the mistake of trying to juggle the women while you figured out who you really wanted to date. Or you saw the minefield ahead of you and decided not to risk precious body parts by alienating matchees. Or matchmakers."

"You can laugh, but I'm rather fond of all my body parts."

She grinned. "I imagine you are. My guess is it was the former. There are a lot of nice ladies with single relatives in town."

"So there are." He chucked her under the chin. "No need to blow your vow now. Use all the soap you want."

With that he closed the door in her face.

She blinked at the wooden barrier. Oh, he wasn't getting away with that. She wasn't through playing with him yet. She yanked the door open and stepped into the hall. Nate was at the end and before she could challenge him he turned. Light flowed over his broad back, highlighting a vivid scar running from his left collarbone across his shoulder blade and under his arm.

It was a shocking blight on the perfect canvas of his muscular body. Between one thundering heartbeat and another she knew he would hate for her to mention it. Wouldn't want to talk about it.

Here was his reason for keeping to himself.

She remembered her dad telling her his new deputy sheriff had been in the army, that he'd been a Ranger or something. Everything she knew about special forces told her his body was a weapon. Which probably told her why he was a sheriff in Podunk River Run instead of still fighting the good fight.

As a woman who knew the value of beauty, she understood his inclination to hide the imperfection. And she respected his right to privacy.

She retreated into the bathroom and closed the door.

Wrapped in Nate's throw, Michelle cuddled under the comforter, clenching her teeth to keep them from chattering. It galled her big-time, but Nate had been right. The couch sat under the window. And the distance from the fire was too great to offset the icy glass over her.

Giving in, she gathered her covers and her pillow and used the dim light of the fire to make her way to the middle of the room and the cozy bed where Jack and Nate slept.

Just being closer to the fire helped and she eyed the makeshift bed, wondering if there was a way she could join them without waking Nate. Hearing him gloat was the last thing she wanted at two in the morning.

He slept on his back and easily took up half the space on the mattress. Jack slept about a foot to the left of Nate, which left about eighteen inches for Michelle to squeeze into.

No way she could climb into the sleeping bag without waking both males so she wouldn't even try. She set the pillow down next to Jack, drew the comforter around herself and, trying for stealth, lay down on the edge of the mattress.

She sighed, but before her head even hit the pillow, Nate erupted into action.

He leaped over Jack, caught her around the middle and rolled with her. Comforter and pillow went flying. Instinctively Michelle threw her arms up in self-defense.

Nate blocked the move, caught her right arm, twisted and flipped her. She screamed, in pain and fright.

The baby began to cry.

"Nate." She spit out carpet fibers and called his name. "Nate, it's me—Michelle."

"Michelle?"

The weight he used to contain her shifted, tensing then relaxing, and suddenly the fight went out of him and he sprawled full-length over her body. He went into a rant of creative and foul curses.

"Hell, woman, are you insane? I'm a soldier. You can't sneak up on me when I'm sleeping. I could have broken your neck."

"My neck is fine. But you may break something else if you don't move," she wheezed out, no longer nervous. "Can I have my arm back? Please."

"Good Lord." Two hands appeared on either side of her and his weight disappeared. A moment later, he flipped her again, gently this time, and his hands ran lightly over her, checking for injuries. "I'm sorry. Are you hurt? Where?"

"Nate. Stop." She grabbed his hands and held them still. She couldn't get her breath back with his hands on her. "I'm fine. You were right. I got cold and moved to the mattress. I didn't mean to startle you."

"Right." He scrubbed his face. Glanced at Jack, who'd been jostled awake by Nate's abrupt departure from the bed, and then back at her. "Look, some habits die hard. Do me a favor, next time announce you're joining me in bed."

"Next time?" She swallowed hard. "You are feeling lucky."

His eyebrows drew together as he processed her comment while clearly still shaken. He shook his head. "Smart-ass."

"What can I say? You bring out the best in me."

"Jack's crying and I'm freezing my butt off. Let's go to bed."

Currently her body was overheated from proximity to him. Maybe she should rethink the whole sleeping-together thing?

No, then he'd know she was running scared.

She allowed him to help her to her feet. She grabbed the crying baby, singing softly to soothe him, while Nate straightened the bedding.

Wrapping the throw around the baby, she watched with interest as Nate unzipped the sleeping bags.

"Why are you unlinking them?"

"With the extra body heat and the comforter we don't need the additional warmth."

"And with the three of us it would be a tad cozy?"

He lifted one bare shoulder, let it drop. "Yeah, there's that."

"Good plan."

"I thought so." He nodded toward Jack. "He's probably hungry. Christy was still taking a bottle at night at that age."

"Christy? You have a daughter?"

His head whipped around and there was no sign of sleep in the gaze that cut through her. "Christy is my friend's daughter. He died in combat."

"And you came to River Run to check up on her?" The guy really did have an overactive protective gene.

"Something like that." He was defensive.

Telling herself it was none of her business, Michelle expressed sorrow over the loss of his friend and asked if he'd get the bottle for Jack.

While he went to the kitchen to clean the bottle, she and Jack got settled on the mattress. The baby continued to fuss until Nate finished making the bottle with the water he had warming by the fire.

She concentrated on Jack, paying no attention as Nate joined them in the bed. Right, as if she could ignore a six-foot-three-inch mass of muscle and testosterone. But she was determined to pretend nonchalance.

He settled against his pillow with a sigh.

Jack put his tiny hand on Nate's biceps, and Michelle could swear he sighed, too.

She turned on her side, facing the baby, and plumped up her pillow. Her eyes blinked as she slid her feet over the cool nylon of the sleeping bag. She focused on the bottle, saw it was almost gone. Her feet encountered a firm, warm surface. She sighed and slid into sleep.

Nate sat up to burp Jack and felt Michelle's toes dig into his calf as she moved with him. Sound asleep, she had an innocence about her that belied her tough exterior. And drew him far more than he could afford.

The truth was he found too much about her way too tempting. He dismissed her bravado; saw it for the shield it was. Some might see her aggression as manipulation and her flippancy as fake, but he heard the self-honesty driving it and appreciated the bluntness.

Her patience and connection with Jack awed Nate. He would have been lost without her tonight.

She was beautiful and knew it. Used it. This woman knew games he'd never even heard of. And wanted no part of. High maintenance thy name was Michelle Ross.

She'd been right. He was a simple man, and he wanted a simple life. He'd deal with taking in Jack because he had to, because he was family.

Nate had originally moved here to support his best friend's widow, to watch over his infant daughter. Nate and Kim had been friends for three years. He knew he could count on her help with Jack.

As soon as the storm ended, he'd call Kim; make a date to talk to her about what he needed for Jack.

Now was definitely not the time to let his irrational attraction for Sleeping Beauty sway him from his set path. But as he set the snoozing baby between them and sank back onto his pillow he made no effort to move away from her seeking toes. The human connection felt too good to lose.

His last thought before fading into sleep was a prayer that the storm ended soon. Spending time housebound with a woman he had no business desiring was his idea of torture.

CHAPTER FIVE

THE next two days were absolute torture. Being cooped up with a bear of a man and a traumatized infant did not make for lots of fun.

Luckily Michelle's foot healed up pretty fast and got her off the couch and puttering around between bouts of watching Jack.

Child care was not in her plans when she headed home to sell her dad's house, but poor Jack was miserable. Obviously he missed his mother, plus his experience from the day before had left him with a cold. Bottom line he was unhappy when he was awake and his cold kept him from sleeping more than a few minutes at a time.

She and Nate settled into a grudging truce as they shared baby duty. She thought his patience would run out, but reluctantly acknowledged he held up his end. He'd prop Jack against his shoulder and go about his business. And he was always busy. He kept the fire going, cooked, cleaned, did dishes, handled the trash.

On the first day, she watched him make tuna sandwiches, mostly one-handed, for lunch and later he did paperwork at his desk. She took the baby, and by the second day he'd devised a sling that helped to leave his hands free.

Because she liked to cook, she helped with the meals and left the rest to him. She spent the remainder of her time wandering through the house taking stock.

She was surprised to find her room remained the same as she'd left it, complete with purple curtains, butterflies, musical notes and pop-star posters.

The house was in good shape, better than she would have thought, but then her dad had always demanded she help out with some new project. From gardening and fixing a broken step to repairing a toilet and building her tree house he'd always had something he needed her help with. She had to admit the fix-it knowledge had come in handy over the years.

And she'd loved her tree house. He'd made her a castle. They'd built it together the first year she went to Princess Camp. And she'd used it clear through her senior year in high school.

Late the second day she followed Nate up to the attic to see if there was any baby furniture they could use. There wasn't. Her mother might have kept that kind of thing. Her dad got rid of anything they weren't currently using.

What they did find was a very dusty wooden rocking chair. At her insistence Nate carried it down to the garage.

"This is filthy. And one of the arms is warped." He dusted off his hands after setting it down. "The only thing it's good for is firewood."

"We'll see." She bounced Jack on her hip. "Yes, it's

dirty but it's sturdy. A little sanding and a good cleaning is all it needs."

He lifted a skeptical brow. "You're on your own there.
Speaking of firewood, I have to replenish our supply."

"Okay, let me put my jacket on and I'll help."

"You have Jack." He reached for a hooded coat he
kept in the garage. "I can handle it."

"Stubborn man," she muttered as he headed out the
back door. She carried Jack into the living room, placed
him in the middle of the mattress and piled up a bar-
ricade of pillows between him and the hearth. As he'd
barely mastered turning over, she figured he couldn't
get far in the few minutes it took her to help Nate.

Dragging on her jacket, she arrived back in the garage in time to hold the door open so Nate didn't have to
struggle to get it while carrying the large load of wood.
A gesture he accepted with a less than gracious grunt.

Rolling her eyes at his back, she stepped out the back
door to walk the short distance to the wood shed but
a hard hand wrapped around her elbow and pulled her
to a stop.

"Stay inside," he insisted. "It's too slick out there for
your weak ankle. You'll only end up on your pretty ass."

"Ohh, so you think I have a pretty tush?" She wiggled her butt enticingly. "I think yours is nice, too."

"Nut." He shook his head, but the corner of his mouth
quirked up just a little. "Now go back inside. I can do
this. What I can't do is take care of Jack and you, too."

"Fine." She flounced around on her heel and
promptly felt her foot slide on a frozen patch, going

out from under her. Luckily, his hand on her arm kept her from falling.

"Careful." He pulled her close, clamping her to his sturdy frame.

Humor fled as she clung to him. The last thing she needed was to hurt herself worse than she already had, especially when her ankle was still on the mend.

Breathless from the near fall, she gazed up at him. "Thank you."

He picked her up and set her inside the garage door. "Does everything always have to be about sex with you?"

Indignant, her hands went to her hips. "How is 'thank you' about sex?"

"I don't know." He threw his gloved hands up, revealing his frustration. "It's the way you talk, everything sounds sexy."

Well, yeah. Using her sexuality usually got her what she wanted. And okay, she'd admit to an attraction to all that raw masculinity. But he was being far too sensitive. Sometimes "thank you" just meant "thank you." Defensive, she tossed his argument back at him.

"Or maybe it's the way you hear it. I just came out to help. You're the one who started talking about my ass."

His eyes narrowed in a scowl and he opened his mouth. Then he obviously thought better of it because he closed his mouth with a click of his teeth.

After a deep breath, he said, "Just hold the door. This will only take a few more minutes."

"Yes, sir." She gave him a pert salute.

Looking at the dark clouds and heavy snowfall, she rubbed her hands together for warmth and wished for the storm to end soon.

The attack began with a close-range sniper shot. Nate heard the whining echo as he caught his best friend in his arms. He went down under Quentin's dead weight. Gunfire broke out. Shouts and then screams rent the air. Return mortar fire boomed and the foundation shook.

Nate dragged Quentin inside. Shafts of light were thick with dust and sand. Paper-thin walls offered little protection but Nate bent over Quentin, calling his name, demanding an answer. His heart in his throat, he checked for a pulse and his hand came back bloody.

The building suddenly exploded. Nate threw his body over Quentin. A lancing pain tore through Nate's shoulder. And then everything went black.

Nate sat straight up in bed. The sound of mortar fire rang in his ears. Sweat beaded his brow and he pushed out of the sleeping bag to pace the chilly room. He grabbed a T-shirt to wipe his face, wishing it was that easy to wipe out his memories.

No, that was wrong. Quentin deserved better from Nate.

He'd told Command they needed to change up the routine. A smart soldier knew predictable was deadly. But nothing about the damn war was logical. So the simple changing of the guard had turned bloody. Worse, he'd changed shifts with Quentin. Their positions should have been reversed.

Nate should be dead and Quentin should be with his wife and daughter.

His blood was on Nate's hands. The first shot had killed him and Nate's efforts to shield him from the blast had been worthless and had nearly cost him his arm.

Nate walked to the kitchen, opened the refrigerator and stared at the contents unseeingly.

Quentin had had so little time with his beautiful daughter, Christy, but he'd loved her so much. He never talked about her, as if he wanted to protect her from the vileness of the war and their everyday life. But he showed Nate pictures, would just hand over a stack without a word. And Nate savored every candid shot of the plump little girl with his buddy's nose and hair and her mother's eyes.

Those pictures of home, of an innocent child filled with the joy of life and discovery, were what kept Nate going. When the sand and the heat and the hatred got to be too much, he'd remember Christy's smile and remind himself he was here to make the world a better, safer place for her.

And sometimes he actually believed it.

He closed the refrigerator door and began to pace, the terrazzo tile icy under his bare feet. Wait… He swung back to the refrigerator and pulled the door open. The light was on. Good, the electricity was back. That meant the storm must be abating.

Thank God.

He used to relive the nightmare of that day in his dreams every night. They'd become less frequent over the past year. He knew exactly what brought it on now: his decision to raise Jack.

They'd saved Nate's arm, but his career was over.

He hadn't hesitated when he returned stateside—he'd moved to River Run. He owed it to his friend to look after his family. And that's what he'd done for the past three years.

"Are you okay?" Michelle's soft voice came out of the darkness.

He gave a harsh laugh. "Yeah, I'm just fine."

"Couldn't sleep?" She leaned a hip against the counter and crossed one pink polka-dot-socked foot over the other.

"Touch of heartburn from the chili tonight." He pounded his chest for emphasis. It wasn't a total lie; it just wasn't what woke him.

She opened a cupboard and tossed him a bottle of antacids. "Sorry. I like spicy. Next time I'll go lighter on the jalapeños."

"No," he said, sorry he'd picked on her food. "Don't." He popped the chalky tablets. "It's worth the burn."

Her smile lit up the dark room. Some of the tension eased in his chest. He told himself it was the fast-acting antacids.

"I'm sorry I woke you."

"It wasn't you. Jack was restless." Her eyes went misty soft. "I saw your scar. My father told me you almost lost your arm in the war. Is that what disturbed your sleep? Bad dreams?"

He froze. "I don't talk about that."

"Maybe you should. Maybe it would help you sleep."

"It's over. My arm is fine. No good comes from rehashing old business."

"No good comes from bottling up old wounds. Talking can help."

"I've heard that psychobabble before." He crossed his arms over his chest. "What possible good can come from splitting my veins open and bleeding emotions?"

"Maybe you'd find some peace."

"What do you want to hear? That I cost my best friend his life? Or that I'd give my arm to have him back? What's the cost of a limb compared to the life of a husband and father?"

She blanched but didn't back down. "Life isn't that simple. You were in a war."

"We traded duty. He was shot as I was relieving him. If our positions had been reversed, I'd be the one sent home in a pine box."

"And if you hadn't changed assignments, the shooter might have shot to the right or the left and your friend would still be gone. You can play the if game all night long, but it doesn't change anything," she said softly. "Death happens."

"Quentin's death is on my hands. It's not something I can be philosophical about."

"I guess not. Try remembering you didn't kill him."

"Right." He mocked her. "I'll remember that."

She tried to shrug off his rudeness, but he saw the cringe she couldn't hide. Why didn't she just go back to bed?

"So Christy is Quentin's daughter. She and her mother are what brought you to River Run?"

"How—" Her knowledge stunned Nate until he remembered he'd mentioned Christy their first night to-gether. "They don't concern you."

"Oh." The animation went out of her face. "Good night then."

He was such a moron. This was his problem. And no business of hers. But he figured she'd only been trying to help. He needed to cut her some slack.

"So Jack was restless?" he said quickly before she could leave and go back to bed.

"Yes." She rubbed her hands over her arms, seeking warmth. "He doesn't like the powdered milk bottles as well as his formula bottles. I think it upsets his stomach a little."

"Speaking of which…" He walked past her, inhaled the sweet scent of lotion that made her skin so silky soft and pulled open the refrigerator, showing her the light.

"We have electricity." She clapped her hands. "That means the storm is over, right?"

"It means the hub is up and working."

"Oh, come on, give me some hope here." She closed the refrigerator door and leaned back against it, putting her way too close. "I'm stir-crazy. I need to see something besides the inside of this house. Even the slim pickings in River Run will do."

"For once we're in agreement." He stepped back and bumped into the counter. She smelled too good, looked too soft, and he found it too easy to remember how sweet she tasted. Being alone with her like this was not good. Not for him. "I appreciate your cooking, but I can really go for some of Luigi's Pizza."

"Oh, my God, Luigi's Pizza! How could I forget

Luigi's Pizza? Their pepperoni is to die for. I swear I ate there three times a week my senior year in high school." She sighed over the memory, her breasts rising and falling under the soft fabric of his T-shirt. He forced his eyes back to her face. "You are so on. As soon as the snowplows clear the roads we have a date."

She flounced back to bed, and he scrubbed his hands over his face. That really hadn't gone according to plan.

"Freedom." Michelle flung her arms out wide, embracing the beautiful outdoors. Crisp and clear, the air still held the icy bite of winter but a single ray of sunshine promised the storm truly had ended. "My kingdom for freedom."

And the roads were plowed, including their driveway—one of the perks of living with the sheriff. Nate had taken off at first light promising to be back by early afternoon to take her grocery shopping.

He missed that deadline by several hours. No surprise.

She'd brooded for a while at being under the thumb of another lawman, the pacing and waiting taking her back to too many memories from the past.

Like the time she walked to school through huge drifts of snow one year after a storm knocked out power for three days. The snow had stopped and Dad was gone so she got dressed and trudged to the school four blocks away, only to find out Dad had forgotten to tell her school was canceled for the rest of the week. She was out the next week because of a bad case of bron chitis and missed the field trip to the capitol building in Sacramento.

After a while she shook off the negativity of being out of control. Instead she and Jack went out to the garage and started sanding the rocker. Okay, she sanded and Jack slept in a blanket-draped drawer, the point being they kept busy until Nate showed up.

Now they were off to town for some much-needed supplies.

And much-needed company.

If she had to spend another minute alone with hunky sheriff Nate, she might spontaneously combust. Something about the man kept her body on a low-level buzz.

"Wouldn't that be queendom?" Nate came out of the house carrying Jack in his car seat.

He wasn't immune to her, either. Sometimes she caught him looking at her with such heat she wanted to eliminate the space between them and forget they could barely tolerate being in the same room together.

Oh, yeah, she needed civilization bad.

"Queendom. I like that. But right now I'll settle for River Run."

"I bet that's something you never thought you'd say."

"You got that right." She strapped her seat belt on. "Luigi's, driver, and make it quick."

Nate gave her an askance glance before he put his big SUV in gear and rolled forward.

"You're a little tipsy on your freedom there, aren't you?"

"Yes." She sighed, making no effort to deny it. "It was getting so I couldn't breathe. It didn't seem to bother you. But then you left at the crack of dawn. You've been free all day."

"I've been working. And I hadn't had a break in close to a month. I was glad to be able to get some things done that I'd been putting off."

"I got some song writing done, too. But I'm still happy to be free." She breathed deeply, let it out slowly. "Did you put an arrest warrant out for Jack's mom?"

"No." His hands fisted on the wheel. "But I listed her as a person of interest, which means information on her will be forwarded to me if she shows up on the grid anywhere we share info."

"What will you do when you find her?"

"I don't know," he admitted, surprising her. "I hate how she abandoned Jack. It's hard for me to get past that. He's probably better off without her."

"Probably?"

"Some women aren't meant to be mothers."

Now that was interesting. Did he speak from personal experience or just from what he'd seen?

"And you feel confident in making that decision for him?"

The look he gave her sliced her to the bone. Which made her wonder why. Why was she pushing? Obviously her question pricked a sore spot for him. But it was none of her business. And sure, Jack was a cute kid, but the last thing she needed was to get emotionally involved in this mess.

"Never mind," she said as if his look hadn't cut her off at the knees. "I'm sure you'll work it all out." Seeing they were still in the driveway, she waved her fingers at him. "Luigi's! Forthwith."

"Freak." He sighed and pulled into the street.

"You have no sense of fun," she informed him.

"I know how to have fun," he stated evenly.

"Jack is the one I feel sorry for. You really should put a little effort in for his sake."

"Don't tell me how to raise Jack."

"I'm just saying the kid deserves a chance."

"Cut it out." He sent her a sideways glare. "I know how to have a good time as much as the next guy."

"Doing what?" she demanded, not believing him for a minute. She'd never met a man that was more work-oriented, except for her father and that wasn't saying much. "What do you do for fun? Play football with the guys? Go fishing? My dad liked to fish. Or are you a secret gamer? Confess, you get your thrills on *Grand Theft Auto*, don't you?"

"What's *Grand Theft Auto*?"

She shook her head in exaggerated disappointment. "Now that's just sad."

"I'm a law enforcement officer. Why would I play something called *Grand Theft Auto*?"

"Oh, I don't know, for the vicarious thrill? Or maybe because *it's fun*?"

Now it was a killer glare. "I don't have to explain myself to you."

"No, you don't." Satisfied she'd riled him, she wiggled more comfortably into her seat. "If you put on the siren so we get to Luigi's extra fast, I'll let you play *Grand Theft Auto* when we get home."

"That's not going to happen."

"It would in my queendom."

He shook his head, but she saw the corner of his mouth quirk up. A smile. They rode in silence for several blocks.

"I work out. And I like to bowl," he finally muttered.

Pleased with herself, she drew an exclamation point in the condensation on the window.

CHAPTER SIX

Luigi's was packed. Seemed everyone had a case of cabin fever and decided to eat out tonight. Nate bounced Jack and scanned the room looking for Kim and Christy.

The kid weighed next to nothing. Nate could hold him in one hand. Not that he would. He still worried he might break the little guy.

It was hard to remember Christy was ever this small. He'd thought he was being a help to Kim in those early days. And he probably was, but he knew now she'd needed so much more than he'd given her.

He'd gone ahead with his plan to call her and asked her to meet him here tonight. With Michelle along it wasn't quite what he'd had in mind, but it was a start. And with Kim there nobody was likely to get the wrong idea about him and Michelle. Especially Michelle.

He spotted Kim talking to her neighbor David, an average-size man with dark hair and a trim mustache. She laughed at something he said, and then she caught sight of Nate and waved. The man picked up Christy and the small group started making its way through the restaurant toward him.

"Looks like your friend has company," Michelle observed. "Maybe we should look for a bigger booth."

He turned and found her tucking a high chair in at the end of a booth. "That won't be necessary. David won't be joining us."

"I'm betting he will," she contradicted him, her gaze on the group about to join them. "I hope you don't have any feelings in that direction."

"What do you mean?" he demanded. "Why do you say that?"

"Because it looks to me like the widow is smitten with David."

"You're wrong." He dismissed her claim. Kim still loved Quentin. Nate would know if that had changed. Quentin may be gone but his spirit was irreplaceable.

"Hi, Nate." Kim greeted him with a big hug. "This was a great idea. You know David, right? It's such a crush in here. You don't mind if he joins us, do you?"

Michelle jumped in. "Of course not. Hi, I'm Michelle Ross."

"Sheriff Ross's daughter." Kim patted Michelle's shoulder in unspoken sympathy. "I'm Kim and this is my daughter, Christy. She's three, and she'll talk your ear off if you let her."

"Michelle." David greeted Michelle with a fond smile. "It's good to see you. May I say how sorry I am about your father's passing? The whole town misses him. I would have been at the services, but I covered the office so my father could go."

"Thank you." Michelle graciously offered her hand and Dave swallowed it up in his large mitts. She didn't seem to notice as she continued. "Those two did like to cast a line together. I was always happy when your dad was free on Saturday mornings. It meant I got some extra beauty sleep."

Nate scowled at the chitchat. He didn't care for the way David hung on to Michelle's hand. The man needed to move on. Didn't he see they were blocking traffic standing around the table?

He made a point of scanning the area. "Sorry, buddy," he told David, "but it doesn't look like any of the bigger booths are available."

"Don't be ridiculous, Nate." Kim waved him off. "We can squeeze in here." She slid onto the bench seat and pulled David in beside her. "Here, there's room in the window for the baby seat." She lowered the handle and shoved the seat on the window ledge.

Unhappy with the way things were shaking out, Nate glanced at Michelle. She winked and scooted in to sit across from Kim. He narrowed his eyes at her, but she just smiled and released Jack from his seat.

"I see you finally got that peach-fuzz mustache to grow in properly," she teased David.

"Brat." He grinned and swiped fingers over the hair framing his upper lip.

"He had such a baby face when he first joined his dad's dental practice, the older ladies gave him a bad time. So he decided to grow a mustache to look older."

"It worked, too." He shook a finger at Michelle. "And it was never as bad as you make out."

"Of course not." She looked at Kim and mouthed, "Peach fuzz."

Kim laughed. She inspected David. "I like it."

Nate shifted in his seat, feeling like an outsider. Thankfully, the waitress arrived to take their order. After a brief consult he ordered one vegetarian and one meat-lover's pizza.

"Mommy, can I have my juice?" Christy asked.

Kim pulled a sippy cup from her purse and David passed it to the little girl.

Once she had her drink, Christy patted Nate's hand and pointed at Jack. "Baby."

"That's right." He bopped her nose with a finger. "That's Jack."

"He sure is a cutie," Kim told Michelle. "How old is he?"

"Around four months."

"I didn't know you had a son," David said. "I'm surprised your dad wasn't crowing about his grandson every chance he got."

"Oh, no." Michelle shook her head, her gold hair brushing over her shoulders. She cocked her thumb in his direction. "He's Nate's."

Clearly shocked, Kim's gaze ricocheted around as if she didn't know where to look. She finally took refuge in snagging David's gaze.

Nate realized he should have taken charge of the introductions. Found a time to make an explanation to Kim when they didn't have an audience. He wanted her help, but he didn't want to put his life on display for strangers.

"Ah, Nate," Michelle whispered.

Used to hiding his emotions, he flicked an expressionless glare at David, wishing him away. He'd prefer Michelle wasn't there, either, and not just because she kept digging her elbow into his ribs.

"Kim, I can explain," he began.

"Nate, you don't have to—"

"I want to. We've been friends for years—"

"Nate—" Michelle suddenly shoved at him "—I really need to talk to you."

He turned his head and looked down at her. "Not now." He focused on Kim. "Jack was a surprise."

"Please, you two, don't argue," Kim implored. "This is a special time for you."

"Kim, it's not what you think," Michelle countered.

Again Kim's gaze went to David, and Nate thought she was wishing for some privacy. He echoed that sentiment. He knew he was handling this badly. He should have planned out what he was going to say, but he'd been distracted by Michelle. And Jack, of course.

"Kim, I was really hoping—"

Michelle stopped him by turning his head toward her, and grinding her mouth on his.

For a moment his mind went blank. And his body took over, responding to the sweet softness of her lips under his. He opened his mouth, tasting her, devouring, her before his brain reengaged.

Furious, he grabbed her hand and pulled her from the booth.

Michelle let Nate drag her away from the table, stopping only long enough to hand Jack over to Kim with a grateful smile.

He kept hold of her hand until they reached the video games at the back of the room near the restrooms.

"Are you insane?" he demanded. "I'm trying to explain the situation to Kim. I have a personal interest in making sure she fully understands what's going on."

"I know." She tugged at the hem of her waist-length sweater. "You're welcome."

"That settles it. You are nuts."

"No, I'm saving you from yourself. I get it, okay. I know your grand plan was to get together with the widow and raise your kids together." She was pretty good at reading people—as a songwriter she observed life—and interpersonal relationships. Plus, the man was as transparent as cellophane.

"You couldn't be more wrong. Her husband was my best friend. She's like a sister to me." His affront couldn't be more obvious, and she realized she'd misread the situation. His ire showed in his stance. "You have no right interfering in my personal affairs. Or giving Kim the impression that something is going on between us."

"Me? The way you bumbled that explanation, the woman thinks I had your baby!"

"No."

"Yes. Look, I know you think you need to play hero because you feel responsible for Kim being a widow—"

"You don't know anything about me, or my intentions. The last thing I am is a hero."

"Whatever. This is what I see, you're fixated on the past and she's ready to move on."

"What? Who with—David?" He scoffed. "Now you're being ridiculous. Kim still loves Quentin."

She sighed. Men could be so dense. "She'll always love Quentin but she's also a young vital woman with a full life ahead of her. She's found a new love. She and David are a couple. You're going to have to deal."

"You don't know what you're talking about." He dismissed her claim. "How could you? You haven't spoken to anyone in town for seven months."

"How can you be a law enforcement officer and not see what's in front of your eyes?"

"Maybe because there's nothing to see."

Aggravated by his failure to listen to her, she grabbed his broad shoulders and tried to turn him toward the table they'd just left.

He didn't budge.

With a sigh she walked around him, forcing him to turn to keep track of her or stand facing the back wall.

When he faced her, she waved her hand, inviting him to take in the couple cooing at the baby. As they watched, Kim lifted her face to David's for a kiss. Ouch.

Michelle rolled her gaze up to Nate. He stood, hands on hips, his eyes locked on the wife of his best friend embracing another man. His expression never changed as the seconds ticked by and she wondered what he was thinking.

Deciding she'd give him a moment alone, she patted his arm and headed back to the booth. She went two steps before his arm wrapped around her waist and he swept her into his arms.

"Hey…" She pushed against his chest.

"Just saying thanks." He bent his head to hers and claimed her mouth. Slanting his head, he deepened the kiss with a sweep of his tongue. No hesitation, no holding back, no distractions, this kiss was unlike any others they'd shared. He held her with care, with urgency. He tasted good and felt better.

The pizza parlor disappeared as she melted against him, and his heat surrounded her. The buzz she constantly fought to ignore ignited into full-blown tingles. Desire flowed hot through her blood as she opened to his sensual demand.

Needing to get closer she went onto her tiptoes and circled his neck with her arms. And suddenly she felt like she floated on air, Nate her only anchor in a swirling mist of sensation.

Someone jostled her from behind.

"Excuse me," a young voice said, followed by teen-aged giggles.

"Sheriff Nate has a girl."

The shrill announcement echoed through Michelle's head, disrupting her passionate haze.

"That kiss was hot," a girlish voice replied in awe.

Michelle's eyes popped open and she stared into Nate's heated gaze. A breath shuddered through his wide chest, her body moving along with his. That's when she realized the floating sensation came from the fact he held her aloft.

"You…" She cleared her throat. "You should put me down."

He leaned over and her feet gently settled on the

ground. For a moment his hands lingered on her waist and then he released her.

She brushed the back of her fingers down his cheek. "Well done."

"What?" She took satisfaction in hearing the rasp of desire in the word.

"You used me. And I don't even care."

"You started it."

She held up a hand. "Don't push it. Your pride needed a booster shot and I was handy. I get it. Don't do it again."

Facing the room, she tugged at the hem of her purple sweater and willed her overheated body to settle down.

"You know you have to correct the impression Jack is our child."

"Nobody would believe that."

She shook her head at his obtuseness. "You'll see."

"Come on." A hand in the small of her back ushered her forward.

The man really had no clue. They'd gone half a dozen steps when a couple stopped them to congratulate them on their little bundle of joy. Michelle flicked him a telling glance, smiled at the couple and moved on to their booth.

She scooted in, slid a piece of meat-lover's pizza onto her plate and took a big bite. Jack slept against Kim's shoulder. Michelle eyed the hands clasped together on the table and felt a smidgen of sympathy for Nate.

A moment later he slid in beside her and reached for his own slice. In a disconnected part of her brain she noticed that both of them had taken the meat pie while Kim and David had both chosen the veggie.

"Please tell them the truth," she prompted him.

He shrugged. "It's my business."

"And my reputation," she countered.

"You're leaving town, what do you care?"

"I care." She faced the couple avidly drinking in their debate. "Kim, Jack isn't my child. He's Nate's cousin's boy."

"Oh." Kim looked confused. "I thought Jack passed away a few months ago."

"Yes, and his girlfriend was pregnant. She left the baby on Nate's porch the first night of the storm."

"Oh, my God," Kim exclaimed. She softly rubbed the sleeping baby's back. "His mother left him in the storm? He could have died."

"Luckily, I heard him crying."

Kim glanced back and forth between Michelle and Nate, her expression a curious combination of understanding and skepticism.

"Why didn't you just say so?" Kim asked Nate.

His cheeks turned ruddy. "This didn't seem the place to go into it. I'm not used to discussing my business in such an open forum."

Kim's gaze shifted to Michelle, pinning her to her seat. "And where do you fit into the picture?"

"I was at the house when Nate found the baby. We've been stuck together for three days."

"Because she broke into my house."

"My house," she corrected through clenched teeth. "And that's what you choose to share?"

Smug, he lifted one shoulder, let it drop.

Aggrieved all over again. Michelle turned to David. "Who is this gal Dad was shacked up with? I didn't know he'd moved out of the house."

"Ah." David blinked in surprise at suddenly being in the hot seat of the volatile conversation. "You know, he and Dolly had been friends for years. That mild heart attack he had just before his birthday last year scared him. Shortly after your visit he moved in with her."

Silence followed the explanation. Dad and Dolly... lovers? Michelle would never have guessed. Then again, she tended to shy away from any notion of Dad and a lover in the same thought.

"More pizza, please." Christy's small voice piped into the stillness. Kim reached for a veggie slice, but the little girl spoke up. "No, Mommy, I want pepperoni."

"Here you go, sweet thing." Nate placed a small slice on her plate.

"Thank you, Uncle Nate." She smiled, grabbed a round bite of pepperoni and popped it in her mouth.

Kim reached over and patted Nate's hand. "Jack couldn't be in better hands."

"Yet, I'm already making mistakes."

Annoyed as she was at his closemouthed attitude, Michelle felt a little sorry for him. Tonight was definitely not going as he'd planned. Time for a change of mood.

"You'll fix it," she stated confidently. "You better—" she smiled at him, showing a lot of teeth "—or I'll sue you for child support."

Next to her Nate went very still, and then he threw

back his head and laughed out loud. He pushed a fall of hair behind her ear.

"You'd probably get it, too."

"Oh, believe it. Judge Austin is my godfather."

Still chuckling, he groaned. "Of course he is."

"You know, Nate, I have Christy's baby furniture stored in the garage. You're welcome to use it for Jack. There's a crib, and a changing table. Plus I think I still have her baby swing."

"Kim, that would be great. I don't know what to say."

"Thank you?"

"Of course. Thank you. I'll pick it up tomorrow."

"I have a truck," David said. "You must be really busy with the aftermath of the storm. Why don't I pack it up and bring it over? Then, if you're not available, I can help set it up."

Nate nodded and expressed his thanks. He managed to sound sincere even though Michelle knew deep down he was totally frustrated.

His phone beeped. He pulled it from his pocket and checked the screen. "I have to take this," he said and slid from the booth to step into the lobby.

"Mommy, can I ride the pony?" Christy pointed at a shiny brown pony with a red saddle.

"I'll take her," David volunteered and lifted the girl into his arms. They wandered off toward the pony.

"Here." Michelle reached for Jack's carrier. "Let's put him in his seat. Your poor arm is probably ready to fall off." She stood, gently took the baby and tucked him into place.

"You're good for him," Kim observed.

"Jack? He's a sweetheart."

"I meant Nate."

"Ha." Michelle made no effort to hide her derision. "We're lucky we didn't kill each other during the storm."

"Hmm. Like that killer kiss?"

"Please. He was punishing me because I was right."

Kim lifted one fine eyebrow. "And it hurt so good?"

Michelle grinned and fanned herself. "I didn't say I didn't like it."

"I've never seen him laugh like that. We're usually lucky to get a few chuckles out of him."

Michelle set Jack's carrier on the bench seat and sat down next to him, her attention wandering to Nate, who stood staring intently out the front window while he dealt with his call.

"Yeah, well, he's not a lighthearted guy."

"No, he's not," Kim agreed with a sigh. "And that's what I love about David."

"Nate seemed a little surprised by David." Michelle liked Kim; she was smart, perceptive and not threatened by Michelle, which sometimes women were. "I think he's put you on a pedestal."

"Which is why I haven't mentioned David." She met Michelle square in the eye. "I think you saved us both from an embarrassing moment."

Michelle simply stared back. Kim sighed.

"I love Nate like a brother. He was a lifesaver after Quentin died. But I'm not a stone statue. I deserve true love. I had it once and I won't settle for less this time. Nate is one of the best men I know. But he doesn't understand because a strong relationship is not something he's ever known. I want it for him. He deserves to be loved. He deserves someone who can make him laugh out loud."

CHAPTER SEVEN

STILL half-asleep Michelle pushed open the bathroom door and stepped inside. She promptly bumped into a steam-slicked body.

Instantly alert she stepped back and ogled Nate in nothing but a towel. His shoulders looked impossibly wide over a broad chest and a rippling six-pack.

The man was fine. And better than a cup of Joe first thing in the morning.

"Mmm. Good morning."

She got a growl in response.

Too bad he was a bad-tempered Neanderthal.

She reached for her toothbrush and took a peek at her own reflection. Her hair was a wild explosion of curls and her face devoid of makeup, but she wore her midnight-blue shorty pajamas. Not too bad a showing first thing in the morning.

"The room is taken," he said around his own toothbrush.

"I don't mind sharing," she assured him.

"I do," he barked.

She ignored him, enjoying instead the play of muscles in his arm and abdomen as he cleaned his teeth.

"Why aren't you using the master suite?" she asked him. "You could have a bathroom all to yourself there."

"I was already settled in my room when your dad decided to move out. I had the house to myself so I saw no reason to move. You take it."

"I'm good in my old room. I won't be here long enough to need the bigger room."

"Thank God."

"Hey, I'm helping you out here," she reminded him. "Have you thought what you're going to do now your girlfriend has found someone new?"

"Not funny. I need to talk to Kim," he declared as he rinsed his brush and returned it to the medicine cabinet, which was meticulously in order. "This thing with David may not be serious."

She rolled her eyes, amazed at his ability for self-deception. "She was kissing him in public."

"We were kissing in public. There's nothing serious between us."

He had her there. And if his easy dismissal of their embrace stung a little, she pretended not to notice.

"It looked serious to me."

"That's not what I need to talk to her about. I want to discuss Jack's care. She'll be able to help me explore my options."

She relaxed and nodded. "Closure is a good thing."

"Ouch!" He pulled his razor away from a bleeding nick. "There's no need for anything girly like closure." He glared at her reflection in the mirror. "Can I have some privacy, please?"

Sighing, she tugged at the hem of her pajama top and

for a moment it molded to the naked breasts beneath the thin cloth. His gaze lowered and his jaw clenched.

Satisfied, she turned on her heel.

"Seems to me you're the one acting like a girl," she ventured. "Next time lock the door if you're so modest."

A curse sounded from the other side of the closed door.

She smirked, suddenly looking forward to the day.

Twenty minutes later she shuffled down the stairs, Jack in her arms, to find Nate walking out the front door.

"Hey." She stopped him. "We need to make plans for shopping. The cupboards are bare and Jack has needs."

He turned to face her, a scowl drawing his dark brows together. He rubbed his temple as his gaze glazed over and his thoughts focused inward.

They'd planned to do some grocery shopping after dinner last night, but it turned out he needed to go back to the office. Instead they swung by the market and he ran in to pick up some formula and diapers. She'd almost kissed him again when she also found coffee and milk in the bag.

But kissing the man was getting to be a habit she needed to break. Seriously, did she have no sense of self-preservation?

He came toward her almost as if he'd read her mind and meant to test her resolve. It took everything in her to hold her ground. He stopped next to her and bent to kiss Jack on the top of his head.

"We're not going to get everything we need here in

River Run. We need to drive down to Sacramento to hit one of the big warehouse stores and a Wal-Mart."

Her heart sung at that decree. "Excellent idea."

"I'll work it out so I leave early. Can you be ready at three?"

"You bet. Jack and I'll be here with our shopping shoes on."

"Uncle Nate is going to be late," Michelle informed Jack after getting off the phone with Nate. He was a cop. Of course he was going to be late. "Get used to it."

She used the extra time to wander out into the backyard. She already had a list of supplies for work on the rocking chair, and changes she'd decided on for updating the kitchen, master suite and downstairs bathroom.

She intended to do the inside work herself; the outside work, not so much. Gardening had been her dad's thing, not hers. The yard work she'd hire out. But she spied the tree house and her heart melted.

That was something her dad had really done right.

Some of her happiest memories were the two years she went to Princess Camp and the hours spent in her castle tree house. The castle started out painted lavender, but in her teen years she toned the color down to a soft gray. By the weathered look of it her dad hadn't done anything with it since she moved away. She mentally added lavender paint to her list.

And a note to call Elle and Amanda. Thoughts of Princess Camp reminded her she hadn't spoken to her longtime friends since before she arrived in River Run.

Her cell rang and she fished her phone from her jeans pocket. Speak of the princesses.

"Elle, I was just thinking about you and Amanda."

"Really? Am I supposed to be telepathic to communicate now? What's wrong with the phone? See I picked up my cell, punched a number and there you were on the other end."

"Witch. Don't pick on me. I'm stuck in the middle of nowhere and until yesterday a storm had knocked out electricity and phone services. It's downright primitive."

"A storm knocked out services for three days?"

"Technically two days, but spring is a day away and we have snow on the ground. You live in San Diego. You wouldn't understand."

"Hmm. You have me there. So how long are you planning to stay in the back of beyond? I'm anxious to see you."

"Bad news. It's going to be longer than I thought. Turns out my dad rented his house to the new sheriff. His lease isn't up for a few months."

"So you can't work on the house?" Elle demanded, eagerness adding a lilt to the question. "Come stay with me, we can scope out L.A. on weekends and find you a place while you're waiting for the tenant to vacate the house."

Everything in Michelle leaped at the suggestion, but she'd given her word to help Nate with Jack. And with Jack's light weight resting trustingly against her shoulder, she couldn't discount her promise.

"I can't."

"What? Why not? If you're thinking of the rent, don't. I have it covered."

"You are the greatest. But you have to stop tempting me, because I have to stay. I made a commitment."

"You hate that place."

"I know. It's complicated."

"Ah." A knowing quality entered Elle's voice. "There's a man involved."

A vision of Nate half-naked in the bathroom this morning streamed through her mind. She sighed and kissed Jack's downy-soft hair.

"Two actually."

"Hmm." Elle hummed knowingly. "That would be complicated. Promise me it's not going to keep you from moving south."

"Not a chance."

"Good. Listen, I have a meeting. Keep in touch, and I don't mean telepathically."

"Very funny. Can you tell what I'm thinking now?"

She laughed. "There's the Michelle I know and love. Tootles."

Michelle disconnected, a grin lifting her mood. She missed her friends.

The time on the phone caught her attention. Nate should be here soon. She moved inside to finish getting ready. In case he arrived on time she wanted to be waiting when he got there.

Too late. Apparently he was early, which was almost as bad as being late.

He came skipping down the stairs as she entered the

front hall. He must have been faster than he'd thought because he'd obviously showered and changed.

He wore black slacks and a long-sleeved, light blue shirt with a navy pin-striped tie and carried a black blazer.

She whistled her appreciation. "Don't you look pretty? Do you always dress so formal to go shopping?"

"I have an appointment with an attorney about assuming custody of Jack," Nate said, hooking his jacket over the end of the banister. "I had to put the mayor off and hurry home because the attorney couldn't adjust the appointment without moving it back two weeks. Child Protective Services needs a copy of the petition. So I'm going to have to drop you at the warehouse store and catch up with you after the meeting."

"Of course you have to make the appointment." She indicated her sweater and jeans. "It'll just take me a minute to change."

"There's no need. And we're already running late."

"I can't go like this. I'll be quick." She thrust Jack into Nate's arms and waved to the baby's gear. "I'll be there before you get Jack loaded up and strapped in." She dashed up the stairs.

Knowing she'd never live it down if she didn't meet her promised speed limit, she kicked her shoes off on the way to the closet, pulled out black pumps and a short black skirt. It took two minutes to shimmy out of her jeans and into the skirt. She looked into the mirror and nodded—the light pink sweater was fine. She clicked a wide black belt around her waist and ran out the door.

At the bottom of the stairs she slipped into the

pumps, grabbed her purse and the jacket she noticed Nate had left hanging over the banister and strolled out to the SUV.

Nate was just closing the garage door as she walked up. The once-over he gave her was gratifying. The obvious male approval stroked her ego. But when he opened his mouth she knew it wouldn't be to compliment her shoes.

"You forgot your jacket," she said and thrust the black garment into his hands. And then she made a point of reaching her seat before he slid into his.

While strapping in she glanced behind her to make sure Jack was properly situated and noticed he sat in a new seat. He was scoring big today. Along with the furniture they dropped off earlier Kim had brought a bag of clothes Christy had outgrown. Gender neutral, of course.

He wore a pair of brown jeans with a pale yellow shirt with a bee buzzing along the front. Under it he wore a white onesie and on top should be a bib that read Got Formula.

"What happened to Jack's bib?" she asked Nate as they hit the road.

"I threw it away."

"What? Why?"

"It was purple."

"It was white."

"With purple writing. He's a boy, he's not going to wear purple."

"He can't read, doesn't know the difference between

purple and polka dots and—pay attention here because this is really important—he's only four months old."

"Which only means I have to protect his manhood until he can do it himself."

"And purple lettering is over the line?"

"Yes."

She shook her head at his unrelenting masculine stance. No wonder men and women didn't understand each other. They were taught from birth to be contrary.

"What time is your appointment?" she asked, changing the subject.

"Four-thirty."

She glanced at her watch—three-twenty. Sacramento was a good hour and a half from River Run.

"Will he wait if you're late?"

"He said he'd wait as long as he could."

"You'd better go straight there." She stated the obvious. "Jack's future is more important than a few supplies. How did you choose this lawyer?"

"Dolly recommended him."

Dolly, retired attorney and Dad's girlfriend. Michelle knew she'd have to go see the woman, but she dreaded the thought. She really didn't want to talk about her dad's relationship or their mutual loss.

He turned right onto the on ramp to Highway 80 and then glanced her way. "You're sure you don't mind waiting?"

"Not when it's best for Jack."

"Best? I'm a sheriff," he said, facing forward again. "I heard you warning him against the perils of living with a lawman."

"There's that, but you've been very good with him, patient and caring. And at least you're trying, which is more than can be said for the woman who dropped him off."

"I thought you were giving her the benefit of the doubt."

"I never said that. I said she may have knocked and we didn't hear her. That didn't mean it was acceptable for her to leave him in the freezing cold."

"I'm glad to hear it." He loosened the tie around his neck.

Michelle meant what she said. And she meant to leave it at that but she couldn't.

"I know she doesn't deserve a second chance. That there's no excuse for leaving her baby in a dangerous situation. I get that, I really do. But there's this tiny part of me that keeps saying I'd have done anything to know my mom."

Silence met her revelation, leaving her feeling exposed. She glanced at Nate's hard profile, found no hint of his thoughts and turned her gaze to the tree-rich scene out her window.

"I guess it's not something you can understand if you grew up with your mom."

There was a sigh beside her. "My mom should never have had a child. She had the maturity of a fifteen-year-old. Which is a personal assessment, not a professional one. Everything was always about her. And if it was too hard, or took too long, she didn't want to be bothered."

"Sounds rough." She'd longed for some freedom, a

little less supervision, but it seemed you could have too much of a good thing.

"It wasn't bad when my dad was alive. He loved taking care of her. He was proud of his home and his family. He took care of everything. She cooked. She had a weekly menu that she repeated week after week."

Okay, that part didn't sound so bad. The Lord knew her dad hadn't been very imaginative in the kitchen.

"And then Dad died."

She flinched. That was bad. "How old were you?"

"Six."

"That's pretty young."

"She could barely function after my dad died. Everything fell to me. I had to get us up for work and school. I had to remind her to shop for food and to pay the bills. I kept expecting her to become the mom, but she never did. She loved me but my needs were always second to hers. I don't want that for Jack."

Of course he wouldn't. His mother had robbed him of a childhood. Michelle understood where he was coming from, but that little voice continued to call to her.

"But you loved her, too."

His shoulders tensed and for a moment she didn't think he'd respond.

"Yeah." It was grudgingly offered.

"Do you think your life would have been better without her?" she wondered aloud.

"It's hard to say," he answered, unsure. "Foster care is no picnic. But there are good people in the system, as well."

"So you're sure this is what you want to do? You want full custody?"

"I owe it to Jack, to my Uncle Stan."

And that wasn't a hard choice to contemplate. The silence grew between them until finally she had to ask.

"Have you heard anything on his mother's whereabouts?"

He slid Michelle a sideways glance. "You're like a dog with a bone, aren't you?"

"That must mean yes." She grinned. "What have you learned?"

"Not much. She and Jack lived in Carson City. Searching across states complicates things, but I'll find her."

"And then?"

He lifted one shoulder, let it drop. "I don't know. The letter made it clear she was done with Jack. She wanted me to assume custody. Or give him to a good home. She couldn't be any clearer in her intentions. Finding her probably won't change anything."

"But you don't know that."

"I know Jack's future is too important to base it on maybes and what-ifs. And the attorney made it clear on the phone if I wait to assume custody, Child Services may step in."

Traffic was light so Nate pulled up to the attorney's office only ten minutes late. It helped that Michelle had agreed to wait.

She surprised him sometimes. She wore her siren facade so well that when she showed signs of depth it caught him off guard. Heaven help him, but he'd told her more about himself than anyone else, ever.

Why was that? What was there about her that made him open up?

She wondered why he had so little sympathy for Jack's mom; he could tell her he knew how it felt to be left in a storm.

He'd been a latchkey kid. They'd lived only a block from the school so he walked, and one day when he was in the first grade he'd run home through the rain only to huddle wet and cold on the doorstep for over an hour waiting for her to get home.

As he'd told Michelle, he firmly believed some women weren't meant to be mothers.

He stepped out of the vehicle and grabbed his jacket. When he saw no movement from her, he bent down to ask, "Aren't you going to come in and wait in the lobby?"

She shook her head, causing her hair to shimmer like gold in the dying sunshine. "Jack is asleep. We'll wait here. Take as long as you need."

He nodded and turned to enter the modern glass building. The entrance faced the small parking lot and Ted Watkins was waiting at the door.

They shook hands and he gestured to the SUV where he could clearly see Michelle.

"Would your friend like to come in? We have a nice waiting room."

"Thank you. But the baby is asleep."

"You have Jack with you?" Ted's gaze went back to the SUV. "Good. I'd like to meet him."

"Why?" Nate's protective hackles rose.

"Because it makes it more personal when I see and talk to the people involved in a case. Child custody cases are extremely personal so I want that connection. I'd also like to document his condition, take some pictures for the file."

"For what reason?" This really wasn't going how Nate had expected. "The trauma he experienced from being left in the storm has passed."

He spread his hands. "It may not ever come into play, but I prefer to be prepared. And as an officer of the court I can add my evaluation along with the custody documentation."

Watkins cocked his head and met Nate stare for stare.

"Is there a reason you don't want me to meet the boy?" the attorney asked point-blank.

"No." Nate relaxed a little. He got the impression Ted Watkins wouldn't relent until he determined for himself that Jack was okay. Nate knew his size and air of command intimidated most people. The fact that Watkins didn't let that deter him told Nate everything he needed to know. The man was tough, not afraid of a fight.

He was in the right hands.

"Good, then shall we ask your friend and Jack to join us?"

CHAPTER EIGHT

"I saw the baby furniture in the room across the hall. I guess David delivered everything."

"He did." Keeping her attention on the array of stains and paint on the shelf, Michelle smiled at Nate's terse tone. "Between the three of us we got it all upstairs and put together. I like Kim. And David. They seem really happy together."

"You already made your point there," he said grimly. "We're not going to talk about their relationship."

"Okay, fine. What did the attorney say?" After being introduced to the lawyer, she and Jack had waited in the reception area while Nate finished his business.

"Can't we talk about the weather?"

Concerned, she stopped and faced him. "It was that bad?"

"No." His expression softened and he cupped the side of her face in his large hand. Briefly, gently, he swept his thumb along her cheek before dropping his hand.

"I liked him. He doesn't anticipate any problem with the court granting me full custody."

"Good." She forced a smile, pretending she didn't already miss his touch. He was an uptight lawman, in a go-nowhere town, and he stood between her and what she needed to do to get out of said nowhere town. Yet a single caress melted her insides.

That was just wrong.

Intent on self-preservation, she turned back to the shelves. They'd already been to the warehouse store to pick up food and baby supplies. They were now at Wal-Mart and had half the baby section loaded into two carts. Jack sat propped up between her oversize purse and a Spider-Man fleece blanket Nate insisted he needed.

Her last chore was to gather the items on her home improvement list. Best to stay on task.

"Whoa." Nate's hand closed around the tin of lavender paint Michelle moved toward her cart. "I said no purple."

"It's not purple. It's lavender."

"Which is just froufrou for purple." He put it back on the shelf. "It's not going in Jack's room."

Michelle tried to reach around him to retrieve the can of paint, but he blocked the shelves with his big body. Hands crossed over his chest, he sidestepped every time she did.

"It's not for Jack's room," she assured him, feinting one way then quickly back the other hoping to catch him off guard. He simply wrapped one long arm around her waist and reeled her in.

"I don't want it anywhere in the house," he declared.

Suddenly breathless and way too close to his taut, muscular body she went still, ending their crazy dance for power.

"Enough." She planted both hands on her hips. "It's not for the house, either. It's for outside."

"You want to paint my house purple? Oh, hell no."

That got her back up. "My house," she corrected. "I'll paint it any color I choose."

"Not while I'm living there," he responded. "New rule, I get veto power over all improvement projects."

"I don't think so. You haven't put a single bit of yourself in the house. And for the baby's room your idea of decorating is a stuffed bear, a dump truck and a Spider-Man blanket."

"It's a really cool truck."

She threw up her hands. "He's four months old!"

"He's a boy. And he's not going to live in a purple house."

"I give up." She sighed. "The paint is for my castle."

He blinked at her. "What?"

"My castle in the backyard." He still looked blank so she laid it out for him. "Castle. In the tree. In the backyard."

"The tree house?" Comprehension dawned. "That eyesore? I've been waiting for a free day to tear that thing down. It would already be gone by now except for the storm."

Anxiety ripped through her. She was lucky she'd made it home in time to save her beloved haven.

"Is the structure even sound? It's probably ready to fall to the ground."

"It's sound. I had to add a couple of nails here and there but it felt sturdy when I climbed up there yesterday."

"Good Lord." Clearly appalled, he demanded, "Tell me you didn't take Jack up there."

"Oh, yeah, we're a team. I had him in the sling while I was swinging the hammer." Sarcasm screamed through her chipper tone.

"Well, who knows about someone who'd paint any type of house purple?" But he stepped aside and let her retrieve the lavender paint.

An overwhelming sense of sadness hit her as she set the can in the cart. It had nothing to do with the stupid argument—the silly dance had almost been fun. But hearing how close she'd come to losing the tree house made her realize she'd soon be walking away from all of it—the house, the yard, the town. Reality brought on a melancholy she couldn't hide as tears burned her eyes.

"Hey," Nate said softly. He stepped closer, patted her shoulder. "Are you okay? Come on, this can't be about the color of the house."

She shook her head. "It's not that."

"Then what is it?"

His hand fell to the small of her back, a comforting touch. Without thought she leaned into him about to confess her unexpected wave of nostalgia.

Good God. She stopped, straightened away from him, then carefully put the length of the cart between them.

What was she thinking? She knew better than to reveal her weaknesses. Especially to a lawman trained to spot and exploit the weaknesses of his adversaries.

And despite their close circumstances, they were adversaries.

"It's nothing." She dismissed his concern with a dab at the corner of her eye. "I got a speck of dust in my eye."

"Dust?" He lifted one dark brow.

"Yes." That was it. No more letting her affection for Jack soften her toward his uncle. Surely that's all it was, a little residual connection. "I'm starved. Didn't you promise me dinner? Italian sounds good."

It simply wasn't possible she was falling for the sheriff.

Jack's cries reached Michelle in stereo through the barely open door and the baby monitor on her nightstand. She peeled one eye open, sighed and then forced the other open and her body into motion.

The first move had her moaning as muscles rarely used screamed in discomfort. With the near loss of her beloved tree house fresh in her mind, she went right to work on the remaining repairs and repainting. Nate may consider it a waste of time, stating the new owners could simply tear it down, but it was important to Michelle to bring it to its original glory. It represented the best part of her childhood, a visual reminder her dad had cared for her.

With the help of an electric sander she spent the day getting it ready for its pretty dressing of lavender paint. But tonight her arms and shoulders were feeling the pain of her gain.

No time to stretch with Jack demanding attention from across the hall, but she'd peek in Nate's medicine cabinet for some muscle rub before she went back to bed.

She frowned when the cries suddenly stopped. Not a good sign. A good baby, Jack rarely cried except for his 2:00 a.m. feeding. He'd already figured out if he didn't make himself heard there would be no bottle, and so he announced himself—loudly—until he saw the whites of her eyes.

At least that had been their schedule for the past four nights.

She pushed the door all the way open and found the reason for the change in routine. Nate stood with the baby cradled against his bare chest, Jack's head resting on Nate's shoulder as he rocked him slowly back and forth.

The sight of man and baby together took Michelle's breath away. Her heart wrenched and she wondered what it was about a tough man holding a baby that made a woman's knees go weak? A psychologist would probably explain it as something primal, dealing with procreation and survival of the species.

Whatever. She felt primal all right, lust at its purest level.

Dressed only in lightweight knit pajama bottoms, he personified masculine perfection—broad shoulders, trim torso, taut butt. Muscles flexed and flowed with the controlled back-and-forth motion.

Just yum.

He was gorgeous. Not even the scar detracted from the sheer beauty of his form.

"Hey," he said, sleep giving him a sexy rumble.

She shifted restlessly, and the satin of her nightie brushed over her sensitive nipples. She shivered even as heat raced through her blood.

"Hey." She crossed her arms over her chest, because her body had ideas she had more sense than to give in to. "Nothing wrong with this boy's lungs."

He laughed. "No. What are you doing up?"

"We agreed I'd watch the kid."

"Sure. During the day. I figured we'd split night duty. You had last night. Tonight is my turn."

"Seriously?"

"Yeah." Jack whimpered and began to wiggle, showing his displeasure with the chitchat delaying his feeding. "But since you're up, can you take him while I get his bottle?"

She took Jack and sung to him softly while Nate disappeared. A few minutes later she heard a ding too close to be from the kitchen downstairs. Curious, she stepped into the hall and encountered Nate coming back from the fourth bedroom, which he'd converted into his office.

He was shaking a bottle he'd obviously just made.

"Are you cheating?" she demanded.

He grinned. "Did I forget to tell you I have a mini-fridge and microwave in my office?"

"You didn't." She would have noticed when she prowled through the house.

"Okay, I bought them off one of my deputies, who was moving in with his girlfriend. It seemed like a good idea."

"Hmm." She accepted the bottle, fed it to Jack and

moved back into the baby's room and the office chair Nate had brought into the room.

He continued to surprise her with his dedication to the whole father thing. "Is it really so easy for you to assume this role?"

He shrugged, a sensual roll of bone and muscle. "Hell no. But it was my choice, no point in moaning about it."

"No, but it's got to be an adjustment."

"You have no idea." He ran both hands through his hair, sending the sleep-tousled mass into further disarray. "Everything has changed. I have to factor him in to every decision I make. Even at work I'm aware there's someone counting on me at home."

"I know," she empathized. "He's young enough and good enough I can put him in the portable crib while I'm working, but I'm constantly aware of him. And not only do I have to think about feeding and changing him, I worry about the logistics of keeping him in view but safe from paint fumes or dust particles."

"I saw the paint you got. It's kid-safe."

"Yes, but I still don't want him breathing in a lot of it. We're becoming a great team. He's a real guy's guy. He was kicking it to the sound of the power tools today."

Nate barked out a laugh and then his gaze turned intense.

"I know I've given you grief, but you've been a life-saver. I really couldn't have done this without you."

"Thanks. I guess we're a team, too." She shifted her gaze away from the half-naked glory of him to the baby in her arms. Nice guy Nate combined with the fabulous body made him way too appealing.

"Have you thought about what you're going to do when I'm gone?" She pushed the reminder of her looming departure at him along with an internal lecture to take note.

Her goal was to spiff up the house, sell it and move to Los Angeles to get on with her life. She needed to stick to the plan.

Jack chose that moment to smile at her around the nipple in his mouth and he reached out and petted her cheek.

Her insides melted at the trust looking at her from that tiny face. She closed her eyes and pictured L.A.

"I've thought about it." Nate huffed out a frustrated breath in answer to her question about his future plans. "And I talked to Kim. She's given me a list of names to contact for nanny service. She says he's too young for most day-care centers and that they won't take a baby until they're potty-trained."

"A nanny is probably better with your hours anyway."

"True." He propped himself against the doorjamb, his broad frame nearly filling the opening. "It doesn't happen often but there are nights when I'm called out." He gave her a lazy smile. "Fair warning, you might have to cover for me some night."

"Familiar territory," she assured him.

"Right. You would understand. Anyway, it's pretty clear I'm going to need someone to live in."

"I was right, wasn't I? You were thinking you and Kim could team up to raise the kids. That a wife might be a better bet than a nanny?"

"It crossed my mind." He grimaced. "It wasn't my finest moment."

"No," she agreed. "You both deserve better."

He hung his head, shook it in despair. "I vowed I'd always take care of Kim and Christy. It's the least I can do."

"And I'd say you've met that vow." She carefully removed the bottle. Jack made a few sucking motions and then settled into sleep.

"I'll burp him." Nate came over and gently took Jack. She handed him a receiving blanket to use as a burp cloth and then crossed her legs and unabashedly watched man and baby.

She couldn't help herself. It was like constantly playing with a sore tooth—it wasn't good for you but you couldn't stop doing it.

"Maybe it wouldn't be such a bad solution," she conceded, thinking about his reaction to David. Maybe it was more than protecting his friend's place in her heart. Could Nate be jealous?

"Do you love her?" Something had driven her to ask the question. She shouldn't care. Didn't, she assured herself. It was only for Jack's sake that she pushed. It wouldn't be fair to him if Nate jumped into a relationship for the wrong reasons.

He went still. The question obviously caught him off guard. And she could see him thinking it through. So what did that mean?

"Yes," he finally declared.

She nodded, not surprised by his response. She knew Kim meant a lot to him, first because of what she'd meant to Quentin, but also from what Kim told her, the two of them had been through a lot together these last few years.

Now the pinch of resentment Michelle felt, *that* surprised her.

She cocked her head, and met him stare for stare. "Do you want her?"

"Ah, hell." No hesitation now, no need to think it through.

She had him. He cared for Kim, but it was clear his feelings for the other woman were no more romantic than hers were for him. And that wasn't going to change.

"So not a solution."

"It was only a passing thought."

"Why did you trade duty with him?"

"What?" Nate alternated rubbing Jack's back and patting him gently. She found it enthralling to watch his big hands tenderly handle the boy.

"With Quentin," she clarified. "Why did you guys switch duty?"

He sighed. "It was his anniversary and he had a chance to do a video chat with Kim, but it had to be early, so I took his shift."

"So you would have chosen to take that from him?"

He scowled. "Of course not. I knew how much he missed her. How he longed to see his kid."

"If you wouldn't change what led to the two of you being where you were when Quentin got shot, you can't continue to blame yourself."

"Wait." He rubbed a fist over his forehead, as if trying to push the information through. "No. If we hadn't traded—"

"Then Kim wouldn't have those last fond memories of him."

His eyes flashed. "But he'd be alive."

"You don't know that," she said softly. "If you're going to change one element, then other factors could change, as well. The sniper may have chosen the other target and Quentin could still be dead."

"No. You're mixing things up."

"I'm saying the only way to change what happened is to have denied Quentin time with his wife and daughter. And even then there's no guarantee he wouldn't still be gone."

Jack burped, the sound loud in the sudden silence. Nate spent the next few minutes putting Jack back in his bed.

She realized she wasn't going to get an answer. That she'd pressed Nate as far as she could. She pushed to her feet and walked to the door, satin sliding sensually over her body. Halfway through the door she stopped and glanced at him over her shoulder.

"You're a good guy, Nate. You should give yourself a break."

CHAPTER NINE

ON Michelle's first day off, she gratefully left Jack in Nate's care, strapped on the tool belt her dad had given her when she was eight and strolled out the front door. The belt felt familiar on her hips and she ran her finger along the notches her dad added to fit her growing figure through the years.

She was supposed to have yesterday off. But it got postponed when the mayor demanded Nate participate in a meeting with the local school district.

Putting aside her annoyance at having her schedule disrespected—she'd expected it, hadn't she—she skipped down the porch steps and strode across the yard.

She'd noticed a couple of fence boards were loose after the storm so she walked the perimeter of the property making repairs where she could and taking notes on boards that needed replacing.

For the front she decided a new coat of paint would do a lot to perk up the curb appeal. Luckily the yard was in good repair because she didn't mind wielding a hammer, but gardening had never been her thing.

Not that Dad hadn't recruited her help there, too. She eyed the early-blooming irises, remembering how helping Dad plant the flower bed around the stone bird-bath had earned her freedom from being grounded to go to the Spring Fling Ball with Timothy Smart in junior high. She deemed the dirt under her fingernails a worthwhile payment when Timmy gave her her first kiss at the dance.

Oh, yeah, she had a fondness for irises. She grinned. How Dad would have freaked if he knew. Then she shook her head—who was she kidding? Of course he'd known. He may not have made it to her graduation from junior high to high school, but he always knew what was happening with her. He'd had spies everywhere. It was one of the reasons she'd been so hot to skip town.

With a sigh she walked down the side of the house, along the cement walk her father had put in when she was all of four or five. Even then he had her helping him. She remembered holding the hose over the wheelbarrow while he mixed the concrete.

At the end of the walk she stopped and stared down at her tiny handprints imbedded in the cement, her father's large prints were there, too, on either side of hers. She remembered how he'd tickled her neck with his whiskers making her laugh, as he leaned over her to press his hands in the wet cement.

Now he was gone. There'd be no more projects. Tears stung her eyes and she ran her finger along the notches again. The tool belt would be a reminder of her dad for the rest of her life.

Ten minutes after his shift ended Nate got a text message from Michelle advising him he'd invited Kim and

David for dinner to thank them for their help last week and he should get home as soon as possible.

He'd invited them? No.

Guilt tightened the muscles across his shoulders as he acknowledged he should have. Worse, he would have but the whole David thing continued to annoy him. Kim should have told him she was seeing someone.

Obviously Michelle had picked up his slack and made the arrangements. Not that it was any of her business.

And he told her so thirty minutes later when he confronted her in his kitchen.

"Well, if you would have handled it, I wouldn't have had to," she informed him. "And you're late."

"It's not a nine-to-five job. I was wrapping up a meeting with a neighborhood watch group when I got your text."

"You could have let me know you'd be late." She gave him a chiding glare along with a set of pot holders. "I'm trying to put on a party here. Can you drain the noodles?"

"I didn't ask for a party. Kim is my friend. She knows I'm grateful for the furniture. I already told her so." He dumped the noodles into the colander, turning his face away from the rising steam.

He noticed she'd hung new curtains. Gone were the dull white ruffles and in their place a soft yellow wafted in the light breeze. They looked fresh and clean against the crisp white of the newly painted trim.

"Oh? So you've talked to her since they delivered the furniture?"

"Well, no." He set the pan back on the stove. "Come on. Friends don't have to keep repeating themselves."

"Not usually, but this was a big favor and it involved more than Kim. You barely know David and he put in a big effort."

Replacing Nate at the stove, she pulled another pan forward and lifted the lid. The scents of garlic and bacon filled the air.

"Him." He used his hip to push her aside and lifted the heavy pan to pour the contents over the noodles. "This looks great. What is it?"

"Yes, David. Kim cares for him." She edged in next to him and began to fold the creamy mixture into the noodles. "If you care for Kim like you say you do, you'll make an effort with David. It's spaghetti carbonara."

He licked a finger. "Tasty."

"Glad you like it. You can set the table."

"I'll tell you what I don't like." He opened the cupboard with the plates. "David."

"You don't know him. This dinner will help remedy that."

Catching her looking at him from the corner of her emerald eyes Nate braced himself for what was coming. He'd already revealed way too much to her the other night. Sitting there in a pink little bit of nothing that clung to her curves as faithfully as a lover, she'd raked him over the coals both emotionally and physically.

"She told me you're like a brother to her."

"Yeah," he admitted with no small sense of relief, "which doesn't make it any easier to see her with David."

"She deserves to be loved, Nate. After all she's suffered, she deserves to be happy. You want that for her, don't you? And for her to be taken care of? Isn't that what Quentin would want for her?"

God, she had his number. Knew just what keys to tap. And she was right about all of it. He wanted Kim and Christy to have everything they needed and wanted. Whether it was him to give it to them or not.

"David makes her happy," Michelle said in a whisper as if the softness would make it easier to accept. And then she turned brisk. "Never mind the table. I've got the rest of this. You should go change if you plan to. They'll be here in fifteen minutes. Oh, and I invited Dolly, too."

"Of course," he muttered as he left the room. "The more the merrier."

Actually Dolly was a great addition to the party. It gave him someone to talk to other than David.

Michelle picked up the plates and followed Nate from the room, watching as he jogged up the stairs. He moved with a lithe grace that was a pure joy to see.

But he was totally off-limits. She'd lectured herself severely on staying detached. This whole dinner party was just an excuse to talk to Dolly.

This morning it had finally clicked with Michelle, duh, that if Nate was renting the house, he must be paying rent. When she asked where he was sending the payments to, he told her Dolly because that was where he had been sending it and he'd never been notified to send it anywhere else.

Dolly was a retired attorney. It stood to reason she'd know where the money was. Michelle should have thought about her dad's affairs before now. She knew he didn't own much beyond the house and a truck older than she was, but there may be something she should take care of.

Michelle liked Dolly. She and Dad had been friends forever. But Michelle didn't know what to think about her dad and Dolly hooking up. It was just such a foreign concept for Michelle to think of him in that way. Anyway, she preferred this meeting with the woman be informal.

So far so good. The carbonara was a hit. Nate actually appeared to be giving David a fair shake, helped along by Dolly's easy chatter. Christy was enthralled with Jack and wanted to treat him like a doll, but otherwise so far so good.

The chill brought on by the storm a week ago was gone, replaced by the warm days of spring. With both the front and back doors open a breeze blew through the house making it easy for them to linger at the table.

Now came the hard part. They'd all carried their plates into the kitchen and the others were headed for the living room. It was Michelle's chance to get the older woman alone.

"Dolly, would you like to see the work I've done refurbishing my dad's old rocking chair?"

"Sure." The petite, white-haired woman turned at Michelle's invitation. "I don't remember him having a rocker."

"We found it in the attic when we went looking for baby furniture. None of my baby stuff was there. I'm kind of surprised the rocker was. Dad believed in use it or lose it."

"That's exactly how he was." Dolly laughed. "I swear if I didn't eat fast enough, half my meal ended up in the trash."

"He was always after me to eat, so he didn't do that to me. But I did have to explain to a teacher once that he'd thrown my homework away."

"Oh, goodness." Dolly's brown eyes danced with mirth. "That ranks right up there with the dog eating it."

"Exactly." Feeling justified even after all these years, Michelle led the way into the garage. "The teacher wouldn't let me make it up until I had my dad call him and admit he'd trashed it."

Laughing together, she met Dolly's gaze and suddenly her throat swelled up and tears filled her eyes. She swallowed and blinked, seeking control. Instead the tears overflowed and rained down her cheeks.

She missed her dad.

While she was in San Francisco it hadn't been so bad, probably because she was used to being alone there. She'd had her friends, especially Amanda, but her dad had little to do with her life in the city. He'd visit a couple of times a year, always made a point to come to her gigs. And she'd always been so proud when he sat in the audience.

Coming home and not finding Dad here felt wrong. The situation with Nate and Jack kept her busy and distracted, but the truth was she kept expecting to see her dad, to run into him when she entered a room.

Of course she didn't. Not physically, but there was evidence of him everywhere.

She tried to pretend she was fine, because if she pretended hard enough eventually she really would be fine. It was hard, though,

"Oh, my dear." Dolly's arms wrapped her in sympathy, in comfort. "I miss him, too. Every day."

They stood, tears flowing, locked together in love and sorrow for a man gone but not forgotten, who'd been important to each of them in different ways.

After a few minutes, Michelle pulled away, walked to the workbench and brought back a box of tissues. She offered a couple to Dolly.

"Thank you." The older woman mopped her eyes and dabbed at her nose. She looked dewy but none the worse for wear.

Michelle knew her eyes were red-rimmed and her nose rivaled Rudolph's, but she pushed the notion aside.

"I've been so mad at him," she confessed.

"Oh, my dear. Why?"

"For not telling me he was sick." She plucked at the damp tissue. "I could have spent more time with him if I'd known. Made him take better care of himself."

"After his scare, he did change his diet and begin exercising more. He was trying."

More tears leaked out. "I never thought of us as being that close. He was always rushing off to take care of business. And the distance just got worse when I moved to the city."

"Oh, sweetheart. I loved your father, but when it came to expressing his emotions, he was a complete cotton head. You don't want to know how long it took him to kiss me the first time."

Michelle threw up a staying hand.

"No, I really don't." She confirmed with a half-hysterical laugh. "That's not a picture I want in my head."

"Of course," Dolly said with a bit of a twinkle. "What I'm trying to say is he may not have said so often, but he loved you very much."

Michelle shook her head and tossed the used tissues in a bin at the end of the workbench. Not often?

Try rare as fairy dust.

She'd only ever heard him say those three little words once a year on her birthday, and then only when he thought she was asleep. She heard it for the first time when she was eight. Every birthday after that, she'd pretended to be asleep early, just to hear the words.

"With Mom gone, it was just the two of us. We should have been tight. But—"

"He put you second." Dolly nodded, her well-defined brows puckered in a frown. "I saw it as you were growing up. It's one of the few things we argued about. It was his self-defense mechanism after your mom died. He needed work and the sense of duty to help him cope, to give him focus. He genuinely couldn't see what it was doing to you."

Choked up, Michelle stared at her feet, focusing on the black sneakers with the bright pink trim. She frowned at a white smudge of paint on the toe.

"He was the job."

"Yes, beyond anything else, he was the job. But I also know it hurt him to know he failed you."

"He didn't fail me," she insisted. "I learned to cope,

too. And I knew if I truly needed him, he'd be there for me."

"I'm glad you realize that." Dolly's smile was sad. "He had his way, you know, of showing his love. Taking out the trash without being asked. Handling little fix-its around the house before they became big fix-its. Drawing me into projects so we spent time together."

Michelle thought of the reminders of her dad she'd found while updating the house to sell, how she kept coming across projects he insisted they work on together. She thought of her tool belt and swallowed hard.

Yes, that was exactly his way.

"I want him back."

"Me, too." Dolly kissed Michelle's cheek. "We'll just have to keep him close in our hearts. Now, where is that rocking chair?"

"Rocking chair?" Michelle blanked for a minute, and then remembered her gambit to get Dolly alone. She still needed to talk to the woman about her father's affairs. She hadn't meant to get so emotional.

"It's over here." She hit the button to lift the garage door and let in the light, then led Dolly to where the mission-style rocker sat on a tarp on the far side of the garage.

"I've stripped it, sanded the treads until they were even and used wood glue to tighten the dowels. Now it's ready to be stained."

"Oh, my dear. You've done a wonderful job. This is a beautiful piece." She sighed. "And I know why your dad kept it."

"Really?" Surprised, Michelle demanded, "Why? How?"

"Your father had a picture of this chair in his things. It's of you and your mother. She's holding you against her shoulder and you're both asleep. It's very Madonna-like."

"Oh." The vision left Michelle speechless.

"It's beautiful. And was obviously a prized possession of your father's."

"Can I have the picture?"

"Of course." Dolly squeezed her hands. "I have all his things for you. And we can go over his estate whenever you're ready."

"His estate? I didn't think he had anything besides the house. I was just going to ask after the rent for this place."

"There's that, yes. But your father lived simply and saved. He had a college fund for you that you never used. And of course there was his life insurance, which has been placed in an account for you at his bank."

"I had no idea." Stunned, Michelle's mind whirled. She'd pulled into town with the last of her savings in her pocket and a desperate plan to turn it into a nest egg to finance a new life in Los Angeles.

It never occurred to her Dad had any assets beyond the house. The windfall was bittersweet, she could use the money, but it came at such a high price.

"I'm sorry." Dolly's voice trembled a little. "I should have made a better attempt to talk to you at the funeral, but it was such a difficult time for me."

"Stop." Michelle hugged the woman. "I understand. Tell me the rest."

"I tried to reach you afterward, but the contact information I found was no longer good."

Michelle grimaced, remembering the loss of yet another job, of having to mooch off Amanda while she tried to find something new in an ever shrinking job market.

"It was a difficult time for me, too."

"I'd like to hear about it," Dolly said with sincerity. "Why don't you come over some day this week? We can talk and I can give you your dad's things."

Michelle had been so reluctant going into this meeting but at the end she felt closer to both her father and Dolly.

She nodded. "I'd like that."

"So you're serious about this David guy?" Nate followed Kim to a small SUV parked at the curb. She'd brought another box of baby things and he'd volunteered to carry them inside.

Michelle's instincts appeared to be on target where Kim and David were concerned, but he wanted to hear it from Kim.

"Come on, Nate. He's not that 'David guy.' You two have met a couple of times. He's a well-respected member of the community." She popped her trunk and then stood back so he could reach the box.

"Huh." In no hurry, he leaned a hip against the dark green vehicle and crossed his arms over his chest.

"We've bumped into each other at a few events. But I don't know the man."

"Considering your occupation, that's a good thing." Both her tone and posture challenged.

He had to concede her point. And her defense of David indicated her emotions were engaged.

Seemed emotions were on the playbill today. From where he stood he saw Michelle and Dolly wrapped together with the waterworks flowing. A frown drew his brows together. It wasn't like Michelle to get all weepy.

"Nate." Kim called his name and he shifted his gaze to her.

"Yeah."

"I want you to give David a chance," she implored him. "He's important to me."

"I see." Well, there was his confirmation. He flicked a glance toward the garage. Michelle had been right. She appeared more composed and he nodded.

"I'm glad you understand." Kim wrapped him in a hug. "You're important to me, too. In a different way."

He patted her on the back. "I'll always be here if you need me."

"I know you don't have to be." She stepped back and gave him a watery smile. "But you will be. You were a good friend to Quentin."

"I'm your friend, too."

"Yes. But you came here and helped me and Christy because of him. I'm not too proud to say we needed you. That I was glad for your help even though you owed us nothing."

He shoved his hands in his pockets and looked away. Michelle and Dolly were inspecting the rocker.

"I wouldn't say nothing."

"I would," Kim insisted. "Quentin was a soldier to the bone, he knew the drill, accepted the risks. We both did. He wouldn't have wanted you to take a bullet because of his choices."

"It's not fair. He had a wife and child. Nobody would have missed me."

"Oh, my God, Nate." Kim pushed the strawberry-blond hair away from her face with both hands. "That is so not true. I hope you don't believe that."

"It's true enough," he argued gruffly. "Nobody depended on me like you depended on Quentin."

"Your cousin Jack needed you. He would have been lost without you."

"Not even Jack could help Jack."

"But you did. He tried because of you."

"I didn't do him any favors. He joined the service because of me. And the war killed him, in a slow and painful process."

"Stop it this instant. You are not responsible for the decisions other people make. War is hell. It breaks the strong and the weak. Jack loved you. He respected you. And he deserves your respect in return." Impassioned she pointed toward the house. "And if you want to talk about someone needing you, let's talk about Jack's son."

"Okay." He pulled her in for a fierce hug. "Settle down."

"Let me go." She pushed away, fire flashing in her blue eyes. "I won't listen to you bad-mouth yourself.

You're one of the best men I know and no one gets to trash talk my friend, not even you."

"All right. You win." Unable to meet her gaze he stared at the toes of his boots. "I'm wonderful."

"Darn right," she snapped, clearly unappeased. "Now say it with a little more conviction. You talk some sense into him. I'm done trying."

Nate looked up to see whose mercy Kim had tossed him to and saw Michelle stood on the curb a few feet away. Why would Kim think Michelle had any sway over him?

He wondered how much she'd heard. Not that it mattered. She pretty much poked her little nose wherever she wanted.

Kim reached into the back of the SUV and lifted the box out. He held out his hands but she walked right by him.

"Hey, I thought I was carrying that."

"That was before I was mad at you. Now I can get it myself." She jutted her chin and narrowed her eyes at him. "And make friends with David, you big lug. You'll like each other if you give it half a chance."

She stormed up the walk and David came out when she reached the porch and took the box. Great.

With a sigh Nate closed the rear door of the SUV. Michelle came over and leaned against it next to him.

"I'll never understand women."

"That's because you're a man and you have to complicate things."

"Me? She's mad because I said Quentin should be here instead of me."

"She's mad because you devalued yourself. And if your life means nothing, does that mean the last three years spent helping her mean nothing?"

"Of course not."

"You blame yourself for both Quentin's and Jack's deaths, but have you ever thought that by taking responsibility you're robbing them of their dignity?"

Appalled, he shook his head. "I'd never do that."

"Life is a series of decisions, actions and consequences. They put us in a certain place at a certain time and life happens. Sometimes you meet that special someone. Or make the deal of a lifetime. Or you could die. Jack struggled in the end, but the same man that raised you raised him. I have to believe at one point he was a strong, capable man. As was Quentin. By honoring their choices you honor their memories."

"Kim said something like that." He rubbed a hand around the back of his neck. He felt like he'd been put through the spin cycle. First Kim and then Michelle questioned his motives when he was just trying to do his best.

Funny how when Kim talked to him, his defenses crackled, but Michelle had a way of offering him options that empowered him.

"Smart woman. You should listen to her." She punched him in the arm and headed inside. After a few steps, she stopped and waved him along. "Come on. We're having ice-cream floats for dessert."

He followed her retreat with brooding eyes.

He had all the respect in the world for Jack and Quentin. But how was he supposed to shrug off their deaths when they seemed so pointless? And when they'd had so much to live for?

Still he needed to think about what Michelle and Kim were saying because he'd rather cut off his right arm than do anything to dishonor Quentin or Jack.

His cell buzzed in his pocket. He fished the phone out and flipped it open. A couple of minutes later, he went inside to make his excuses. He'd have to miss out on the ice-cream floats. There'd been an incident at Pete's Hardware and Nate had to go.

Luckily he escaped before he had to admit the women were right.

CHAPTER TEN

A WEEK later Michelle slowly rocked Jack as he took his bottle at 2:00 a.m. Tonight was Nate's turn, but he'd been called out to an accident on the main highway.

Her muscles ached with each motion of the chair. She'd finished painting the castle today. It looked great—soft lavender with white trim, a true castle in the sky.

She was a little surprised she was still here. As they'd planned, she'd met up with Dolly for lunch earlier in the week. Her dad had provided well for her in his death. She should have known he would, because he'd provided well for her in life, physically if not emotionally.

Excited, her immediate reaction was to take the money and run, waving to River Run via her rearview mirror.

And then she left the meeting and had her first hesitation when she strapped Jack into his car seat. How could she think of leaving him? He'd already lost his father and his mother. Yes, he loved Nate, the two of them were as close as a dog and his bone, but losing someone else would no doubt affect his little psyche.

Not to mention Nate had yet to find a sitter or nanny to take her place.

He'd allowed her to stay and start on the house in exchange for helping with Jack. Nate had needed the help, but so had she and he'd come through for her.

And truthfully living with him wasn't so bad. Sure his schedule could be erratic, but she'd also arrived home from running errands or visiting Kim to find Nate had started dinner or folded the laundry. They'd fallen into a rhythm and it worked.

Sure her circumstances had changed but she still needed to deal with selling the house. If she left now, she'd just have to come back to finish what she'd started. Once she got to Los Angeles she wanted to concentrate on the future, not be drawn back to the past.

Better to stay and see it through now.

Jack whimpered. Poor guy was in a bit of a mood tonight. She began to hum and when he opened his eyes to look at her she sang softly.

My American man opens his arms, opens his home
To a fatherless child, lost and alone.
He heats up the bottle, rocks him to and fro.
My American man is an everyday hero.

Jack smiled and her heart lurched. Yeah, here was the true reason she was staying. And oh, she had it bad.

She sang a while longer playing with the words to a song she'd been working on and he slid into sleep. She kissed him softly and put him in his crib, and then lingered for a moment, tucking the blanket around him, making sure he was sleeping soundly.

With a sigh, she turned to leave and found Nate standing in the doorway watching her. She stopped, caught by something in his expression. He looked tired, but more than that he looked tormented. And she knew it must have been bad tonight.

That he was in need tonight.

Again her heart lurched. Oh, man. She knew better than to let him close, to allow him in. That wasn't why she was staying.

But the pain in his eyes cut through all that.

"Hey," she said softly.

Without a word he walked to her, cupped her face in his hands and took her mouth with his. She tasted his desperation, his need, and gave him everything he craved, going on her toes to get closer to him.

He groaned and wrapped his arms around her, hugging her near and deepening the kiss. For long moments he ravaged her mouth, stealing her breath and her senses.

She thrilled to his touch, to the heat building between them. Inching closer she pressed her body to his, aligning thigh to thigh, hip to hip, breast to chest. Oh, yeah.

He lifted his head, pressed his forehead to hers. Breath ragged, he demanded, "My bed or yours?"

"I have a twin." She imagined the two of them squeezed onto the small bed and thought it wouldn't be such a bad thing. But bigger would be better.

"Mine then." He took her hand and turned for the door.

"The master has a king."

A smoldering glance pinned her over his shoulder. "Too much space."

Yeah, plus she really needed to make changes in there before she'd be comfortable thinking of it as anything other than Dad's room.

To prove she liked how Nate thought she pushed him through his door and followed him inside. Closing it behind her, she leaned back against wood. A quick glance confirmed Nate's baby monitor was active on his nightstand. Good.

Biting her lower lip in a sexy moue, she beckoned to him. His eyes blazed with desire, and he prowled back to her. Placing both hands on the wooden barrier either side of her head, he lowered his head and claimed her mouth with his. He ran his tongue along the seam of her mouth and softly nipped her bottom lip, punishing her for taunting him.

Or rewarding her.

"Ouch." She sighed. And then returned the favor, using her teeth on him, and rejoiced in his groan of need. Circling his neck with her arms, she allowed him to carry her to his bed, to lower her to her feet. "More." She threaded her fingers in his hair and pulled him to her for another heated kiss.

"This is probably a bad idea," she said when they came up for air. And then, her eyes on his, she slipped the straps of her cotton camisole off her shoulders. Anticipation flaring in his gaze, he hooked his thumbs in the sides and pushed the garment down her body, catching the waist of her pajama shorts along the way.

"Oh, I'm sure we'll regret it," he agreed, nibbling on her ear. "But I don't want to stop. Do you?"

"You could try to stop." Shivering under his intent stare, she reached for the buttons of his uniform. "But I'd hate to have to hurt you so early in our relationship."

He laughed. But he shook his head and stopped her. Instead he swept the covers back, letting them fall off the end, and then he pushed her gently down.

"No danger of that." He assured her, making quick work of stripping off his clothes. And lowering himself next to her.

He went to kiss her but she placed a finger against his lips to halt him. He nipped her finger then lifted a dark brow in question.

"Are you sure you wouldn't rather talk?"

"You're kidding me, right?"

"You're obviously upset from the accident."

"It was a fatality. Two dead, a child and his mother. I really don't want to talk about watching a man lose his family. I want to forget." He dipped his head and did something with his mouth that made lightning sing through her body.

"Make me forget," he said against her skin.

"Forget what?" She gasped, already lost under the skill of his hands and lips, arching as he played her like a delicate instrument.

She wrapped herself around him, giving, taking, wondering. From one moment to the next caress became demand, became the need for more, for harder, deeper, higher until she bowed under the exquisite flow of sensation. With a cry she clung to him, her ballast in the storm, and soared with him through the night.

Jack's soft whimpering woke Nate the next morning. Instantly alert, he opened his eyes to see it was before seven. No need for the woman in his arms to be up yet. God, she felt good against him, soft and warm and female. How could something that felt so right, be so wrong?

He kissed the bare curve of her shoulder and eased away from the temptation of her. Pulling on his jeans he crossed the hall to tend Jack.

"Hi, buddy." He greeted the baby. At the sound of his voice Jack stopped whimpering and smiled. "Sorry I missed your feeding last night. It couldn't be avoided."

He'd been feeling raw when he'd gotten home last night. Death was never easy. And the Lord knew Nate had seen more than his fair share of it. But it's not something a guy became accustomed to. At least he hoped he never got that callous.

He'd asked Michelle to help him forget. And she had helped. He hadn't truly forgotten, the victims deserved better than that, but she'd given him the distance he needed to cope with the memories.

Finding her standing over Jack dressed in a skimpy T-shirt and shorts, singing softly to the baby about everyday heroes, instantly relieved his distress. Her sensual beauty and sweet voice soothed him, the perfect foil for the devastation he'd come from.

Every day he fought the need to taste her again, to feel her in his arms. He understood she didn't fit in his life, that when she got the money from the house she'd be gone in a blink.

Last night, he hadn't cared.

Need overrode common sense and in the wee hours of a difficult night, he'd been drawn across the room, compelled to inhale her scent, to surround himself in her warmth. And her eager response eased his troubled soul.

He lifted Jack from his bed, made quick work of changing his diaper and carried him downstairs to prep his bottle. While the formula heated in the microwave, Nate got the coffee going.

He amazed himself with how adept he'd become with the routine. He should thank Michelle for that, too. She was so impressed with his decision to take in Jack, Nate hated the thought of looking like a freaked-out pansy handling the baby—which was how he'd really felt—so he'd faked it.

Reading instructions on the formula can, total pansy, making note of how the snaps and tapes and buckles went as he undid them so he could put them back. Watching Michelle, seeing how she did things. He'd been a total cheat. But it had worked. Now he only occasionally freaked out.

Jack squeaked and shifted to look at the microwave, a clue to Nate he'd missed hearing the bell.

He grinned at Jack. "I'll tell you this—" he lifted the boy so they met eye to eye "—my head may be all over the place, but I feel great."

"I'm feeling pretty good myself," Michelle drawled from the doorway.

He tucked Jack against his shoulder and met her gaze across the width of the room. "Hey."

"Good morning." She strolled over, circled his neck with one arm and kissed him softly. With a sigh she pulled away and walked to the coffeemaker to pour herself a cup of the strong brew.

"What's wrong with your head?" she asked after her first sip.

Jack began to protest the delay of his breakfast, so Nate pulled the baby's bottle from the microwave and fed it to him before responding.

She smelled of soap and a hint of mint and looked beautiful without a speck of makeup. His body tightened as images of her in his arms woke up his libido.

Forget Wheaties, the breakfast of champions stood in front of him, her sweet butter hair, cherry lips and peaches-and-cream skin made her look good enough to eat.

Oh, yeah, he wanted him some for breakfast.

Too bad all that sweetness was bad for him.

And he still had night mouth.

"I was messed up last night." Definitely not thinking straight. And her kiss just sent his morning ricocheting off course. What did it mean? "You helped. Thanks."

Was it a morning-after kiss? Or was it a she-thought-they'd-started-something kiss?

"A fatality must be difficult to deal with. Especially a child," she sympathized.

"You know, hold that thought." He pushed Jack into her arms. "And Jack. I'll be right back."

Either way she meant the kiss, he didn't want the final

marker of last night to be a mere peck on the mouth. Not when it was going to have to last him a lifetime.

He shot upstairs, hit the bathroom for a quick spit and shine, grabbed a shirt and headed back downstairs.

In the kitchen he rewrote history. Jack played with a rattle in the portable crib under the window and Michelle whisked something at the counter.

Grabbing her hand he whirled her into his arms and captured her mouth with his in a lover's kiss, swift and needy, a dance of tongues in a heated embrace. He drowned himself in her, sipping from the minty freshness of her lips.

He lifted his head once, but it was too soon. So he shifted to a new angle and sank into her again. And she was right there with him. She climbed onto his feet, lifted onto her toes and took him prisoner by circling him in her arms, surrendering to the passion consuming them.

The need to breathe broke them apart. Forehead to forehead he sawed for air as if he'd run a four-minute mile. She sighed and swayed into him. He had to set his knees to hold them up. He buried his nose in her hair, breathed deep of sunshine and hibiscus.

She turned her head and bit him on the arm.

"Ow!" He set her at arm's length. "What the hell?"

"My thought exactly." She threw back her head and propped her hands on her hips. "I know goodbye when it smacks me in the mouth. I shouldn't be surprised. You said you'd have regrets."

"But I don't," he denied.

"Looks like boo-hoo from where I'm standing."

The woman donned attitudes like other women wore accessories. Different occasions requiring different 'tudes. He saw just enough hurt in her defiant eyes to recognize her attack as a defensive move.

Fine. She wanted a fight?

He got right up in her grill. "No regrets." He made it clear. "Not a single one. You were the best time I've ever had."

"You bet your derriere I am."

She didn't blink. Didn't back down an inch, which was seriously hot. And an unwanted distraction.

He bit back a smile, knowing any show of amusement would only antagonize her more.

"I'm not a gambling man."

Her vibrant green eyes narrowed suspiciously.

"But?"

"No buts."

"Seriously?"

"There were no promises made. None inferred." This close to her, with the air sizzling between them, he almost regretted that. "We're both adults who know the score."

"Yet it won't happen again." It was a statement, which told him she'd come to the same conclusion.

"It's for the best."

Each breath brought her scent into him until he longed to eliminate the space between them. Instead he carefully stepped back.

"Don't you agree?"

"Yes." An odd twitch of her head accompanied the

agreement and then she swung around and picked up the whisk. "It's for the best."

She beat furiously at the poor concoction in the bowl.

He ached to go to her, to pull her stiff body into his and re-create the magic they'd made last night. But good as it had been there was no future in it.

And he knew in that moment why none of the women he'd interviewed for Jack's nanny were working out. None of them were Michelle.

Until he worked that out, he needed her help with Jack. It wouldn't be smart to get involved with her in any other capacity. Not for such a short amount of time.

Not when he was already half in love with her.

CHAPTER ELEVEN

It was her own fault, Michelle bemoaned as she bounced Jack on her hip and watched three little girls play ring-around-the-rosie with the coffee table. She allowed Kim and Dolly to gang up on her.

It took all her energy and ingenuity to take care of one little boy. What made them—or her—think she could take on four kids at one time?

The thing was Dolly and Kim were friends with two of Michelle's old classmates who had opened an internet cupcake pop business. It was a good news-bad news scenario. Good news for her classmates' business, bad news for Michelle, who was called on to babysit while everyone baked, dipped and shipped.

"Girls, let's head outside. I have apples and oranges for everyone."

As the girls shrieked their excitement, she ushered them outside.

No doubt about it, she'd gotten the rough end of the arrangement. She'd been looking forward to four o'clock, when the moms were supposed to pick up their young. That was before the phone call saying they needed another hour. Or two!

Nate was going to freak when he got home.

"Castle." Awe colored Christy's voice and lit up her big blue eyes as she took in the refurbished tree house. "I wanna go in the castle."

"Castle, castle." The other girls began to chant. They were all under four.

"Oh, no. No. No. No." Michelle tried to stop the stampede of three-year-olds, but it was no contest. They almost knocked her off her feet. She hugged Jack to her and prayed for a miracle.

"Girls, I can't take the baby up there and you can't go alone. Girls!" She glanced helplessly at the table and then back at the heads bobbing around the base of the tree. "There's fruit."

Giving up, she crossed the lawn at a trot, catching Christy around the waist and lifting her off the ladder leading up.

"Sorry, kids, but you're too small."

Too small and too many for her to handle on her own while also taking care of Jack.

The wailing started.

The girls scattered like cats after pigeons, each trying to get to the ladder when she chased another away. Delighted with the game, Jack giggled. Not so thrilled, Michelle growled under her breath.

"Stop. I said stop." Her stern tone had no impact on the tiny tots. Their merry shrieks were loud enough to pierce the eardrum.

"What's going on out here?" a male voice demanded.

Of course Nate was early. You could never count on a lawman's schedule. Late when you wanted them home, early when you needed extra time. But today she didn't care.

She swung around and found the sight of Nate standing on the back patio such a sight for frazzled nerves her standoffish attitude of the last two weeks vanished in an instant.

Rushing to his side, she thrust Jack into his arms.

"I'm never having kids," she announced. And turned back to corral the girls. She shook her head as she saw Christy was halfway up the ladder again. Definitely the instigator in this crowd.

Nate quickly passed Michelle, moving Jack into one arm and snagging Christy safely with his other. He blocked the ladder so the other little girls couldn't get up and turned to face Michelle, the two children perched smugly in his embrace, obviously unfazed by his stern demeanor.

"I asked what was going on."

Happy for a moment's respite, Michelle plopped down in a patio chair, grabbed an apple slice and bit off the end. Flavor exploded in her mouth, the sweetness and crunch as satisfying as the joy of handing over authority. Even if it only lasted for a brief moment.

"Where's Mama?" Christy asked.

"Good question," Nate told her. His gaze pinned Michelle. "Spill."

With a sigh she filled him in on the whole babysitting gig.

"How long ago did Kim call?"

She glanced at her watch. "An hour and a half."

The corner of his mouth lifted in a grim half smile and he pulled his cell out of his pocket.

"Hey," he said into the phone. "Your daughter is asking for you." Pause. "No, I'm not early. How's it going over there?" He listened for a few minutes, throwing in an occasional grunt. "How much longer do you think that's going to take? Another hour and a half?"

Michelle's heart sank. She threw up both hands in a staying motion and frantically shook her head. After five hours, she was more than ready to throw in the towel. In fact, give her a towel—a bubble bath sounded really good right about now.

Listening to him agree to additional time, she thought she better get some cupcake pops out of this or someone would pay.

"I can't believe you caved," she groused when he hung up. "Chump."

He laughed and set Christy down to play with her friends. "You started it."

"Last time I make that mistake," she assured him. It was good to hear him laugh again. The last couple of weeks had been very stiff between them. She'd missed him. "I thought I was such hot stuff because I've been taking care of Jack. But he's sweet and happy, and quiet. I'm telling you these girls are from a whole other planet."

"Michelle." He was totally patronizing.

"And they don't talk on their planet. They scream."

"You're tired."

"Completely wiped."

"Uncle Nate." Christy tugged on his pant leg. "We want to go in the castle."

"Yeah." The other two girls cheered. "We want to go in the castle!"

"That's their latest thing, but they can't go up alone and I couldn't help them and hold Jack, too." She waved to the fruit on the table. "I made them a snack. But I brought them out here and now all they're interested in is the castle."

"Well, they are little girls."

"Yeah."

"And you did spiff it up so it looks pretty enchanting."

"Yeah, it's pretty dope." He was trying to butter her up, and darned if it wasn't working.

"Well, we have the girls for another hour or more." Without shifting his attention from her, he carefully removed his badge from Jack's grasp and tucked it in his pants pocket. "Why don't we add some sandwiches and have a picnic in the *c-a-s-t-l-e*."

She perked up in an instant. She loved the idea. A tea party in the castle, how perfect. It had been way too long since she played princess.

"Excellent." She popped up, threw her arms around him, kissed him on the cheek and Jack on the mouth. "Tiaras! We're going to need tiaras."

"Hold it," Nate called after her as she skipped into the house. "We are not playing dress-up."

She simply wiggled her fingers at him over her shoulder. Of course they were playing dress-up. Why hadn't she thought of it sooner?

In her room she found everything she needed.

For all his quickness to toss clutter, her dad had left her room pretty much alone. After her conversations with Dolly, Michelle began to see signs of his affection all over the house. Here was another. And her heart warmed as she headed for the closet.

Since she'd always been a princess in her heart she had plenty of fluff and frills from the past. In her zest to clean things out she'd bagged most of it for Goodwill, so she knew right where to go.

She dumped the bag on the bed, plucked out the items they couldn't use and a couple of things with sharp edges and put the rest back in the bag. Draping a pink boa around her neck, she grabbed the bag and hurried downstairs.

In the kitchen Jack was in the portable crib, the girls sat like perfect angels at the table—yeah, she believed that—and Nate stood in front of the open refrigerator. She grabbed the grape jelly from the door and handed it to him.

"Three peanut-butter-and-jelly sandwiches cut into four triangles each," she instructed him. "And then can you find a box or a basket we can use to carry all the food?"

"Sure."

Ten minutes later they packed his sandwiches along with the ham-and-cheese she'd made, the sliced fruit, cookies, water, soda and juice packs into a huge basket.

"Ready," she announced and handed the food to Nate to carry.

"Yeah!" The girls clapped and jumped from their seats to follow him outside.

Michelle picked up Jack and then decided to detour by the living room for the throw and some pillows.

"Am I going to fit up there?" Nate demanded when she caught up with them at the ladder of the tree house.

She eyed his broad shoulders and had a moment's doubt. But she looked up and saw the opening and figured it might be tight, but he'd make it.

"My dad did, so you should," she assured him.

She went first and laid out the blanket and pillows, and then Nate handed her Jack and she tucked him between two of the pillows. Next the girls climbed up one at a time. And finally Nate joined them.

Instantly the spacious six-by-nine-foot room shrank to dollhouse proportions. Man, he was huge. And totally out of place at a princess tea party.

Yet here he was. And after they'd spent the last two weeks avoiding each other. He sat with his back to the wall, legs drawn up in front of him. The man was all male, all the time. The Lord knew she'd had a heck of a time pretending he didn't exist.

And yet he let Christy and her friends dress him up for the tea party. They wrapped a gauzy scarf around his neck, beads around his thick wrist and put stickers on his boots.

The pained expression on his face spoke volumes. And still he accepted a tiny sandwich triangle on a pink napkin as if Michelle offered him a gourmet treat.

"Thanks." He devoured the triangle in one bite. "I

have to say I'm impressed with the job you did on this tree house. I was ready to tear it down."

She threw him a chiding glare as she wrapped a sparkling pink necklace around a headband. "It was weathered but it's built well. A few nails and a fresh coat of paint was all it needed."

"You're making it sound easier than it was. You're such a girly girl, how do you even know how to do all the home repair stuff?"

"My dad." She put the makeshift tiara on Christy's head and pulled her fine brown hair free of the headband. "He was always dragging me into helping on some project or another. Building, plumbing, gardening—we did all kinds of stuff. Everything but electrical. I only got to watch him do electrical."

"That's actually smart. Electrical can be dangerous."

Christy preened and posed for the other two girls and they crowded closer, wanting tiaras of their own. Michelle reached for the shimmering blue beads and a plastic purple headband.

"Yeah, it didn't hurt my feelings not to mess with electricity."

"I suppose not."

"Dolly said drawing me into working with him was Dad's way of showing his love. Working on the house, seeing all the different projects we worked on together, it's like I've found him again."

"Then it's a good thing you came back."

Tears burned at the back of her eyes. She blinked them away, determined to keep them happy memories.

"Yes." She met his gaze. "I'm glad I came."

Red crystals woven through a soft cream scarf and wrapped around blond pigtails made up the last tiara. The girls giggled and practiced bowing to each other.

Michelle laughed and pulled out the plate she'd tucked into the bottom of the basket. Loading it with sandwiches, fruit and cookies, she handed it to Nate with both hands.

His eyes lit up and he eagerly reached for it. She held on to to the edge until he looked up with a question on his face.

"Thank you," she told him. "This is special for them. For me. We couldn't have done it without you."

He winked. "Just call me Prince Charming."

"Today has been so great," Amanda told Michelle as they settled at an outdoor table in a café on the wharf. "I'm going to miss you heaps when you move to Los Angeles. Promise you'll visit often."

"Now that I have some funds, you can bet I will. Los Angeles doesn't even seem real to me yet. It's going to be tough. And lonely."

"Elle is just down the road in San Diego. She's excited about your move. And this song is a winner, Mich. If you sent it to the record companies instead of the artists, they'd snap you up in a heartbeat."

"I'm a behind-the-scenes girl. Have been ever since that first year at Princess Camp."

Amanda rolled her eyes. "Most people get over stage fright."

Michelle just shook her head and ignored the years-long disagreement. The waiter came and went with their coffee order.

"You really think it will sell?" She bit her lip. "Everyday Hero" was so close to her heart, she had no objectivity on this one.

"I do." Amanda squeezed her hand in encouragement. "He sounds pretty special. Tell me about him."

Michelle hesitated; she was usually the one in control of her relationships. She never had trouble walking away. This time it didn't feel so easy. With a sigh she spilled her guts, telling Amanda all about Nate and Jack, and of finding peace with her father's memory.

"Girl, you are in trouble," Amanda declared after a sip of latte.

"I know. It feels like I'm a different person now than when I moved to River Run two months ago. I still want to succeed with my music, but the overwhelming desire to get to Los Angeles has eased up."

"Do you love him?"

"Jack? Yeah. He's such a sweetheart I defy anyone not to love him."

"You're so full of it. You know who I mean. If you care about this guy, maybe you should give it a chance."

"He's a cop, he lives in River Run, and he has enough baggage to fill a jumbo jet. Three strikes and he's out."

"Don't do that," her friend implored her. "Don't dismiss your feelings just because they're inconvenient. Love is worth fighting for."

"It's not love," Michelle denied emphatically. "I have more self-respect than to put myself second to a man's job again."

"Michelle, most relationships require compromise of some type. It's okay if you don't love him, but don't let childhood grievances keep you from finding true happiness."

"He's testing out a prospective nanny today." Michelle forced cheer into her voice. "Soon he won't need me and I'll be in Los Angeles glad that a fun time didn't keep me from pursuing my dreams."

"Or you could show a little backbone, fight for what you want and start a family with your sweetheart. And his little boy."

"Oh, you think you're funny." Michelle shook her finger at Amanda. "You are so not funny."

"I'm a little funny." Amanda grinned as she reached for her purse. "Coffee is my treat."

Michelle argued for the bill, but inside she thought Amanda wasn't funny, and the picture she painted held way too much appeal.

"How did you know it was Nate's birthday?" Kim demanded. "I've tried to pry the information from him for three years."

"He left his wallet on the sink, so I checked out his driver's license."

"You looked in his wallet?" Kim sounded awestruck over the phone line.

"Of course. There's a lot to learn about a man in his wallet. Just like a woman's purse. For instance, he's an organ donor, but no surprise there."

"Still it's pretty bold snooping behind his back."

"Oh, he was in the room."

Kim laughed. "That's bolder still."

"So I've reserved the event room at the bowling alley for Friday night. It has the four lanes right in the room. I need you to handle the invitations."

"Sure, I can do that. This is a great idea. A lot of people will be excited to attend."

Michelle believed it. People responded to Nate's strength of character and decency. But who knew she'd find those characteristics so appealing?

"Remember, it's a surprise."

"Got it. How are you going to get him there?"

"It's covered. Hank is going to call and report a fight about a half hour before Nate's shift ends. He's going to specifically ask for Nate to come out."

"That should work. This is a fine thing you're doing, Michelle. You've been good for him."

Michelle had no response to that. They'd certainly been good together, but a lack of any future scared him off. Actually the thought of a future would probably freak him out just as much. The good Lord knew it terrified her.

"He'll probably hate it. He's not one for drawing attention to himself. But he needs a little fuss made over him. I don't think he's had much of that in his life."

"Like I said, you're good for him."

CHAPTER TWELVE

NATE heard from his attorney around two on Friday afternoon. The courts had granted him full custody of Jack.

Raw emotion gripped Nate. He straight-up loved the boy. The depth of it shocked him.

When Jack first arrived Nate hadn't hesitated to accept responsibility for the child. Duty was as familiar to him as brushing his teeth, starting when he was six years old, and it fell to him to care for his mother.

Hell, he'd made a career of it.

With Jack it had become so much more than obligation.

Which was what made him reach into his bottom drawer and pull out the file on Alicia Carlton, Jack's mother. Nate had received notice of her whereabouts shortly after his first meeting with the attorney. Michelle's fervent wish for a mother's love and guidance was the only reason he hadn't pursued legal action against the woman.

She lived in Carson City, Nevada, not much more than an hour away, but clearly out of his jurisdiction.

Thirty-five and divorced, she had a lengthy file.

Mostly petty stuff, drug-related, but she spent a year in a secured facility five years ago for being in possession of stolen property.

No doubt about it Jack was better off without her in his life. Yet even with that thought ringing in his head, he closed the file and headed for the door.

He stopped at the dispatcher's desk. "I'm taking a couple of hours of personal time. I'll have my cell on. Hit me if you need me."

She nodded and Nate gave his second in command the same message on his way to his vehicle. An hour and twenty minutes later he pulled into the parking lot of a national restaurant chain and walked inside. He grabbed a seat at the counter and ordered a coffee while he assessed the situation.

One thing he couldn't get out of his head was the timing. Today was his birthday and his cousin Jack had always made a point of talking to him on his birthday. How odd the decision regarding Jack Jr. should be on today of all days. It was almost like Jack Sr. was giving a nod of approval. Nate didn't put a lot of stock in woo-woo stuff. But this felt right.

It took him a few minutes to spot Alicia.

He hardly recognized her. When he last saw her, she'd been four months pregnant, strung out, with sallow skin and her black hair a shaggy, matted mess. She'd barely acknowledged him as he spoke to Jack. His cousin had insisted she was clean, that it was the pregnancy that made her tired. Seemed she suffered from morning sickness.

She looked good today. Her hair was clean and pulled

back in a ponytail. Her skin had a healthy sheen and she smiled as she worked.

For the first time Nate saw what had attracted Jack to the woman. She sure didn't appear to be missing her son.

She must have felt the weight of his stare because she glanced up and spotted him. And there it all was for him to see. Fear first, followed by despair, and then hope, and finally resignation.

A lot of emotion in a flash of time, but she didn't try to bolt. She waved him over to a booth by the window before telling her boss she was taking a break.

"How is he?" she demanded as soon as she sat across from him.

Okay, she got points for going there first.

"You left him on the porch in the middle of a snow storm. I could be here to tell you he's dead."

She went white, all the healthy color leaving her face in a rush. "No." She shook her head in denial. "I'd know if he were gone. Somehow, I'd know."

"How could you know? You didn't even wait for me to open the door."

"No, but I saw you. I watched you go in. I couldn't stay, couldn't face you. I was at the lowest point in my life, but I knocked. And I left him in a better place."

"He could have died."

"Could have." She grabbed on to that. "So he's okay?"

"He's fine. Healthy. My attorney just notified me the courts have granted me full custody." He gave it to her straight, no sugar coating.

She went totally still, and then she nodded and her

whole body relaxed as she dropped her head into her hands on the table. No sound reached him, but by the way her shoulders shook, it appeared she was sobbing her heart out.

Her boss started toward the table. Nate flashed his badge and shook his head. The man backed off, but only as far as the cash register, where he kept an eye on the booth.

"Ms. Carlton," Nate said after a moment, and when she didn't respond he said, "Alicia."

One hand broke loose to grab a napkin, there were motions of mopping up, and then she slowly lifted her head.

"I'm okay," she told him and straightened her shoulders. She met his gaze with water-drenched brown eyes. "It was the right thing to do."

"You haven't changed your mind?" he asked her point-blank. If she was having doubts, he wanted to know now.

"No." Her body shuddered with a heavy sigh. "I said I reached my lowest point before I dropped him off at your place. I was wrong. Losing him was my lowest point. I went on a real bender after that. I was free, right? No baby to hold me back or to force me to work to take care of him."

She dabbed her eyes with the damp napkin. "But no matter what I did, or what I took or drank, I'd see his sweet face in my head. And I'd look at where I was or who I was with and I knew I'd done the right thing in giving him to you. I knew you'd keep him fed and warm and safe. Jack had such faith in you, I knew I could trust you, too."

"You look clean," he stated bluntly. Drugs were not something to tiptoe around.

"I am," she said with her chin up. "For over a month now. I'm doing the best I ever have before. Because of Jack. I was hoping if I stayed clean for a year, you might let me come see him."

He stared at her, searching for a break in her sincerity. He found none.

"But you don't want him back."

Her lips pressed together until they disappeared as if she had to force the words back, but she firmly shook her head. Tears welled again, but she pushed them back.

"I want what's best for him. And that ain't me. A month clean seems like forever. And I got to work at it every day. Real hard. It's best if you keep him." She nodded emphatically and dabbed at the corner of her eye, smiling sadly. "I thought he was a drag on me, but truth is I would be the drag on him. If you want to adopt him, I'll sign whatever you need."

"I'll have my attorney put the papers together." Nate climbed to his feet and put a twenty down for his coffee. "I'll be watching you," he told her, keeping his tone stern. She needed to know he meant what he said. "If you're clean for a year, we'll talk, see if you feel the same way. If you aren't clean, you won't get anywhere near him."

She swallowed hard, then nodded.

He turned away, took a couple of steps and then stopped. He reached into his pocket and pulled out his wallet again. This time he placed a picture Michelle had taken of Jack on the table.

The twenty still sat there and she reached right over it to snap up the picture. Tears flowed down her cheeks. "Thank you."

"Get ready," Kim squealed in excitement. "Hank just called to say a sheriff's car pulled into the lot."

Excited murmurs went around the room as people jockeyed for a good position to view Nate's surprise.

Michelle stared down at the text on her phone and knew it wasn't Nate driving up. He was going to be late. He'd been to Carson City and was still twenty minutes away. He had something to tell her, but he'd just gotten tagged for a call. He hoped it would be cleared before he got to town. He wanted her to put on something pretty and get Jack ready; they were going out to celebrate tonight.

Her first gut-wrenching reaction was disappointment. The same angry letdown she always experienced when her dad failed to show as expected for some special event.

Well, she knew just how to speed Nate along. Knowing he'd been called to a fight at Hank's Bowl, she texted back: Take your time, Jack and I are at a birthday party at the bowling alley. See you soon.

Her phone immediately rang. Before answering, she walked up next to the bowling lanes where the noise was the loudest. "Hey. I got your text."

"Michelle, are you okay?"

"What?"

"Are you and Jack okay? There was report of a fight."

"You're fighting traffic? Don't worry. We're fine here. Oh, my goodness. What a ruckus."

"Michelle! Go home."

"What? Home? I can barely hear you. Listen, we won't be much longer. We'll see you at the house. Say bye-bye to Daddy, Jack."

Jack cooed on cue, making Michelle grin.

"Wait," Nate demanded.

"Bye." She clicked shut the phone just as Nate's deputy entered the room and a loud boo went up.

Kim rushed up to the man to find out what was up, but Michelle wandered out to watch the parking lot.

Guilt racked her. But she was tired of the men in her life making her wait. Yes, she knew it was part of the job, but she hadn't chosen the job.

Sometimes family should come first.

It didn't help at all that Nate wasn't family. That she had no claim on him or Jack. Or that Nate knew nothing about the party. It didn't even matter that he was much better at keeping her informed of his whereabouts and schedule than her father ever was.

She'd wanted to give him something special and it was ruined because he was late. Glancing around at the crowd waiting to cheer his arrival, she almost regretted putting the surprise together. Almost.

But no. She reined in her emotions. Nate was not her father and she was no longer twelve years old waiting for him to show up at Princess Camp.

The truth was Nate deserved this moment of joy and

recognition. She had the feeling he'd had very few happy birthdays. Very few happy moments really.

She bit her lip. Well, it sounded like he'd gotten some good news today; hopefully it would be enough to put him in the mood for the party.

Okay, maybe it was a little mean to let Nate think they were in danger. But she made sure he knew they were both fine. And now he felt compelled to reach the bowling alley as quickly as possible, which was the point.

Ten minutes later Nate's SUV whipped into the lot. He looked grim as he made his way to the building.

Michelle bit her lip and backed into the event room. She hoped she hadn't spoiled his birthday by putting him in a bad mood with her call.

"He's here," she announced to the room.

"Are you sure?" Kim asked after the false alarm earlier.

"Yeah. I saw him."

The blonde clapped her hands. "Goody." She wrapped her arm around David's and dragged him over to crowd close to Michelle near the entrance. "My mother-in-law will probably only stay a short while. She's going to keep Christy overnight and she said she'd be happy to take Jack, too, so you and Nate can enjoy yourselves."

"That would be great." Michelle rubbed Jack's back, disconcerted at the thought of an evening without him. He'd become such a part of her life. "We'll see what Nate says."

A moment later he came charging into the room.

"Surprise!" voices shouted out from all around them.

Nate stopped as if he'd run into a brick wall. He surveyed all the people surrounding him, clearly surprised. Finally he grinned and reached out to shake hands. His gray gazed snagged hers with a promise of retribution before he disappeared in the crush of people.

She sighed and kissed Jack's cheek. "It's going to be all right."

Good. Let him wallow in the attention of his community for a while. He cared for these people whether he knew them as individuals or not. It was time he saw they recognized his dedication.

Yep, let them mellow him out a bit before he hunted her down.

Just as she relaxed with that notion, he appeared in front of her. His eyes flared with heated intent.

"You'll pay for this," he promised as he took Jack, holding the alert baby against his solid shoulder.

She thought that might be it for now. But no, he snaked a hard arm around her waist and jerked her close.

"And never scare me like that again." His head lowered and he kissed her, a slow deep claiming of her mouth by his. Not so much a caress as another promise.

Oh, yeah, if this was her punishment, give her more. She angled her head and challenged him to do his worst. Best? Hmm. Whatever.

A slap in the face, literally, brought her out of the sensual interlude.

She and Nate both pulled back to find Jack giggling and bouncing. Every day he gained better use of his limbs and he reached out and clocked her again.

"Whoa, kid." Nate caught Jack's arm. "We don't hit women in this family."

"He's just trying to show his love." Michelle grabbed the baby's fist and pretended to take a bite.

"Well, he's going to have to find a different way," Nate stated, pleasant but firm. "Because starting now, no hitting girls."

"You're right," she agreed, rubbing at the smudge of lipstick on his lower lip rather than look into his eyes. He was going to make such a good father and every day her departure loomed closer. "Good job, Daddy."

"Eeek." Jack squealed and waved his arms.

"Are you jealous?" Michelle demanded. "That's it, isn't it?" she teased the baby. "You want all my kisses for yourself."

Jack proved her right by leaning forward to give her a sloppy kiss on the mouth.

"Um." She laughed as she blotted her lips with the back of her hand. "I guess that says it all."

"Now I'm the jealous one," Nate complained.

"Don't worry." She leaned close to whisper. "I'm sure you'll get better with practice."

He caught her chin to hold her near for a lingering kiss where their only connection was mouth to mouth. Slowly, softly, he showed her he knew exactly how to excite her senses. When he lifted his head, she sighed.

"We'll practice more later."

Oh, my. Promises, promises. She didn't know whether to be thrilled or scared. She did know she should discourage him, but she couldn't quite bring herself to do so.

"Nate," a voice called out from the bowling lanes. "We need a man to complete our team."

"Go bowl," she ordered him. "There'll be dancing and karaoke later. It's your party. Have a good time."

"I intend to." He winked and turned to join the bowlers.

While he bowled she kept busy checking on the food and the music. With everything flowing nicely, she slipped out to the car to retrieve the jeans and black polo shirt she'd brought for Nate to change into.

While she was outside, she called the sheriff's office and asked the dispatcher to invite everyone to stop by when they had a chance. The woman was excited to hear from Michelle and assured her everyone would be contacted, both on and off duty because everyone would want to attend or at least stop by.

Tears welled in Michelle's eyes at the show of enthusiasm from Nate's coworkers. He thought he was so alone. But the truth was he collected people and didn't even know it.

Blinking back emotion, she told herself he hadn't worked his magic on her. She may not be running away from River Run anymore. Finding explanations for her father's behavior and seeing his actions through the eyes of an adult had helped her put the ghosts of her childhood behind her. But she was still determined to get to Los Angeles. That's where her future lay.

Back inside she handed off Nate's change of clothes and made a swing around the room, checking that all was well. She got caught up in the noise and gaiety of the party revelers, grabbed a beer, and strolled over to watch Nate bowl and let her momentary melancholy melt away.

CHAPTER THIRTEEN

NATE reluctantly let Jack go home with Kim's mother-in-law. Nate's plan earlier had been to spend the night with Jack and Michelle and it was hard to give that up. But the party was in full swing and she'd gone to a lot of trouble to give him this surprise. So he did his best to get out and mingle.

This was so not his thing. If not for Michelle, he would have been lost. As it was, he kept her in sight. Watching her having fun allowed him to relax and enjoy himself, too.

He killed it at bowling, beating both David and his dad. Okay, so maybe David wasn't so bad. And now Kim belted out a decent rendition of "Redneck Woman." Michelle rocked to the chorus, her hips swaying in sexy rhythm to the beat.

She wore a red minidress, the luxurious material shimmering when she moved. It was a turtleneck halter dress, blousy on the top and snug around her hips. Sheer vixen from head to toe.

He stepped up behind her and wrapped his arms around her waist, pulling her close and swaying along with her. She shimmied against him and then turned in the circle of his arms to face him.

"There's the birthday boy." She linked her arms around his neck. "Having fun?"

"I am."

She laughed. "No need to sound so surprised."

"I'm not a social guy," he said with a shrug.

"That was before you took on the community," she corrected him. "Now they've adopted you."

"Because of you." He had no illusions about that.

"Oh, no." The emphatic shake of her head echoed her denial. "It's all you. I just gave them a venue." She ran her hands over his shoulders, straightened his collar. "What did you want to tell me?"

He made a quick scan of the crowd filling the space. This wasn't the time or the place he'd planned, but good news was good news wherever they were.

"I heard from my attorney today. Jack is officially mine."

Her eyes lit up and she threw her body against him, hugging him tightly. "That is good news. He's so lucky to have you."

Her encouragement eased some of Nate's anxiety. "I'm glad you think so."

"I know so. I've watched the two of you together for the past six weeks. He loves you."

"This is different. The last six weeks felt temporary. This is the rest of our lives. And it is different, stronger. It's as if a link binds us now."

"That makes sense. It's official now."

"Yeah." The tightness in his gut eased even more.

"That sounds right. My feelings are the same. I love Jack either way, but now I know no one can take him from me." He told her about his trip over to Carson City and his talk with Jack's mother. "She offered to let me adopt him."

"Really? She said she wanted you to keep him?"

"Yes."

Michelle nodded. "See, even she sees it."

"You were right, that she needs to be a part of his life. If she stays clean, I think they'll be good for each other. If not, then I'll protect him any way I can."

"I have no doubt."

"Okay, everyone," Kim announced from the stage. "We're going to take a break from the karaoke entertainment so someone can give Nate a very special birthday present. Everyone, Michelle Ross."

Applause broke out. And Michelle wiggled out of his grasp.

"That's me." She stepped away, her gaze locked on his. "I hope you like it."

Nate followed her, stopping short of the stage. He crossed his arms over his chest and watched as she picked up a guitar and moved to the stool Kim had set in the middle of the raised dais.

Michelle adjusted the microphone, strummed an introductory riff and began to sing.

My American man wears a uniform,
Does his duty with honor and pride
He suffers every loss both friend and foe
My American man is an everyday hero.

She had the voice of an angel, low and rich, it grabbed him by the heart and squeezed.

My American man wears a badge and a gun.
Protects every man, woman, daughter and son.
His life he'd give and never say no.
My American man is an everyday hero.

My American man opens his arms, opens his home
To a fatherless child, lost and alone.
He heats up the bottle, rocks him to and fro.
My American man is an everyday hero.

My American man takes care of me just right.
He loves me passionately all through the night.
His kisses so sweet, his touch, oh, oh!
My American man is my everyday hero.

The words ended and the music faded away. Silence reigned for a beat of time, and then another before applause broke out, thundering through the room.

Without a word, Nate stepped up to the stage, took Michelle's hand and assisted her down.

"Did you like it?" Her eyes held both excitement and anxiety as she joined him.

Too choked up for words, he kissed her hand and drew her with him across the room.

As he got close to the door, he cleared his throat and called out a deputy's name. When he answered, Nate tossed the man the keys to his SUV. "Drop my vehicle off at my place on your way home."

Nate received a nod. Satisfied, he told Michelle, "Get your purse."

She shook her head. "I locked it in my car."

"Good. Give me the keys." He took them, and laced his fingers through hers. He waved to the crowd and then gave her hand a tug. "Let's go."

He talked little on the trip home, because he didn't know what to say.

She finally broke under the silence. "Are you really mad about the party?"

"No."

"Good." More silence followed. "Then why are you so quiet?"

"Nobody's ever gone to so much trouble for my birthday. Hell, nobody's ever gone to any trouble at all. Mom only remembered events where she got gifts. I got a token present or two at Christmas, but most of the gifts were from her to her. I had to remind her of my birthday." After he turned eight he gave up.

"Did it get any better when you moved in with your uncle?"

"Uncle Stan was simple—birthday, holiday, whatever—he'd pack Jack and me into the car and take us out to dinner. It marked the occasion and that was enough for him."

"My dad and your uncle Stan would have got along real well. That's what he always wanted to do. No surprise I always wanted a party."

"My money is on you."

"And you'd win."

Tonight he couldn't quite grasp it was all for him. Not until Michelle's birthday present. From the moment she stepped onstage, he'd wanted to be alone with her. She looked so pretty in the spotlight. Her silky blond hair flowing like liquid gold around bare white shoulders, lips as red as the dress inching up her long legs. Making him sound like a hero in a voice meant for the bedroom.

It was a gift he'd never forget.

Come to think of it, he'd received a few cards tonight, but thank God nobody else brought gifts. How uncomfortable would that be?

Only when he heard his voice fade did he realize he'd spoken his thought aloud.

"We put it on the invitation not to bring a gift," Michelle explained. "If someone wanted to give something they were encouraged to donate to the River Run Community Improvement Fund."

"I'm not sure you can do that."

"Sure we could. Nobody had to donate. But plenty did. Last I heard you raised twelve hundred dollars for the fund."

"Seriously?" He flashed a glance her way, watched her smother a yawn.

"Yeah." She grinned, her white teeth showing in the spill of a streetlight. "Pretty smart, huh? I knew you wouldn't want people giving you anything, but they're preprogrammed to give for birthdays, so I came up with the donation. The Community Improvement Fund

seemed like a good choice, because everyone bene-
fits."

"Brilliant. Are you going to spend the night with
me?"

"Is that what you want?"

"More than anything."

"Even if it's not for the best?"

He pulled into the drive, put the car in Park and
flipped off the ignition. He turned to her, reached out
and cupped the back of her neck, the move instinctive,
primal.

"You're leaving. I get that. I want the time we have
left to be special."

"It's not the smart thing to do," she reminded him
softly.

He drew her close until they were forehead to forehead. "I don't care." He angled his head, placed his lips
on hers and gently, oh, so gently, kissed her.

She hesitated, but his care paid off. With a sigh she
sank into the caress. Yes, this was what he needed, her
in his arms. The taste of her, the warmth of her, his for
the taking.

Minutes later he had her upstairs, slowly undressing
her like the gift she was. He savored her, with his lips,
with every stroke of his hands, with his whole body. And
she responded beautifully. Embraced him wholeheart-
edly, even his scars, her acceptance giving him peace
even as his body burned for her.

So receptive, so giving, her pleasure brought him
pleasure. And he rocked them ever higher, sensation

building on sensation, until anticipation splintered into indescribable satisfaction.

Heaven—he rolled them so he wouldn't crush her—must be something like this.

"Thank you," he said around a throat choked with emotion, "for everything."

Her hand trailed over his chest. "So you liked your song?"

"It's beautiful." He cleared his throat. "More than I deserve."

"Don't say that." She lifted onto her elbow next to him. "You are one of the best men I've ever met."

"There's nothing special about me," he denied.

She laid a finger over his lips, shushing him.

"Everything in that song is true. If you see the value of it, you have to see the value in yourself."

He frowned, wanting to argue with her logic but unable to do so.

Seeing she'd stumped him, she smiled and cuddled next to him again. "My agent loved it. She's sending it to an up-and-coming star in Nashville."

"Good luck." He sighed, feeling something deep inside settle. Life had never been better.

Jack was his now, safe and sound. As contentment led him into sleep, Nate tightened his arms around the beauty sleeping bonelessly beside him. Michelle was his, too. For as long as she stayed.

Michelle put the finishing touch to the chair rail in the master bedroom. She stepped back and admired the freshness of the room. As with all the renovations she'd done to the house, her improvements in here were mostly cosmetic, bringing the interior design from mid-eighties to the new millennium.

The chair rail circled the room in a soft cream; above it a mellow green paint three shades lighter than the sage green below the rail gave the room a serene feel. Cream curtains held back with sage ties dressed the window. A luxurious light green comforter with dark green vines flowing over it and mounds of pillows propped at the head made the bed an inviting bower. An artful rug in reverse colors and pattern from the comforter brought life to the serviceable beige carpet.

Pleased with the room she did a little happy dance. It hit the perfect balance, pretty without being too feminine. The dark wood of the furniture added the right masculine touch.

Satisfied, she headed in to check on the progress of the electrician in the master bath. She'd bought new light fixtures for the whole house. The electrician started the day inspecting the wiring throughout, and Michelle was happy to hear everything was in good shape. Now he was wrapping up the installation of the new fixtures.

Her cell rang before she reached the bathroom. She saw her agent's name and anticipation tingled up her spine.

"Hi, Denise. Tell me quick so I can breathe, do you have news about the song?"

"Girl, would I mess with you? Would I chatter on about nothing while you waited breathlessly for me to give you exciting news? It's not like you haven't been waiting for this news forever—"

"Denise, tell me now or I swear to you I will come through this line and scuff up your Jimmy Choos."

A husky laugh sounded. "Is that any way to talk to the woman who is going to make all your dreams come true?"

"Oh, my God." Michelle's heart stuttered. "She wants to buy the song?"

"She wants to buy the song."

Michelle screamed. Too excited to contain it she danced for real and when the electrician came running to see what happened, she grabbed him and danced some more.

"Ah, congratulations." Balding and in his fifties, the man gave her a twirl and a hug and then wiggled free and escaped back to the bathroom.

Michelle laughed and finally heard Denise calling her name. She put the cell back to her ear. "Sorry about that, I got a little carried away."

"You're entitled." Denise sounded almost as excited as Michelle felt. "It's a great song. I heard a man's voice, the inspiration for your song perhaps?"

"Electrician. Poor man now knows how it feels to be groped."

"It's his lucky day. And yours, too. I hope you're done with that house, because it's time to move to L.A."

"She's really, seriously interested in the song? Don't mess with me about this, Denise."

"Michelle, this is serious business. I would never mess with you over the sale of your song."

"I need to sit down." Michelle sank right down to the green rug.

"She loved the song. Wants to make it a lead on her next album."

"Shut up." This was so surreal. "Are you going to tell me who she is?"

"Rikki West, she won *Idol* a couple of years ago. Has been riding a wave to the top ever since."

"I can't believe it." Michelle couldn't be more thrilled. She loved Rikki West's voice. "I thought of her when I was writing it. This is perfect."

"It gets better." Denise practically purred. "She wants to meet you, to see what else you have."

"When? Where?" Okay, this had to be a dream. Michelle pinched herself because it was just too good to be true. The sting on her left arm did little to convince her she wasn't in some alternate reality.

"She's going to be in L.A. for an awards show next week. You need to get yourself down here now."

"Right." Michelle frowned, there was no reason the request should throw her. She'd always known the time would come for her to leave.

The first time Denise mentioned it Michelle had been too swept up in the moment to make the connection that going to L.A. meant leaving River Run. And Jack.

It meant the end of what she had with Nate.

Denise gave Michelle a few more details and signed off with another nudge to finish her business in River Run and get her butt to Los Angeles.

Her stomach churned and she flopped back on the carpet to stare up at the ceiling and try and make sense of what she was feeling.

Oh, God. She didn't want to go.

The biggest break of her career and her heart broke at the idea of leaving River Run and the family she'd found here.

No, she just felt attached because she was missing her dad, that's all. She'd reassigned her affections to keep from being so lonely. And sure she'd miss Nate and the baby for a few days. But her new life would soon distract her.

And she'd see them again. She still had to come back and sell the house. So no more moping. Today was going to be all about celebrating.

Needing her buzz back, she called Amanda in San Francisco and linked in Elle in San Diego. Both screamed when they heard her news.

"I knew it would happen." Elle calmed first. "You're so talented it was only a matter of time."

"And it's a great song," Amanda added. "I heard it when she came to town to record it. Patriotic is always in and it ends kind of like a love song, which is a nice touch. Makes me wonder if there's anything you want to tell us?"

No, not a thing. Michelle wasn't going down that road again.

"I can tell you Denise wants me in Los Angeles yesterday."

"Let me know when you make your reservations," Elle told her. "I'll drive up and help you find a place to live. We can celebrate."

"Count me in," Amanda demanded. "I'll take the weekend off from the museum and fly down, too. Heck, I'll bring the champagne."

CHAPTER FOURTEEN

"HEY, I got your message and yes, I'll be home at the regular time. See you tonight."

After leaving Michelle the voice mail, Nate flipped his cell closed and returned it to his pocket. She wanted to tell him something at dinner. He had a bad feeling he knew what it was.

She was leaving.

And he wasn't ready to hear it.

A glance at his watch told him he had two hours before end of shift. He bent his head down and put his attention into completing the budget report for the mayor. But Nate's mind soon wandered.

The two weeks since his birthday had shown him what it meant to be part of a loving family. Waking up to Michelle each morning, watching Jack learn something new every day, knowing she had his back at home— Nate never expected to know such joy.

After half an hour, he acknowledged the report was a no-go. He couldn't concentrate, couldn't stand to sit still. Pushing to his feet, he left his office. He needed to be busy. Stay busy.

He stopped at dispatch. "What do we have going on?"

"It's quiet," she told him. "But I just got a call from Frank over at the Sleepy Bear Motel. He says someone broke into all his units and stole the complimentary toiletries. I was going to send Nelson."

"I'll take it." A nuisance call was a perfect time-suck. And it would keep him distracted for the rest of his shift. "Have Nelson come in if it looks like Peters needs help."

Michelle sounded excited on the phone. He knew she'd scheduled the electrician to come today. She'd come to refurbish and sell the house. The electrician marked the end of that project. There was nothing more to hold her in town until his lease ended in two months.

The thought of her leaving tore him apart.

He could deny it no longer. He loved her.

He didn't know what he was going to do when she left town. He'd finally found the peace he sought in the arms of a siren. Michelle was not the shallow woman he'd first thought. Beautiful and strong, clever and funny, she was a survivor, like him. And he'd fallen in love.

Ten minutes later he arrived at the Sleepy Bear Motel to find the owner—Frank—nose to nose with Beverly, the owner of the local B and B. Uh-oh. Everyone knew of the ongoing feud between the gangly, gray-haired Frank and the plump, grandmotherly redhead.

This might take a little longer than he thought.

"Okay, let's break it up here." Nate quickly put himself between the two of them before the heated argument got out of control.

"Frank accused my grandson of stealing the toiletries." Beverly tried to get around Nate. "No one is going to call my grandson a thief."

It took him a few minutes to calm them down and separate them so he could conduct interviews. And then he had to find a spot to speak to one while keeping an eye on the other.

Just when he was wrapping up the statements, pleased to be only ten minutes past his end of shift, Frank's granddaughter showed up. She went ballistic when she heard Frank had accused the grandson.

"Grandpa, I told you he's smart. He doesn't have to steal. I love him."

Nate smothered a groan. He was tempted to order the lot of them down to the station, but that would only drag this out and he was already late. He reached for his phone to call Michelle and the grandson stormed in and, like his grandmother, immediately went nose to nose with Frank.

Nate pushed his phone into his pocket and went to break it up.

Tears blurring her vision, Michelle blew out the candles on the dining room table. In the kitchen she ditched the chicken medallions in artichoke sauce, pan and all, into the trash. Followed by the bread, the salad and the baked potatoes.

Ruined. Everything was ruined.

The food, the dinner, the joy in sharing her news with Nate, all of it ruined because of his tardiness, because he couldn't be bothered to call and tell her he was going to be late.

Bad enough to be late, but at least call, then she knew better than to expect him at any minute, knew to do something with the food before it grew cold, dry and wilted. Then she knew that her excitement had no foundation, that she was second to the job, again.

She scrubbed the tears from her face, furious at their appearance. She would not cry today.

It was the best day of her life.

She'd be damned if she'd cry.

She'd be damned if she'd stay in this hick town one more night.

She was right to leave River Run when she was younger, right that there was nothing here for her. Tonight proved that.

Her phone rang. She looked at the caller ID. Nate. Looked at the time, over an hour late. She rejected the call.

Chin up, shoulders back, she raced upstairs. In her room she threw her suitcases on the bed and began piling in clothes. She tried for order but folding was beyond her.

She shook with anger, with disappointment.

The betrayal was her own. He wasn't supposed to matter. Men were for fun and a means to an end. She knew that, had learned early to rely only on herself.

Because it hurt when she trusted someone with her heart and they let her down. And they always let her down. Second to the job again. It was the one thing she promised herself in a relationship. She must come first.

The disillusionment was all her fault. He was a lawman, so of course giving her priority was the one thing he couldn't promise her. And yeah, she'd been lying to herself every time she pretended she could walk away without looking back.

All the more reason to be gone when he got home. No need to put her pain on display. He didn't deserve her tears, didn't deserve her love.

Suddenly weak, she sank down on the side of the bed. Oh, God. She loved him.

Oh, yeah, she was a monster liar. How could she let this happen? She knew better than to leave her heart vulnerable. But he'd stolen past her guard with his broken soul and ready acceptance of Jack.

Jack. Oh, Lord.

Her throat tightened and she surged to her feet, seeking action to offset the need to think, to stop the emotions bombarding her from all sides.

The closet and drawers were empty so her gaze went to the walls, the bed. She hadn't touched this room mostly because she didn't want the mess in here where she slept but also because the nostalgia of it, in the face of her father's loss, made her feel safe, loved.

Another illusion.

Armed with anger and righteousness she stripped the walls of posters and pictures, of butterflies and musical notes. Books and trinkets got tossed into a box as she removed all evidence of herself from the room.

That done she carried her bags downstairs.

And there her emotion-driven adrenaline rush gave out on her. She looked at the door and couldn't bring herself to walk through it.

Her phone rang again. Nate again. She rejected it again.

As much as she hurt, the truth was Nate and Jack had her heart. She couldn't just leave. Instead she turned and headed out back, going where she always went as a child when she didn't know what to do and she needed to think.

She escaped to her castle.

By the time Nate got everything sorted out—all signs pointed to the new maid, who had missed her shift and was nowhere to be found—and got on the road home, he was nearly two hours late.

He tried Michelle's cell again. He'd finally managed a try twenty minutes ago but it went to voice mail. And it was the same now.

Aggravated, he tossed the phone into the passenger seat. Her refusal to answer was not good. Told him just how much trouble he faced.

He wasn't eager to hear her departure was imminent, yet he didn't want to hurt her, either. And this whole episode smacked of her father's neglect. Nate usually managed to connect with her to let her know he'd be late, but today's situation had been too volatile. Petty, yes, but emotions had been running hot.

He nearly tripped over her bags when he walked through the door. It reminded him of the day she arrived, of finding her asleep on his couch. Of the kiss that brought him to life. From that moment on, he hadn't been able to get her out of his head.

"Michelle," he called out and dread weighed heavy on him when silence answered him.

The very notion of losing her tore his soul in half. Yes, he had to let her go, but not like this, not on bad terms.

His nose led him to the kitchen. The savory scent of dinner lingered in the air and he found the remains of it in the trash. He rescued the pan, considered it another bad sign and continued his search for her.

Her room broke his heart. Seeing her childhood memories torn from the walls and stuffed in the trash shredded something deep inside him. It also told him he may be wrong about what she wanted to tell him. This was not careful packing. This was rage fueled by hurt.

More than ever he regretted taking the nuisance call. Not that he could know it would turn into such a fiasco, except a cop always knew a call could turn into something more.

He needed to find her. Needed to make this better. He backed into the hall and stared into Jack's empty room. It struck him, where was the baby?

He flipped open his phone, called Kim.

"Yeah, I have Jack. Michelle asked me to take him for the night. Are you sure she's not there? She was headed home to make dinner when she left here."

"The dinner is here." What was left of it. "She's not."

"She was excited about something but said she'd tell me about it tomorrow. She wanted to tell you first."

"I was a little late."

"Uh-oh."

"Yeah. Hey, thanks for watching Jack."

"Good luck."

He went back, checked every room looking for Michelle. She was nowhere yet everywhere. She'd taken a house stuck in the eighties and turned it into a modern, comfortable home. With paint and molding, new rugs and fixtures and a lot of hard work she'd changed it from sorry and dated to fresh and inviting.

He'd thought about buying the house from her, but no. He couldn't live here without her.

The quiet ate at him. He used to live in silence. There had been times when lack of noise meant the difference between survival or death. But that wasn't who he was anymore.

He was a dad now. Noise came with the territory.

He hadn't made a big deal of it when Michelle, talking to Jack, had first referred to him as Daddy, but the name felt good. He probably wouldn't have claimed the title without her, would just have gone on as Uncle Nate. But he wanted to be a dad, wanted the bond and responsibility implied by the title. Wanted to give Jack the love and connection he deserved.

And still it wouldn't be enough for Nate. Michelle completed their little family. These last couple of weeks of playing make-believe family showed him just what he'd be missing.

Sure he could hire someone to do the things she did but it wouldn't be the same. She challenged him, encouraged him, made him laugh. She sang like an angel and made love like a vixen. She wanted to be catered to yet worked like a dog when it mattered to her. He'd miss how she enjoyed cooking but got lazy over the laundry.

Most of all he'd miss her smile and the look in her eyes when she said his name.

The look in her eyes. The look that said she thought the world revolved around him. How could she look at him like that and not love him?

Ha. He laughed out loud. She loved him.

Hope energized him. If she loved him, he had a chance. Spurred to new action he moved from the hall to the kitchen.

He puzzled over whether the wreck in her bedroom happened before the trashing of the dinner when a light in the tree house caught his attention. Of course.

"Michelle," he called as he stepped outside. No response. Not surprised he powered his way up the ladder and shouldered through the child-size door.

Wrapped in a soft pink throw she slept with her head on a purple pillow shaped like a crown. The light behind her made her hair glow like ribbons of flowing gold. Again he remembered the day she first arrived.

Unhesitating he claimed his sleeping beauty with a kiss. He ran his tongue along the seam of her mouth and nibbled lightly on her bottom lip. Soon she blossomed under his attention, her passion awakening with her senses.

Michelle came awake to a warm embrace and the familiar taste of Nate. His kiss took her from slumberous to aroused from one racing heartbeat to the next. She longed to wrap her arms around his neck and hold on tight.

Instead she sighed and pushed against his chest. "I'm mad at you."

"Yeah, I got that from the pan in the trash."

"I worked hard on that dinner."

"I'm sorry I missed it. Sorry I upset you."

She narrowed her eyes at him. "You can do better than that."

"You're right." He swept a curl back from her face, his gaze following the gesture. And then his glance met hers and the intensity in his gray eyes made her breath catch. "I love you."

"Oh, no." Her heart rejoiced even as she denied his words. "Don't say that." Unable to hold his gaze she looked away. "Don't make this harder."

"I am going to make it hard." He kissed her cheek, the line of her jaw. "I'm going to fight for you."

"We're totally wrong for each other," she reminded him. "You love this town and I've been waiting to leave since the moment I got here."

"We belong together." He nudged her nose with his, then dipped down to kiss the corner of her mouth. She turned into the caress, instinctively seeking more, but he'd already moved on. "And you made your peace with River Run when you made peace with your father's memory."

"You're a cop." Let him argue that one after leaving her sitting for nearly two hours tonight. "I vowed never to be with a cop."

"Too late." He lowered his head to the curve of her neck. "We've been lovers for a month. These last two weeks waking up next to you have been magical."

"No."

"Ah, ah. Your honesty is one of the things I love most

about you." The heat of his tongue tasted her skin. "And we're more than lovers, we're a family."

"No." She shook her head. "No fair bringing Jack into this."

"All's fair in love and war." He breathed against her ear, making the cliché a carnal threat. "I'm a warrior in love. I'm going to fight to win."

"Nate."

"He loves you. We love you."

"Unfair, unfair." He was destroying her with his relentless pursuit combined with a delicious physical attack. How did she fight him when she couldn't think straight?

"I'm leaving."

"Stay. Marry me. Be Jack's mom."

"I sold my song," she whispered desperately as he nibbled on her earlobe. She needed a reminder of where her future was. "The one I wrote about you."

That stopped him. He lifted onto his elbow, ending his sensual assault to stare down at her. His expression revealed nothing but she could practically see his mind at work.

She held her breath. It was her song, but his, too, and he was a very private man.

Finally he nodded and she breathed. And then his face lit up with pride and joy for her. "Congratulations."

And that was the moment he won her over. His approval and excitement for her warmed her heart. She'd been waiting for this minute since she got the call. But everything she'd always wanted was suddenly at odds with what she'd never wanted but had found where she least expected.

"I need to be in Los Angeles next week."

She loved Nate, loved Jack, but how did she give up her dream?

"Michelle…" He cradled her face in his hands, demanded she look him in the eyes. "I was late tonight because a call went long. I hurt you and I'm sorry. I'm not going to lie to you. There are times you'll have to be second to my job, but I'm willing to be second to yours occasionally, too. We'll decide on a nanny so you can write and fly when you need to. As long as I'm first in your heart like you are in mine, we can make it work. Go to L.A. but come home to me."

"I can go to Los Angeles? And Nashville?" First in his heart. She liked the sound of that. Was it possible she could have it all? Love, a family and her career?

"Tell me you love me and I'll drive you to the airport. But you have to promise to marry me first."

She threw her arms around his neck and dragged him down to her, kissing him with everything in her. He wrapped her close and delivered on his erotic onslaught.

"Yes," she accepted, feeling lucky as the princess she used to dream of being. "I love you. Yes, I'll marry you. Yes, I'll be Jack's mom. But be warned. You proposed in a castle. I'll settle for nothing less than happily ever after."

He grinned. "No problem. I have my very own sleeping beauty." To prove it, he kissed her again.

* * * * *

Give a 12 month subscription to a friend today!

Call Customer Services
0844 844 1358*

or visit
millsandboon.co.uk/subscriptio

The World of
MILLS & BOON®

With eight paperback series to choose from, there's a Mills & Boon series perfect for you. So whether you're looking for glamorous seduction, Regency rakes or homespun heroes, we'll give you plenty of inspiration for your next read.

Experience the ultimate rush of falling in love.
12 new stories every month

Romantic Suspense
INTRIGUE

A seductive combination of danger and desire
8 new stories every month

Desire™

Passionate and dramatic love stories
6 new stories every month

n o c t u r n e™

An exhilarating underworld of dark desires
2 new stories every month

For exclusive member offers go to
millsandboon.co.uk/subscribe

The World of
MILLS & BOON®